Early Canadian Short Stories

Canadian Critical Editions

General Editors

John Moss and Gerald Lynch

Canadian Critical Editions offer, for academic study and the interested reader, authoritative texts of significant Canadian works within a comprehensive critical setting. Where appropriate, each edition provides extensive biographical and bibliographical background, reprints of documents, commentary to illuminate the context of its creation and the history of its reception, new essays written from a variety of critical perspectives, and a biography. These critical editions provide an excellent opportunity for appreciation of the works themselves, for understanding their place in the developing tradition, and for participating in the critical discourse surrounding each work. Making the best accessible, this is the key concept behind the Canadian Critical Editions.

Other titles in the Canadian Critical Editions available from Borealis Press

Stephen Leacock, *Sunshine Sketches of a Little Town*, editor Gerald Lynch, 1996.
Sara Jeannette Duncan, *The Imperialist*, editor Thomas E. Tausky, 1996.
Susanna Moodie, *Roughing It in the Bush; or, Life in Canada*, editor Elizabeth Thompson, 1997.
John Richardson, *Wacousta*, editor John Moss, 1998.
A Northern Romanticism; Poets of the confederation, editor Tracy Ware, 2000.

Titles in Preparation

Stephen Leacock, *Arcadian Adventures with the Idle Rich*, editor David Bentley.
James De Mille, *A Strange Manuscript Found in a Copper Cylinder*, editor Gwendolyn Davies.
Thomas Chandler Haliburton, *The Clockmaker*, editor Carrie MacMillan.
Frances Brooke, *The History of Emily Montague*, editor Laura Moss.
Charles G.D. Roberts, *Charles G.D. Roberts: Animal Stories*, editor Terry Whalen.

Early Canadian Short Stories

Short Stories in English
before World War I

A Critical Edition

Edited by
Misao Dean

The Tecumseh Press Ltd.
Ottawa, Canada
2000

Copyright © by The Tecumseh Press Ltd., 1999

Permission has been sought for all articles used, where appropriate (for any omissions, please contact the publishers) and bibliographic information supplied.

All rights reserved. No part of this book may be used or reproduced in any manner whatsoever without written permission except in the case of brief quotations embodied in critical articles and reviews.

We acknowledge the financial support of the Government of Canada through the Book Publishing Industry Development Program (BPIDP), and of the Canada Council, and the Ontario Arts Council, for our publishing activities

Canadian Cataloguing in Publication Program

Main entry under title:

Early Canadian short stories: short stories in English before World War I

(Canadian critical editions)
Includes bibliographical references.
ISBN 1-896133-13-4 (bound) -
ISBN 1-896133-15-0 (pbk.)

1. Short stories, Canadian (English) 2. Canadian fiction (English)—20th century. I. Dean, Misao II, Series.

PS8325.E27 1999   C813'.0108052   C99-901362-9
PR9197.32.E27 1999

Canadian Cataloguing in Publication Program

Cover design by Greg Betts, Victoria
Typesetting by Chisholm Communications, Ottawa

Printed and bound in Canada on acid-free paper

for my Dad, who reads for fun

Acknowledgements

Thank you to Carole Gerson, who has again generously shared her knowledge of early Canadian periodicals and of Canadian women writers in response to my queries. Celeste Derksen brought the Pauline Johnson essay to my attention. My research assistant Pat Atkins provided valuable help in searching out the originals of many stories, and checking editorial emendations.

Thanks also to Gerald Lynch, who invited me to undertake this project and who has provided valuable feedback and many bad jokes during the process of its completion. Jamie Dopp kindly commented on several versions of the introduction. Gerry Walsh deserves thanks for everything.

The articles in the "Criticism" section appear by the kind permission of their authors, and I thank Frank Davey, James Doyle, Daniel Francis, W.H. New, Mary Louise Pratt and Stephen Scobie for the opportunity to include their work and for their encouragement.

The cover image was created by Greg Betts using graphic "quotations" from the following sources: Provincial Archives of British Columbia; Public Archives of Canada Photography Collection C:68854; *Profiles in Canadian Literature* (ed. Jeffrey Heath, Toronto: Dundurn Press) vols 3, 5, 7; *The Bookman* (London) XIV (June 1898) 67; Queen's Archives; The Atkins-Dixon Album.

Table of Contents

Introduction xi

Stories

The Trotting Horse
Thomas Chandler Haliburton 1

Brian, the Still Hunter
Susanna Moodie 7

My Visit to Fairview Villa
Rosanna Leprohon 25

The Idyl of the Island
Susan Frances Harrison 51

Old Man Savarin
E.W. Thomson 61

Three Outlaws
Gilbert Parker 73

A Red Girl's Reasoning
Pauline Johnson 81

Witchcraft
Lily Dougall 99

Lobo, The King of Currumpaw
Ernest Thompson Seton 113

When Twilight Falls on the Stump Lots
Charles G.D. Roberts 129

A Mother in India
Sara Jeannette Duncan 135

Charcoal
Duncan Campbell Scott 175

Dinner for Seven in the Temple
Robert Barr 185

Sowing Seeds in Danny
Nellie McClung 205

Its Wavering Image
Edith Eaton (Sui Sin Far) 219

The Marine Excursion of the Knights of Pythias
Stephen Leacock 227

The Third Generation
Marjorie Pickthall 247

Backgrounds and Contexts

Documents

Sara Jeannette Duncan: The Heroine of
  Old-Time (1886) 261
J. MacDonald Oxley: Periodical Literature in
  Canada (1888) 264
Pauline Johnson: On the Indian Girl in Modern
  Fiction (1892) 266
Lily Dougall: The Leaven of the Pharisees (1900) 274
Charles G.D. Roberts: The Animal Story (1904) 278
Edith Eaton (Sui Sin Far): Leaves from the Mental
  Portfolio of an Eurasian (1909) 283

Criticism

James Doyle: Canadian Women Writers and the
 American Literary Milieu of the 1890s 299
W. H. New: *from* Back to the Future: The Short Story
 in Canada and the Writing of Literary History 306
Mary Louise Pratt: *from* The Short Story: the Long
 and the Short of It 319
Frank Davey: Genre Subversion in the English
 Canadian Short Story 322
Stephen Scobie: *from* The Deconstruction of Writing ... 333
Daniel Francis: On Pauline Johnson 341

Bibliography 352

Introduction

This anthology contains some of the best-known stories by the best-known writers from the nineteenth and early twentieth centuries—including Thomas Chandler Haliburton, Stephen Leacock, and Susanna Moodie. It also contains examples of some of the most popular forms of the short story from the nineteenth century, including the local colour "sketch," the detective story and the wilderness adventure. But it also provides an introduction to some lesser-known stories and writers (such as Edith Eaton and Susan Frances Harrison), and reintroduces many—such as Gilbert Parker and E.W. Thomson—who have become less popular in the last thirty years. In choosing these stories, I have been guided less by an aesthetic model of "the good story" than by my own interests in the reading and writing of prose fiction in the late nineteenth and early twentieth centuries, the interests that I concentrate on when I teach my courses on early Canadian writing: the material conditions of production, publication and distribution of literary texts; the form of the short story itself; its representations of Canada in relation to imperial power, and of gendered, marginalized and racialized subjects within anglo-Canadian society. The selection navigates between the extremes of commercial fiction and "serious literature," and between the canonically sanctioned and the marginalized, in order to be at once historically representative, inclusive and open to a variety of critical approaches. The stories are arranged chronologically according to their date of first publication; the text is that of the first book publication (unless otherwise specified) with obvious errors corrected and US and British spellings regularized.

Like the previous books in the *Canadian Critical Editions* series, this anthology also includes "Documents," "Criticism," and a Bibliography. In the "Documents" section are journalism, literary essays and autobiographical writing that construct a particular kind of historical context for the literary works, focusing on genre, on markets and on issues of representation. In the "Criticism" section I have departed from the format established by the previous editors in this series; instead of attempting to create a comprehensive survey of important reviews and critical statements (an unreasonable task, given that the anthology contains seventeen authors), I have chosen a group of important recent articles to illustrate the wide range of critical approaches to Canadian short stories. I hope these articles, in conjunction with the Bibliography section at the end of the book, will encourage readers to look further for criticism on specific authors as well as on the genre itself.

The variety and popularity of short prose fiction as a genre in the nineteenth and early twentieth centuries in Canada was partly a result of the material conditions of its production and consumption. In the early nineteenth century, book publishing was risky and expensive; an audience for fiction had not yet been located and analysed, and the system for wholesaling and distributing books, to the extent that one existed, was oriented towards the selling of imports. Literacy rates grew slowly over the century, and the small population was widely distributed, linked by bad roads and unreliable ferries. Canadians, on the whole, were not rich, and had little money to spend on luxuries like books. Newspapers were necessary to the growing political infrastructure, and their distribution by mail was subsidized by government. Thus the first publishing opportunities for Canadian authors were newspapers.

In early Canadian newspapers, fiction quite literally filled up the space between the ads on slow news days. Idealistic publishers saw literature as a mark of the maturity of the new society, and encouraged submissions of "sketches" by local authors. The sketch, whose name suggests an analogy between visual and literary representation, was a flexible prose form of varying length that could include description, anecdote, autobiography and moral commentary. Their publication in newspapers which were known for their political partisanship and a no-holds-barred approach to political debate also suggested political opinion and satire as chief contents. Sketches might be re-tellings of local legends, accounts of interesting "characters," or descriptions of picturesque neighbourhoods, bound together less by conventional plot or character development than by the consistent voice of the narrator. Such a form appealed to the colonial taste for factual reading, and allowed the facts to be placed in the moral context which was held to be part and parcel of "improving" and tasteful literature.

Sketches published in a series in a newspaper or magazine created a ready-made audience for later publication in book form. Haliburton's *Clockmaker* series appeared initially as installments in Joseph Howe's magazine, *The Novascotian*; the six sketches which formed the basis of Moodie's *Roughing It in the Bush* appeared in John Lovell's *Literary Garland*. Both books eventually found publishers in England, initiating what would become a pattern for successful publishing: local periodical appearances leading to foreign book publication.

Prose sketches which documented Canada's unique landscape and social practices formed a contrast to the actual fiction published in newspapers and literary periodicals in the early nineteenth century. Most early fiction followed British models; though Rosanna Leprohon's romantic tale, "My Visit to Fairview Villa," takes place in Quebec, it follows the conventions of British domestic fiction and makes little of its setting. But the public discourse of nationhood which dominated the years following Confederation in 1867 included a call for a distinctively Canadian literature which would legitimate our sense of ourselves as a nation. The early sketches provided the basis for the articulation of Canada as a unique place, and of uniquely Canadian cultural traditions, in the stories that began to appear in the 1880s in popular publications such as *The Canadian Magazine* and *Dominion Illustrated*.

The dominance of the growing Canadian periodical market by US and British publications forced many Canadian periodicals out of business after a few years; their unstable publishing histories and low rates of pay suggested to Canadian writers that they look elsewhere for a reliable and on-going market for their work. Canadian writers knew that they could reach their Canadian readers, as well as a much larger international audience, by writing in a style that would gain acceptance in foreign publications. By late in the century, the international magazine story had developed into several conventional varieties—the detective story, the romantic love tale, the "local colour" story and the animal story among them—that had reliable commercial appeal. Foreign editors, in particular, seemed to have an unending appetite for tales of "wilderness adventure" by Canadian authors. Canadians found they could make a living writing such stories, and publishers by publishing them.

Genre stories, stories written to conform to the set conventions of a particular commercial genre, were written by the score by Canadians such as Gilbert Parker, Norman Duncan, Isabel Ecclestone Mackay, Robert Barr, and Charles G.D. Roberts. They catered directly to the cultural assumptions of their intended audiences. Parker's habit of inventing locales, "Indian" legends and "Indian tribes," is stunningly racist as well as frighteningly inaccurate, yet his stories were highly respected by his British and Canadian audiences and considered realistic, because they accorded with the cultural codes of racial degeneracy and cultural absence that signified "the wilderness" or "the West" for such readers. The traces of racist and masculinist ideologies are clearly identifiable in Roberts' representations of animals, and in Thomson's French Canadians; not surprisingly, these writers have often been neglected in recent surveys of Canadian prose. But repugnance for the ideological "content" of such texts should not necessarily lead to their expulsion from the teaching canon: as Alan Lawson has argued, the literatures of "settler" colonies like Canada are "the very place where the processes of colonial power as negotiations, as transactions of power, are most visible." The stories in this anthology illustrate the ways that Canadians have signified themselves as members of a national community; the ways this community has constructed its racialized other; the ways that the white settler subject both contests and participates in the operations of imperial power. Their inclusion in this anthology provides the opportunity for a new and more rigorous critical approach to the ways that race and gender were constructed in nineteenth- and early twentieth-century Canadian culture.

The monologic discourse of empire which stories by Parker and Roberts enact did not go unchallenged, though often the challenge is muted and ironic. While Sara Jeannette Duncan deconstructs the ideal of motherhood in "A Mother In India,"

Introduction

she also constructs a discourse of the British in India which erases Indians and represents the white rulers of the Raj as victims of British cultural ignorance. Pauline Johnson's witty objections to the stereotype of the "Indian princess" in contemporary fiction provide a context for her story "A Red Girl's Reasoning." Edith Eaton's powerful and naive account of growing up racialized in nineteenth-century Montreal is undercut by her own frequent representation of Chinese North Americans as conservative, "little," and inscrutable. In Marjorie Pickthall's "The Third Generation" the desire of the white "explorer" for indigenization encounters its limit in his responsibility for the extermination of the First Nations. In all of these stories, meaning is uncertain and ambiguous, mediated by an irony which, as Linda Hutcheon suggests, may be the characteristic voice of Canadians when addressing issues of power and dominance.

Johnson, Duncan, Eaton, and Pickthall were only four among the many Canadian women who achieved success as writers at the turn of the century. While the market was still dominated by men like Parker, Norman Duncan, Roberts, and J. Macdonald Oxley, the debate about women's nature that took place in public discourse at the end of the century privileged women writers as authorities on the subject, and resulted in opportunities to publish what British critic W.T. Stead called fiction of the "Modern Woman": "written by a woman about women from the standpoint of Woman." The prominence of women in the "social reform" movement of 1880-1920 also provided an opportunity for women writers to address issues such as poverty, child labour, domestic violence, and women's demands for education and admission to the professions. The battle for women's suffrage was fought in the *Grain Grower's Guide* and the Toronto *Globe* by first wave feminists like Francis Marion Beynon and Sara Jeannette Duncan, who published fiction as well as journalism. The magazine story came to be a forum for the dramatization of feminist issues like temperance, spiritual reform, and the emancipation of women in the work of authors such as Nellie McClung and Lily Dougall.

As W.H.New suggests, turn-of-the-century commentators had their own theories to account for the popularity of the short story, and had very fixed criteria for its aesthetic judgment. The fast pace of "modern" life and the demand of readers for intense experiences seemed to suggest a correspondingly short and intense prose form, leading to the conventional and highly formalized generic definition of the short story as a "fragment of a life": a story unified in place, action and time, whose dramatization of a revelatory and emotionally intense moment manages to suggest the outcome of a complete "life story" in a concentrated form. "The Idyl of the Island" is an elegant early example of the highly unified, "fragment of a life" which became the critical norm for the modern anthology story. Yet not all short fiction conformed to this model: "Brian, the Still Hunter" is almost its opposite, diffuse and unstructured, filled with seemingly irrelevant autobiography and domestic detail. The documentary detail of Duncan Campbell Scott's "Charcoal" and the rambling plot of Ernest Thompson Seton's "Lobo" might be justified by the aesthetic preference for the construction of "histories" in the early critical works surveyed by New, or by the traditional description of the short story as apprentice or occasional work for a writer whose main interest was the novel. Stories such as "Witchcraft" might be analysed as hybrids, revealing their genesis in sketches of character and folk culture from the early nineteenth century while at the same time constructing a dramatic "epiphany" in the lives of the characters.

In retrospect, contemporary critics have suggested that the implied "generic contract" understood by readers of the short story influenced its popularity, specifically among colonial writers. In an article included in this volume, Mary Louise Pratt argues that the short story typically introduces new materials into an established literature. Early Canadian writers, at a loss as to how to interpret the "experiences" that signified Canada for them, chose the genre which was already defined as appropriately focussed on the local, the unique, the different. American and British readers (and anglo-Canadians who retained their European and metropolitan identification) were more likely to accept new and unfamiliar settings and themes when conventionalized by the short story form. According to such arguments, the development of new forms such as the linked short-story series or the story cycle (Leacock's *Sunshine Sketches of a Little Town* or Alice Munro's *Lives of Girls and Women* are examples) represents the struggle of colonial writers to resist the hegemony of the novel form, and its implicit judgments about suitable methods, contents and cultural norms. Certainly some of the stories in this volume seem to illustrate what Frank Davey suggests is the Canadian penchant for evading or re-writing generic restrictions; but many seem entirely conventional as well, and this tension provides an interesting area for further investigation.

Introductions of this kind often end with an exhortation to students, in pompous and formal language, to remember that Canadian history is good for you, and it can be fun. Believe it or not I do find it fun—but to end here is to trivialize our mutual efforts, as students of Canadian culture, to process, comprehend and situate ourselves within the ideology that determines us. I made this anthology because these stories offer the opportunity to study and discuss some of the most important and interesting issues in current literary studies, and because I hope to convey to readers some of my enthusiasm for these stories as stories, and for the study of early Canadian prose in general. I hope they will stimulate readers to look beyond the requirements of the particular course in which this might be a required text, and as students of their own culture, and politically situated subjects, to think productively about the issues they suggest.

Thomas Chandler Haliburton (1796-1865)

Thomas Chandler Haliburton began his career as a lawyer in 1820, and soon became both a judge and a member of the Nova Scotia House of Assembly. He conceived of his writing as a vehicle for promoting moral and political reforms among the "bluenoses"; a life-long Tory, he advocated strong ties to Britain, the preservation of the existing social hierarchy and specific measures for economic development such as railroads and canals. Disappointed by the financial failure of his first serious work, *A Historical and Statistical Account of Nova Scotia* (1829), he initiated the series of sketches that became *The Clockmaker* with the goal of persuading his readers by a different method; as Sam Slick explains, "when reason fails to convince, there is nothin' left but ridicule." "The Trotting Horse" introduces the Yankee Clockmaker whose conversations with "The Squire" dominate all three series of *The Clockmaker*. Sam Slick's energy and direct, critical speech skewers the complacency of the bluenoses, whose motto, according to Slick, should be, "He sleeps all the days of his life." The first series of sketches appeared in *The Novascotian*, a newspaper edited by Haliburton's friend and political ally, Joseph Howe. This text of "The Trotting Horse" is taken from its first book publication in 1836.

The Trotting Horse

I was always well mounted; I am fond of a horse, and always piqued myself on having the fastest trotter in the Province. I have made no great progress in the world, I feel doubly, therefore, the pleasure of not being surpassed on the road. I never feel so well or so cheerful as on horseback, for there is something exhilirating in quick motion; and, old as I am, I feel a pleasure in making any person whom I meet on the way put his horse to the full gallop, to keep pace with my trotter. Poor Ethiope! you recollect him, how he was wont to lay back his ears on his arched neck, and push away from all competition.

He is done, poor fellow! the spavin spoiled his speed, and he now roams at large upon 'my farm at Truro.' Mohawk never failed me till this summer. I pride myself, (you may laugh at such childish weakness in a man of my age,) but still, I pride myself in taking the conceit out of coxcombs I meet on the road, and on the ease with which I can leave a fool behind, whose nonsense disturbs my solitary musings. On my last journey to Fort Lawrence, as the beautiful view of Colchester had just opened upon me, and as I was contemplating its richness and exquisite scenery, a tall thin man, with hollow cheeks and bright twinkling black eyes, on a good bay horse, somewhat out of condition, overtook me; and drawing up, said, I guess you started early this morning, Sir? I did, Sir, I replied. You did not come from Halifax, I presume, Sir, did you? in a dialect too rich to be mistaken as genuine Yankee. And which way may you be travelling? asked my inquisitive companion. To Fort Lawrence. Ah! said he, so am I, it is *in my circuit*. The word *circuit* sounded so professional, I looked again at him, to ascertain whether I had ever seen him before, or whether I had met with one of those nameless, but innumerable limbs of the law, who now flourish in every district of the Province. There was a keenness about his eye, and an acuteness of expression, much in favour of the law; but the dress, and general bearing of the man, made against the supposition. His was not the coat of a man who can afford to wear an old coat, nor was it one of 'Tempest & More's,' that distinguish country lawyers from country boobies. His clothes were well made, and of good materials, but looked as if their owner had shrunk a little since they were made for him; they hung somewhat loose on him. A large brooch, and some superfluous seals and gold keys, which ornamented his outward man, looked 'New England' like. A visit to the States, had perhaps, I thought, turned this Colchester beau into a Yankee fop. Of what consequence was it to me who he was—in either case I had nothing to do with him, and I desired neither his acquaintance nor his company—still I could not but ask myself who can this man be? I am not aware, said I, that there is a court sitting at this time at Cumberland? Nor am I, said my friend. What then could he have to do with the circuit? It occurred to me he must be a Methodist preacher. I looked again, but his appearance again puzzled me. His attire might do—the colour might be suitable—the broad brim not out of place; but there was a want of that staidness of look, that seriousness of countenance, that expression, in short, so characteristic of the clergy. I could not account for my idle curiosity—a curiosity which, in him, I had the moment before viewed both with suspicion and disgust; but so it was—I felt a desire to know who he could be who was neither lawyer nor preacher, and yet talked of his *circuit* with the gravity of both. How ridiculous, I thought to myself, is this; I will leave him. Turning towards him, I said, I feared I should be late for breakfast, and must therefore bid him good morning. Mohawk felt the pressure of my knees, and away we went at a slapping pace. I congratulated myself on conquering my own curiosity, and on avoiding that of my travelling companion. This, I said to myself, this is the value of a good horse; I patted his neck—I felt proud of him. Presently I heard the steps of the unknown's horse—the clatter increased. Ah, my friend, thought I, it won't do; you should be well mounted if you desire my company; I pushed Mohawk faster, faster, faster—to his best. He outdid himself; he had never trotted so handsomely—so easily—so well.

I guess that is a pretty considerable smart horse, said the stranger, as he came beside me, and apparently reined in, to prevent his horse passing me; there is not, I reckon, so spry a one on *my circuit*.

Circuit, or no circuit, one thing was settled in my mind; he was a Yankee, and a very impertinent Yankee, too. I felt humbled, my pride was hurt, and Mohawk was beaten. To continue this trotting contest was humiliating; I yielded, therefore, before the victory was palpable, and pulled up. Yes, continued he, a horse of pretty considerable good action, and a pretty fair trotter, too, I guess. Pride must have a fall—I confess mine was prostrate in the dust. These words cut me to the heart. What! is it come to this, poor Mohawk, that you, the admiration of all but the envious, the great Mohawk, the standard by which all other horses are measured—trots next to Mohawk, only yields to Mohawk, looks like Mohawk—that you are, after all, only a counterfeit, and pronounced by a straggling Yankee to be merely 'a pretty fair trotter!' If he was trained, I guess that he might be made do a little more. Excuse me, but if you divide your weight between the knee and the stirrup, rather most on the knee, and rise forward on the saddle, so as to leave a little daylight between you and it, I hope I may never ride *this circuit again*, if you don't get a mile more an hour out of him. What! not enough, I mentally groaned, to have my horse beaten, but I must be told that I don't know how to ride him; and that, too, by a Yankee—Aye, there's the rub—a Yankee what? Perhaps a half-bred puppy, half Yankee, half Blue Nose. As there is no escape, I'll try to make out my riding master. *Your circuit*, said I, my looks expressing all the surprise they were capable of—your circuit, pray what may that be? Oh, said he, the eastern circuit—I am on the eastern circuit, sir. I have heard, said I, feeling that I now had a lawyer to deal with, that there is a great deal of business on this circuit—pray, are there many cases of importance? There is a pretty fair business to be done, at least there has been, but the cases are of no great value—we do not make much out of them, we get them up very easy, but they don't bring much profit. What a beast, thought I, is this; and what a curse to a country, to have such an unfeeling pettifogging rascal practising in it—a horse jockey, too—what a finished character! I'll try him on that branch of his business.

That is a superior animal you are mounted on, said I—I seldom meet one that can travel with mine. Yes, said he coolly, a considerable fair traveller, and most particular good bottom. I hesitated, this man who talks with such unblushing effrontery of getting up cases, and making profit out of them, cannot be offended at the question—yes, I will put it to him. Do you feel an inclination to part with him? I never part with a horse sir, that suits me, said he—I am fond of a horse—I don't like to ride in the dust after every one I meet, and I allow no man to pass me but when I choose. Is it possible, I thought, that he can know me; that he has heard of my foible, and is quizzing me, or have I this feeling in common with him. But, continued I, you might supply yourself again. Not on *this circuit*, I guess, said he, nor yet in Campbell's circuit. Campbell's circuit—pray, sir, what is that? That, said he, is the western—and Lampton rides the shore circuit; and as for the people on the shore, they know so little of horses, that Lampton tells me, a man from Aylesford once sold a hornless ox there, whose tail he had cut and nicked for a horse of the Goliath breed. I should think, said I, that Mr. Lampton must have no lack of cases among such enlightened clients. Clients, sir, said my friend, Mr. Lampton is not a lawyer. I beg pardon, I thought you said he rode the *circuit*. We call it a circuit, said the stranger, who seemed by no means flattered by the mistake—we divide the Province, as in the Almanack, into circuits, in each of which we separately carry on our business of manufacturing and selling clocks. There are few, I guess, said the Clockmaker, who go upon *tick* as much as we do, who have so little use for lawyers; if attorneys could wind a *man up again*, after he has been fairly *run down*, I guess they'd be a pretty harmless sort of folks. This explanation restored my good humour, and as I could not quit my companion, and he did not feel disposed to leave me, I made up my mind to travel with him to Fort Lawrence, the limit of *his circuit*.

Susanna Moodie (1803-1885)

Susanna Strickland Moodie had some success as a writer of sketches and poetry for British annuals and gift-books before she emigrated to Canada with her husband, John Moodie, in 1832. The couple first settled on a cleared farm near Cobourg in Upper Canada, but by 1834 had moved to their grant of bush land in Douro near Peterborough. Their Cobourg neighbour, Brian Bouskill, provided the model for "Brian, the Still Hunter."

"Brian, the Still Hunter" was one of a series of six "Canadian Sketches" which appeared in the influential periodical *The Literary Garland* (published by John Lovell and edited by his brother-in-law, John Gibson) in 1847-48. These autobiographical sketches formed the basis of Moodie's best-known book, *Roughing it in the Bush* (London: Bentley, 1852), which drew on her experience as a pioneer. The success of *Roughing It in the Bush* established Moodie's reputation, and she went on to publish numerous works with Bentley, including another book about Canada, *Life in the Clearings* (1853).

This version of "Brian, the Still Hunter," appeared in the *Literary Garland* 5:10 (October 1847): 460-67. Students who have studied *Roughing It* will find it interesting to compare this version with the book, and note the way Moodie re-wrote the periodical text for a British audience.

Brian, the Still Hunter

O'er mem'ry's glass I see his shadow flit,
Though he was gathered to the silent dust
Long years ago:—a strange and wayward man,
Who shunn'd companionship, and lived apart.
The gleamy lakes, hid in their gloomy depths,
Whose still, deep waters never knew the stroke
Of cleaving oar, or echoed to the sound
Of social life—contained for him the sum
Of human happiness. With dog and gun,
Day after day he tracked the nimble deer
Through all the tangled mazes of the forest:
                                    Author

It was early day, in the fall of 1832. I was alone in the old shanty, preparing breakfast for my husband, and now and then stirring the cradle with my foot, to keep little Katie a few minutes longer asleep, until her food was sufficiently prepared for her first meal—and wishing secretly for a drop of milk, to make it more agreeable and nourishing for the poor weanling—when a tall, thin, middle-aged man, walked into the house, followed by two large, strong dogs.

Placing the rifle he carried across his shoulder, in a corner of the room, he advanced to the hearth, and, without speaking, or seemingly looking at me, lighted his pipe, and commenced smoking. The dogs, after growling and snapping at the cat, who had not given the strangers a very courteous reception, sat down on the hearth-stone, on either side of their taciturn master, eyeing him, from time to time, as if long habit had made them understand all his motions. There was a great contrast between the dogs: the one was a brindled, grey and white, bull-dog, of the largest size,—a most formidable and powerful brute; the other, a staghound, tawny, deep-chested, and strong-limbed. I regarded the man and his hairy companions with silent curiosity. He was between forty and fifty years old: his head, nearly bald, was shaded at the sides by strong, coarse, black, curling hair. His features were high, his complexion brightly dark; and his eyes, in size, shape, and colour, resembled the eyes of a hawk. The expression of his face was sorrowful and taciturn; and his thin, compressed lips, looked as if they were not much accustomed to smiles, or, indeed, often served to hold communication with any one. He stood at the side of the huge hearth, silently smoking, his keen eyes fixed on the fire; and now and then he patted the head of his dogs, and reproved their exuberant expressions of attachment, with— "Down, Chance! Down, Music!"

"A cold, clear morning," said I, in order to attract his attention, and draw him into conversation.

A nod, without raising his head, or taking his eyes off the fire, was my only answer; and turning from my unsociable guest, I took up the baby, who just then awoke, sat down on a low stool by the table, and commenced feeding her. During

Brian, the Still Hunter

this operation, I once or twice caught the stranger's keen eye fixed upon me; but word spoke he none; and presently after, he whistled to his dogs, resumed his gun, and strode out.

When M—— and Monaghan came in to breakfast, I told them what a strange visitor I had; and they laughed at my vain attempts to get him to talk.

"He is a strange, mysterious being," I said. "I must find out who, or what he is."

In the afternoon, an old soldier called Layton, who had served during the American war, and got a grant of land, about a mile in the rear of our location, came in to trade for a cow. Now, this Layton was a perfect ruffian,—a man whom no one liked, and whom all feared. He was a deep drinker, a great swearer, and a perfect reprobate, who never cultivated his land, but went jobbing about, from farm to farm, trading horses and cattle, and cheating in a pettifogging way. Uncle Joe had employed him to sell M—— a young heifer, and he had brought her for him to look at.

When he came in to be paid, I described the stranger of the morning; and as I knew that he was familiar with every person in the neighbourhood, I asked if he knew him.

"No one should know him better than myself," he said. "'Tis old Brian, the hunter, and a near neighbour of yourn. A sour, morose, queer chap he is, and as mad as a 'March hare.' He's from Lancashire, in England, and came to this country some twenty years ago, with his wife, Deb, who was a pretty young lass in those days. He had lots of money, too; and he bought four hundred acres of land, just at the corner of the concession line, where it meets the main road—and excellent land it is; and a better farmer, while he stuck to his business, never went into the bush. He was a dashing, handsome fellow too, and did not hoard the money either. He loved his pipe and his pot too well; and, at last, he left off farming, and stuck to them altogether. Many a jolly booze he and I have had, I can tell you. But Brian was an awful passionate man; and when the liquor was in, and the wit was out, as savage and as quarrelsome as a bear. At such times, there was no one but Ned Layton dared go near him. We once had a pitched battle, and I whipped him; and ever after he yielded a sort of sulky obedience to all I said to him. After being on the spree for a week or two, he would take fits of remorse, and return home to his wife—would go down upon his knees, and ask her forgiveness, and cry like a child. At other times, he would hide himself up in the woods, and steal home at night, and get what he wanted out of the pantry, without speaking a word to any one. He went on with these pranks for some years, till he took a fit of the 'blue devils.'

"'Come away, Ned, to the Rice Lake, with me,' said he. 'I'm weary of my life, and I want a change.'

"'Shall we take the fishing-tackle,' says I: 'The black bass are in prime season; and F—— will lend us the old canoe. He's got some capital rum up from Kingston. We'll fish all day, and have a spree at night.'

"'It's not to fish I'm going,' says he.

"'To shoot, then? I've bought Reckwood's new rifle.'

"'It's neither to fish nor to shoot, Ned: it's a new game I'm going to try; so, come along.'

"Well, to the Rice Lake we went. The day was very hot, and our path lay through the woods, and over those scorching plains, for sixteen miles; and I thought I should have dropped by the way; but all that distance, my comrade never opened his lips. He strode on before me, at a half run, never once turning his hard leather face.

"'The man must be the devil,' says I, 'and accustomed to a warmer place, or he must feel this. Hollo, Brian! stop there: do you mean to kill me?'

"'Take it easy,' says he; 'you'll see another day after this: I've business on hand, and cannot wait.'

"Well, on we went, at this awful rate; and it was mid-day when we got to the little tavern on the lake shore, kept by one F——, who had a boat for the convenience of strangers who came to visit the place.

"Here we got our dinner, and a good stiff rum to wash it down: but Brian was moody; and to all my jokes he only made a sort of grunt; and while I was talking with F——, he slips out, and I saw him crossing the lake in an old canoe.

"'What's the matter with Brian?' says F——; 'all does not seem right with him, Ned. You had better take the boat, and look after him.'

"'Phoo!' says I, 'he's often so; and grows so glum now-a-days, that I will cut his acquaintance altogether, if he does not improve.'

"'He drinks awful hard,' says F——, 'there is no telling what he may be up to at this minute.'

"My mind misgave me, too; so I e'en takes the oars, and pushes out, right upon Brian's track; and, by the Lord Harry! if I did not find him, upon my landing on the opposite shore, lying, wallowing in his blood, with his throat cut.

"'Is that you, Brian?' says I, giving him a kick with my foot. 'What upon earth tempted you to play F—— and me this dirty, mean trick; to go and stick yourself like a pig—bring such a discredit on the house—and you so far from home, too, and those who should nurse you!'

"I was so wild with him, that, saving your presence, ma'am, I swore awfully, and called him names that would be undacent to repeat here; but he only answered by groans, and a horrid gurgling in his throat.

"'It's choking you are,' said I; 'but you shan't have your own way, and die so easily either, if I can punish you, by keeping you alive.' So I just turned him upon his belly, with his head down the steep bank; but he still kept choking, and growing black in the face. I then saw that it was a piece of flesh of his throat that had been carried into his wind-pipe. So, what do I do, but puts in my finger and thumb, and pulls it out, and bound up his throat with my handkerchief, dipping it first in the water to stanch the blood. I then took him, neck and heels, and threw him into the bottom of the boat, and pushed off for the tavern. Presently, he came to himself a little, and sat up in the boat, and, would you believe it? made several attempts to throw himself into the water. 'This will not do,' says I: 'you've done mischief enough already, by cutting your wizzand: if you dare to try that again, I will kill you with the oar.' I held it up, threatening him all the while; and he was scared, and lay down as quiet as a lamb. I put my foot upon his breast. 'Lie still, now, or you'll catch it.' He looked piteously at me, but he could not speak; but he seemed to say—'Have pity upon me, Ned; don't kill me.' Yes; this man, who had cut his throat, and who, twice after that, tried to drown himself, was afraid that I should knock him on the head, and kill him. Ha! ha! I never shall forget the work F—— and I had with him.

"The doctor came, and sewed up his throat; and his wife—poor crater!—came to nurse him; and he laid bad there for six months; and did nothing but pray to God to forgive him; for he thought the devil would surely have him, for cutting his own throat. And when he got about again—which is now twelve years ago—he left off drinking entirely, and wanders about the country, with his dogs, hunting. He seldom speaks to any one, and his wife's brother carries on the farm for him and the family. He is so shy of strangers, that it is a wonder he came in here. The old wives are afraid of him; but you need not heed him: his troubles are to himself: he harms no one."

Layton departed, and left me brooding over the sad tale he had told in such an absurd and jesting manner. It was evident, from the account he had given of Brian's attempt at suicide, that the hapless hunter was not wholly answerable for his conduct—that he was a harmless maniac.

The next morning, at the very same hour, Brian again made his appearance; but instead of the rifle across his shoulder, a large stone jar was suspended by a stout leathern thong. Without speaking a word, but with a truly benevolent smile, that flitted slowly over his stern features, and lighted them up, like a sunbeam breaking from beneath a stormy cloud—he advanced to the table, and, unslinging the jar, set it down before me, and in a low, gruff, but not unfriendly voice, said:

"Milk, for the child," and vanished.

"How good it was of him!—how kind!" I exclaimed, as I poured the precious gift, of four quarts of pure new milk, out into a deep pan— "and I never asked him—never said that the poor babe wanted milk. It was the courtesy of a gentleman—of a man of benevolence and refinement."

For weeks did my strange friend steal silently in, take up the empty jar, and supply its place with another, replenished with milk. The baby knew his step, and would hold out her hands to him, and cry— "Milk!" and Brian would stoop down and kiss her, and his two great dogs lick her face.

"Have you any children, Mr. B——?"

"Yes, five; but none like this—"

"My little girl is greatly indebted to you for your kindness."

"She's welcome, or she would not get it. You are strangers; but I like you all. You look kind; and I would like to know more about you."

M—— shook hands with the old hunter, and assured him that he should always be glad to see him.

After this invitation, Brian became a frequent guest. He would sit and listen with delight to M——, while he described to him elephant-hunting at the Cape; grasping his rifle with a determined air, and whistling an encouraging air to his dogs. I asked him one evening what made him so fond of hunting?

"'Tis the excitement," he said: "it drowns thought, and I love to be alone. I am sorry for the creatures, too, for they are free and happy; but I am led, by an impulse I cannot restrain, to kill them. Sometimes the sight of their dying agonies recalls painful feelings; and then I lay aside the gun, and do not hunt for days. But 'tis fine to be alone, with God, in the great woods—to watch the sunbeams stealing through the thick branches—the blue sky breaking in upon you in patches; and to know that all is bright and shiny above you, in spite of the gloom that surrounds you."

After a long pause, he said, with much solemn feeling in his look and tone:

"I lived a life of folly for years—for I was well born and educated before I left home for the woods, and should have known better; but if we associate long with the depraved and ignorant, we learn to become even worse than them. I felt I had become the slave to low vice and sin. I hated myself; and in order to free myself from the hateful tyranny of evil passions, I did a very rash and foolish action. I need not mention the manner in which I transgressed God's laws—all the neighbours know it, and must have told you long ago. I could have borne reproof, but they turned my sorrow into indecent jests;

and, unable to bear their ridicule, I made companions of my dogs and gun, and went forth into the wilderness. Hunting became a habit—I could no longer live without it—and it supplies the stimulant which I lost, when I renounced the cursed whiskey bottle.

"I remember the first hunting excursion I took alone in the forest, how sad and gloomy I felt. I thought that there was no creature in the world so miserable as me; I was tired and hungry, and I sat down upon a fallen tree to rest. All was still as death around me; and I was fast sinking to sleep, when my attention was aroused by a long, wild cry. My dog—for I had not Chance then, and he is no hunter—pricked up his ears, but instead of answering with a bark of defiance, he crouched down, trembling, at my feet. 'What does this mean?' I said; and I cocked my gun, and sprang upon the log. The sound came nearer upon the wind. It was like the deep baying of a pack of hounds in full cry. Presently, a noble deer rushed past me, and fast upon his trail— I see them now, like so many black devils—swept by, a pack of ten or fifteen large fierce wolves, with fiery eyes and bristling hair, and paws that seemed scarcely to touch the ground, in their eager haste. I thought not of danger, for, with their prey in view, I was safe; but I felt every nerve within me tremble for the fate of the poor deer. The wolves gained upon him at every step: a close thicket intercepted his path; and rendered desperate, he turned at bay. His nostrils were dilated, and his eyes seemed to send forth long streams of light. It was wonderful to witness the courage of the beast—how bravely he repelled the first attack of his deadly enemies—how gallantly he tossed them to the right and left, and spurned them from beneath his hoofs; yet all his struggles were useless, and he was quickly torn to pieces by his ravenous foes. At that moment, he seemed more unfortunate than me; for I could not see in what manner he had deserved his fate. All his speed and energy, his courage and fortitude, had been given to him in vain. I had tried to destroy myself; but he, with every effort vigorously made for self-preservation, was doomed to meet the fate he dreaded. Is God just to his creatures?"

With this sentence in his throat, he started abruptly from his seat, and left the house.

One day he found me painting some wild flowers, and was greatly interested in watching the progress I made in the group. Late in the afternoon of the following day, he brought me a large bunch of splendid spring flowers.

"Draw these," said he: "I have been all the way to the Rice Lake Plains to find them for you."

"Oh! pretty, pretty flowers," lisped Katie, grasping them with infantine joy, and kissing, one by one, every lovely blossom.

"These are God's pictures," said the hunter; "and the child, who is all nature just now, understands them in a minute. Is it not strange, Mrs. M——, that these beautiful things are hid away in the wilderness, where no eyes but the birds of the air, and the wild beasts of the woods, and the insects that live upon them, ever see them? Does God provide, for the pleasure of such creatures, these flowers? When I am alone in the forest, these things puzzle me."

Knowing that to argue with Brian was only to call into action the slumbering fires of his fatal malady, I asked him why he called the dog Chance?

"I found him," he said, "forty miles back in the bush. He was a mere skeleton. At first I took him for a wolf, but the shape of his head undeceived me. I opened my wallet, and called him to me. He came slowly, stopping and wagging his tail at every step, and looking me wistfully in the face. I offered him a bit of cooked venison, and he soon became friendly, and followed me home, and has never left me, night or day, since. I called him Chance, after the manner I happened with him; and I would not part with him for twenty dollars."

Alas! for poor Chance! he had, unknown to his master, contracted a private liking for fresh mutton; and one night he killed no less than eight sheep that belonged to Mr. D——, on the front road; who, having long suspected, caught him in the very act; and this mischance cost him his life. Brian was very sad and gloomy for many weeks after his favourite's death.

"I would have restored the sheep, four-fold," he said, "if he would but have spared the life of my dog."

All my recollections of Brian seem more particularly to concentrate in the adventures of one night, when I happened to be left alone, for the first time since my arrival in Canada. I cannot now imagine how I could have been such a fool, as to give way for four and twenty hours to such childish fears; but so it was, and I will not disguise the truth from my readers. M—— had bought a very fine cow of a black man named Mollineux, who lived twelve miles distant through the woods, and one fine, frosty spring day, he and John Monaghan took a rope and the dog to fetch her home. M—— said that they should be back by six o'clock in the evening, and to mind and have something cooked for supper when they returned, as their long walk and the sharp air would give them a great appetite. This was during the time that I was without a female servant, and lived in old Mrs. H——'s shanty.

The day was so bright and clear, and Katie was so full of frolic and play, rolling about the floor or toddling from chair to chair, that the day passed on without my feeling remarkably lonely. At length the evening drew nigh, and I began to expect the return of my beloved, and to think of the supper I was to prepare for his reception. The red heifer came lowing to the door to be milked, but I did not know how to milk in those days, and was terribly afraid of the cattle. Yet as I knew milk must be had for the tea, I ran across to Mrs. Joe, and begged that one of her girls would be so kind as to milk for me. My request was greeted with a rude burst of laughter from the whole set.

"If you can't milk," said Mrs. Joe, "it is high time you should learn. My galls are above being helps."

"I would not ask you but as a favour; I am afraid of cows."

"Afraid of cows!" Here followed another horse laugh; and indignant at the refusal of the first request I had ever made, when they had all borrowed so much from me, I shut the door, and returned home.

After many ineffectual attempts I succeeded at last, and bore my half pail of milk in triumph to the house. Yes! I felt prouder of that milk than the best thing I ever wrote, whether in verse or prose; and then it was doubly sweet, when I considered that I had procured it without being under any obligation to my ill-natured neighbours.

Brian, the Still Hunter

I fed little Katie and put her to bed, made the hot cakes for tea, boiled the potatoes, and laid the ham cut in nice slices in the pan, ready to cook the moment I saw the men enter the clearing, and arranged the little room with scrupulous care and neatness. A glorious fire was blazing on the hearth, and everything was ready for their supper, and I began to look out anxiously for their arrival. The night had closed in cold and foggy, and I could no longer distinguish any object a few yards from the door. Bringing in as much wood as I thought would last me for a few hours, I closed the door, and for the first time in my life, found myself in a house entirely alone. Then I began to ask myself a thousand torturing questions, as to the reason of their unusual absence. "Had they lost their way in the woods? could they have fallen in with wolves?—one of my early bugbears—could any fatal accident have befallen them?" I started up, opened the door, held my breath, and listened. The little brook lifted up its voice, in loud hoarse wailing, or mocked, in its bubbling to the stones, the sound of human voices. As it became later, my fears increased in proportion. I grew too superstitious to keep the door open; and not only closed it, but dragged a heavy box in front of it. Several ill-looking men had asked their way to Toronto during the day; and I felt alarmed lest such rude wayfarers should come to-night, and find me alone and unprotected. Once I thought of running across to Mrs. Joe, and asking her to let one of the girls stay with me until M—— returned; but the way in which I had been repulsed in the evening deterred me. Hour after hour wore away, and the crowing of the cocks proclaimed midnight, and yet they came not. I had burnt out all my wood, and I dared not open the door to fetch in more. The candle was expiring in the socket, and I had not courage to go up into the loft, before it went finally out, to set up another. Cold, heart-weary, and faint, I sat in the middle of the floor, and cried. The furious barking of the dogs at the neighbouring farms, and the cackling of the geese upon our own place, made me hope that they were coming; and then I listened, till the beating of my own heart excluded all other sounds. Oh! that weary brook! how it sobbed and moaned, like a fretful child! What unreal terrors, and fanciful illusions, my too active mind conjured up, while listening to its mysterious tones! Just as the moon rose, the howling of a pack of wolves, from the great swamp in our rear, filled the whole air. Their yells were answered by the barking of all the dogs in the vicinity; and the geese, unwilling to be behind hand in the general confusion, set up the most discordant screams. I had often heard, and even been amused, during the winter, particularly on thaw nights, by the howls of these formidable wild beasts; but I had never before heard them alone, and my fears reached a climax. They were directly on the track that M—— and Monaghan must have taken,—and I now made no doubt that they had been attacked, and killed, on their return, and I wept and cried, until the grey cold dawn looked in upon me through the small dim windows. I have passed many a long, cheerless night; but that was the saddest and longest I ever remember. Just as the day broke, my friends, the wolves, set up a parting benediction, so loud and wild, and so near the house, that I was afraid that they would come through the windows, or come down the chimney, and rob me of my child. But the howls died away in the distance; the bright sun rose up, and dispersed the long horrors of the night; and I looked once more timidly around me. The sight of the uneaten supper for a few minutes renewed my grief, for I could not divest myself of the idea that M—— was dead. I opened the door, and stepped forth into the pure air of the early day. A solemn and beautiful repose still hung, like a veil, over the face of nature. The mists of night still rested upon the majestic woods; and not a sound, but the flowing of the waters, went up in the vast stillness. The earth had not yet raised her matin hymn to the Throne of the Creator. Sad at heart, and weary and worn in spirit, I went down to the spring, and washed my face and head, and drank a deep draught of its icy waters. On returning to the house, I met, near the door, old Brian the hunter, with a large fox across his shoulder, and the dogs following at his heels.

"Good God! Mrs. M——, what is the matter? you are early up, and look dreadfully ill. Is anything wrong at home? Is the baby or your husband sick?"

"Oh no!" I cried, bursting into tears: "I fear he is eaten by the wolves."

The man stared at me, as if he doubted the evidence of his senses, and well he might; but this one idea had taken such strong possession of my mind that I would admit no other. I then told him, as well as I could, the cause of my alarm, to which he listened very kindly and patiently.

"Set your heart at rest, Mrs. M———, he is safe. It is a long journey, on foot, to Mollineux's, and they have stayed all night at his shanty. You will see them back at noon."

I shook my head, and continued to weep.

"Well, now, in order to satisfy you, I will saddle my mare, and ride over to Mollineux's, and bring you word, as fast as I can."

I thanked him sincerely for his kindness, and returned in somewhat better spirits to the house. At ten o'clock, my messenger returned, with the glad tidings that M——— was safe, and on his way home.

The day before, when half the journey was accomplished, John Monaghan had let go the rope by which he had led the cow, and she had returned to her old master; and when they again reached his place, night had set in, and they were obliged to wait until the return of day.

Brian's eldest son—a lad of fourteen—was not exactly an idiot, but what, in the Old Country, the common people designate a *natural*. He could feed and assist himself; and even go on errands to and from the town, and to the neighbouring farm-houses; but he was a strange creature, who evidently inherited, in no small degree, the father's malady. During the summer months he lived entirely in the woods, near his father's house, and only returned to obtain food, which was generally left for him in an out-house. In the winter, driven home by the severity of the weather, he would sit for days together moping in the chimney corner, without taking notice of anything passing around him. Brian never mentioned this boy—who had a strong active figure, and rather a handsome, though perfectly inexpressive, face—without a deep sigh; and I feel certain that half his own dejection was caused by painful reflections, occasioned by the mental aberrations of his child.

One day he sent the lad with a note to our house, to know

if we would purchase the half of an ox that he was going to kill. There happened to stand in the corner of the room, an open wood-box, into which several bushels of apples had been thrown; and, while M—— was writing an answer to the note, the eyes of the idiot were fastened, as if by some magnetic influence, upon the apples. Knowing that they had a very fine orchard, I did not offer him any, because I thought it would be useless to do so.

When the note was finished, I handed it to him. The lad grasped it mechanically, without removing his fixed gaze from the apples.

"Give that to your father."

The lad answered not: his ears, his eyes, his whole soul, were concentrated in the apples. Ten minutes elapsed; but he stood motionless, like a pointer at a dead set.

"My good boy, you can go."

Still, he did not stir.

"Is there anything you want?"

"I want," said the lad, without moving his eyes from the objects of his intense desire, and speaking in a slow, pointed manner, which ought to have been heard to be fully appreciated— "I want apples!"

"Oh! if that's all; take what you like."

The permission once obtained, the boy flung himself upon the box, with the rapacity of a hawk upon its prey, after being long poised in air, to fix its certain aim. Thrusting his hands to the right and left, in order to secure the finest specimens of the coveted fruit, scarcely allowing himself time to breathe, until he had filled his old straw hat and all his pockets. To help laughing was impossible; while this new "Tom o' Bedlam" darted from the house, and scampered across the field, for dear life, as if afraid that we should pursue him, to rob him of his prize.

It was during this winter, that our friend Brian was left a fortune of three hundred pounds per annum; but it was necessary for him to return to his native country, and county, in order to take possession of the property. This he positively refused to do; and when we remonstrated with him on the apparent imbecility of this resolution, he declared, that he would not risk his life in crossing twice the Atlantic, for twenty times that sum. What strange inconsistency was this, in a being who had three times attempted to take away that life which he dreaded so much to lose accidentally!

I was much amused with an account, which he gave me, in his quaint way, of an excursion he went upon, with a botanist, to collect specimens of the plants and flowers of Upper Canada.

"It was a fine spring day, some ten years ago; and I was yoking my oxen to drag in some oats I had just sown, when a little, fat, punchy man, with a broad, red, good-natured face, and carrying a small black leathern wallet across his shoulder, called to me over the fence, and asked me if my name was Brian. I said, 'Yes; what of that?'

"'Only, you are the man I want to see. They tell me that you are better acquainted with the woods than any person in these parts; and I will pay you anything in reason if you will be my guide for a few days.'

"'Where do you want to go?' said I.

"'No where in particular,' says he. 'I want to go here, and there, in all directions, to collect plants and flowers.'

"'That is still-hunting with a vengeance.' said I. 'To-day I must drag in my oats. If to-morrow will suit, we will be off.'

"'And your charge?' said he: 'I like to be certain of that.'

"'A dollar a-day. My time and labour just now, upon my farm, is worth that.'

"'True,' said he. 'Well, I'll give you what you ask. At what time will you be ready to start?'

"'By day-break, if you wish it.'

"Away he went; and by day-light, next morning, he was at my door, mounted upon a stout French pony.

"'What are you going to do with that beast?' said I. 'Horses are of no use on the road that you and I are to travel. You had better leave him in my stable.'

"'I want him to carry our traps,' said he. 'It may be some days that we shall be absent.'

"I assured him that he must be his own beast of burden, and carry his axe, and blanket, and wallet of food, upon his own back. The little body did not much relish this arrangement; but as there was no help for it, he very good-naturedly complied. Off we set, and soon climbed the hills at the back of your farm, and got upon the Rice Lake Plains. The woods were flush with flowers; and the little man grew into such an extasy, that at every fresh specimen he uttered a yell of joy, cut a caper in the air, and flung himself down upon them, as if he were drunk with delight.

"'Oh! what treasures! what treasures!' he cried. 'I shall make my fortune!'

"'It is seldom I laugh,' quoth Brian, 'but I could not help laughing at this odd little man; for it was not the beautiful blossoms that drew forth these exclamations, but the queer little plants, which he had rummaged for at the roots of old trees, among the moss and long grass. He sat upon a decayed tree, which lay in our path, for an hour, making a long oration over some greyish things which grew out of it, which looked more like mould than plants; declaring himself repaid for all the trouble and expense he had been at, if it were only to obtain a sight of them. I gathered him a beautiful blossom of lady's slipper; but he pushed it back when I presented it to him, saying:

"'Yes, yes; 'tis very fine: I have seen that often before; but these lichens are splendid!'

"The man had so little taste, that I thought him a fool, and left him to talk to his dear plants, while I shot partridges for our supper. We spent six days in the woods; and the little man filled his wallet with all sorts of rubbish, as if he wilfully shut his eyes to the beautiful flowers, and chose only to admire the ugly, insignificant plants, that even a chipmunk would have passed without noticing, and which, often as I had been in the woods, I never had observed before. I never pursued a deer with such earnestness as he continued his hunt for what he called 'specimens.' When we came to the Cold Creek, which is pretty deep in places, he was in such a hurry to get at some plants that grew under the water, that he lost his balance, and fell, head over heels, into the stream. He got a thorough ducking, and was in a terrible fright; but he held on to the flowers which had caused the trouble, and thanked his stars that he had saved them, as well as his life. Well, he was an innocent man," continued Brian— "a very little made him happy; and at night he would sing and amuse himself, like a little child. He gave me ten dollars for my trouble, and I never saw him again; but I often think of him, when hunting in the woods that we wandered through together; and I pluck the wee plants that he used to admire, and wonder why he preferred them to the fine flowers."

When our resolution was formed to sell our farm and go upon our grant of land, in the back-woods, no one was so earnest in trying to persuade us from our ruinous plan, as our friend Brian, who became quite eloquent in his description of the trials and troubles which awaited us. During the last week of our stay, he visited us every evening, and never bade us goodnight without a tear moistening his eyes. We parted with the hunter as with an old friend, and we never saw him again.

His fate was a sad one. He fell into a moping melancholy, which ended in self-destruction—but a kinder or warmer-hearted man, while he enjoyed the light of reason, has seldom crossed our path.

Rosanna Leprohon (1829-1879)

Born and educated in Montreal, Rosanna Mullins began to publish poems and stories in *The Literary Garland* shortly after she left convent school. In 1851 she married French-speaking Jean-Baptiste Lukin Leprohon, a medical doctor, and they had thirteen children during the course of a long and happy marriage. Leprohon's unique position as an English Catholic whose allegiances bridged both French and English-speaking communities allowed her to write with conviction about both. Her most famous novel, *Antoinette de Mirecourt* (1864) depicts marriage between a Quebeçoise heroine and English hero; it remained in print in French translation long after it lost its popularity in English Canada.

"My Visit to Fairview Villa" appeared in the *Canadian Illustrated News* 14, 21 and 28 May 1870; this version is taken from the reprint in the *Canadian Illustrated News* New Series of Original Novels 1 (Montreal: George Desbarats, 1871).

My Visit to Fairview Villa

"Love! Pshaw! I don't believe in it, and I really think I shall live and die an old maid, lest I should be wooed and married for my money. Men are such selfish, grasping, egotistical creatures!"

Such was the uncompromising judgment I heard pronounced on my sex as I entered the pleasant shady drawing-room of my friend, Stephen Merton, in compliance with a pressing invitation lately received, to spend a few weeks of the hot, dusty summer months at his pleasant residence, Fairview Villa, situated on the beautiful Saint Foy Road, some short distance from picturesque old Quebec.

The moment of my arrival was rather unpropitious, and I think I would have retreated had not my hostess caught sight of my rather embarrassed countenance. Instantly rising, she came forward and kindly welcomed me, introducing me afterwards to her two daughters, Fanny and Charlotte Merton, her niece, Miss Gray, and a young lady guest, Miss Otway.

"Hem!" thought I, when fairly seated, and replying with tolerable composure to the liberally gay small talk addressed me on all sides: "Which of these fair ladies has just proclaimed so unequivocally her contempt for mankind?" and my glance here travelled round the fair circle. "Oh, that is the one," I pronounced, as my gaze rested on Miss Geraldine Otway, who stood haughtily erect beside the mantlepiece, twisting a piece of honey-suckle round her taper fingers. The scorn was yet lingering in the dark eyes that met mine so fearlessly—in the rosy lips so contemptuously curved, and a yet more femininely beautiful being I had rarely met. Features of childish delicacy, a varying, transparent complexion, and a figure of the most fragile, though graceful proportions, were hers; all forming a striking contrast to the words and manner of this determined hater of mankind.

"Pray, Mr. Saville, did you overhear any part of the discussion we were engaged in when you opportunely entered to prevent its animation degenerating into animosity?" enquired Miss Gray, with a mischievous glance towards Miss Otway.

"Only the concluding sentences," I replied.

"If Mr. Saville wishes, I am ready to repeat what I have already said, and to defend it," exclaimed the lovely occupant of the hearth-rug, nibbling with superb indifference at the spray of honey-suckle in her hand.

"No, Miss Otway," I rejoined with a low bow, "that would be unnecessary, for I acknowledge the justice of your remarks. More than that, I will say you were not half severe enough."

I had flattered myself that my ironical acquiescence in her stern views would have slightly disconcerted this fair Amazon with the tender bloom of eighteen summers still fresh on her cheek, but so far from that, she merely averted her long fringed azure eyes contemptuously from me, as if judging me unworthy of further notice.

"Why, Mr. Saville," interposed little Charlotte Merton, "you should blush for subscribing so unreservedly to such a sweeping, odious accusation against your sex!"

"I beg pardon, Miss Merton, but since you take me up so seriously, I must say that I assent only in part to Miss Otway's opinions."

"And pray what part does Mr. Saville judge fit to dispute?" questioned my fair enemy, pursuing her fragrant repast without deigning to cast a glance in my direction.

The overwhelming contempt for my humble self and judgment, conveyed in the clear cold tones and averted eyes, was something really wonderful in its way, and would have utterly annihilated a more sensitive individual than myself. I contrived, however, with tolerable composure, to rejoin:

"As to the selfishness and rapacity of men, we will leave it an open question; but with regard to Miss Otway's intention of living and dying in single blessedness, holding as she does, so poor an opinion of our sex, I highly applaud her wisdom."

"Oh!" thought I, inwardly elated, "what a magnificent thrust! She'll scarcely get over it!"

Slowly she brought her full clear eyes to bear on mine, and having steadily stared at my hapless countenance a full moment, quietly said:

"It is barely possible I may yet be induced to change my present opinion of the lords of creation for a more favourable one; to commit the egregious folly of trusting in them; but I do not think," and here she came to a pause expressive of the most unutterable scorn; "I do not think that Mr. Saville, or any person at all resembling him, will be the one who shall succeed in making me do so."

I was vanquished, for I could not descend to vulgar retort and tell her she might rest assured that Mr. Saville would never seek her capricious favour, so making her a low bow I retired from the lists, intercepting as I did so a deprecating look from dove-eyed Fanny Merton towards Miss Otway, which that young lady answered by a slight toss of her graceful head. My gentle hostess here compassionately hastened to my assistance, and became suddenly interested in the health of my married sister and her olive branches, till the entrance of Mr. Merton, his two sons, and a couple of gentlemen guests, completely restored my equanimity.

Smarting as I still was under the unsparing onslaught Miss Otway had just made on me, I found my gaze involuntarily following and I fear admiring her every movement, so full of careless grace, of easy elegance. Of course she was surrounded, flattered, courted, for she was an heiress as well as a beauty, not to speak of her being a matchless and most capricious coquette. How bewitchingly she would smile one moment on the suitor from whom she would scornfully turn the next!— how she would overwhelm with contemptuous raillery this hour the unlucky being to whose whispered flatteries she had perhaps silently listened a short time before!

Beautiful, wonderfully beautiful she was, and changeable in her loveliness as an April day; now all smiles, sparkling epigram and repartee, then full of quiet, graceful dignity, a creature formed surely to bewilder, fascinate, utterly bewitch a man, do anything but make him happy. Such were my reflections, despite all efforts to the contrary, as I sat beside pretty, gentle Miss Merton, vainly endeavouring to concentrate my attention on herself. My folly, however, went no farther and I never joined the group paying Miss Otway such assiduous court. I felt instinctively that my nature was capable of conceiving a deep and lasting attachment, one which, if unhappy, would cloud a great part perhaps of my future life, and I knew that Geraldine Otway was one formed to inspire such a feeling, and after winning her aim, to laugh at the sufferings of her victim. Warned in time, I resolved to be prudent, and to keep without the charmed circle surrounding this modern Circe.

After the lapse of a few days, during the course of which we had barely exchanged a few words of commonplace civility, she seemed to become gradually aware of my existence, and then came my fiery ordeal. When she would ask with her bewildering smile, "Mr. Saville, please turn my music for me?" how could I say no, and then, when I would make a feeble effort to get away from her side, from the witchery of her sparkling eyes, and she would softly say, "What, tired so soon?" I would struggle like a bird in the grasp of the fowler; and for the time submit. I began to fear it was my destiny to love this beautiful, wayward syren, and well I knew what my reward would be if I weakly allowed myself to do so. I never deceived myself by indulging any illusory hopes. I knew that I was passably good-looking, young, and not a dunce. My family was as good as her own. My income, though likely to appear small in the eyes of an heiress, was a comfortable one, but these advantages never induced me to hope even for one moment that I would have any chance with her. I knew that she had spent a winter in Quebec and another in Montreal, during both of which she had been a reigning *belle*, had discarded men far superior to myself in wealth and position, and would probably yield up her freedom only to some great magnet whose social standing would elevate him, at least in her estimation, above the greater part of his fellow-men.

Life would have been very pleasant to me during my visit at Fairview Villa had it not been for the constant struggle between judgment and inclination. Could I have blindly yielded myself up to her fascinations, living only for the present, careless—oblivious of the future, all would have been sunshine; but I knew that an awakening from the intoxicating trance, bringing with it an hour of reckoning for me, not for her, would come, when she would say "good-bye for ever," and go on her way careless and smiling, leaving me to the misery of shattered hopes and an aching heart. I repeated inwardly, over and over again, that it should never come to this—that I would turn a deaf ear to her soft words, be marble to her wiles. We shall see with what success.

Pic-nics, boating and riding parties; walks by moonlight, sunlight, starlight; croquet on the lawn; billiards in the parlour; music in the drawing-room, succeeded each other with bewildering rapidity, and through all, Geraldine Otway shone, and glittered, and queened it, till I sometimes feared my only chance of safety lay in instant flight. Prudence whispered it would be my surest protection, but weak will found many excuses for avoiding the step. My sudden departure might offend Mrs. Merton; I wanted change of air; I was conscious of danger, and therefore able to take care of myself, and—in short, I stayed.

Pic-nics were a favourite pastime with us, and we often resorted to the beautiful woods that lay about a mile from Fairview Villa, and spent a pleasant time with green foliage and sunbeams overhead, and soft moss and wild flowers beneath our feet.

On one occasion that our wandering had extended into the green depths of the wood farther than usual, a sudden and violent rainstorm set in. I happened to be somewhat behind my companions, intent on gathering a bouquet of wild flowers for Charlotte Merton, a duty she had laughingly charged me with, when the deluge came down, and finding myself in a comparatively open clearing, where my choice summer suit was receiving more than a fair share of the shower, I quickened my steps to a run. On reaching a dense part of the wood I slackened my pace, and casting a glance of satisfaction at the thick roof of verdure overhead, suddenly perceived Miss Otway standing drenched and draggled (no other word for it, dear reader) under the shelter of a huge maple.

"Why, you are all wet, Miss Otway," I hastily said. "And alone, too!"

"Yes, that stupid Willy Merton worried me into standing here whilst he should go back to the carriages in search of an umbrella and shawls," was her petulant answer. "I do not think I will wait, though. I will try a race through the shower."

I held up my finger warningly as the rain suddenly poured down with renewed violence, whilst a vivid flash of lightning rent the sky, and was succeeded by a sullen peal of thunder.

She turned pale as death, murmuring:

"I do not fear many things, but I certainly stand in awe of lightning and thunder."

What was to be done? The rain pouring down with added force was penetrating the thick foliage, literally drenching my delicate companion. After a moment I removed my light over-coat and, with considerable hesitation, asked might I wrap it around her. She was generally so haughty and independent I made the offer timidly, fearing perhaps a sharp rebuff, but instead, she gratefully thanked me, and nestled her little cheek inside the collar with a child-like satisfaction at the additional shelter it afforded. Wrenching off the little dainty fabric of tulle and rosebuds that had done duty as a bonnet a few minutes before, but which was now a shapeless, gaudy pulp, she flung it away, saying:

"Now, I have an excuse for getting a new one to-morrow. It shall be illusion, trimmed with honeysuckle."

"But you must not let the rain pour down on your uncovered head in this way," I remonstrated.

"Oh, it will do no harm. There are no false tresses embellishing it."

How very lovely she was! Disordered, drenched, still the face looked out so calmly beautiful from amid the shining wet masses of hair on either side. I felt the spell of her rare loveliness stealing over me, and I knew I must strengthen myself against its dangerous influence, doubly insidious in the soft, feminine mood that ruled her at the moment.

Another vivid flash with accompanying sullen rumble, and again the colour left her cheek, and a look of terror crept over her face.

"What are we to do?" she piteously asked, turning to me.

She was so touching, so winning in her girlish tremors and helplessness that a wild impulse to tell her there and then how loveable, how fascinating she was, took possession of me, and afraid of myself, of my own want of self-control, I stood silent at her side. Another flash, another peal, and she convulsively clutched my arm, bowing her head on it to shut out the lightning from her sight. She was trembling in every limb, her very lips white with terror, and I, weak fool, was as unnerved as herself, though from a very different cause. Ah, my fears, my presentiments had all pointed to the truth, and I had learned to love her in spite of prudence, judgment, and common sense. Yes, I had fallen into the snare I had so firmly resolved on avoiding, but she, at least, should never know my folly, never have an opportunity of curling her lip in scorn at my audacity—of trampling on feelings that to me, alas! were only too earnest. Was I not tried—tried almost beyond my strength with her clinging, trembling and helpless to my arm in the recesses of that dim wood? Surely I would betray myself. Ability to act or speak with outward calmness was fast deserting me. Again another terrible flash. The very elements were leagued against me. Closer she clung, whispering:

"Lawrence, Mr. Saville, I shall die with terror."

The sound of my Christian name, which seemed to have escaped her lips involuntarily, the close, but soft pressure of her little fingers as they closed so imploringly on my arm, the graceful head bowed almost on my shoulder, all combined to rout completely my presence of mind—the calmness so necessary to me then, and I felt that unless I made a mighty and immediate effort, my doom was sealed.

"Miss Otway," I quietly said, "there is really no danger. Pray be calm, and allow me to seat you here, under the tree, where you will be more sheltered from the rain."

Whether owing to the struggle going on within me, my voice had assumed a degree of coldness I had not intended it should, or that the words in themselves, containing a sort of implied wish to rid myself of the duty of supporting her, incensed her proud spirit, she instantly raised her head from my arm, and with the look and bearing of an offended queen, flung my coat from her and walked forth in the midst of the deluge coming down still with undiminished violence.

"Miss Otway," I besought, I urged, "for heaven's sake wait a few moments longer. This heavy rain will soon be over!"

She made no reply beyond slightly contracting her dark eyebrows, and pursued her course. It was distressing beyond measure to see that delicate frail creature exposed to such a storm, and I renewed my entreaties for her to return to the shelter of the wood, but received no reply, nothing but contemptuous silence. Again a vivid flash of lightning, a crashing peal of thunder overhead. "Ah, poor girl, she will stop now," thought I. But I was mistaken. Her indomitable pride triumphed over every feeling, and though her cheek became if possible of a still more deathly whiteness, she steadily kept on her way. I came closer to her, proffering my arm, my coat, which were both mutely but disdainfully rejected. Thus, I following her in an ignominious, valet style of companionship, we plashed on through rain and mire till we at length reached our party, the men of which had constructed a temporary shelter for the ladies by drawing the carriages together.

"Why, you are in a shocking plight, Miss Otway. I hope friend Saville has taken good care of you," said Mr. Merton.

"Oh yes," she rejoined with stinging sarcasm; "he is such a very prudent young gentleman."

"Come, Geraldine, don't be cross because your pretty bonnet is among the things that were," interrupted Miss Merton, who always kindly came to my rescue.

"But did you not meet Willy and the shawls?" questioned our host. "He set off some time ago with a sufficient quantity to construct a wigwam if you had desired it, not to mention two umbrellas and a parasol."

"We did not meet him, Mr. Merton. I suppose he has been seeking for a short cut through the wood, which instead has proved a long one."

"Geraldine, quick, step into the carriage. We have plenty of place for you," called out Miss Gray.

"Yes, if you are not afraid of getting your dresses wet or spoiled, or of my fatiguing you otherwise," she replied, darting another withering look towards my hapless self.

"What an unlucky fellow I am," I mournfully thought when, fairly started some time later on our homeward route, I wondered over the events of the day. "I have made myself fairly odious to her; and heavens! what a fire-brand she is!" But, alas, I vainly sought to fortify myself by the latter uncharitable reflection, and I was no sooner in my own room, whither I had instantly retired on arriving at the house, to change my wet clothes, than I found myself kissing like a verdant school boy the silk lining of my coat collar against which her soft cheek had so prettily nestled a short while ago.

"Fool! idiot! mad-man!" I groaned, as the full meaning of this act of folly rose suddenly upon me, revealing that love for this peerless creature had indeed, spite of all my resolutions and efforts, crept into my heart. "All I can do now is to hide my madness from every eye, but from hers above all others. She hates, scorns me now, but, so help me heaven, she shall never laugh at me!"

On entering the drawing-room, there was Miss Otway in a fresh, delicate tinted robe, showing no signs of the late great fatigue and exposure she had undergone beyond a brighter flush on her cheek and a greater brilliancy in her dark eyes. She never noticed me all the evening beyond launching at my devoted head, on one or two occasions, some sarcasms as cutting as they were wholly unprovoked, and from which I sought refuge in the society of Miss Merton. The companionship of the latter really pretty, amiable girl was always agreeable to me, principally for two reasons. First, she was quite in love, I well knew, with the gallant Captain Graham, of the ———th, a handsome young officer who had lately joined our party, (and who by the way was hopelessly in love himself with Miss Otway) so I saw no risk of my attentions being misinterpreted; secondly, she was an intimate, or as young ladies call it, a bosom friend of the wilful mistress of my heart, and often chose her for the theme of our long chats together, recounting so many instances of the generosity, kindness and better nature of the latter that my chains after each such dangerous dialogue were more closely riveted than if I had been in company with Miss Otway herself. The conduct of that young lady continued the same for a few days as it had been on the evening of the luckless pic-nic, I, all the time, even whilst smarting under her petulant injustice, finding a gloomy satisfaction in the thought that my secret was safe. Then again her mood changed, and she became friendly and conciliating even to the point of making advances which I certainly did not meet more than half way, even if I went that far.

One beautiful afternoon that several of us had gone on an exploring expedition on horseback to some fine view in the neighbourhood, I found myself by her side with Capt. Graham as we were turning our horses' heads homewards. Suddenly she discovered that "she had forgotten her lace handkerchief, and hoped that Captain Graham would have gallantry enough to go for it." The directions, to say the least, were rather vague, and the accomplished son of Mars departed on his mission, smiles on his lips and weary disgust in his heart. Turning towards me she said with her softest smile:

"Spur up, Mr. Saville. We can ride two abreast here."

Ah! merciless coquette! arch traitress! she was determined on leading me into a confession. How could I resist her? Would that she had been a serf—a peasant girl, anything that I might have hoped to have room for my own, but instead she was the petted heiress, the merciless flirt, and I a miserable captive with nothing to console me under the weight of my chains save the certainty that none knew I wore them. Very calmly I accepted her invitation to ride beside her, and we journeyed on, the golden sunlight quivering through the green branches overhead, the soft summer winds caressing our foreheads, and yet our talk was as dull and prosaic as if we had been a couple of elderly respectable people with the cares of the state, or of a family, on our shoulders. Suddenly she turned full towards me, saying with a charming smile:

"Now for a race, Mr. Saville. If you win, you may name your reward."

With a look of laughing defiance that wonderfully heightened her exquisite beauty, she glanced archly at me and then set off at full speed. Easily I could have overtaken her and she must have known that well, for few horses excelled in speed my own good steed kindly accommodated with a comfortable stall in the stables at Fairview Villa, but I had no intention of jeopardizing my secret which this girl seemed bent on wringing from me, and at a very moderate rate of speed I followed in her wake. After a time she looked sharply round, and either angered by the slowness of my pace, or by my preoccupied look, she struck her spirited little mare angrily across the ears, and the latter catching the fiery mood of her mistress, gave a bound forward and set off at break-neck speed. Anxious beyond measure, I spurred forward, dreading every moment some accident to the frail girlish creature I saw flying before me through the interstices of the wood with such reckless disregard of caution. Now, had I not firmly determined when commencing this humble recital, that it should possess the merit of being at least veracious, even at the expense of dullness, I should here enliven it by a rapid, brilliant account of some deadly peril which would suddenly menace Miss Otway, say for instance, her horse rearing on the brink of a precipice, from which strait she would be delivered entirely by my strength of arm and presence of mind; but resisting manfully the temptation, doubly strong in the present case, as I feel convinced I could make a graphic, indeed splendid sketch of the thing, I will honestly confess that she at length drew rein, safe though flushed and panting, at Fairview Villa.

I hastily dismounted so as to assist her to alight, but without waiting for my help, she sprang to the ground at the risk of a sprained ankle if not of more serious injury, and as I pressed towards her, uttered the one word, "Laggard!" with a look and voice of indignant contempt, striking at the same time her horse another light but angry blow over its neck. From her expression as she swept by me, I knew she would much rather have applied the whip to my own shoulders, but had she done so, I would not only have borne it, but spaniel-like have caressed the hand that struck me, for alas! my desperate struggles were but rivetting my chains the more securely, and I felt I was beginning to love Geraldine Otway with a love almost terrible in its intensity. Surely, surely, I was foolish—mad—to remain longer exposed to the fascinations of this temptress. I must leave without delay, leave before yielding to the impulse of some moment of passion, I should utter words of love which would be answered by smiles of ridicule; before laying bare feelings too sacred and secret to be made the jest of a hollow-hearted coquette and her friends.

How she persecuted, lashed, taunted me that evening! More than once I retorted, sharply if not rudely, for my own character was beginning to suffer from the peculiar irritation engendered by mental suffering. Really this girl was trying me in every way beyond my strength! On my pillow, that night, I made up my mind that the next day should be my last at Fairview Villa and that I should tear myself away from the fascinations of this Eden, the memories of which would embitter many a long hour in the dreary future.

With the sunshine of the following morning, Miss Otway's smiles had returned, and as the day was bright but pleasantly cool, Miss Gray proposed a botanizing excursion to the woods, indignantly protesting against baskets of refreshments which would give our expedition the air of a vulgar, every day pic-nic, instead of a scientific exploration. "Papa" Merton quietly smiled at this, and in despite of the warning, some hampers containing the *materiel* of a very dainty lunch, were slipped into the carriage, proving I may as well say before hand, as welcome to Miss Gray as to the rest of our hungry party when luncheon hour came round.

The members of the coming expedition were already standing in groups on the verandah when I joined them, and Miss Otway, radiant in fresh loveliness, and in the coolest and most becoming of morning toilettes, was standing chatting to Miss Gray who, armed with a basket and some tiny garden implement for transplanting, looked as if she intended business.

"Who knows anything about plants, their classes, orders and genera?" inquired Miss Otway.

As she fixed her eyes on me at the conclusion of the sentence, I muttered something about having forgotten Botany since I had left college. The other gentlemen of the party murmured a similar confession.

"Well, as I do not intend that Miss Gray, who is really well versed in it, shall have all the glory of the expedition to herself, I propose we make it a sort of generally scientific thing. Each member shall pursue the study for which he or she has most aptitude, be it geology, mineralogy, botany, so that all may return learned-looking and triumphant. What do you think Mr. Saville?"

"I have forgotten them all," I pleaded. A general and significant cough of acquiescence, each on his own count, again ran round the gentlemen of the circle, when Miss Otway reported:

"I see Mr. Saville is bent on demoralizing our scientific forces, so to punish his indolence and keep him out of mischief, I shall condemn him to hold my specimens. He will at least be able to do that."

Thus enlisted in her train, and only too happy, if the truth be told, for the circumstance, I approached her side, inwardly thinking that as it was my last day (for her smiles and charms had but strengthened my resolve of leaving her) I might take one more sip of the intoxicating happiness I found in her society ere I renounced it for ever.

Started on our way, she turned to me, saying, "Now, every little weed or wild flower you see, gather it so that in such a number we may chance on getting some verdant treasure with which to astonish and delight the real botanists of the party."

Oh, what a walk that was! Loitering among sunshine and flowers—stooping sometimes to gather plant or fern.

"It is fortunate for me," thought I, "that this is the last day of temptation, or otherwise I should surely make a fool of myself."

"Come, show me the fruits or rather flowers of your industry, Mr. Saville. What! common clover—dandelion—catnip—why, what are you thinking of? If this is a specimen of your abilities, I fear I will never be able to teach you even the little botany I know myself."

I looked steadily, earnestly at her as she stood beside me, smiling up in my face, and then suddenly said, it seemed in spite of myself:

"You have taught me one lesson too many already—one which I only hope I may be able to speedily forget."

I was unprepared for the crimson tide that so abruptly rushed to her face, flushing even the tiny shell-shaped ears showing so daintily from under her little hat, and I was equally unprepared for the suddenness with which her eyes, abashed and half frightened-looking, sought the ground. A long silence followed, I inwardly ruminating on my rashness and resolving on more circumspection; when at length raising her eyes, but still looking away from me, she hesitatingly said in a low tone, very unlike her usual clear ringing accents,

"Explain your words, Mr. Saville."

Ah, Syren! She had brought me to the very verge of a declaration—another moment and I would have been at her feet, almost kissing the hem of her garments, but summoning all my self-command, my manhood's pride to my aid, I replied with a tone of gay politeness that cost me a mighty effort, for I had to bite my lip till the blood almost started.

"You have taught me, Miss Otway, how charming, how irresistible a pretty woman can render herself."

Her face flushed again, but this time angrily and proudly.

"Good!" thought I, finding even in the midst of my own secret suffering, a satisfaction in the pang I had just inflicted on her vanity.

"Diamond cut diamond, wily coquette! You have robbed me of happiness and hope, but not of self-respect. You shall have one *scalp* the less to hang on to your girdle of feminine triumphs."

Another pause, during which I assiduously commenced gathering another handful of the first weeds that came within reach, to replace the former specimens which she had thrown away. As usual, she first broke silence by carelessly asking,

"Are you going to row for Mrs. Merton's silver arrow in the boat race coming off this week?"

"I won't be here, Miss Otway. I am obliged to leave."

"Yes—when?" she calmly asked, as she carefully shook off a little insect resting on a pretty fern, forming part of her collection.

"To-morrow," was my brief rejoinder.

If I had unconsciously calculated on the sudden announcement of my approaching departure producing an impression on her flinty heart, I had good cause to feel wofully disappointed. There was no regret, no emotion exhibited, not even as much interest as she displayed in getting rid of the tiny beetle on which her eyes were fixed. Chatting freely on different topics, expressing much interest in the forthcoming race in which Captain Graham was to ply an oar, accompanied by a carelessly polite regret that I should miss it, as well as a moonlight drive and some other pleasures in contemplation, we hastened our steps and soon rejoined the party, finding Miss Gray severely lecturing some of its members on the nature of the botanical collections they had made.

"The charity-school children might have known better than to have gathered such trash," she indignantly exclaimed, tossing aside bundles of what she sarcastically suggested might be useful to the cook at Fairview Villa as "greens." Lunch was immediately produced, however, and in the welcome prospect thus afforded to all, Miss Gray's denunciations were borne with considerable philosophy. Our return home was very cheerful, the mineralogists of the party amusing themselves by firing their specimens at each other, or at a given mark.

Miss Otway was in excellent spirits, brilliant, witty, playful, a strong contrast to my own self, wrapped up in moody taciturnity, brooding over the woful thought that on the morrow I should be far away from the enchantress who, despite prudence, reticence, resolve, had called to life so strong a passion in my aching heart.

After our return the ladies sought their rooms to dress for dinner. She (what other woman than Geraldine Otway did I give a thought to now) came down soon in one of the light, transparent, soft-tinted toilets that became her delicate beauty so well, and looking so childishly lighthearted as she fondled and teazed a pretty King Charles given her by Captain Graham, that I was divided between a wish to strangle the dog on one hand, and on the other to curse the day on which I had first met its radiant mistress. After a time Mr. Merton came in with some papers and letters, one of which he handed to Miss Otway. She opened it and then retired into the embrasure of the window to read it at her leisure behind the lace curtains. Restless and wretched, I strolled out on the lawn. Capt. Graham accosted me—I turned shortly from him. Then Miss Merton, but for once she failed to please. Next I encountered my hostess to whom I had not as yet spoken of my intended departure, but I wanted energy to meet and resist the kind entreaties which I knew would be forthcoming to induce me to change my intention.

After a listless half hour I re-entered the drawing-room, like the moth returning to the flame that had already singed my heart, I suppose I must say, instead of wings. No one was there except Miss Otway, who was still standing near the window, looking absently from it, and mechanically twisting and creasing the corners of the envelope she held in her hand. Approaching her, I made some slight common-place remark which she as indifferently answered, and then suddenly, without word or warning, she burst into tears. Grieved, shocked, I ventured to hope that Miss Otway had received no painful news from her correspondents.

Springing to her feet, she exclaimed:

"Dolt! Don't you know that nine times out of ten a woman cries without cause?"

Ere I could recover from my astonishment, she was gone, whilst I remained rooted dumbly to the spot, not so much by the unprovoked epithet flung at my head with such a wrathful glance, as by the wondering surmise of what had I done to offend her, to call forth such an exhibition of anger.

What a termagant she was, and yet what would I not have given for the privilege of taking that termagant to my heart for life.

I saw no more of her till evening, when returning from a short stroll with my host, in which I had declared my resolve of starting, notwithstanding his hospitable entreaties, the following morning, I noted Geraldine's slight figure step forth on the verandah. Anxious for a kindly farewell word, for I knew my departure would take place the following morning ere she should have left her couch, I broke off a sprig of ivy twining round one of the pillars of the porch, and approached her.

"May I offer this as a species of olive branch, Miss Otway? I leave to-morrow."

"But we have not quarrelled," she coldly said, drawing back from me.

"Because I would not quarrel with you," I retorted, with considerable bitterness, for the thought of all she was making me suffer in the present, as well as what I would suffer in the future, awoke angry feelings within me. "Provocation on your part was certainly not wanting. Accept, however, my token, and our parting will at least be friendly. Ignorant as I am of botany, I know this leaf signifies friendship. Pray take it?"

"Why should I?" she asked. "It would be even more utterly worthless than the vegetable phenomena which Miss Gray suggested this morning might answer for greens," and with a scornful look she flung my offering away and turned back into the house. Ah, she had had the best of our singular duel, and she was still heart-free, unfettered, able to heap scorn on me which burned like fire into my very soul. Cruel, merciless flirt! Why had destiny ever permitted us to meet?

But we learn to dissemble through life, and as I sauntered round the grounds later that evening, for the glorious beauty of the moonlight tempted us all into the open air, no one would have suspected from my calm cheerful look and easy playful retorts to friendly witticisms, that I had already entered on what I feared would be to me a life-long, absorbing sorrow. Still I yearned for solitude, for quiet, and on seeing Miss Merton step forth from the library on the lawn, I quietly fell back into the shade of the trees to avoid her. My heart was too sore for even her gentle companionship then; and as soon as chance favoured me, I stole up into the room she had just left. It was as I expected, quite deserted, and lit only by the arrowy beams of moonlight that streamed through the half-drawn curtains. It was a welcome haven, and peering about through the semi-obscurity, I saw a small sofa, deep in shadow, on which I seated myself, and which probably had just been vacated by Miss Merton, for her handkerchief, recognizable by her favourite perfume, Mignionette, lay yet upon it. I took it up and inhaled the fragrance its folds gave forth, thinking all the while how feminine was the gentle owner, how different to the mocking Circe on whom I had so idly lavished the treasured love of an honest heart.

Suddenly a light figure entered from the garden and approached my obscure sofa. "Ah! here comes Miss Merton," I thought. "I will give her a surprise."

But the figure quietly seated itself beside me, saying, "I have kept you waiting, Fanny, dear; but I could not get away from that tiresome Graham before;" and the speaker was not Fanny Merton but Geraldine Otway.

And now had I not so exactly and fearlessly told the plain truth up to this present moment, I should feel tempted here to depart from it, and slur over matters a little, for instead of instantly rising, and saying as any honourable, high principled man would have done, "Miss Otway, it is Lawrence Saville, not Miss Merton," I treacherously and silently retained my seat, still keeping the handkerchief to my face.

"I promised you, dear friend, to tell you what I was crying for before I should go to bed to-night," she said in a low, sweet tone, which, alas! was almost unknown to me, so rarely had she employed it in my presence.

"It was not the letter as you thought. No, it is because that wretch, Saville, who does not care one farthing for me, is going away to-morrow, and, God help me, Fanny! I dearly love him."

Here a little soft arm stole round my neck, and with a gasping sob she laid her head upon my breast.

Suddenly, involuntarily, I pressed her to my heart with a

rapture beyond the power of words to express. Whether the fervour of my embrace awoke her suspicions; or, that her soft cheek had come in contact with my rough bearded one, she suddenly sprang from my side, and in a voice thrilling in its agonized shame and terror, gasped forth,

"For God's sake, who are you?"

In a moment I was at her feet, telling I was one who loved as no man had ever loved her yet, loved her in silence, in hopeless despair, almost from the moment we had first met.

"What! Lawrence Saville?" she whispered.

I renewed my prayers, my vows; but she recoiled from me in horror.

"False, cruel, treacherous!" she faltered. "How dare you allow me to betray myself thus?"

Almost forgetting in my sympathy with the terrible humiliation of that proud though noble nature, my own boundless joy to know myself beloved by her, I still knelt at her feet, imploring her to forgive—to listen to me.

"Begone from my sight, for ever," she passionately exclaimed.

"I believe not in this story of your new-found love, and even if it be true, I shall go down unwedded to my grave before you shall ever place a ring on my finger."

At this moment the door opened, and Mrs. Merton, bearing a waxen taper, entered. Her look of offended amazement on seeing Miss Otway's terrible agitation, and I kneeling at her feet, was indescribable.

"What is it?" she asked. "Tell me, Geraldine, at once."

"He, that man has insulted me," she answered, with death-pale face and glittering eyes.

My hostess turned majestically towards me, and I rose to my feet.

"How dare you, sir," she angrily questioned. "How dare you insult a young lady under my protection—under my roof. It is fortunate that you intend leaving without delay, or I should be under the necessity of saying to you—go. Mr. Saville, I have been terribly deceived in you. You are one of the very last I would have suspected capable of such conduct!"

I listened in silence to all this, for a firm resolution was taken by me in that moment to never give to man or woman explanation of the present scene; and if she chose to leave me open to obloquy and blame, was it not a cheap price to pay for the knowledge that the priceless treasure of her love was mine?

"Leave me, sir, and never let me see you again under my roof," continued Mrs. Merton, waving me imperiously from the room, whilst Miss Otway, turning to still more marble whiteness, leaned against her for support.

Resolving to make my preparations for departure without delay, I proceeded to my own room, but 'ere I had been long there, a slight tap sounded at my door, and opening it, I found it was Captain Graham.

"Mr. Saville," he said, "we are both men of the world, so a few words will suffice. I happened to be in the hall when Miss Otway made her indignant complaint to Mrs. Merton that you had insulted her. Though having no legal right to defend that young lady, she is very dear to me, and without waiting for further formalities, I ask at your hands reparation for the insult she alleges having received from you?"

"At your own time and hour, Captain Graham," I stiffly replied.

"Well, if I mistake not, you intend leaving for town early to-morrow, and I will run down the day after. We can then settle everything, as well as invent a cause for our quarrel, for the young lady's name must not be mixed up in it."

I handed him my card with place of residence on it, inwardly thinking he was a manly and spirited, if not successful wooer; and with a formal interchange of bows, we parted.

Then I sat down to think for my brain was almost giddy. I who had never yet been engaged in a duel, even as a second, was now pledged to one with an adversary who was a practical hand; then again, I, a most peaceful, unoffending man by disposition, found myself lying under the grave charge of having grossly insulted a young lady in a house where I was a guest. But what mattered it all? I was beloved by her whom I had so blindly worshipped in secret, and even though she might never consent to look on me again (a thing possible with that wayward, proud spirit), the blissful consciousness that her love was mine, was amply worth all I had suffered or might suffer.

When my parting arrangements were completed, I sat down and wrote to Geraldine Otway a letter such as a man on the brink of parting from life might write to her who was the chief link that bound him to it. There was no mocking smile to dread now, no scornful taunt to fear; and I poured out my whole soul in the letter I was writing. All was earnest between her and I now. I told her, my proud, beautiful darling, how, from the first, I had struggled against loving her, how when affection for her, despite my efforts, had crept into my heart, I had striven to tear it thence, never daring to dream it could be returned, but had been foiled, worsted in the combat, succeeding only in hiding my secret, and finding the only sure means of doing that—flight. I went over it all; my struggle with self in the wood the day of the storm; during our ride; our botanical excursion; and then, when my letter was finished, I sealed, pressed it to my lips for her sake, and rose to my feet.

Day was dawning cold and chill; and I resolved to hasten down to the stables and get out my horse myself, but the bridle was not to be found, and the servants were still in bed. Action was necessary to me, and finding the keen sharp air of early morning welcome to my hot cheek and temples, I decided on a stroll down the road. On my return I saw a sleepy stable boy lounging near the gate, and I gave him the requisite directions. Whilst he was attending to them, I scribbled a line to my host containing farewell thanks and excuses for my early departure, mentioning I should send for my luggage the ensuing day. This note I left on the hall table, then with one long yearning look towards the closely curtained window of Miss Otway's room, one wild agonized wish that we might yet meet again, were it only for a moment, I descended the stairs and took my solitary way.

It was hard, too, loving and loved, to part thus, but earth gives only a certain portion of happiness to each of her children, and I had had probably my share, surely an ample one, when leaning her head on my breast she had avowed her love. Would she ever relent later? Well, it did not matter much, for though no coward, I was also no shot, Graham a sure one, so in all probability, my heart so restless and full of throbbing emotions now, would soon be quiet enough. Suddenly, who should confront me emerging from a side alley but Miss Otway herself. Despite the great agitation of the moment, I noticed she looked very ill, and her eyes were swollen as if with weeping.

Almost as much embarrassed as herself, I was silent for a moment and then entreatingly said:

"Miss Otway, dare I hope that your hand will touch mine in friendly greeting before we part? I am leaving now."

"Ah, so you and that tiresome Captain Graham are really running to town to have a quiet shot at each other. What redoubtable Don Quixotes you both are!"

This was said with a very wretched attempt at her usual careless sarcasm, and then suddenly bursting into tears, she covered her face with hands, whispering:

"Forgive me, Lawrence, forgive me! Your noble letter (I have already stolen and mean to always keep it) has softened at last my icy, selfish heart, and I can bring myself not only to confess my follies, but also plead for your pardon."

My darling! Surely the rapture of that moment was worth a life's ransom! Then we walked to a garden seat near us, and with the soft twittering of birds overhead and the glorious hues of sunrise rolling up in the east, bringing morning's pure fragrant breath to us, she entered on her short tale. I have never witnessed a summer sunrise since that memorable morning without recalling with gratitude to the Giver of all Good the happiness its soft dawning once brought me.

"Well, Lawrence, for so I will henceforth call you," she faltered, her charming colour and frequent pauses betraying an agitation that rendered her so feminine, so doubly dear to me, "after you left us last night, I went at once to my room, and throwing myself on a sofa, sobbed and raved alternately at myself and you, till I was almost exhausted. It was so inexpressibly mortifying to have betrayed myself so utterly to you, who had always recoiled from my advances; as to your avowal of love, I looked on it as a fiction, invented at the moment to meet that which I had so openly declared for yourself. After a time reason regained some little sway, and then Mrs. Merton knocked at my door and entered, full of wrath against you and compassion for myself. Oh, Lawrence, it was decreed that you should be an instrument in cruelly humbling my overweening pride, for there, sitting at her feet, my burning face bowed on her motherly lap, I had to do you justice and tell my tale clearly and plainly. Once finished she gently stroked my head and said: "Noble young man, how generously he bore for your sake unmerited obloquy and reproach!" Whilst Mrs. Merton was yet speaking, her quick ear caught the sound of cautious footsteps in the passage. She carefully peered out and saw Capt. Graham enter your room. The circumstance was unusual, for all the household had retired to rest, and divining some mischief, she lay in wait for him, and on his return pounced on and dragged him into the small sitting-room where we often sew and chat on rainy mornings. When smilingly but abruptly interrogated as to his business with yourself, he hesitated and stammered, upon which Mrs. Merton, who immediately began to suspect the true state of things, subjected him to a most searching cross-examination. He was yet blundering through a confused, equivocating reply, through which, however, a portion of truth penetrated, when she called my trembling self in. Again, Lawrence, you were avenged of all I had made you suffer, as I stammered forth a declaration that not only were you entirely guiltless of having insulted me in any manner, but that, I know not how it came out, you were anything but an object of dislike to me. I found some consolation for my own overwhelming mortification in the knowledge of the pang I inflicted at the same time on my luckless admirer whose officiousness had rendered the explanation necessary.

"This hard task over, Mrs. Merton brought me back to my room, and insisted on my lying down, as all danger of a duel between yourself and Captain Graham was now over. But I could not rest. I still feared some rashness on your part, some treachery on his, and I resolved to have an explanation with yourself in the morning before you should leave, a coldly polite one of course, containing a final farewell, something very different to this; so that anything like mischief should be entirely precluded. Worn out with watching, I fell into a doze on the sofa, a little before day-break.

"Awoke by the sound of a door closing, I sprang to the window, and saw you leaving the house. Oh, in that moment, Lawrence, I first realized how dear you were to me, and trembling with anxiety, I hurried in the direction of your room, the door of which was open, to gather, if possible, some indication of where or for what you had gone so early. This letter (my darling pressed it to her lips as she spoke) was lying on the table. It was addressed to me, and breaking the seal, I read it. Need I say its generous devotion touched me even to the inmost core of my wayward heart; need I tell you I sobbed and cried over it, fearing you had left me for ever. Ah, my selfish pride was utterly and completely subdued! Suddenly I heard the front gate unclose, and looking out, saw you enter the grounds. No time for delay, for hesitation now, and with a beating heart I hastened down the side staircase. A few moments of irresolution, a last short, sharp struggle with myself, as I saw you hastening away, and the end is told."

It was my turn now, and at the risk of being tedious, I went over all that I had previously said in my letter, and she listened in blushing, quiet happiness. After a long, blissful hour together, my promised wife left me to dress for breakfast, and I, still almost unable to believe in my unhoped for happiness, sat on, listening in a sort of dream-like rapture to the pleasant sounds of morning.

A more prosaical turn was given to my thoughts after a time by seeing Captain Graham coming leisurely down the walk. He certainly did not look so miserable as I expected, but the latent fierceness with which he occasionally decapitated some harmless flower that grew within reach of his tiny cane proved his thoughts were not of a very pleasant character. Scarcely decided how to meet him, I silently waited his approach, but as soon as he saw me, he languidly said:

"Aw! Good morning Saville. I'm deuced glad there's no necessity for that little affair between us coming off. 'Tis really as unpleasant to shoot at a fellow as to be shot at. Must say I was never in my life so taken aback, indeed, I may say stunned, as when Geraldine, hem! Miss Otway, I should say, informed me in one breath that I was an officious noodle, whom she hated as much as she liked yourself. You are a deuced sly fellow, Saville! Thought all along you were in love with that pretty little Merton girl."

"So I might have been at one time, only her affections were otherwise engaged," I answered, anxious to give my blue eyed friend a "lift."

"Really! To that big shouldered Chester, I suppose. Some women are so fond of giants. Yet no, she'd often cut him confoundedly short when he'd go up to talk to her. Perhaps it is that clever Canadian party who came from town last week, and wrote smart verses in French about her eyes and golden tresses. Wonder if he meant that Japanese switch, as the ladies call it, which she coils round her head?"

"The fact is, Captain Graham, Miss Merton never made me her confidant, but I have a considerable amount of sharpness, hem! where I am not concerned myself," I suddenly added remembering my own late inveterate blindness in a case somewhat analogous, "and I have only to say that you are no coxcomb."

The significant emphasis, and significant look I favoured my companion with here must have been very eloquent indeed, for all at once opening his sleepy blue eyes very wide, his cheek slightly flushing at the same time, he said:

"You don't mean to say that I'm the favoured man?"

I smiled, but maintained a prudent silence.

"Well, I never dreamed of such a thing. I was so taken up with that shrewish, hem! with Miss Otway, I mean. But, say, hadn't you better try to look a little more like a man going to breakfast, and a little less like Speke, Livingston, or any of those other great travellers?"

Thanking him for the really serviceable hint, for my actual equipment was certainly not a proper breakfast costume where ladies were expected to be present, my beard, owing to mental agitation, having remained unshorn, whilst my portmanteau lay prostrate on the ground a few paces from me, I left him, inwardly hoping that the saying about hearts being easily caught at a rebound, might hold good in his case and that of my fair ally.

Later it really did, and Fanny Merton, long since Mrs. Captain Graham, is still an intimate friend of Geraldine Saville, my well-loved wife.

In justice to the latter I must say before closing this short episode of my life, that Miss Otway showed me more temper and waywardness during the short period I knew her, than Mrs. Saville has done in the course of the sixteen years that have elapsed since we joined our destinies together, a step, I may safely aver, neither of us have ever once regretted.

— Comedy of manners — Jane Austin-ish.

— Sitting room, parlour, dance etc. — place for womens stories to unfold

Susan Frances Harrison (1859-1935)

Susan Frances Harrison was a prominent contributor of reviews, interviews, poems, songs and stories to the influential Toronto literary periodical *The Week*, as well as a variety of Canadian, American and British magazines and newspapers. She was well-known as a professional pianist and singer, and was particularly interested in the folk culture of Quebec. She was born in Toronto and educated there and in Montreal; in 1879 she married John Harrison, a professional musician, and lived with him and their two children in Ottawa and Toronto. Harrison often published under pseudonyms: the best-known was "Seranus," which she explained was invented by an editor who misread her signature, S. Frances Harrison.

Harrison's first book was a collection of short stories, *Crowded Out! And other Sketches* (Ottawa: 1886). She subsequently published two novels and numerous collections of poetry.

The Idyl of the Island

There lies mid-way between parallels 48 and 49 of latitude, and degrees 89 and 90 of longitude, in the northern hemisphere of the New World, serenely anchored on an ever-rippling and excited surface, an exquisitely lovely island. No tropical wonder of palm-treed stateliness, or hot tangle of gaudy bird and glowing creeper, can compare with it; no other northern isle, cool and green and refreshing to the eye like itself, can surpass it. It is not a large island. It is about half-a-mile long and quarter of a mile broad. It is an irregular oval in shape, and has two distinct and different sides. On the west side its grey limestone rises to the height of twenty feet straight out of the water. On the east side there occurs a gradual shelving of a sumach-fringed shore, that mingles finally with the ever-rippling water. For the waters in this northern country are never still. They are perpetually bubbling up and boiling over; seething and fuming and frothing and foaming and yet remaining so cool and clear that a quick fancy would discover thousands of banished fountains under that agitated and impatient surface. Both ends of the island are as much alike as its sides are dissimilar. They taper off almost to a distinct blade-point of rock, in which a mere doll's flagstaff of a pine-tree grows; then comes a small detached rock, with a small evergreen on it, then a still smaller rock, with a tuft of grass, then a line of partially submerged stones, and so out to the deep yet ever-bubbling water. This island might seem just the size for two, and there were two on it on a certain July morning at five o'clock. One of these was a lady who lay at full length and fast asleep upon a most unique couch. These northern islands are in many places completely covered with a variety of yellowish-green moss, varying from a couple of inches to a foot and a half in thickness; and yielding to the pressure of the foot or the body as comfortably as a feather bed, if not more so, being elastic in nature. A large square of this had been cut up from some other part of the island and placed on the already moss-grown and cushioned ground, serving as a mattrass, while two smaller pieces served as pillows. A sumach tree at the head of the improvised couch gave the necessary shade to the face of the sleeper, while a wild grape-vine, after having run over and encircled with its moist green every stone and stem on the island, fulfilled its longing at length in a tumultuous possession of the sumach, making a massive yet aerial patched green curtain or canopy to the fantastic bed, and ending seemingly in two tiny transparent spirals curling up to the sky.

    If there were a fault in the structure it was that it was too clever, too well thought out, too rectangular, too much in fact like a bed. But it told certainly of a skilful pair of hands and of a beautiful mind and the union of art with nature perfectly suited the charms—contradictory yet consistent—of the occupant. For being anything but a beautiful woman she was still far from a plain one, which though no original mode of putting it does convey the actual impression she made upon a gentleman in a small boat who rowing past this island at the hour of five o'clock in the morning was so much struck with this curious sight, quite visible from the water below, that he was

Imprisoned — from Brit literary World —

rude enough to stand up that he might see better. The lady was dressed in some dark blue stuff that evidently covered her all over and fitted tightly where it could be seen. A small linen collar, worn all night and therefore shorn of its usual freshness was round her neck, and she was tucked up from the waist under a Scotch woollen rug. Her hair, of a peculiar red-brown, was allowed to hang about her and was lovely; her mouth sad; her nose, rather too prominent; her complexion natural and healthy, but marred by freckles and moles, not many of either but undeniably scattered over the countenance. All told but her eyes which, if they proved to match with her hair, would atone for these other shortcomings. The gentleman sat down again and reflected.

"How still it is!" he said under his breath. "Absolutely not a thing stirring. This is the time when the fish bite. I ought to be fishing I suppose. Going to be warm by-and-bye."

It was indeed almost absolutely silent. The sun climbed higher but the lady slept on, and the gentleman gazed as if fascinated. The only sound that broke the beautiful early morning silence was the occasional weird laugh of the loon. It came twice and then a third time. The sleeper stirred.

"If that thing out there cries again she will wake," said the gentleman to himself. "I must be off before that happens. But I *should* like to see her eyes. What a pretty picture it is!" Once more the loon gave its maniacal laugh and the lady started, sat bolt upright and wide awake. Her admirer had not time to retreat but he took his oars up and confronted her manfully. It was an awkward moment. He apologized. The lady listened very politely. Then she smiled.

"Most of the islands in this lake are owned by private people," she said, "who use them during the summer months for the purpose of camping out upon them. I should advise you, if you row about much here, to keep to the open water, unless you wish to be seriously handled by the fathers and mothers of families."

"Thank you very much," returned the gentleman, standing up in his boat, "I assure you I intended no rudeness, but I have never seen so charming a summer couch before, and I was really fascinated by the—ah,—the picture you made. May I ask what you mean by 'camping out'? Is it always done in this fashion?"

The lady stared. "Have *you* never camped out?"

"Never in my life," said the gentleman. "I am an Englishman, staying at the hotel near the point for a day or two. I came out to see something of the country."

"Then you should at least have camped out for a week or so. That is a genuine Canadian experience," said the lady with a frankness which completely restored the equanimity of the Englishman.

"But how do you live?" he went on in a puzzled manner that caused the lady with the red-brown hair, still all hanging about her, much amusement.

"O, capitally! Upon fish and eggs, and gooseberry tarts, and home-made bread and French coffee. Just what you would get in town, and much better than you get at the hotel."

"O, that would be easy!" the gentleman groaned. "I eat my meals in a pitch-dark room, in deadly fear and horror of the regiments of flies that swarm in and settle on everything the minute one raises the green paper blinds"

The lady nodded. "I know. We tried it for two or three seasons, but we could not endure it; the whole thing, whitewash and all, is so trying, isn't it? So we bought this lovely island and bring our tent here and live *so* comfortably." The gentleman did not reply at once. He was thinking that it was his place to say "Good morning," and go, although he would much have liked to remain a little longer. He hazarded the remark:

"Now, for instance, what are you going to breakfast on presently?"

The lady laughed lightly and shook her red-brown hair.

"First of all I have to make a fire."

"Oh!"

"But that is not so very difficult."

"How do you do it?"

"Would you like to know?"

"Very much indeed. I should like to see, if I may."

The lady reflected a moment. "I suppose you may, but if

you do, you ought to help me, don't you think?" The gentleman much amused and greatly interested.

"Ah but you see, it is you I want to see make it. I am very useless you know at that sort of thing, still, if you will allow me, I will try my best. Am I to come ashore?"

"Certainly, if you are to be of any use."

The lady jumped lightly off the pretty couch of moss and wound her plentiful hair round her head with one turn of her arm. Her dress was creased but well-fitting, her figure not plump enough for beauty but decidedly youthful. She watched her new friend moor his boat and ascend with one or two strides of his long legs up the side of the cliff that was not so steep. He took off his hat.

"I am at your service," he said with a profound bow. The lady made him another, during which all her long hair fell about her again, at which they both laughed.

"What do we do first?" said he.

"O we find a lot of sticks and pieces of bark, mostly birch bark, and anything else that will burn—you may have to fell a tree while you are about it—and I'll show you how to place them properly between two walls of stones, put a match to them and there is our fire. Will you come with me?"

He assented of course, and they were soon busy in the interior of the little wood that grew up towards the centre of the island. I must digress here to say that the gentleman's name was Amherst. He was known to the world in latter life as Admiral Amherst, and he was a great friend of mine. When he related this story to me, he was very particular in describing the island as I have done—indeed he carried a little chart about with him of it which he had made from memory, and he told me besides that he never forgot the peculiar beauty of that same little tract of wood. The early hour, the delicious morning air, the great moss-grown and brown decaying tree trunks, the white, clammy, ghostly flower or fungus of the Indian Pipe at his feet, the masses of ferns, the elastic ground he trod upon, and the singular circumstance that he was alone in this exquisite spot with a woman he had never seen until five minutes previously, all combined to make an ineffaceable impression upon his mind.

The lady showed herself proficient in the art of building a fire and attended by Amherst soon had a fine flame rising up from between the fortifications evidently piled by stronger hands than her own.

"What do we do now?" asked Amherst. "I should suggest—a kettle."

"Of course, that is the next step. If I give it to you, you might run and fill it, eh?"

"Delighted!" and away went Amherst. When he returned the lady was not to be seen. The place was shorn of its beauty, but he waited discreetly and patiently, putting the kettle on to boil in the meanwhile.

"It's very singular," said he, "how I come to be here. I wonder who are with her in her party; no one else appears to be up or about. That striped red and white thing is the tent, I see, over there. Ah! that's where she has gone, and now she beckons me! Oh! I'll go, but I don't want to meet the rest of them!"

But when he reached the tent, it was quite empty, save rugs and wraps, boxes, etc., and the lady was laughingly holding out a loaf of bread in one hand and a paper package in the other.

"You will stay and breakfast with me?"

"What will you give me?" said Amherst, smiling.

"I can only give eggs boiled in the kettle, coffee and bread and butter. The fish haven't come in yet."

"What can be nicer than eggs—especially when boiled in the kettle, that is, if you make the coffee first."

"Certainly I do."

"And is it really French coffee?"

"Really. Café des Gourmets, you know; we—I always use it—do not like any other."

Amherst was fast falling in love. He told me that at this point his mind was quite made up that if it were possible he would remain in the neighbourhood a few days at least, in order to see more of this charming girl. She seemed to him to be about twenty-six or seven, and so frank, simple and graceful, one could not have resisted liking her. Her hair and eyes were identical in colour and both were beautiful; her expression was arch and some of her gestures almost childish, but a certain dignity appeared at times and sat well upon her. Her hands were destitute of any rings as Amherst soon discovered, and were fine and small though brown. While she made the coffee, Amherst threw himself down on the wonderful moss, the like of which he had never seen before and looked out over the water. An unmistakeable constraint had taken the place of the unaffected hilarity of the first ten minutes. A reaction had set in. Amherst could of course only answer to me in telling this for himself, but he divined at the time a change in his companion's manner as well.

"I hope you like your eggs," she said presently.

"They are very nice, indeed, thank you," rejoined Amherst.

"And I have made your coffee as you like it?"

"Perfectly, thank you. But you—you are not eating anything! Why is that?"

As he asked the question he turned quickly around, in order to rise that he might help her with the ponderous kettle that she was about lifting off the camp-fire, when a long strand of her hair escaping from its coil blew directly across his face. Amherst uttered a radiant "Oh!" and taking it to his lips forgot himself so far as to press kiss after kiss upon it. The lady stood as if transfixed and did not move, even when Amherst actually swept all her hair down over one arm and turning her face to his, pressed one long kiss on her forehead.

The moment he had done this his senses returned and he stepped back in indignation with himself. But his companion was still apparently transfixed. Amherst looked at her in dismay. She did not seem to see him and had grown very pale. He touched her gently on the arm but she did not show that she felt the touch. He retreated a few paces and stood by himself, overcome with shame and contrition. What had he done? How should he ever atone for such an unwarrantable action? Had it been the outcome of any ordinary flirtation, he would have felt no such scruples, but the encounter, though short, had been one of singular idyllic charm until he had by his own rash act spoilt it. A few minutes passed thus in self contemplation appeared like an eternity. He must speak.

"If you would allow me—"

But the lady put out her left hand in deprecation as it were and he got no further. The silence was unendurable. Amherst took a step or two forward and perceived great tears rolling down her cheeks.

"Oh!" he began desperately, "won't you allow me to say a word to tell you how very, very sorry I am, how grieved I am and always shall be? I never—I give you my word of honour—I never do those sort of things, have never done such a thing before! But I can't tell what it was, the place is so beautiful, and when all that lovely hair came sweeping past my face, I could not help doing as I did, it was so electrical! Any man would have done the same. I know it sounds like a miserable, cowardly excuse, but it is true, perfectly true." The lady seemed to struggle to appear calm and with a great effort she turned her face towards Amherst.

"I know one man," she said, in a voice choked with sobs, "who would not have done it."

Amherst started. "I am sorrier than ever, believe me. I might have known you were engaged, or had a lover—one so charming"—

"It is not that," said the lady. "I am married." She was still struggling with her emotion.

Amherst recoiled. He was torn with conflicting thoughts. What if he had been seen giving that involuntary salute? He might have ruined her peace for ever. Who would believe in the truth of any possible explanation?

"I will leave you at once;" he said stiffly "there is nothing more to be said."

"Oh! you will reproach me now!" said his companion, wiping her eyes as the tears came afresh.

"I will try not to;" said Amherst, "but you could so easily have told me; I do not think it was—quite—fair." Yet he could not be altogether angry with the partner of his thoughtlessness, nor could he be entirely cold. Her beautiful eyes, her despairing attitude would haunt him he knew for many a day. She had ceased weeping and stood quietly awaiting his departure. Amherst felt all the force of a strong and novel passion sweep along his frame as he looked at her. Was she happy, was she a

The Idyl of the Island

loved and loving wife? Somehow the conviction forced itself upon him that she was not. Yet he could not ask her, it must remain her secret.

Amherst looked at his watch. It aroused her.

"What is the time?" she said lifting her head for the first time since he had kissed her.

"Ten minutes past six," Amherst replied.

"You must go," she said, with an effort at self-control. "I shall have much to do presently."

He cast one look about and approached her.

"Will you forgive me"—he began in a tone of repression, then with another mighty and involuntary movement he caught her hands and pressed them to his breast. "My God," he exclaimed, "how I should have loved you!"

A moment after he flung her hands away and strode down the cliff, unfastened his boat and rowed away in the direction of the hotel as fast as he could. Rounding a sharp rock that hid what lay beyond it, he nearly succeeded in overturning another boat like his own, in which sat a gentleman of middle age, stout and pleasant and mild of countenance. The bottom of the boat was full of fish. Amherst made an incoherent apology, to which the gentleman answered with a good-natured laugh, insisting that the fault was his own. He would have liked to enter into conversation with Amherst, but my friend was only anxious to escape from the place altogether and forget his recent adventure in the hurry of departure from the hotel. Three days after he embarked at Quebec for England, and never revisited Canada. But he never married and never forgot the woman whom he always asserted he might have truly and passionately loved. He was about twenty-eight when that happened and perfectly heart-whole. Why—I used to say to him, why did you not learn her name and that of her husband? Perhaps she is a widow now, perhaps you made as great an impression upon her mind and affections as she did upon yours.

But my friend Admiral Amherst, as the world knew him, was a strange, irrational creature in many ways, and none of these ideas would he ever entertain. That the comfortable gentleman in the boat was her husband he never doubted; more it was impossible to divine. But the cool northern isle, with its dark fringe of pines; its wonderful moss, its fragrant and dewy ferns, its graceful sumachs, just putting on their scarlet tipped leaves, the morning stillness broken only by the faint unearthly cry of the melancholy loon, the spar-dyked cliffs of limestone, and the fantastic couch, with its too lovely occupant, never faded from his memory and remained to the last as realities which indeed they have become likewise to me, through the intensity with which they were described to me.

Edward William Thomson (1849-1924)

E.W. Thomson trained as a civil engineer and land surveyor, but by the age of thirty had left this profession for journalism. He spent twelve years as an editorial writer and correspondent for *The Globe* in Toronto and Montreal, and subsequently worked as a "revising editor" for *Youth's Companion*, a Boston magazine. He returned to Canada in 1901 as Ottawa correspondent for the *Boston Evening Transcript*. Thomson maintained an active correspondence with fellow writers D.C. Scott and Ethelwyn Wetherald, and was close friends with poet Archibald Lampman.

Thomson's first collection of stories was published in 1895, and "Old Man Savarin," which had previously appeared in *Two Tales* 1:1 (March 12, 1892): 279-304, was the title story. Its use of dialect and its technique of "othering" francophone Canadians by describing them as "quaint" and uneducated is racist by contemporary standards; such representations were typical of the turn-of-the-century "local colour" story set in Quebec. Thomson subsequently published two books for children, a collection of poems and several other works.

Old Man Savarin

Old Ma'ame Paradis had caught seventeen small doré, four suckers, and eleven channel-catfish before she used up all the worms in her tomato-can. Therefore she was in a cheerful and loquacious humour when I came along and offered her some of my bait.

"Merci; non, M'sieu. Dat's 'nuff fishin' for me. I got too old now for fish too much. You like me make you present of six or seven doré? Yes? All right. Then you make me present of one quarter dollar."

When this transaction was completed, the old lady got out her short black clay pipe, and filled it with *tabac blanc*.

"Ver' good smell for scare mosquitoes," said she. "Sit

down, M'sieu. For sure I like to be here, me, for see the river when she's like this."

Indeed the scene was more than picturesque. Her fishing-platform extended twenty feet from the rocky shore of the great Rataplan Rapid of the Ottawa, which, beginning to tumble a mile to the westward, poured a roaring torrent half a mile wide into the broader, calm brown reach below. Noble elms towered on the shores. Between their trunks we could see many white-washed cabins, whose doors of blue or green or red scarcely disclosed their colours in that light.

The sinking sun, which already touched the river, seemed somehow the source of the vast stream that flowed radiantly from its blaze. Through the glamour of the evening mist and the maze of June flies we could see a dozen men scooping for fish from platforms like that of Ma'ame Paradis.

Each scooper lifted a great hoop-net set on a handle some fifteen feet long, threw it easily up stream, and swept it on edge with the current to the full length of his reach. Then it was drawn out and at once thrown upward again, if no capture had been made. In case he had taken fish, he came to the inshore edge of his platform, and upset the net's contents into a pool separated from the main rapid by an improvised wall of stones.

"I'm too old for scoop some now," said Ma'ame Paradis, with a sigh.

"You were never strong enough to scoop, surely," said I.

"No, eh? All right, M'sieu. Then you hain't nev' hear 'bout the time Old Man Savarin was catched up with. No, eh? Well, I'll tol' you 'bout that." And this was her story as she told it to me.

* * *

"Der was fun dose time. Nobody ain't nev' catch up with dat old rascal ony other time since I'll know him first. Me, I'll be only fifteen den. Dat's long time 'go, eh? Well, for sure, I ain't so old like what I'll look. But Old Man Savarin was old already. He's old, old, old, when he's only thirty; an' *mean— baptême!* If de old Nick ain' got de hottest place for dat old stingy—yes, for sure!

Old Man Savarin

"You'll see up dere where Frawce Seguin is scoop? Dat's the Laroque platform by right. Me, I was a Laroque. My fader was use for scoop dere, an' my gran'fader—the Laroques scoop dere all de time since ever dere was some Rapid Rataplan. Den Old Man Savarin he's buyed the land up dere from Felix Ladoucier, an' he's told my fader, 'You can't scoop no more wisout you pay me rent.'

"'Rent!' my fader say. '*Saprie!* Dat's my fader's platform for scoop fish! You ask anybody.'

"'Oh, I'll know all 'bout dat,' Old Man Savarin is say. 'Ladoucier let you scoop front of his land, for Ladoucier one big fool. De lan's mine now, an' de fishin' right is mine. You can't scoop dere wisout you pay me rent.'

"'*Baptême!* I'll show you 'bout dat,' my fader say.

"Next mawny he is go for scoop same like always. Den Old Man Savarin is fetch my fader up before de magistrate. De magistrate make my fader pay nine shillin'!

"'Mebbe dat's learn you one lesson,' Old Man Savarin is say.

"My fader swear pretty good, but my moder say: 'Well, Narcisse, dere hain' no use for take it out in *malediction*. De nine shillin' is paid. You scoop more fish—dat's the way.'

"So my fader he is go out early, early nex' mawny. He's scoop, he's scoop. He's catch plenty fish before Old Man Savarin come.

"'You ain't got 'nuff yet for fishin' on my land, eh? Come out of dat,' Old Man Savarin is say.

"'*Saprie!* Ain't I pay nine shillin' for fish here?' my fader say.

"'*Oui*—you pay nine shillin' for fish here *wisout* my leave. But you ain't pay nothin' for fish here *wis* my leave. You is goin' up before de magistrate some more.'

"So he is fetch my fader up anoder time. An' de magistrate make my fader pay twelve shillin' more!

"'Well, I s'pose I can go fish on my fader's platform now,' my fader is say.

"Old Man Savarin was laugh. 'Your honour, dis man tink he don't have for pay me no rent, because you'll make him pay two fines for trespass on my land.'

"So de magistrate told my fader he hain't got no more right for go on his own platform than he was at the start. My fader is ver' angry. He's cry, he's tear his shirt; but Old Man Savarin only say, 'I guess I learn you one good lesson, Narcisse.'

"De whole village ain't told de old rascal how much dey was angry 'bout dat, for Old Man Savarin is got dem all in debt at his big store. He is grin, grin, and told everybody how he learn my fader two good lesson. An' he is told my fader: 'You see what I'll be goin' for do wis you if ever you go on my land again wisout you pay me rent.'

"'How much you want?' my fader say.

"'Half de fish you catch.'

"'Monjee! Never!'

"'Five dollar a year, den.'

"'*Saprie*, no. Dat's too much.'

"'All right. Keep off my lan', if you hain't want anoder lesson.'

"'You's a tief,' my fader say.

"'Hermidas, make up Narcisse Laroque bill,' de old rascal say to his clerk. 'If he hain't pay dat bill to-morrow, I sue him.'

"So my fader is scare mos' to death. Only my moder she's say, '*I'll* pay dat bill, me.'

"So she's take the money she's saved up long time for make my weddin' when it come. An' she's paid de bill. So den my fader hain't scare no more, an' he is shake his fist good under Old Man Savarin's ugly nose. But dat old rascal only laugh an' say, 'Narcisse, you like to be fined some more, eh?'

"'*Tort Dieu*. You rob me of my place for fish, but I'll take my platform anyhow,' my fader is say.

"'Yes, eh? All right—if you can get him wisout go on my land. But you go on my land, and see if I don't learn you anoder lesson,' Old Savarin is say.

"So my fader is rob of his platform, too. Nex' ting we hear, Frawce Seguin has rent dat platform for five dollars a year.

"Den de big fun begin. My fader an Frawce is cousin. All de time before den dey was good friend. But my fader he is go to Frawce Seguin's place an' he is told him, 'Frawce, I'll goin' lick you so hard you can't nev' scoop on my platform.'

"Frawce only laugh. Den Old Man Savarin come up de hill.

"'Fetch him up to de magistrate an' learn him anoder lesson,' he is say to Frawce.

"'What for?' Frawce say.

"'For try to scare you.'

"'He hain't hurt me none.'

"'But he's say he will lick you.'

"'Dat's only because he's vex,' Frawce say.

"'*Baptême! Non!* my fader say. 'I'll be goin' for lick you good, Frawce.'

"'For sure?' Frawce say.

"'*Saprie!* Yes; for sure.'

"'Well, dat's all right den, Narcisse. When you goin' for lick me?'

"'First time I'll get drunk. I'll be goin' for get drunk dis same day.'

"'All right, Narcisse. If you goin' get drunk for lick me, I'll be goin' get drunk for lick you'—*Canadien* hain't nev' fool 'nuff for fight, M'sieu, only if dey is got drunk.

"Well, my fader he's go on old Marceau's hotel, an' he's drink all day. Frawce Seguin he's go 'cross de road on Joe Maufraud's hotel, an' *he's* drink all day. When de night come, dey's bose stand out in front of de two hotel for fight.

"Dey's bose yell an' yell for make de oder feller scare bad before dey begin. Hermidas Laronde an' Jawnny Leroi dey's hold my fader for fear he's go 'cross de road for keel Frawce Seguin dead. Pierre Seguin an' Magloire Sauve is hold Frawce for fear he's come 'cross de road for keel my fader dead. And dose men fight dat way 'cross de road, till dey hain't hardly able for stand up no more.

"My fader he's tear his shirt and he's yell, 'Let me at him!' Frawce he's tear his shirt and he's yell, 'Let me at him!' But de men hain't goin' for let dem loose, for fear one is strike de oder ver' hard. De whole village is shiver 'bout dat offle fight—yes, seh, shiver bad!

"Well, dey's fight like dat for more as four hours, till dey hain't able for yell no more, an' dey hain't got no money left for buy wheeskey for de crowd. Den Marceau and Joe Maufraud tol' dem bose it was a shame for two cousins to fight so bad.

An' my fader he's say he's ver' sorry dat he lick Frawce so hard, and dey's bose sorry. So dey's kiss one anoder good—only all their close is tore to pieces.

"An' what you tink 'bout Old Man Savarin? Old Man Savarin is just stand in front of his store all de time, an' he's say: 'I'll tink I'll fetch him *bose* hup to de magistrate, an' learn him bose a lesson.'

"Me, I'll be only fifteen, but I hain't scare 'bout dat fight same like my moder is scare. No more is Alphonsine Seguin scare. She's seventeen, an' she wait for de fight to be all over. Den she take her fader home, same like I'll take my fader home for bed. Dat's after twelve o'clock of night.

"Nex' mawny early my fader he's groaned and he's groaned: 'Ah—ugh—I'm sick, sick, me. I'll be goin' for die dis time, for sure.'

"'You get up an' scoop some fish,' my moder she's say, angry. 'Den you hain't be sick no more.'

"'Ach—ugh—I'll hain't be able. Oh, I'll be so sick. An' I hain' got no place for scoop fish now no more. Frawce Seguin has rob my platform.'

"'Take de nex' one lower down,' my moder she's say.

"'Dat's Jawnny Leroi's.'

"'All right for dat. Jawnny he's hire for run timber to-day.'

"'Ugh—I'll not be able for get up. Send for M'sieu le Curè—I'll be goin' for die for sure.'

"'*Misère*, but dat's no *man!* Dat's a drunk pig,' my moder she's say, angry. 'Sick, eh? Lazy, lazy—dat's so. An' dere hain't no fish for de little chilluns, an' it's Friday mawny.' So my moder she's begin for cry.

"Well, M'sieu, I'll make de rest short; for de sun is all gone now. What you tink I do dat mawny? I take de big scoop-net an' I'll come up here for see if I'll be able for scoop some fish on Jawnny Leroi's platform. Only dere hain't nev' much fish dere.

"Pretty quick I'll look up and I'll see Alphonsine Seguin scoop, scoop on my fader's old platform. Alphonsine's fader is sick, sick, same like my fader, an' all de Seguin boys is too little for scoop, same like my brudders is too little. So dere Alphonsine she's scoop, scoop for breakfas'.

"What you tink I'll see some more? I'll see Old Man Savarin. He's watchin' from de corner of de cedar bush, an I'll know ver' good what he's watch for. He's watch for catch my fader go on his own platform. He's want for learn my fader anoder lesson. *Saprie!* dat's make me ver' angry, M'sieu!

"Alphonsine she's scoop, scoop plenty fish. I'll not be scoop none. Dat's make me more angry. I'll look up where Alphonsine is, an' I'll talk to myself:—

"'Dat's my fader's platform,' I'll be say. 'Dat's my fader's fish what you catch, Alphonsine. You hain't nev' be my cousin no more. It is mean, mean for Frawce Seguin to rent my fader's platform for please dat old rascal Savarin.' Mebby I'll not be so angry at Alphonsine, M'sieu, if I was able for catch some fish; but I hain't able—I don't catch none.

"Well, M'sieu, dat's de way for long time—half-hour mebby. Den I'll hear Alphonsine yell good. I'll look up de river some more. She's try for lift her net. She's try hard, hard, but she hain't able. De net is down in de rapid, an' she's only able for hang on to de hannle. Den I'll know she's got one big sturgeon, an' he's so big she can't pull him up.

"*Monjee!* what I care 'bout dat! I'll laugh me. Den I'll laugh good some more, for I'll want Alphonsine for see how I'll laugh big. And I'll talk to myself:—

"'Dat's good for dose Seguins,' I'll say. 'De big sturgeon will pull away de net. Den Alphonsine she will lose her fader's scoop wis de sturgeon. Dat's good 'nuff for dose Seguins! Take my fader platform, eh?'

"For sure, I'll want for go an' help Alphonsine all de same—she's my cousin, an' I'll want for see de sturgeon, me. But I'll only just laugh, laugh. *Non, M'sieu;* dere was not one man out on any of de oder platform dat mawny for to help Alphonsine. Dey was all sleep ver' late, for dey was all out ver' late for see de offle fight I told you 'bout.

"Well, pretty quick, what you tink? I'll see Old Man Savarin goin' to my fader's platform. He's take hold for help Alphonsine, an' dey's bose pull, and pretty quick de big sturgeon is up on de platform. I'll be more angry as before.

"Oh, *tort Dieu!* What you tink come den? Why, dat Old

Man Savarin is want for take de sturgeon!

"First dey hain't speak so I can hear, for de Rapid is too loud. But pretty quick dey's bose angry, and I hear dem talk.

"'Dat's my fish,' Old Man Savarin is say. 'Didn't I save him? Wasn't you goin' for lose him, for sure?'

"Me—I'll laugh good. Dass *such* an old rascal.

"'You get off dis platform, quick!' Alphonsine she's say.

"'Give me my sturgeon,' he's say.

"'Dat's a lie—it hain't your sturgeon. It's *my* sturgeon,' she's yell.

"'I'll learn you one lesson 'bout dat,' he's say.

"Well, M'sieu, Alphonsine she's pull back de fish just when Old Man Savarin is make one grab. An' when she's pull back, she's step to one side, an' de old rascal he is grab at de fish, an' de heft of de sturgeon is make him fall on his face, so he's tumble in de Rapid when Alphonsine let go de sturgeon. So der's Old Man Savarin floating in de river—and *me!* I'll don' care eef he's drown one bit!

"One time he is on his back, one time he is on his face, one time he is all under de water. For sure he's goin' for be draw into de *culbute* an' get drown' dead, if I'll not be able for scoop him when he's go by my platform. I'll want for laugh, but I'll be too much scare.

"Well, M'sieu, I'll pick up my fader's scoop and I'll stand out on de edge of de platform. De water is run so fast, I'm mos' 'fraid de old man is boun' for pull me in when I'll scoop him. But I'll not mind for dat, I'll throw de scoop an' catch him; an' for sure, he's hold on good.

"So dere's de old rascal in de scoop, but when I'll get him safe, I hain't able for pull him in one bit. I'll only be able for hold on an' laugh, laugh—he's look *ver'* queer! All I can do is to hold him dere so he can't go down de *culbute*. I'll can't pull him up if I'll want to.

"De ole man is scare ver' bad. But pretty quick he's got hold of de cross-bar of de hoop, an' he's got his ugly old head up good.

"'Pull me in,' he say, ver' angry.

"'I'll hain't be able,' I'll say.

Old Man Savarin 69

"Jus' den Alphonsine she's come 'long, an' she's laugh so she can't hardly hold on wis me to de hannle. I was laugh good some more. When de old villain see us have fun, he's yell: 'I'll learn you bose one lesson for this. Pull me ashore!'

"'Oh! you's learn us bose one lesson, M'sieu Savarin, eh?' Alphonsine she's say. 'Well, den, us bose will learn M'sieu Savarin one lesson first. Pull him up a little,' she's say to me.

"So we pull him up, an' den Alphonsine she's say to me: 'Let out de hannle, quick'—and he's under de water some more. When we stop de net, he's got hees head up pretty quick.

"'*Monjee!* I'll be drown' if you don't pull me out,' he's mos' cry.

"'Ver' well—if you's drown, your family be ver' glad,' Alphonsine she's say. 'Den they's got all your money for spend quick, quick.'

"M'sieu, dat scare him offle. He's begin for cry like one baby.

"'Save me out,' he's say. 'I'll give you anything I've got.'

"'How much?' Alphonsine she's say.

"He's tink, and he's say, 'Quarter dollar.'

"Alphonsine an' me is laugh, laugh.

"'Save me,' he's cry some more. 'I hain't fit for die dis mawny.'

"'You hain't fit for live no mawny,' Alphonsine she's say. 'One quarter dollar, eh? Where's my sturgeon?'

"'He's got away when I fall in,' he's say.

"'How much you goin' give me for lose my big sturgeon?' she's ask.

"'How much you'll want, Alphonsine?'

"'Two dollare.'

"'Dat's too much for one sturgeon,' he's say. For all he was not feel fit for die, he was more 'fraid for pay out his money.

"'Let him down some more,' Alphonsine she's say.

"'Oh, *misère, misère!* I'll pay de two dollare,' he's say when his head come up some more.

"'Ver' well, den,' Alphonsine she's say; 'I'll be willin' for save you, *me*. But you hain't scooped by *me*. You's in Marie's net. I'll only come for help Marie. You's her sturgeon'; an' Alphonsine she's laugh an' laugh.

"'I didn't lost no sturgeon for Marie,' he's say.

"'No, eh?' I'll say mysef. 'But you's steal my fader's platform. You's take his fishin' place. You's got him fined two times. You's make my moder pay his bill wis *my* weddin' money. What you goin' pay for all dat? You tink I'll be goin' for mos' kill mysef pullin' you out for noting? When you ever do someting for anybody for noting, eh, M'sieu Savarin?'

"'How much you want?' he's say.

"'Ten dollare for de platform, dat's all.'

"'Never—dat's robbery,' he's say, an' he's begin to cry like *ver'* li'll baby.

"'Pull him hup, Marie, an' give him some more,' Alphonsine she's say.

"But de old rascal is so scare 'bout dat, dat he's say he's pay right off. So we's pull him up near to de platform, only we hain't big 'nuff fool for let him out of de net till he's take out his purse an' pay de twelve dollare.

"*Monjee,* M'sieu! If ever you see one angry old rascal! He not even stop for say: 'T'ank you for save me from be drown' dead in the *culbute!* He's run for his house an' he's put on dry clo'es, and' he's go up to de magistrate first ting for learn me an' Alphonsine one big lesson.

"But de magistrate hain' ver' bad magistrate. He's only laugh an' he's say:—

"'M'sieu Savarin, de whole river will be laugh at you for let two young girl take eet out of smart man like you like dat. Hain't you tink your life worth twelve dollare? Didn't dey save you from de *culbute? Monjee!* I'll tink de whole river not laugh so ver' bad if you pay dose young girl one hunder dollare for save you so kind.'

"'One hunder dollare!' he's mos' cry. 'Hain't you goin' to learn dose girl one lesson for take advantage of me dat way?'

"'Didn't you pay dose girl yourself? Didn't you took out your purse yourself? Yes, eh? Well, den, I'll goin' for learn you one lesson yourself, M'sieu Savarin,' de magistrate is say. 'Dose two young girl is ver' wicked, eh? Yes, dat's so. But for why? Hain't dey just do to you what you been doin' ever since you was in beesness? Don' I know? You hain' never yet got advantage of nobody wisout you rob him all you can, an' dose wicked young girl only act just like you give dem a lesson all your life.'

"An' de best fun was de whole river *did* laugh at M'sieu Savarin. An' my fader and Frawce Seguin is laugh most of all, till he's catch hup wis bose of dem anoder time. You come for see me some more, an' I'll tol' you 'bout dat."

Gilbert Parker (1862-1932)

Gilbert Parker left Canada in 1885 after obtaining a degree from the University of Toronto; he became an assistant editor of the Sydney *Morning Herald* in Australia and in 1889 moved to England. There he became a well known and popular author, and eventually a member of Parliament (1900-1918); he directed the British Government's propaganda campaign to move US opinion in a pro-British direction during the First World War. Parker's (over twenty) books of adventures were highly regarded by critics; he was knighted in 1902, and created a baronet in 1915.

Parker had no first-hand knowledge of the North-West; nonetheless he became famous for his stories of "the North" and "the West," inaugurated in *Pretty Pierre and his People* (1892), which went through twenty-seven editions in twenty years. Pretty Pierre the gambler is the recurrent character who links these stories, a "half-breed" who is racially determined as sophisticated and well-read but also cunning and "wild."

Three Outlaws

The missionary at Fort Anne of the H.B.C. was violently in earnest. Before he piously followed the latest and most amply endowed batch of settlers, who had in turn preceded the new railway to the Fort, the word *scandal* had no place in the vocabulary of the citizens. The H.B.C. had never imported it into the Chinook language, the common meeting-ground of all the tribes of the North; and the British men and native-born, who made the Fort their home, or place of sojourn, had never found need for its use. Justice was so quickly distributed, men were so open in their conduct, good and bad, that none looked askance, nor put their actions in ambush, nor studied innuendo. But this was not according to the new dispensation: that is, the dispensation which shrewdly followed the settlers, who as shrewdly preceded the railway. And the dispensation and the missionary were known also as the Reverend Ezra Badgley, who, on his own declaration, in times past had "a call" to preach, and in the far East had served as local preacher, then probationer, then went on circuit, and now was missionary in a district of which the choice did credit to his astuteness, and gave abundant room for his piety and holy rage against the Philistines. He loved a word for righteous mouthing, and in a moment of inspiration *pagan* and *scandal* came to him. Upon these two words he stamped, through them he perspired mightily, and with them he clenched his stubby fingers: such fingers as dug trenches, or snatched lewdly at soft flesh, in days of barbarian battle. To him all men were Pagans who loved not the sound of his voice, nor wrestled with him in prayer before the Lord, nor fed him with rich food, nor gave him much strong green tea to drink. But these men were of opaque stuff, and were not dismayed, and they called him St. Anthony, and with a prophetic and deadly patience waited. The time came when the missionary shook his denouncing finger mostly at Pretty Pierre, who carefully nursed his silent wrath until the occasion should arrive for a delicate revenge which hath its hour with every man, if, hating, he knows how to bide the will of Fate.

The hour came. A girl had been found dying on the roadside beyond the Fort by the drunken doctor of the place and Pierre. Pierre was with her when she died.

"An' who's to bury her, the poor colleen?" said Shon McGann afterwards.

Pierre musingly replied: "She is a Protestant. There is but one man."

After many pertinent and vigorous remarks, Shon added: "A Pagan is it he calls you, Pierre: you that's had the holy water on y'r forehead, and the cross on the water, and that knows the book o' the Mass like the cards in a pack? Sinner y' are, and so are we all, God save us! say I; and weavin' the stripes for our backs He may be, and little I'd think of Him failin' in that: but Pagan! —faith, it's black should be the white of the eyes of that preachin' sneak, and a rattle of teeth in his throat—divils go round me!"

The half-breed, still musing, replied: "An eye for an eye, and a tooth for a tooth—is that it, Shon?"

"Nivir a word truer by song or by book, and stand by the text, say I. For Papist I am, and Papist are you; and the imps from below in y'r fingers whin poker is the game; and outlaws as they call us both—you for what it doesn't concern me, and I for a wild night in ould Donegal;—but Pagan! Wurra! whin shall it be, Pierre?"

"When shall it be?"

"True for you. The teeth in his throat and a lump to his eye, and what more be the will o' God. Fightin' there'll be, av coorse; but by you I'll stand, and sorra inch will I give, if they'll do it with sticks or with guns, and not with the blisterin' tongue that's lied of me and me frinds—for frind I call you, Pierre, that loved me little in days gone by. And proud I am not of you, nor you of me; but we've tasted the bitter of avil days together, and divils surround me, if I don't go down with you or come up with you, whichever it be! For there's dirt, as I say on their tongues, and over their shoulder they look at you, and not with an eye full front."

Pierre was cool, even pensive. His lips parted slightly once or twice, and showed a row of white, malicious teeth. For the rest, he looked as if he were politely interested but not moved by the excitement of the other. He slowly rolled a cigarette and replied: "He says it is a scandal that I live at Fort Anne. Well, I was here before he came, and I shall be here after he goes—yes. A scandal—Tsh! what is that? You know the word *Raca* of the Book? Well, there shall be more *Raca* soon—perhaps. No, there shall not be fighting as you think, Shon; but—" here Pierre rose, came over, and spread his fingers lightly on Shon's breast— "but this thing is between this man and me, Shon McGann, and you shall see a great matter. Perhaps there will be blood, perhaps not—perhaps only an end." And the half-breed looked up at the Irishman from under his dark brows so covertly and meaningly that Shon saw visions of a trouble as silent as a plague, as resistless as a great flood. This noiseless vengeance was not after his own heart. He almost shivered as the delicate fingers drummed on his breast.

"Angels begird me, Pretty Pierre, but it's little I'd like you for enemy o' mine; for I know that you'd wait for y'r foe with death in y'r hand, and pity far from y'r heart; and y'd smile as you pulled the black cap on y'r head, and laugh as you drew the life out of him, God knows how! Arrah, give me, say I, the crack of a stick, the bite of a gun, or the clip of a sabre's edge, with a shout in y'r mouth the while!"

Though Pierre still listened lazily, there was a wicked fire in his eyes. His words now came from his teeth with cutting precision: "I have a great thought to-night, Shon McGann. I will tell you when we meet again. But, my friend, one must not be too rash—no, not too brutal. Even the sabre should fall at the right time, and then swift and still. Noise is not battle. Well, *au revoir!* To-morrow I shall tell you many things." He caught Shon's hand quickly, as quickly dropped it, and went out indolently singing a favourite song,— "*Voici le Sabre de mon Père!*"

It was dark. Pretty Pierre stood still, and thought for a while. At last he spoke aloud: "Well, I shall do it now I have him—so!" And he opened and shut his hand swiftly and firmly. He moved on, avoiding the more habited parts of the place, and by a roundabout came to a house standing very close to the bank of the river. He went softly to the door and listened. Light shone through the curtain of a window. He went to the window and looked beneath the curtain. Then he came back to the door, opened it very gently, stepped inside, and closed it behind him.

A man seated at a table, eating, rose; a man on whom greed had set its mark—greed of the flesh, greed of men's praise, greed of money. His frame was thick-set, his body was heavily nourished, his eye was shifty but intelligent; and a close observer would have seen something elusive, something furtive and sinister, in his face. His lips were greasy with meat as he stood up, and a fear sprang to his face, so that its fat looked sickly. But he said hoarsely, and with an attempt at being brave:— "How dare you enter my house without knocking? What do you want?"

The half-breed waved a hand protestingly towards him. "*Pardon!*" he said. "Be seated, and finish your meal. Do you know me?"

"Yes, I know you."

"Well, as I said, do not stop your meal. I have come to speak with you very quietly about a scandal—a scandal, you understand. This is Sunday night, a good time to talk of such things." And Pierre seated himself at the table, opposite the man.

But the man replied: "I have nothing to say to you. You are—"

The half-breed interrupted: "Yes, I know, a Pagan fattening—" here he smiled, and looked at his thin hands— "'fattening for the shambles of the damned,' as you have said from the pulpit, Reverend Ezra Badgley. But you will permit me—a sinner as you say—to speak to you like this while you sit down and eat. I regret to disturb you, but you *will* sit, eh?"

Pierre's tone was smooth and low, almost deferential, and his eyes, wide open now, and hot with some hidden purpose, were fixed compellingly on the man. The missionary sat, and, having recovered slightly, fumbled with a knife and fork. A napkin was still beneath his greasy chin. He did not take it away.

Pierre then spoke slowly: "Yes, it is a scandal concerning a sinner—and a Pagan... Will you permit me to light a cigarette? Thank you... You have said many harsh things about me: well, as you see, I am amiable. I lived at Fort Anne before you came. They call me *Pretty* Pierre. Why is my cheek so? Because I drink no wine; I eat not much. *Pardon!* pork like that on your plate—no! no! I do not take green tea as there in your cup; I do not love women, one or many. Again, *pardon!* I say."

The other drew his brows together with an attempt at pious frowning and indignation; but there was a cold, sneering smile now turned upon him, that changed the frown to anxiety, and made his lips twitch, and the food he had eaten grow heavy within him.

"I come to the scandal slowly. The woman? She was a young girl travelling from the far East, to search for a man who had—spoiled her. She was found by me and another. Ah, you start so! ... Will you not listen? ... Well, she died to-night."

Here the missionary gasped, and caught with both hands at the table.

"But before she died she gave two things into my hands: a packet of letters (a man is a fool to write such letters!) and a small bottle of poison—laudanum, old-fashioned but sure. The letters were from the man at Fort Anne— *the man,* you hear! The other was for her death, if he would not take her to his arms again. Women are mad when they love. And so she came to Fort Anne, but not in time. The scandal is great, because the man is holy—sit down!"

The half-breed said the last two words sharply, but not loudly. They both sat down slowly again, looking each other in the eyes. Then Pierre drew from his pocket a small bottle and a packet of letters, and held them before him. "I have this to say: there are citizens of Fort Anne who stand for justice more than law; who have no love for the ways of St. Anthony. There is a Pagan, too, an outlaw who knows when it is time to give blow for blow with the holy man. Well, we understand each other, eh?"

The elusive, sinister look in the missionary's face was etched in strong lines now. A dogged sullenness hung about his lips. He noticed that one hand only of Pretty Pierre was occupied with the relics of the dead girl; the other was free to act suddenly on a hip pocket. "What do you want me to do?" he said, not whiningly, for beneath the selfish flesh and shallow outworks there were the elements of a warrior—all pulpy now, but they were there.

"This," was the reply: "for you to make one more outlaw at Fort Anne by drinking what is in this bottle—sit down, quick, by God!" He placed the bottle within reach of the other. "Then you shall have these letters; and there is the fire. After? Well, you will have a great sleep, the good people will find you, they will bury you, weeping much, and no one knows here but me. Refuse that, and there is the other, the Law—ah, the poor girl was so very young! —and the wild Justice which is sometimes quicker than Law. Well? well?"

The missionary sat as if paralysed, his face all grey, his eyes fixed on the half-breed. "Are you man or devil?" he said at length.

With a slight, fantastic gesture Pierre replied: "It was said that a devil entered into me at birth, but that perhaps was mere scandal. You shall think as you will."

There was silence. The sullenness about the missionary's lips became charged with a contempt more animal than human. The Reverend Ezra Badgley knew that the man before him was absolute in his determination, and that the Pagans of Fort Anne would show him little mercy, while his flock would leave him to his fate. He looked at the bottle. The silence grew, so that the ticking of the watch in the missionary's pocket could be heard plainly, having for its background of sound the continuous swish of the river. Pretty Pierre's eyes were never taken off the other, whose gaze, again, was fixed upon the bottle with a terrible fascination. An hour, two hours passed. The fire burned lower. It was midnight: and now the watch no longer ticked; it had fulfilled its day's work. The missionary shuddered slightly at this. He looked up to see the resolute gloom of the half-breed's eyes, and that sneering smile, fixed upon him still. Then he turned once more to the bottle.... His heavy hand moved slowly towards it. His stubby fingers perspired and showed sickly in the light.... They closed about the bottle. Then suddenly he raised it, and drained it at a draught. He sighed once heavily, and as if a great inward pain was over. He rose and took the letters silently pushed towards him, and dropped them in the fire. He went to the window, raised it, and threw the bottle into the river. The cork was left: Pierre pointed to it. He took it up with a strange smile and thrust it into the coals. Then he sat down by the table; he leaned his arms upon it, his eyes staring painfully before him, and the forgotten napkin still about his neck. Soon the eyes closed, and, with a moan on his lips, his head dropped forward on his arms.... Pierre rose, and, looking at the figure soon to be breathless as the baked meats about it, said: "Well, he was not all coward. No."

Then he turned and went out into the night.

Pauline Johnson (1861-1913)

Pauline Johnson toured Canada performing her writing as "The Mohawk Princess," but her relationship to her native heritage was ambiguous. Though her father was a Mohawk from the Six Nations Reserve near Brantford, her upbringing and education were strongly influenced by her English mother and by the surrounding white culture. As an adult she embraced her native background, writing poems and stories which advocated for native Canadians and giving readings in an "Indian" costume of her own devising. After she retired to Vancouver she became friends with Chief Joe Capilano, and published a book, *Legends of Vancouver* (1911), based upon their conversations about Squamish history and legends.

"A Red Girl's Reasoning" appeared in *Dominion Illustrated Magazine* February 1893: 19-28; this version is from the collection, *The Moccasin Maker* (Toronto: William Briggs, 1913). The plot has some basis in historical fact: the legality of marriages contracted according to the "custom of the country" was denied by Canadian courts in 1886 (see Van Kirk, 240-42).

A Red Girl's Reasoning

"Be pretty good to her, Charlie, my boy, or she'll balk sure as shooting."

That was what old Jimmy Robinson said to his brand new son-in-law, while they waited for the bride to reappear.

"Oh! you bet, there's no danger of much else. I'll be good to her, help me Heaven," replied Charlie McDonald, brightly.

"Yes, of course you will," answered the old man, "but don't you forget, there's a good big bit of her mother in her, and," closing his left eye significantly, "you don't understand these Indians as I do."

"But I'm just as fond of them, Mr. Robinson," Charlie said assertively, "and I get on with them too, now don't I?"

"Yes, pretty well for a town boy; but when you have lived forty years among these people, as I have done; when you have had your wife as long as I have had mine—for there's no getting over it, Christine's disposition is as native as her mother's, every bit—and perhaps when you've owned for eighteen years a daughter as dutiful, as loving, as fearless, and, alas! as obstinate as that little piece you are stealing away from me to-day—I tell you, youngster, you'll know more than you know now. It is kindness for kindness, bullet for bullet, blood for blood. Remember, what you are, she will be," and the old Hudson Bay trader scrutinized Charlie McDonald's face like a detective.

It was a happy, fair face, good to look at, with a certain ripple of dimples somewhere about the mouth, and eyes that laughed out the very sunniness of their owner's soul. There was not a severe nor yet a weak line anywhere. He was a well-meaning young fellow, happily dispositioned, and a great favourite with the tribe at Robinson's Post, whither he had gone in the service of the Department of Agriculture, to assist the local agent through the tedium of a long census taking.

As a boy he had had the Indian relic hunting craze, as a youth he had studied Indian archaeology and folk-lore, as a man he consummated his predilections for Indianology by loving, winning and marrying the quiet little daughter of the English trader, who himself had married a native woman twenty years ago. The country was all back-woods, and the Post miles and miles from even the semblance of civilization, and the lonely young Englishman's heart went out to the girl who, apart from speaking a very few words of English, was utterly uncivilized and uncultured, but had withal that marvellously innate refinement so universally possessed by the higher tribes of North American Indians.

Like all her race, observant, intuitive, having a horror of ridicule, consequently quick at acquirement and teachable in mental and social habits, she had developed from absolute pagan indifference into a sweet, elderly Christian woman, whose broken English, quiet manner, and still handsome copper-coloured face, were the joy of old Robinson's declining years.

He had given their daughter Christine all the advantages of his own learning—which if truthfully told, was not universal;

but the girl had a fair common education, and the native adaptability to progress.

She belonged to neither and still to both types of the cultured Indian. The solemn, silent, almost heavy manner of the one so co-mingled with the gesticulating Frenchiness and vivacity of the other, that one unfamiliar with native Canadian life would find it difficult to determine her nationality.

She looked very pretty to Charles McDonald's loving eyes, as she reappeared in the doorway, holding her mother's hand and saying some happy words of farewell. Personally she looked much the same as her sisters, all Canada through, who are the offspring of red and white parentage—olive complexioned, grey eyed, black haired, with figure slight and delicate, and the wistful, unfathomable expression in her whole face that turns one so heart-sick as they glance at the young Indians of to-day—it is the forerunner too frequently of "the white man's disease," consumption—but McDonald was pathetically in love, and thought her the most beautiful woman he had ever seen in his life.

There had not been much of a wedding ceremony. The priest had cantered through the service in Latin, pronounced the benediction in English, and congratulated the "happy couple" in Indian as a compliment to the assembled tribe in the little amateur structure that did service at the post as a sanctuary.

But the knot was tied as firmly and indissolubly as if all Charlie McDonald's swell city friends had crushed themselves up against the chancel to congratulate him, and in his heart he was deeply thankful to escape the flower pelting, white gloves, rice-throwing, and ponderous stupidity of a breakfast, and indeed all the regulation gimcracks of the usual marriage celebrations, and it was with a hand trembling with absolute happiness that he assisted his little Indian wife into the old muddy buckboard, that, hitched to an underbred-looking pony, was to convey them over the first stages of their journey. Then came more adieus, some hand-clasping, old Jimmy Robinson looking very serious just at the last, Mrs. Jimmy, stout, stolid, betraying nothing of visible emotion, and then the pony, roughshod and shaggy, trudged on, while mutual hand-waves were kept up until the old Hudson Bay Post dropped out of sight, and the buckboard with its lightsome load of hearts, deliriously happy, jogged on over the uneven trail.

* * *

She was "all the rage" that winter at the provincial capital. The men called her a "deuced fine little woman." The ladies said she was "just the sweetest wildflower." Whereas she was really but an ordinary, pale, dark girl who spoke slowly and with a strong accent, who danced fairly well, sang acceptably, and never stirred outside the door without her husband.

Charlie was proud of her; he was proud that she had "taken" so well among his friends, proud that she bore herself so complacently in the drawing-rooms of the wives of pompous Government officials, but doubly proud of her almost abject devotion to him. If ever human being was worshipped that being was Charlie McDonald; it could scarcely have been otherwise, for the almost godlike strength of his passion for that little wife of his would have mastered and melted a far more invincible citadel than an already affectionate woman's heart.

Favourites socially, McDonald and his wife went everywhere. In fashionable circles she was "new"—a potent charm to acquire popularity, and the little velvet-clad figure was always the centre of interest among all the women in the room. She always dressed in velvet. No woman in Canada, has she but the faintest dash of native blood in her veins, but loves velvets and silks. As beef to the Englishman, wine to the Frenchman, fads to the Yankee, so are velvet and silk to the Indian girl, be she wild as prairie grass, be she on the borders of civilization, or, having stepped within its boundary, mounted the steps of culture even under its superficial heights.

"Such a dolling little appil blossom," said the wife of a local M.P., who brushed up her etiquette and English once a year at Ottawa. "Does she always laugh so sweetly, and gobble you up with those great big grey eyes of hers, when you are togetheah at home, Mr. McDonald? If so I should think youah pooah brothah would feel himself terribly *de trop*."

He laughed lightly. "Yes, Mrs. Stuart, there are not two of Christie; she is the same at home and abroad, and as for Joe, he doesn't mind us a bit, he's no end fond of her."

"I'm very glad he is. I always fancied he did not care for her, d'you know."

If ever a blunt woman existed it was Mrs. Stuart. She really meant nothing, but her remark bothered Charlie. He was fond of his brother, and jealous for Christie's popularity. So that night when he and Joe were having a pipe he said:

"I've never asked you yet what you thought of her, Joe." A brief pause, then Joe spoke. "I'm glad she loves you."

"Why?"

"Because that girl has two possibilities regarding humanity—love or hate."

"Humph!—Does she love or hate *you*?"

"Ask her."

"You talk bosh. If she hated you, you'd get out. If she loved you I'd *make* you get out."

Joe McDonald whistled a little, then laughed.

"Now that we are on the subject, I might as well ask—honestly, old man, wouldn't you and Christie prefer keeping house alone to having me always around?"

"Nonsense, sheer nonsense. Why, thunder, man, Christie's no end fond of you, and as for me—you surely don't want assurances from me?"

"No, but I often think a young couple—"

"Young couple be blowed. After a while when they want you and your old surveying chains, and spindle-legged tripod telescope kick-shaws, further west, I venture to say the little woman will cry her eyes out—won't you Christie?" This last in a higher tone, as through clouds of tobacco smoke he caught sight of his wife passing the door-way.

She entered. "Oh, no, I would not cry; I never do cry, but I would be heart-sore to lose you, Joe, and apart from that"— a little wickedly— "you may come in handy for an exchange some day, as Charlie does always say when he hoards up duplicate relics."

"Are Charlie and I duplicates?"

"Well—not exactly"—her head a little to one side, and eyeing them both merrily, while she slipped softly on to the arm of her husband's chair— "but, in the event of Charlie's failing me"—everyone laughed then. The "some day" that she spoke of was nearer than they thought. It came about in this wise.

There was a dance at the Lieutenant Governor's, and the world and his wife were there. The nobs were in great feather that night, particularly the women, who flaunted about in new gowns and much splendour. Christie McDonald had a new gown also, but wore it with the utmost unconcern, and if she heard any of the flattering remarks made about her she at least appeared to disregard them.

"I never dreamed you could wear blue so splendidly" said Captain Logan, as they sat out a dance together.

"Indeed she can, though," interposed Mrs. Stuart, halting in one of her gracious sweeps down the room with her husband's private secretary.

"Don't shout so, captain. I can hear every sentence you uttah—of course Mrs. McDonald can wear blue—she has a morning gown of cadet blue that she is a picture in."

"You are both very kind," said Christie. "I like blue; it is the colour of all the Hudson's Bay posts, and the factor's residence is always decorated in blue."

"Is it really? How interesting—do tell us some more of your old home, Mrs. McDonald; you so seldom speak of your life at the post, and we fellows so often wish to hear of it all," said Logan eagerly.

"Why do you not ask me of it, then?"

"Well-er, I'm sure I don't know; I'm fully interested in the Ind—in your people—your mother's people I mean, but it always seems so personal I suppose; and-a-a—."

"Perhaps you are like all other white people, afraid to mention my nationality to me."

The captain winced, and Mrs. Stuart laughed uneasily. Joe McDonald was not far off and he was listening, and chuckling, and saying to himself, "That's you, Christie, lay 'em out; it won't hurt 'em to know how they appear once in a while."

"Well, Captain Logan," she was saying, "what is it you would like to hear—of my people, or my parents, or myself?"

"All, all, my dear," cried Mrs. Stuart clamorously. "I'll speak for him—tell us of yourself and your mother—your father is delightful, I am sure—but then he is only an ordinary Englishman, not half as interesting as a foreigner, or—or, perhaps, I should say a native."

Christie laughed. "Yes," she said, "my father often teases my mother now about how very native she was when he married her; then, how could she have been otherwise? She did not know a word of English, and there was not another English-speaking person besides my father and his two companions within sixty miles."

" Two companions, eh? one a Catholic priest and the other a wine merchant, I suppose, and with your father in the Hudson Bay, they were good representatives of the pioneers in the New World," remarked Logan, waggishly.

"Oh, no, they were all Hudson Bay men. There were no rumsellers and no missionaries in that part of the country then."

Mrs. Stuart looked puzzled. "*No missionaries?*" she repeated with an odd intonation.

Christie's insight was quick. There was a peculiar expression of interrogation in the eyes of her listeners, and the girl's blood leapt angrily up into her temples as she said hurriedly, "I know what you mean; I know what you are thinking. You are wondering how my parents were married—."

"Well-er, my dear, it seems peculiar—if there was no priest, and no magistrate, why—a—." Mrs. Stuart paused awkwardly.

"The marriage was performed by Indian rites," said Christie.

"Oh, do tell me about it; is the ceremony very interesting and quaint—are your chieftains anything like Buddhist priests?" It was Logan who spoke.

"Why, no," said the girl in amazement at that gentleman's ignorance. "There is no ceremony at all, save a feast. The two people just agree to live only with and for each other, and the man takes his wife to his home, just as you do. There is no ritual to bind them; they need none; an Indian's word was his law in those days, you know."

Mrs. Stuart stepped backwards. "Ah!" was all she said. Logan removed his eye-glass and stared blankly at Christie. "And did McDonald marry you in this singular fashion?" he questioned.

"Oh, no, we were married by Father O'Leary. Why do you ask?"

"Because if he had, I'd have blown his brains out to-morrow."

Mrs. Stuart's partner, who had hitherto been silent, coughed and began to twirl his cuff stud nervously, but nobody took any notice of him. Christie had risen, slowly, ominously—risen, with the dignity and pride of an empress.

"Captain Logan," she said, "what do you dare to say to me? What do you dare to mean? Do you presume to think it would not have been lawful for Charlie to marry me according to my people's rites? Do you for one instant dare to question that my parents were not as legally—."

"Don't, dear, don't," interrupted Mrs. Stuart hurriedly; "it is bad enough now, goodness knows; don't make—" Then she broke off blindly. Christie's eyes glared at the mumbling woman, at her uneasy partner, at the horrified captain. Then they rested on the McDonald brothers, who stood within earshot, Joe's face scarlet, her husband's white as ashes, with something in his eyes she had never seen before. It was Joe who saved the situation. Stepping quickly across towards his sister-in-law, he offered her his arm, saying, "The next dance is ours, I think, Christie."

Then Logan pulled himself together, and attempted to carry Mrs. Stuart off for the waltz, but for once in her life that lady had lost her head. "It is shocking!" she said, "outrageously shocking! I wonder if they told Mr. McDonald before he married her!" Then looking hurriedly round, she too saw the young husband's face—and knew that they had not.

"Humph! deuced nice kettle of fish—and poor old Charlie has always thought so much of honourable birth."

Logan thought he spoke in an undertone, but "poor old Charlie" heard him. He followed his wife and brother across the room. "Joe," he said, "will you see that a trap is called?" Then to Christie, "Joe will see that you get home all right." He wheeled on his heel then and left the ball-room.

Joe *did* see. He tucked a poor shivering, pallid little woman into a cab, and wound her bare throat up in the scarlet velvet cloak that was hanging uselessly over her arm. She crouched down beside him, saying, "I am so cold, Joe; I am so cold," but she did not seem to know enough to wrap herself up. Joe felt all through this long drive that nothing this side of Heaven would be so good as to die, and he was glad when the poor little voice at his elbow said: "What is he so angry at, Joe?"

"I don't know exactly, dear," he said gently, "but I think it was what you said about this Indian marriage."

"But why should I not have said it? Is there anything wrong about it?" she asked pitifully.

"Nothing, that I can see—there was no other way; but Charlie is very angry, and you must be brave and forgiving with him, Christie, dear."

"But I did never see him like that before, did you?"

"Once."

"When?"

"Oh! at college, one day, a boy tore his prayer-book in half, and threw it into the grate, just to be mean, you know. Our mother had given it to him at his confirmation."

"And did he look so?"

"About, but it all blew over in a day—Charlie's tempers are short and brisk. Just don't take any notice of him; run off to bed, and he'll have forgotten it by the morning."

They reached home at last. Christie said good night quietly, going directly to her room. Joe went to his room also, filled a pipe and smoked for an hour. Across the passage he could hear her slippered feet pacing up and down, up and down the length of her apartment, There was something panther-like in those restless footfalls, a meaning velvetyness that made him shiver, and again he wished he were dead—or elsewhere.

After a time the hall door opened, and someone came upstairs, along the passage, and to the little woman's room. As he entered, she turned and faced him.

"Christie," he said harshly, "do you know what you have done?"

"Yes," taking a step nearer him, her whole soul springing up into her eyes, "I have angered you, Charlie, and—"

"Angered me? You have disgraced me; and moreover you have disgraced yourself and both your parents."

"*Disgraced?*"

"Yes, *disgraced;* you have literally declared to the whole city that your father and mother were never married, and that you are the child of what shall we call it—love? certainly not legality."

Across the hallway sat Joe McDonald, his blood freezing; but it leapt into every vein like fire at the awful anguish in the little voice that cried simply, "Oh! Charlie!"

"How could you do it, how could you do it, Christie, without shame either for yourself or for me, let alone your parents?"

The voice was like an angry demon's—not a trace was there in it of the yellow-haired, blue-eyed, laughing-lipped boy who had driven away so gaily to the dance five hours before.

"Shame? Why should I be ashamed of the rites of my people any more than you should be ashamed of the customs of yours—of a marriage more sacred and holy than half of your white man's mockeries?"

It was the voice of another nature in the girl—the love and the pleading were dead in it.

"Do you mean to tell me, Charlie—you who have studied my race and their laws for years—do you mean to tell me that, because there was no priest and no magistrate, my mother was not married? Do you mean to say that all my forefathers, for hundreds of years back, have been illegally born? If so, you blacken my ancestry beyond—beyond—beyond all reason."

"No, Christie, I would not be so brutal as that; but your father and mother live in more civilized times. Father O'Leary has been at the post for nearly twenty years. Why was not your father straight enough to have the ceremony performed when he *did* get the chance?"

The girl turned upon him with the face of a fury. "Do you suppose," she almost hissed, "that my mother would be married according to your *white* rites after she had been five years a wife, and I had been born in the meantime? *No,* a thousand times I say, *no*. When the priest came with his notions of Christianizing, and talked to them of re-marriage by the Church, my mother arose and said, "Never—never—I have never had but this one husband; he has had none but me for wife, and to have you re-marry us would be to say as much to the whole world as that we had never been married before. You go away; *I* do not ask that *your* people be re-married; talk not so to me. I *am* married, and you or Church cannot do or undo it."

"Your father was a fool not to insist upon the law, and so was the priest."

"Law? *My* people have *no* priest, and my nation cringes not to law. Our priest is purity, and our law is honour. Priest? Was there a *priest* at the most holy marriage known to humanity—that stainless marriage whose offspring is the God you white men told my pagan mother of?"

"Christie—you are *worse* than blasphemous; such a profane remark shows how little you understand the sanctity of the Christian faith—"

"I know what I *do* understand; it is that you are hating me because I told some of the beautiful customs of my people to Mrs. Stuart and those men."

"Pooh! who cares for them? It is not them; the trouble is they won't keep their mouths shut. Logan's a cad and will toss the whole tale about at the club before to-morrow night; and as for the Stuart woman, I'd like to know how I'm going to take you to Ottawa for presentation and the opening, while she is blabbing the whole miserable scandal in every drawing room, and I'll be pointed out as a romantic fool, and you—as worse; I *can't* understand why your father didn't tell me before we were married; I at least might have warned you to never mention it." Something of recklessness rang up through his voice, just as the panther-likeness crept up from her footsteps and couched herself in hers. She spoke in tones quiet, soft, deadly.

"Before we were married! Oh! Charlie, would it have—made—any—difference?"

"God knows," he said, throwing himself into a chair, his blonde hair rumpled and wet. It was the only boyish thing about him now.

She walked towards him, then halted in the centre of the room. "Charlie McDonald," she said, and it was as if a stone had spoken, "look up." He raised his head, startled by her tone. There was a threat in her eyes that, had his rage been less courageous, his pride less bitterly wounded, would have cowed him.

"There was no such time as that before our marriage, for we *are not married now*. Stop," she said, outstretching her palms against him as he sprang to his feet, "I tell you we are not married. Why should I recognize the rites of your nation when you do not acknowledge the rites of mine? According to your own words, my parents should have gone through your church ceremony as well as through an Indian contract; according to *my* words, *we* should go through an Indian contract as well as through a church marriage. If their union is illegal, so is ours. If you think my father is living in dishonour with my mother, my people will think I am living in dishonour with you. How do I know when another nation will come and conquer you as you white men conquered us? And they will have another marriage rite to perform, and they will tell us another truth, that you are not my husband, that you are but disgracing and dishonouring me, that you are keeping me here, not as your wife, but as your—your—*squaw*."

The terrible word had never passed her lips before, and the blood stained her face to her very temples. She snatched off her wedding ring and tossed it across the room, saying scornfully, "That thing is as empty to me as the Indian rites to you."

He caught her by the wrists; his small white teeth were locked tightly, his blue eyes blazed into hers.

"Christine, do you dare to doubt my honour towards you? *you*, who I would have died for; do you *dare* to think I have kept you here, not as my wife, but—."

"Oh! God. You are hurting me; you are breaking my arm," she gasped.

The door was flung open, and Joe McDonald's sinewy hands clinched like vices on his brother's shoulders.

"Charlie, you're mad, mad as the devil. Let go of her this minute."

The girl staggered backwards as the iron fingers loosed her

wrists. "Oh! Joe," she cried, "I am not his wife, and he says I am born—nameless."

"Here," said Joe, shoving his brother towards the door, "Go downstairs 'till you can collect your senses. If ever a being acted like an infernal fool, you're the man."

The young husband looked from one to the other, dazed by his wife's insult, abandoned to a fit of ridiculously childish temper. Blind as he was with passion, he remembered long afterwards seeing them standing there, his brother's face darkened with a scowl of anger—his wife, clad in the mockery of her ball dress, her scarlet velvet cloak half covering her bare brown neck and arms, her eyes like flames of fire, her face like a piece of sculptured greystone.

Without a word he flung himself furiously from the room, and immediately afterwards they heard the heavy hall door bang behind him.

"Can I do anything for you, Christie?" asked her brother-in-law calmly.

"No, thank you—unless—I think I would like a drink of water please."

He brought her up a goblet filled with wine; her hand did not even tremble as she took it. As for Joe, a demon arose in his soul as he noticed she kept her wrists covered.

"Do you think he will come back?" she said.

"Oh, yes, of course; he'll be all right in the morning. Now go to bed like a good little girl and—and, I say, Christie, you can call me if you want anything; I'll be right here, you know."

"Thank you, Joe, you are kind—and good."

He returned then to his apartment. His pipe was out, but he picked up a newspaper instead, threw himself into an armchair, and in a half-hour was in the land of dreams.

When Charlie came home in the morning, after a six-mile walk into the country and back again, his foolish anger was dead and buried. Logan's "Poor old Charlie" did not ring so distinctly in his ears. Mrs. Stuart's horrified expression had faded considerably from his recollection. He thought only of that surprisingly tall, dark girl, whose eyes looked like coals, whose voice pierced him like a flint-tipped arrow. Ah, well, they would never quarrel again like that, he told himself. She loved him so, and would forgive him after he had talked quietly to her, and told her what an ass he was. She was simple-minded and awfully ignorant to pitch those old Indian laws at him in her fury, but he could not blame her; oh, no, he could not for one moment blame her. He had been terribly severe and unreasonable, and the horrid McDonald temper had got the better of him; and he loved her so. Oh! he loved her so! She would surely feel that, and forgive him and— He went straight to his wife's room. The blue velvet evening dress lay on the chair into which he had thrown himself when he doomed his life's happiness by those two words, "God knows." A bunch of dead daffodils and her slippers were on the floor, everything—but Christie.

He went to his brother's bedroom door.

"Joe," he called, rapping nervously thereon; "Joe, wake up; where's Christie, d'you know?"

"Good Lord, no," gasped that youth, springing out of his armchair, and opening the door. As he did so a note fell from off the handle. Charlie's face blanched to his very hair while Joe read aloud, his voice weakening at every word:—

"DEAR OLD JOE.—I went into our room at daylight to get that picture of the Post on your bookshelves. I hope you do not mind, but I kissed your hair while you slept; it was so curly, and yellow, and soft, just like his. Good-bye, Joe.

CHRISTIE."

And when Joe looked into his brother's face and saw the anguish settle in those laughing blue eyes, the despair that drove the dimples away from that almost girlish mouth; when he realized that this boy was but four and twenty years old, and that all his future was perhaps darkened and shadowed for ever, a great, deep sorrow arose in his heart, and he forgot all things, all but the agony that rang up through the voice of the fair, handsome lad as he staggered forward, crying, "Oh! Joe—what shall I do—what shall I do?"

* * *

It was months and months before he found her, but during all that time he had never known a hopeless moment; discouraged he often was, but despondent, never. The sunniness of his ever-boyish heart radiated with a warmth that would have flooded a much deeper gloom than that which settled within his eager young life. Suffer? ah! yes, he suffered, not with locked teeth and stony stoicism, not with the masterful self-command, the reserve, the conquered bitterness of the still-water sort of nature, that is supposed to run to such depths. He tried to be bright, and his sweet old boyish self. He would laugh sometimes in a pitiful, pathetic fashion. He took to petting dogs, looking into their large solemn eyes with his wistful, questioning blue ones. He would kiss them, as women sometimes do, and call them "dear old fellow," in tones that had tears; and once in the course of his travels, while at a little way-station, he discovered a huge St. Bernard imprisoned by some mischance in an empty freight-car; the animal was nearly dead from starvation, and it seemed to salve his own sick heart to rescue back the dog's life. Nobody claimed the big starving creature, the train hands knew nothing of its owner, and gladly handed it over to its deliverer. "Hudson," he called it, and afterwards when Joe McDonald would relate the story of his brother's life he invariably terminated it with, "And I really believe that big lumbering brute saved him." From what, he was never known to say.

But all things end, and he heard of her at last. She had never returned to the Post, as he at first thought she would, but had gone to the little town of B——, in Ontario, where she was making her living at embroidery and plain sewing.

The September sun had set redly when at last he reached the outskirts of the town, opened up the wicket gate, and walked up the weedy, unkept path leading to the cottage where she lodged.

Even through the twilight, he could see her there, leaning on the rail of the verandah—oddly enough she had about her shoulders the scarlet velvet cloak she wore when he had flung himself so madly from the room that night.

The moment the lad saw her his heart swelled with a sudden heat, burning moisture leapt into his eyes, and clogged his long boyish lashes. He bounded up the steps— "Christie," he said, and the word scorched his lips like audible flame.

She turned to him, and for a second stood magnetized by his passionately wistful face; her peculiar greyish eyes seemed to drink the very life of his unquenchable love, though the tears that suddenly sprang into his seemed to absorb every pulse in his body through those hungry, pleading eyes of his that had, oh! so often been blinded by her kisses when once her whole world lay in their blue depths.

"You will come back to me, Christie, my wife? My wife, you will let me love you again?"

She gave a singular little gasp, and shook her head. "Don't, oh! don't," he cried piteously. "You will come to me, dear? it is all such a bitter mistake—I did not understand. Oh! Christie, I did not understand, and you'll forgive me, and love me again, won't you—won't you?"

"No," said the girl with quick, indrawn breath.

He dashed the back of his hand across his wet eyelids. His lips were growing numb, and he bungled over the monosyllable "Why?"

"I do not like you," she answered quietly.

"God! Oh! God, what is there left?"

She did not appear to hear the heart-break in his voice; she stood like one wrapped in sombre thought; no blaze, no tear, nothing in her eyes; no hardness, no tenderness about her mouth. The wind was blowing her cloak aside, and the only visible human life in her whole body was once when he spoke the muscles of her brown arm seemed to contract.

"But, darling, you are mine—*mine*—we are husband and wife! Oh, heaven, you *must* love me, you *must* come to me again."

"You cannot *make* me come," said the icy voice, "neither church, nor law, nor even"—and the voice softened— "nor even love can make a slave of a red girl."

"Heaven forbid it," he faltered. "No, Christie, I will never claim you without your love. What reunion would that be? But oh, Christie, you are lying to me, you are lying to yourself, you are lying to Heaven."

She did not move. If only he could touch her he felt as sure of her yielding, as he felt sure there was a hereafter. The memory of times when he had but to lay his hand on her hair to call a most passionate response from her filled his heart with a torture that choked all words before they reached his lips; at the thought of those days he forgot she was unapproachable, forgot how forbidding were her eyes, how stoney her lips. Flinging himself forward, his knee on the chair at her side, his face pressed hardly in the folds of the cloak on her shoulder, he clasped his arms about her with a boyish petulance, saying "Christie, Christie, my little girl wife, I love you, I love you, and you are killing me."

She quivered from head to foot as his fair, wavy hair brushed her neck, his despairing face sank lower until his cheek, hot as fire, rested on the cool, olive flesh of her arm. A warm moisture oozed up through her skin, and as he felt its glow he looked up. Her teeth, white and cold, were locked over her under lip, and her eyes were as grey stones.

Not murderers alone know the agony of a death sentence.

"Is it all useless? all useless, dear?" he said, with lips starving for hers.

"All useless," she repeated. "I have no love for you now. You forfeited me and my heart months ago, when you said *those two words*."

His arms fell away from her wearily, he arose mechanically, he placed his little grey checked cap on the back of his yellow curls, the old-time laughter was dead in the blue eyes that now looked scared and haunted, the boyishness and the dimples crept away for ever from the lips that quivered like a child's; he turned from her, but she had looked once into his face as the Law Giver must have looked at the Land of Canaan outspread at his feet. She watched him go down the long path and through the picket gate, she watched the big yellowish dog that had waited for him, lumber up on to its feet—stretch—then follow him. She was conscious of but two things, the vengeful lie in her soul, and a little space on her arm that his wet lashes had brushed.

* * *

It was hours afterwards when he reached his room. He had said nothing, done nothing—what use were words or deeds? Old Jimmy Robinson was right; she had "balked" sure enough.

What a bare hotelish room it was! He tossed off his coat and sat for ten minutes looking blankly at the sputtering gas jet. Then his whole life, desolate as a desert, loomed up before him with appalling distinctness. Throwing himself on the floor beside his bed, with clasped hands and arms outstretched on the white counterpane, he sobbed. "Oh! God, dear God, I thought you loved me; I thought you'd let me have her again, but you must be tired of me, tired of loving me too. I've nothing left now, nothing! it doesn't seem that I even have you to-night."

He lifted his face then, for his dog, big and clumsy and yellow, was licking at his sleeve.

Lily Dougall (1858-1923)

Born in Montreal to prosperous parents of Scottish descent, Lily Dougall lived as an adult in Scotland and England. She was the author of ten novels variously set in Canada, the United States and England; her numerous religious philosophical works were the focus of a discussion group she hosted at her home in Cumnor, England. Like many women authors at the turn of the century, Dougall found fiction a useful venue for ideas. In her novels and her non-fiction prose she advocated reform of Christian morality and a new vision of its role in modern society; a characteristic Dougall plot constructs a complex moral dilemma within which the main character must take action.

"Witchcraft" first appeared in the *Atlantic Monthly* 76 (December 1895): 740-47; this version is from the collection *A Dozen Ways of Love* (London: A&C Black, 1897).

Witchcraft

A young minister was walking through the streets of a small town in the island of Cape Breton. The minister was only a theological student who had been sent to preach in this remote place during his summer holiday. The town was at once very primitive and very modern. Many log-houses still remained in it; almost all the other houses were built of wood. The little churches, which represented as many sects, looked like the churches in a child's Dutch village. The town hall had only a brick facing. On the hillsides that surrounded the town far and wide were many fields, in which the first stumps were still standing, charred by the fires that had been kindled to kill them. There were also patches of forest still to be seen among these fields, where the land had not yet been cleared. In spite of all this, the town was very advanced, every improvement being of the newest kind because so recently achieved. Upon huge ungainly tree-trunks roughly erected along the streets, electric lamps hung, and telephone wires crossed and recrossed one another from roof to roof. There was even an electric tram that ran straight through the town and some distance into the country on either side. The general store had a gaily dressed lay figure in its window,—a female figure,—and its gown was labelled 'The latest Parisian novelty.'

The theological student was going out to take tea. He was a tall, active fellow, and his long strides soon brought him to a house a little way out of the town, which was evidently the abode of some degree of taste and luxury. The house was of wood, painted in dull colours of red and brown; it had large comfortable verandahs under shingled roofs. Its garden was not old-fashioned in the least; but though it aspired to trimness the grass had not grown there long enough to make a good lawn, so the ribbon flower-beds and plaster vases of flowers lacked the green-velvet setting that would have made them appear better. The student was the less likely to criticise the lawn because a very pretty, fresh-looking girl met him at the gate.

She was really a fine girl. Her dress showed rather more effort at fashion than was quite in keeping with her very rural surroundings, and her speech and accent betrayed a childhood spent among uneducated folk and only overlaid by more recent schooling. Her face had the best parts of beauty: health and good sense were written there, also flashes of humour and an habitual sweet seriousness. She had chanced to be at the gate gathering flowers. Her reception of the student was frank, and yet there was just a touch of blushing dignity about it which suggested that she took a special interest in him. The student also, it would appear, took an interest in her, for, on their way to the house, he made a variety of remarks upon the weather which proved that he was a little excited and unable to observe that he was talking nonsense.

In a little while the family were gathered round the tea-table. The girl, Miss Torrance by name, sat at the head of the table. Her father was a banker and insurance agent. He sat opposite his eldest daughter and did the honours of the meal with the utmost hospitality, yet with reserve of manner caused by his evident consciousness that his grammar and manners were not equal to those of his children and their guest. There were several daughters and two sons younger than Miss Torrance. They talked with vivacity.

The conversation soon turned upon the fact that the abundant supply of cream to which the family were accustomed was not forthcoming. Strawberries were being served with the tea; some sort of cold pudding was also on the table; and all this to be eaten without cream,—these young people might have been asked to go without their supper, so indignant they were.

Now, Mr. Torrance had been decorously trying to talk of the young minister's last sermon and of the affairs of the small Scotch church of which he was an elder, and Miss Torrance was ably seconding his effort by comparing the sentiments of the sermon to a recent magazine article, but against her will she was forced to attend to the young people's clamour about the cream.

It seemed that Trilium, the cow, had recently refused to give her milk. Mary Torrance was about eighteen; she suddenly gave it as her opinion that Trilium was bewitched; there was no other explanation, she said, no other possible explanation of Trilium's extraordinary conduct.

A flush mounted Miss Torrance's face; she frowned at her sister when the student was not looking.

"It's wonderful, the amount of witchcraft we have about here, Mr. Howitt," said the master of the house tentatively to the minister.

Howitt had taken Mary's words in jest. He gave his smooth-shaven face the twist that with him always expressed ideas wonderful or grotesque. It was a strong, thin face, full of intelligence.

"I never could have conceived anything like it," said he. "I come across witch tales here, there, everywhere; and the marvellous thing is, some of the people really seem to believe them."

The younger members of the Torrance family fixed their eyes upon him with apprehensive stare.

"You can't imagine anything more degrading," continued the student, who came from afar.

"Degrading, of course." Mr. Torrance sipped his tea hastily. "The Cape Breton people are superstitious, I believe."

An expression that might have betokened a new resolution appeared upon the fine face of the eldest daughter.

"*We* are Cape Breton people, father," she said, with dignified reproach. "I hope"—here a timid glance as if imploring support— "I hope we know better than to place any real faith in these degrading superstitions."

Howitt observed nothing but the fine face and the words that appeared to him natural.

Torrance looked at them both with the air of an honest man who was still made somewhat cowardly by new-fashioned propriety.

"I never put much o' my faith in these things myself," he said at last in broad accents, "still,"—an honest shake of the head— "there's queer things happens."

"It is like going back to the Middle Ages"—Howitt was still impervious— "to hear some of these poor creatures talk. I never thought it would be my lot to come across anything so delightfully absurd."

"Perhaps for the sake of the ministry ye'd better be careful how ye say your mind about it," suggested Mr. Torrance; "in the hearing of the poor and uneducated, of course, I mean. But if ye like to make a study o' that sort of thing, I'd advise ye to go and have a talk with Mistress Betty M'Leod. She's got a great repertory of tales, has Mistress Betty."

Mary spoke again. Mary was a young woman who had the courage of her opinions. "And if you go to Mistress M'Leod, Mr. Howitt, will you just be kind enough to ask her how to cure poor Trilium? and don't forget anything of what she says."

Miss Torrance gave her sister a word of reproof. There was still upon her face the fine glow born of a new resolution never again to listen to a word of witchcraft.

As for Howitt, there came across his clever face the whimsical look which denoted that he understood Mary's fun perfectly. "I will go tomorrow," he cried. "When the wise woman has told me who has bewitched Trilium, we will make a waxen figure and stick pins in it."

The next day Howitt walked over the hills in search of Mistress Betty M'Leod. The lake of the Bras d'Or held the sheen of the western sun in its breast. The student walked upon green slopes far above the water, and watched the outline of the hills on the other side of the inlet, and thought upon many things. He thought upon religion and philosophy, for he was religious and studious; he thought upon practical details of his present work, for he was anxious for the welfare of the souls under his charge; but on whatever subject his thoughts dwelt, they came back at easy intervals to the fair, dignified face of his new friend, Miss Torrance.

"There's a fine girl for you," he said to himself repeatedly, with boyish enthusiasm. He thought, too, how nobly her life would be spent if she chose to be the helpmeet of a Christian minister. He wondered whether Mary could take her sister's place in the home circle. Yet with all this he made no decision as to his own course. He was discreet, and in minds like his decisions upon important matters are fruits of slow growth.

He came at last to a farm, a very goodly farm for so hilly a district. It lay, a fertile flat, in a notch of the green hillside. When he reached the house yard he asked for Mistress Betty M'Leod, and was led to her presence. The old dame sat at her spinning-wheel in a farm kitchen. Her white hair was drawn closely, like a thin veil, down the sides of her head and pinned at the back. Her features were small, her eyes bright; she was not unlike a squirrel in her sharp little movements and quick glances. She wore a small shawl pinned around her spare shoulders. Her skirts fell upon the treadle of the spinning-wheel. The kitchen in which she sat was unused; there was no fire in the stove. The brick floor, the utensils hanging on the walls, had the appearance of undisturbed rest. Doors and windows were open to the view of the green slopes and the golden sea beneath them.

"You come from Canada," said the old dame. She left her spinning with a certain interested formality of manner.

"From Montreal," he replied.

"That's the same. Canada is a terrible way off."

"And now," he said, "I hear there are witches in this part of the land." Whereupon he smiled in an incredulous cultured way.

She nodded her head as if she had gauged his thought. "Ay, there's many a minister believes in them if they don't let on they do. I mind—"

"Yes," said he.

"I mind how my sister went out early one morning, and saw a witch milking one of our cows."

"How did you know she was a witch?"

"Och, she was a neighbour we knew to be a witch real well. My sister didn't anger her. It's terrible unlucky to vex them. But would you believe it? as long as we had that cow her cream gave no butter. We had to sell her and get another. And one time— it was years ago, when Donald and me was young—the first sacrament came round—"

"Yes," said he, looking sober.

"And all the milk of our cows would give hardly any butter for a whole year! And at house-cleaning time, there, above the milk shelves, what did they find but a bit of hair rope! Cows' and horses' hair it was. Oh, it was terrible knotted, and knotted just like anything! So then, of course, we knew."

"Knew what?"

"Why, that the milk was bewitched. We took the rope away. Well, that very day more butter came at the churning, and from that time on, more, but still not so much as ought by rights to have come. Then, one day, I thought to unknot the rope, and I undid, and undid, and undid. Well, when I had got it undone, that day the butter came as it should!"

"But what about the sacrament?" asked he.

"That was the time of the year it was. Oh, but I could tell you a sad, sad story of the wickedness of witches. When Donald and me was young, and had a farm up over on the other hill, well, there was a poor widow with seven daughters. It was hard times then for us all, but for her, she only had a bit of flat land with some bushes, and four cows and some sheep, and, you see, she sold butter to put meat in the children's mouths. Butter was all she could sell.

"Well, there came to live near her on the hill an awful wicked old man and woman. I'll tell you who their daughter is: she's married to Mr. M'Curdy, who keeps the store. The old man and his wife were awful wicked to the widow and the fatherless. I'll tell you what they did. Well, the widow's butter failed. Not one bit more could she get. The milk was just the same, but not one bit of butter. 'Oh,' said she, 'it's a hard world, and me a widow!' But she was a brave woman, bound to get along some way. So, now that she had nothing to sell to buy meal, she made curds of the milk, and fed the children on that.

"Well, one day the old man came in to see her in a neighbouring way, and she, being a good woman,—oh, but she was a good woman!—set a dish of curds before him. 'Oh,' said he, 'these are very fine curds!' So he went away, and next day she put the rennet in the milk as usual, but not a bit would the curd come. 'Oh,' said she, 'but I must put something in the children's mouths!' She was a fine woman, she was. So she kept the lambs from the sheep all night, and next morning she milked the sheep. Sheep's milk is rich, and she put rennet in that, and fed the children on the curd.

"So one day the old man came in again. He was a wicked one; he was dreadful selfish; and as he was there, she, being a hospitable woman, gave him some of the curd. 'That's good curd,' said he. Next day, when she put the rennet in the sheep's milk, not a bit would the curd come. She felt it bitterly, poor woman; but she had a fine spirit, and she fed the children on a few bits of potato she had growing.

"Well, one day, the eldest daughter got up very early to spin—in the twilight of the dawn it was—and she looked out, and there was the old woman coming from her house on the hill, with a shawl over her head and a tub in her arms. Oh, but she was a really wicked one! for I'll tell you what she did. Well, the girl watched and wondered, and in the twilight of the dawn she saw the old woman crouch down by one of the alder bushes, and put her tub under it, and go milking with her hands; and after a bit she lifted her tub, that seemed to have something in it, and set it over against another alder bush, and went milking with her hands again. So the girl said, 'Mother, mother, wake up, and see what the neighbour woman is doing!' So the mother looked out, and there, in the twilight of the dawn, she saw her four cows in the bit of land, among the alder bushes, and the old neighbour woman milking away at a bush. And then the old woman moved her tub likewise to another bush, and likewise, and likewise, until she had milked four bushes, and she took up her tub, and it seemed awful heavy, and she had her shawl over it, and was going up the hill.

"So the mother said to the girl, 'Run, run, and see what she has got in it.' For they weren't up to the ways of witches, and they were astonished like. But the girl, she said, 'Oh, mother, I don't like.' Well, she was timid, anyway, the eldest girl. But the second girl was a romping thing, not afraid of anything, so they sent her. By this time the wicked old woman was high on the hill; so she ran and ran, but she could not catch her before she was in at her own door; but that second girl, she was not afraid of anything, so she runs in at the door, too. Now, in those days they used to have sailing-chests that lock up; they had iron bars over them, so you could keep anything in that was a secret. They got them from the ships, and this old woman kept her milk in hers. So when the girl bounced in at the door, there she saw that wicked old woman pouring milk out of the tub into her chest, and the chest half full of milk, and the old man looking on! So then, of course they knew where the good of their milk had gone."

The story was finished. The old dame looked at the student and nodded her head with eyes that awaited some expression of formal disapproval.

"What did they know?" asked he.

"Know! Oh, why, that the old woman was an awful wicked witch, and she'd taken the good of their milk."

"Oh, indeed!" said the student; and then, "But what became of the widow and the seven daughters?"

"Well, of course she had to sell her cows and get others, and then it was all right. But that old man and his wife were that selfish they'd not have cared if she'd starved. And I tell you, it's one of the things witches can do, to take the good out of food, if they've an eye to it; they can take every bit of nouriture out of it that's in it. There were two young men that went from here to the States—that's Boston, ye know. Well, pretty soon one, that was named M'Pherson, came back, looking so white-like and ill that nothing would do him any good. He drooped and he died. Well, years after, the other, whose name was McVey, came back. He was of the same wicked stock as the old folks I've been telling ye of. Well, one day he was in low spirits like, and he chanced to be talking to my father, and says he, 'It's one of the sins I'll have to 'count for at the Judgment that I took the good out of M'Pherson's food till he died. I sat opposite to him at the table when we were at Boston together, and I took the good out of his food, and it's the blackest sin I done,' said he.

"Oh, they're awful wicked people, these witches! One of them offered to teach my sister how to take the good out of food, but my sister was too honest; she said, 'I'll learn to keep the good of my own, if ye like.' However, the witch wouldn't teach her that because she wouldn't learn the other. Oh, but I cheated a witch once. Donald, he brought me a pound of tea. 'Twasn't always we got tea in those days, so I put it in the tin box; and there was just a little over, so I was forced to leave that in the paper bag. Well, that day a neighbour came in from over the hill. I knew fine she was a witch; so we sat and gossiped a bit; she was a real pleasant woman, and she sat and sat, and the time of day went by. So I made her a cup of tea, her and me; but I used the drawing that was in the paper bag. Said she, 'I just dropped in to borrow a bit of tea going home, but if that's all ye have'— Oh, but I could see her eyeing round; so I was too sharp for her, and I says, 'Well, I've no more in the paper just now, but if ye'll wait till Donald comes, maybe he'll bring some.' So she saw I was too sharp for her, and away she went. If I'd as much as opened the tin she'd have had every grain of good out of it with her eyes."

At first the student had had the grave and righteous intention of denouncing the superstition, but gradually he had perceived that to do so would be futile. The artistic soul of him was caught by the curious recital. He remembered now the bidding of Mary Torrance, and thought with pleasure that he would go back and repeat these strange stories to Miss Torrance, and smile at them in her company.

"Now, for instance," he said aloud, "if a good cow, that is

a great pet in the family, should suddenly cease to give her milk, how would you set about curing her?"

The dame's small bright eyes grew keener. She moved to her spinning-wheel and gave it a turn. "Ay," she said, "and whose is the cow?"

He was not without a genuine curiosity. "What would you do for *any* cow in that case?"

"And is it Torrance's cow?" asked Mistress Betty. "Och, but I know it's Torrance's cow that ye're speiring for."

The young minister was recalled to a sense of his duty. He rose up with brisk dignity. "I only asked you to see what you would say. I do not believe the stories you have been telling me."

She nodded her head, taking his assertion as a matter of course. "But I'll tell you exactly what they must do," she said. "Ye can tell Miss Torrance she must get a pound of pins."

"A pound of pins!" said he.

"Ay, it's a large quantity, but they'll have them at the store, for it's more than sometimes they're wanted—a time here, a time there—against the witches. And she's to boil them in whatever milk the cow gives, and she's to pour them boiling hot into a hole in the ground; and when she's put the earth over them, and the sod over that, she's to tether the animal there, and milk it there, and the milk will come right enough."

While the student was making his way home along the hillside, through field and forest, the long arm of the sea turned to red and gold in the light of the clouds which the sun had left behind when it sank down over the distant region that the Cape Breton folk call Canada.

The minister meditated upon what he had heard, but not for long. He could not bring his mind into such attitude towards the witch-tales as to conceive of belief in them as an actual part of normal human experience. Insanity, or the love of making a good story out of notions which have never been seriously entertained, must compose the warp and woof of the fabric of such strange imaginings. It is thus we account for most experiences we do not understand.

The next evening the Torrance family were walking to meeting. The student joined himself to Miss Torrance. He greeted her with the whimsical look of grave humour. "You are to take a pound of pins," he said.

"I do not believe it would do any good," she interrupted eagerly.

It struck him as very curious that she should assert her unbelief. He was too nonplussed to go on immediately. Then he supposed it was part of the joke, and proceeded to give the other details.

"Mr. Howitt,"—a tremulous pause,— "it is very strange about poor Trilium, she has always been such a good, dear cow; the children are very fond of her, and my mother was very fond of her when she was a heifer. The last summer before she died, Trilium fed out of mother's hand, and now—she's in perfect health as far as we can see, but father says that if she keeps on refusing to give her milk he will be obliged to sell her."

Miss Torrance, who was usually strong and dignified, spoke now in an appealing voice.

"Couldn't you get an old farmer to look at her, or a vet?"

"But why do you think she has suddenly stopped giving milk?" persisted the girl.

"I am very sorry, but I really don't know anything about animals," said he.

"Oh, then if you don't know anything about them—" She paused. There had been such an evident tone of relief in her voice that he wondered much what would be coming next. In a moment she said, "I quite agreed with you the other night when you said that the superstition about witchcraft was degrading."

"No one could think otherwise." He was much puzzled at the turn of her thought.

"Still, of course, *about animals,* old people like Mistress Betty M'Leod may know something."

As they talked they were walking down the street in the calm of the summer evening to the prayer meeting. The student's mind was intent upon his duties, for, as they neared the little white-washed church, many groups were seen coming from all sides across the grassy space in which it stood. He was an earnest man, and his mind now became occupied with the thought of the spiritual needs of these others who were flocking to hear him preach and pray.

Inside the meeting-room, unshaded oil lamps flared upon a congregation most serious and devout. The student felt that their earnestness and devotion laid upon him the greater responsibility; he also felt much hindered in his speech because of their ignorance and remote ways of thought. It was a comfort to him to feel that there was at least one family among his hearers whose education would enable them to understand him clearly. He looked with satisfaction at the bench where Mr. Torrance sat with his children. He looked with more satisfaction to where Miss Torrance sat at the little organ. She presided over it with dignity and sweet seriousness. She drew music even out of its squeaking keys.

A few days after that prayer meeting the student happened to be in the post-office. It was a small, rough place; a wooden partition shut off the public from the postmistress and her helpers. He was waiting for some information for which he had asked; he was forced to stand outside the little window in this partition. He listened to women's voices speaking on the other side, as one listens to that which in no way concerns oneself:

"It's just like her, stuck up as she is since she came from school, setting herself and her family up to be better than other folks."

"Perhaps they were out of them at the store," said a gentler voice.

"Oh, don't tell me. It's on the sly she's doing it, and then pretending to be grander than other folks."

Then the postmistress came to the window with the required information. When she saw who was there, she said something else also.

"There's a parcel come for Miss Torrance,—if you happen to be going up that way," she simpered.

The student became aware for the first time that his friendship with Miss Torrance was a matter of public interest. He was not entirely displeased. "I will take the parcel," he said.

As he went along the sunny road, he felt so light-hearted that, hardly thinking what he did, he began throwing up the parcel and catching it again in his hands. It was not large; and it was very tightly done up in thick paper, and had an ironmonger's label attached; so that, though he paid small attention, it did not impress him as a thing that could be easily injured. Something, however, did soon make a sharp impression upon him; once as he caught the parcel he felt his hand deeply pricked. Looking closely, he saw that a pin was working its way through the thick paper. After that he walked more soberly, and did not play ball. He remembered what he had heard at the post-office. The parcel was certainly addressed to Miss Torrance. It was very strange. He remembered now with displeasure the assumption of the postmistress that he would be glad to carry this parcel.

He delivered the pound of pins at the door without making a call. His mind had never come to any decision with regard to his feeling for Miss Torrance, and now he was more undecided than ever. He was full of curiosity about the pins. He found it hard to believe that they were to be used for a base purpose, but suspicion had entered his mind. The knowledge that the eyes of the little public were upon him made him realise that he could not continue to frequent the house merely to satisfy his curiosity.

He was destined to know more.

That night, long after dark, he was called to visit a dying man, and the messenger led him somewhat out of the town.

He performed his duty to the dying with wistful eagerness. The spirit passed from earth while he yet knelt beside the bed. When he was returning home alone in the darkness, he felt his soul open to the power of unseen spirit, and to him the power of the spiritual unseen was the power of God.

Walking on the soft, quiet road, he came near the house where he had lately loved to visit, and his eye was arrested by seeing a lantern twinkling in the paddock where Trilium grazed. He saw the forms of two women moving in its little circle of light; they were digging in the ground.

He felt that he had a right to make sure of the thing he suspected. The women were not far from a fence by which he could pass, and he did pass that way, looking and looking till a beam of the lantern fell full on the bending faces. When he saw that Miss Torrance was actually there, he went on without speaking.

After that two facts became known in the village, each much discussed in its own way; yet they were not connected with each other in the common mind. One was that the young minister had ceased to call frequently upon Miss Torrance; the other, that Trilium, the cow, was giving her milk.

Ernest Thompson Seton (1860-1946)

Ernest Thompson Seton shares with Charles G.D. Roberts the distinction of having inaugurated the popular genre of the realistic animal story. Born in England, Seton grew up in the country near Lindsay, Ontario and in Toronto, where his experiences in the (then rural) Don Valley inspired his self-education as a naturalist. Seton's meticulous observations of the appearance and behaviour of birds and animals formed the basis of several scientific works as well as paintings, illustrations and stories of animal life.

Seton and Roberts distinguished their form of the animal story from its predecessors by emphasizing direct observation of animal behaviour and the scientific basis upon which they constructed their "animal psychology"; however, contemporary readers will note the ways that both authors create their animal subjects within a set of unconscious ideological assumptions about gender, economics, the family, and the self.

"Lobo, The King of Currumpaw," is based on Seton's experiences in New Mexico in 1893; it appeared in an early version in *Scribner's Magazine* 16 (November 1894): 618-28. This version appeared in the collection *Wild Animals I Have Known* (Toronto: G.N. Morang, 1899).

Lobo, The King of Currumpaw

I

Currumpaw is a vast cattle range in northern New Mexico. It is a land of rich pastures and teeming flocks and herds, a land of rolling mesas and precious running waters that at length unite in the Currumpaw River, from which the whole region is named. And the king whose despotic power was felt over its entire extent was an old grey wolf.

Old Lobo, or the king, as the Mexicans called him, was the gigantic leader of a remarkable pack of grey wolves, that had ravaged the Currumpaw Valley for a number of years. All the shepherds and ranchmen knew him well, and, wherever he appeared with his trusty band, terror reigned supreme among the cattle, and wrath and despair among their owners. Old Lobo was a giant among wolves, and was cunning and strong in proportion to his size. His voice at night was well-known and easily distinguished from that of any of his fellows. An ordinary wolf might howl half the night about the herdsman's bivouac without attracting more than a passing notice, but when the deep roar of the old king came booming down the cañon, the watcher bestirred himself and prepared to learn in the morning that fresh and serious inroads had been made among the herds.

Old Lobo's band was but a small one. This I never quite understood, for usually, when a wolf rises to the position and power that he had, he attracts a numerous following. It may be that he had as many as he desired, or perhaps his ferocious temper prevented the increase of his pack. Certain is it that Lobo had only five followers during the latter part of his reign. Each of these, however, was a wolf of renown, most of them were above the ordinary size, one in particular, the second in command, was a veritable giant, but even he was far below the leader in size and prowess. Several of the band, besides the two leaders, were especially noted. One of those was a beautiful white wolf, that the Mexicans called Blanca; this was supposed to be a female, possibly Lobo's mate. Another was a yellow wolf of remarkable swiftness, which, according to current stories had, on several occasions, captured an antelope for the pack.

It will be seen, then, that these wolves were thoroughly well-known to the cowboys and shepherds. They were frequently seen and oftener heard, and their lives were intimately associated with those of the cattlemen, who would so gladly have destroyed them. There was not a stockman on the Currumpaw who would not readily have given the value of many steers for the scalp of any one of Lobo's band, but they seemed to possess charmed lives, and defied all manner of devices to kill them. They scorned all hunters, derided all poisons, and continued, for at least five years, to exact their tribute from the Currumpaw ranchers to the extent, many said, of a cow each day. According to this estimate, therefore, the band had killed more than two thousand of the finest stock, for, as was only too well-known, they selected the best in every instance.

The old idea that a wolf was constantly in a starving state, and therefore ready to eat anything, was as far as possible from the truth in this case, for these freebooters were always sleek and well-conditioned, and were in fact most fastidious about what they ate. Any animal that had died from natural causes, or that was diseased or tainted, they would not touch, and they even rejected anything that had been killed by the stockmen. Their choice and daily food was the tenderer part of a freshly killed yearling heifer. An old bull or cow they disdained, and though they occasionally took a young calf or colt, it was quite clear that veal or horseflesh was not their favourite diet. It was also known that they were not fond of mutton, although they often amused themselves by killing sheep. One night in November, 1893, Blanca and the yellow wolf killed two hundred and fifty sheep, apparently for the fun of it, and did not eat an ounce of their flesh.

These are examples of many stories which I might repeat, to show the ravages of this destructive band. Many new devices for their extinction were tried each year, but still they lived and throve in spite of all the efforts of their foes. A great price was set on Lobo's head, and in consequence poison in a score of subtle forms was put out for him, but he never failed to detect and avoid it. One thing only he feared—that was firearms, and knowing full well that all men in this region carried them, he never was known to attack or face a human being. Indeed, the set policy of his band was to take refuge in flight whenever, in the daytime, a man was descried, no matter at what distance. Lobo's habit of permitting the pack to eat only that which they themselves had killed, was in numerous cases their salvation, and the keenness of his scent to detect the taint of human hands or the poison itself, completed their immunity.

On one occasion, one of the cowboys heard the too familiar rallying-cry of Old Lobo, and stealthily approaching, he found the Currumpaw pack in a hollow, where they had 'rounded up' a small herd of cattle. Lobo sat apart on a knoll, while Blanca with the rest was endeavouring to 'cut out' a young cow, which they had selected; but the cattle were standing in a compact mass with their heads outward, and presented to the foe a line of horns, unbroken save when some cow, frightened by a fresh onset of the wolves, tried to retreat into the middle of the herd. It was only by taking advantage of these breaks that the wolves had succeeded at all in wounding the selected cow, but she was far from being disabled, and it seemed that Lobo at length lost patience with his followers, for he left his position on the hill, and, uttering a deep roar, dashed toward the herd. The terrified rank broke at his charge, and he sprang in among them. Then the cattle scattered like the pieces of a bursting bomb. Away went the chosen victim, but ere she had gone twenty-five yards Lobo was upon her. Seizing her by the neck he suddenly held back with all his force and so threw her heavily to the ground. The shock must have been tremendous, for the heifer was thrown heels over head. Lobo also turned a somersault, but immediately recovered himself, and his followers falling on the poor cow, killed her in a few seconds. Lobo took no part in the killing—after having thrown the victim, he seemed to say, "Now, why could not some of you have done that at once without wasting so much time?"

The man now rode up shouting, the wolves as usual retired, and he, having a bottle of strychnine, quickly poisoned the carcass in three places, then went away, knowing they would return to feed, as they had killed the animal themselves. But next morning, on going to look for his expected victims, he found that, although the wolves had eaten the heifer, they had carefully cut out and thrown aside all those parts that had been poisoned.

The dread of this great wolf spread yearly among the ranchmen, and each year a larger price was set on his head, until at last it reached $1,000, an unparalleled wolf-bounty, surely; many a good man has been hunted down for less. Tempted by the promised reward, a Texan ranger named Tannerey came one day galloping up the cañon of the Currumpaw. He had a superb outfit for wolf-hunting—the best of guns and horses, and a pack of enormous wolf-hounds. Far out on the plains of the Pan-handle, he and his dogs had killed many a wolf, and now he never doubted that, within a few days, old Lobo's scalp would dangle at his saddle-bow.

Away they went bravely on their hunt in that grey dawn of a summer morning, and soon the great dogs gave joyous tongue to say that they were already on the track of their quarry. Within two miles, the grizzly band of Currumpaw leaped into view, and the chase grew fast and furious. The part of the wolf-hounds was merely to hold the wolves at bay till the hunter could ride up and shoot them, and this usually was easy on the open plains of Texas; but here a new feature of the country came into play, and showed how well Lobo had chosen his range; for the rocky cañons of the Currumpaw and its tributaries intersect the prairies in every direction. The old wolf at once made for the nearest of these and by crossing it got rid of the horsemen. His band then scattered and thereby scattered the dogs, and when they reunited at a distant point of course all of the dogs did not turn up, and the wolves no longer outnumbered, turned on their pursuers and killed or desperately wounded them all. That night when Tannerey mustered his dogs, only six of them returned, and of these, two were terribly lacerated. This hunter made two other attempts to capture the royal scalp, but neither of them was more successful than the first, and on the last occasion his best horse met its death by a fall; so he gave up the chase in disgust and went back to Texas, leaving Lobo more than ever the despot of the region.

Next year, two other hunters appeared, determined to win the promised bounty. Each believed he could destroy this noted wolf, the first by means of a newly devised poison, which was to be laid out in an entirely new manner; the other a French Canadian, by poison assisted with certain spells and charms, for he firmly believed that Lobo was a veritable 'loup-garou,' and could not be killed by ordinary means. But cunningly compounded poisons, charms, and incantations were all of no avail against this grizzly devastator. He made his weekly rounds and daily banquets as aforetime, and before many weeks had passed, Calone and Laloche gave up in despair and went elsewhere to hunt.

In the spring of 1893, after his unsuccessful attempt to capture Lobo, Joe Calone had a humiliating experience, which seems to show that the big wolf simply scorned his enemies, and had absolute confidence in himself. Calone's farm was on a small tributary of the Currumpaw, in a picturesque cañon, and among the rock of this very cañon, within a thousand yards of the house, old Lobo and his mate selected their den and raised their family that season. There they lived all summer, and killed Joe's cattle, sheep, and dogs, but laughed at all his poisons and traps, and rested securely among the recesses of the cavernous cliffs, while Joe vainly racked his brain for some method of smoking them out, or of reaching them with dynamite. But they escaped entirely unscathed, and continued their ravages as before. "There's where he lived all last summer," said Joe, pointing to the face of the cliff, "and I couldn't do a thing with him. I was like a fool to him."

II

This history, gathered so far from the cowboys, I found hard to believe until in the fall of 1893, I made the acquaintance of the wily marauder, and at length came to know him more thoroughly than anyone else. Some years before, in the Bingo days, I had been a wolf-hunter, but my occupations since then had been of another sort, chaining me to stool and desk. I was much in need of a change, and when a friend, who was also a ranch-owner on the Currumpaw, asked me to come to New Mexico and try if I could do anything with this predatory pack, I accepted the invitation and, eager to make the acquaintance of its king, was as soon as possible among the mesas of that region. I spent some time riding about to learn the country, and at intervals, my guide would point to the skeleton of a cow to which the hide still adhered, and remark, "That's some of his work."

It became quite clear to me that, in this rough country, it was useless to think of pursuing Lobo with hounds and horses, so that poison or traps were the only available expedients. At present we had no traps large enough, so I set to work with poison.

I need not enter into the details of a hundred devices that I employed to circumvent this 'loup-garou'; there was no combination of strychnine, arsenic, cyanide, or prussic acid, that I did not essay; there was no manner of flesh that I did not try as bait; but morning after morning, as I rode forth to learn the result, I found that all my efforts had been useless. The old king was too cunning for me. A single instance will show his wonderful sagacity. Acting on the hint of an old trapper, I melted some cheese together with the kidney fat of a freshly killed heifer, stewing it in a china dish, and cutting it with a bone knife to avoid the taint of metal. When the mixture was cool, I cut it into lumps, and making a hole in one side of each lump, I inserted a large dose of strychnine and cyanide, contained in a capsule that was impermeable by any odor; finally I sealed the holes up with pieces of the cheese itself. During the whole process, I wore a pair of gloves steeped in the hot blood of the heifer, and even avoided breathing on the baits. When all was ready, I put them in a raw-hide bag rubbed all over with blood, and rode forth dragging the liver and kidneys of the beef at the end of a rope. With this I made a ten-mile circuit, dropping a bait at each quarter of a mile, and taking the utmost care, always, not to touch any with my hands.

Lobo, generally, came into this part of the range in the early part of each week, and passed the latter part, it was supposed, around the base of Sierra Grande. This was Monday, and that same evening, as we were about to retire, I heard the deep bass howl of his majesty. On hearing it one of the boys briefly remarked, "There he is, we'll see."

The next morning I went forth, eager to know the result. I soon came on the fresh trail of the robbers, with Lobo in the lead—his track was always easily distinguished. An ordinary wolf's forefoot is $4\,^1/_2$ inches long, that of a large wolf $4\,^3/_4$ inches, but Lobo's, as measured a number of times, was $5\,^1/_2$ inches from claw to heel; I afterward found that his other proportions were commensurate, for he stood three feet high at the shoulder, and weighed 150 pounds. His trail, therefore, though obscured by those of his followers, was never difficult to trace. The pack had soon found the track of my drag, and as usual followed it. I could see that Lobo had come to the first bait, sniffed about it, and finally had picked it up.

Then I could not conceal my delight. "I've got him at last," I exclaimed; "I shall find him stark within a mile," and I galloped on with eager eyes fixed on the great broad track in the dust. It led me to the second bait and that also was gone. How I exulted—I surely have him now and perhaps several of his band. But there was the broad paw-mark still on the drag; and though I stood in the stirrup and scanned the plain I saw nothing that looked like a dead wolf. Again I followed—to find now that the third bait was gone—and the king-wolf's track led on to the fourth, there to learn that he had not really taken a bait at all, but had merely carried them in his mouth. Then having piled the three on the fourth, he scattered filth over them to express his utter contempt for my devices. After this he left my drag and went about his business with the pack he guarded so effectively.

This is only one of many similar experiences which convinced me that poison would never avail to destroy this robber, and though I continued to use it while awaiting the arrival of the traps, it was only because it was meanwhile a sure means of killing many prairie wolves and other destructive vermin.

About this time there came under my observation an incident that will illustrate Lobo's diabolic cunning. These wolves had at least one pursuit which was merely an amusement, it was stampeding and killing sheep, though they rarely ate them. The sheep are usually kept in flocks of from one thousand to three thousand under one or more shepherds. At night they are gathered in the most sheltered place available, and a herdsman sleeps on each side of the flock to give additional protection. Sheep are such senseless creatures that they are liable to be stampeded by the veriest trifle, but they have deeply ingrained in their nature one, and perhaps only one, strong weakness, namely, to follow their leader. And this the shepherds turn to good account by putting half a dozen goats in the flock of sheep. The latter recognize the superior intelligence of their bearded cousins, and when a night alarm occurs they crowd around them, and usually are thus saved from a stampede and are easily protected. But it was not always so. One night late in last November, two Perico shepherds were aroused by an onset of wolves. Their flocks huddled around the goats, which being neither fools nor cowards, stood their ground and were bravely defiant; but alas for them, no common wolf was heading this attack. Old Lobo, the weir-wolf, knew as well as the shepherds that the goats were the moral force of the flock, so hastily running over the backs of the densely packed sheep, he fell on these leaders, slew them all in a few minutes, and soon had the luckless sheep stampeding in a thousand different directions. For weeks afterward I was almost daily accosted by some anxious shepherd, who asked, "Have you seen any stray OTO sheep lately?" and usually I was obliged to say I had; one day it was, "Yes, I came on some five or six carcasses by Diamond Springs;" or another, it was to the effect that I had seen a small 'bunch' running on the Malpai Mesa; or again, "No, but Juan Meira saw about twenty, freshly killed, on the Cedra Monte two days ago."

At length the wolf traps arrived, and with two men I worked a whole week to get them properly set out. We spared no labour or pains, I adopted every device I could think of that might help to insure success. The second day after the traps arrived, I rode around to inspect, and soon came upon Lobo's trail running from trap to trap. In the dust I could read the whole story of his doings that night. He had trotted along in the darkness, and although the traps were so carefully concealed, he had instantly detected the first one. Stopping the onward march of the pack, he had cautiously scratched around it until he had disclosed the trap, the chain, and the log, then left them wholly exposed to view with the trap still unsprung, and passing on he treated over a dozen traps in the same fashion. Very soon I noticed that he stopped and turned aside as soon as he detected suspicious signs on the trail and a new plan to outwit him at once suggested itself. I set the traps in the form of an H; that is, with a row of traps on each side of the trail, and one on the trail for the cross-bar of the H. Before long, I had an opportunity to count another failure. Lobo came trotting along the trail, and was fairly between the parallel lines before he detected the single trap in the trail, but he stopped in time, and why or how he knew enough I cannot tell, the Angel of the wild things must have been with him, but without turning an inch to the right or left, he slowly and cautiously backed on his own tracks, putting each paw exactly in its old track until he was off the dangerous ground. Then returning at one side he scratched clods and stones with his hind feet till he had sprung every trap. This he did on many other occasions, and although I varied my methods and redoubled my precautions, he was never deceived, his sagacity seemed never at fault, and he might have been pursuing his career of rapine to-day, but for an unfortunate alliance that proved his ruin and added his name to the long list of heroes who, unassailable when alone, have fallen through the indiscretion of a trusted ally.

III

Once or twice, I had found indications that everything was not quite right in the Currumpaw pack. There were signs of irregularity, I thought; for instance there was clearly the trail of a smaller wolf running ahead of the leader, at times, and this I could not understand until a cowboy made a remark which explained the matter.

"I saw them to-day," he said, "and the wild one that breaks away is Blanca." Then the truth dawned upon me, and I added, "Now, I know that Blanca is a she-wolf, because were a he-wolf to act thus, Lobo would kill him at once."

This suggested a new plan. I killed a heifer, and set one or two rather obvious traps about the carcass. Then cutting off the head, which is considered useless offal, and quite beneath the notice of a wolf, I set it a little apart and around it placed six powerful steel traps properly deodorized and concealed with the utmost care. During my operations I kept my hands, boots, and implements smeared with fresh blood, and afterward sprinkled the ground with the same, as though it had flowed from the head; and when the traps were buried in the dust I brushed the place over with the skin of a coyote, and with a foot of the same animal made a number of tracks over the traps. The head was so placed that there was a narrow passage between it and some tussocks, and in this passage I buried two of my best traps, fastening them to the head itself.

Wolves have a habit of approaching every carcass they get the wind of, in order to examine it, even when they have no intention of eating of it, and I hoped that this habit would bring the Currumpaw pack within reach of my latest stratagem. I did not doubt that Lobo would detect my handiwork about the meat, and prevent the pack approaching it, but I did build some hopes on the head, for it looked as though it had been thrown aside as useless.

Next morning, I sallied forth to inspect the traps, and there, oh, joy! were the tracks of the pack, and the place where the beef-head and its traps had been was empty. A hasty study of the trail showed that Lobo had kept the pack from approaching the meat, but one, a small wolf, had evidently gone on to examine the head as it lay apart and had walked right into one of the traps.

We set out on the trail, and within a mile discovered that the hapless wolf was Blanca. Away she went, however, at a gallop, and although encumbered by the beef-head, which weighed over fifty pounds, she speedily distanced my companion who was on foot. But we overtook her when she reached the rocks, for the horns of the cow's head became caught and held her fast. She was the handsomest wolf I had ever seen. Her coat was in perfect condition and nearly white.

She turned to fight, and raising her voice in the rallying cry of her race, sent a long howl rolling over the cañon. From far away upon the mesa came a deep response, the cry of Old Lobo. That was her last call, for now we had closed in on her, and all her energy and breath were devoted to combat.

Then followed the inevitable tragedy, the idea of which I shrank from afterward more than at the time. We each threw a lasso over the neck of the doomed wolf, and strained our horses in opposite directions until the blood burst from her mouth, her eyes glazed, her limbs stiffened and then fell limp. Homeward then we rode, carrying the dead wolf, and exulting over this, the first death-blow we had been able to inflict on the Currumpaw pack.

At intervals during the tragedy, and afterward as we rode homeward, we heard the roar of Lobo as he wandered about on the distant mesas, where he seemed to be searching for Blanca. He had never really deserted her, but knowing that he could not save her, his deep-rooted dread of firearms had been too much for him when he saw us approaching. All that day we heard him wailing as he roamed in his quest, and I remarked at length to one of the boys, "Now, indeed, I truly know that Blanca was his mate."

As evening fell he seemed to be coming toward the home cañon, for his voice sounded continually nearer. There was an unmistakable note of sorrow in it now. It was no longer the loud, defiant howl, but a long, plaintive wail; "Blanca! Blanca!" he seemed to call. And as night came down, I noticed that he was not far from the place where we had overtaken her. At length he seemed to find the trail, and when he came to the spot where we had killed her, his heart-broken wailing was piteous to hear. It was sadder than I could possibly have believed. Even the stolid cowboys noticed it, and said they had "never heard a wolf carry on like that before." He seemed to know exactly what had taken place, for her blood had stained the place of her death.

Then he took up the trail of the horses and followed it to the ranch-house. Whether in hopes of finding her there, or in quest of revenge, I know not, but the latter was what he found, for he surprised our unfortunate watchdog outside and tore him to little bits within fifty yards of the door. He evidently came alone this time, for I found but one trail next morning, and he had galloped about in a reckless manner that was very unusual with him. I had half expected this, and had set a number of additional traps about the pasture. Afterward I found that he had indeed fallen into one of these, but such was his strength, he had torn himself loose and cast it aside.

I believed that he would continue in the neighbourhood until he found her body at least, so I concentrated all my energies on this one enterprise of catching him before he left the region, and while yet in this reckless mood. Then I realized what a mistake I had made in killing Blanca, for by using her as a decoy I might have secured him the next night.

I gathered in all the traps I could command, one hundred and thirty strong steel wolf-traps, and set them in fours in every trail that led into the cañon; each trap was separately fastened to a log, and each log was separately buried. In burying them, I carefully removed the sod and every particle of earth that was lifted we put in blankets, so that after the sod was replaced and all was finished the eye could detect no trace of human handiwork. When the traps were concealed I trailed the body of poor Blanca over each place, and made of it a drag that circled all about the ranch, and finally I took off one of her paws and made with it a line of tracks over each trap. Every precaution and device known to me I used, and retired at a late hour to await the result.

Once during the night I thought I heard Old Lobo, but was not sure of it. Next day I rode around, but darkness came on before I completed the circuit of the north cañon, and I had nothing to report. At supper one of the cowboys said, "There was a great row among the cattle in the north cañon this morning, maybe there is something in the traps there." It was afternoon of the next day before I got to the place referred to, and as I drew near a great grizzly form arose from the ground, vainly endeavouring to escape, and there revealed before me stood Lobo, King of the Currumpaw, firmly held in the traps. Poor old hero, he had never ceased to search for his darling, and when he found the trail her body had made he followed it recklessly, and so fell into the snare prepared for him. There he lay in the iron grasp of all four traps, perfectly helpless, and all around him were numerous tracks showing how the cattle had gathered about him to insult the fallen despot, without daring to approach within his reach. For two days and two nights he had lain there, and now was worn out with struggling. Yet, when I went near him, he rose up with bristling mane and raised his voice, and for the last time made the cañon reverberate with his deep bass roar, a call for help, the muster call of his band. But there was none to answer him, and, left alone in his extremity, he whirled about with all his strength and made a desperate effort to get at me. All in vain, each trap was a dead drag of over three hundred pounds, and in their relentless fourfold grasp, with great steel jaws on every foot, and the heavy logs and chains all entangled together, he was absolutely powerless. How his huge ivory tusks did grind on those cruel chains, and when I ventured to touch him with my rifle-barrel he left grooves on it which are there to this day. His eyes glared green with hate and fury, and his jaws snapped with a hollow 'chop,' as he vainly endeavoured to reach me and my trembling horse. But he was worn out with hunger and struggling and loss of blood, and he soon sank exhausted to the ground.

Something like compunction came over me, as I prepared to deal out to him that which so many had suffered at his hands.

"Grand old outlaw, hero of a thousand lawless raids, in a few minutes you will be but a great load of carrion. It cannot be otherwise." Then I swung my lasso and sent it whistling over his head. But not so fast; he was yet far from being subdued, and, before the supple coils had fallen on his neck he seized the noose and, with one fierce chop, cut through its hard thick strands, and dropped it in two pieces at his feet.

Of course I had my rifle as a last resource, but I did not wish to spoil his royal hide, so I galloped back to the camp and returned with a cowboy and a fresh lasso. We threw to our victim a stick of wood which he seized in his teeth, and before he could relinquish it our lassoes whistled through the air and tightened on his neck.

Yet before the light had died from his fierce eyes, I cried, "Stay, we will not kill him; let us take him alive to the camp." He was so completely powerless now that it was easy to put a stout stick through his mouth, behind his tusks, and then lash his jaws with a heavy cord which was also fastened to the stick. The stick kept the cord in, and the cord kept the stick in so he was harmless. As soon as he felt his jaws were tied he made no further resistance, and uttered no sound, but looked calmly at us and seemed to say, "Well, you have got me at last, do as you please with me." And from that time he took no more notice of us.

We tied his feet securely, but he never groaned, nor growled, nor turned his head. Then with our united strength were just able to put him on my horse. His breath came evenly as though sleeping, and his eyes were bright and clear again, but did not rest on us. Afar on the great rolling mesas they were fixed, his passing kingdom, where his famous band was now scattered. And he gazed till the pony descended the pathway into the cañon, and the rocks cut off the view.

By travelling slowly we reached the ranch in safety, and after securing him with a collar and a strong chain, we staked him out in the pasture and removed the cords. Then for the first time I could examine him closely, and proved how unreliable is vulgar report when a living hero or tyrant is concerned. He had *not* a collar of gold about his neck, nor was there on his shoulders an inverted cross to denote that he had leagued himself with Satan. But I did find on one haunch a great broad scar, that tradition says was the fang-mark of Juno, the leader of Tannerey's wolf-hounds—a mark which she gave him the moment before he stretched her lifeless on the sand of the cañon.

I set meat and water beside him, but he paid no heed. He lay calmly on his breast, and gazed with those steadfast yellow eyes away past me down through the gateway of the cañon, over the open plains—his plains—nor moved a muscle when I touched him. When the sun went down he was still gazing fixedly across the prairie. I expected he would call up his band when night came, and prepared for them, but he had called once in his extremity, and none had come; he would never call again.

A lion shorn of his strength, an eagle robbed of his freedom, or a dove bereft of his mate, all die, it is said, of a broken heart; and who will aver that this grim bandit could bear the threefold brunt, heart-whole? This only I know, that when the morning dawned, he was lying there still in his position of calm repose, but his spirit was gone—the old king-wolf was dead.

I took the chain from his neck, a cowboy helped me to carry him to the shed where lay the remains of Blanca, and as we laid him beside her, the cattle-man exclaimed: "There, you *would* come to her, now you are together again."

- Roberts - when under fire for his depiction of animals defended the realism pf what he was doing. Whatever he wrote about he claimed to have seen.

- The childrens aid society came out of the humane society! Children & animals must be protected!

Animal Stories - Important Genre in Canadian Literature - Said to be a true product of Canadian Soil.

* - Roberts - different in that his animal stories are based on history & observations of nature/animals in the wild not on human/moral elements.

- essay in the back by Roberts on his animal stories.

- Local colourist - treating what goes on in a particular place as only a local can.

Charles G.D. Roberts (1860-1943)

Roberts' boyhood rambles in rural New Brunswick and his later hunting and camping trips with friends inspired his highly successful stories about animals. Educated in Classics at the University of New Brunswick, Roberts taught at King's College in Windsor, Nova Scotia until 1895, and published several highly acclaimed books of poetry. From 1895 to 1925 he lived in the United States and in Europe, writing commercial stories, novels and histories to make his living. In later life he returned to poetry and to Canada, where he was celebrated as the "Father of Canadian Literature."

"When Twilight Falls on the Stump Lots" demonstrates typical features of Roberts' animal stories: told from the imagined point of view of the animals themselves, it evokes heroic values only to undermine them with an "objective" Darwinian science. This version of the story is taken from the collection, *Kindred of the Wild* (Toronto: Copp Clark, 1902).

When Twilight Falls on the Stump Lots

The wet, chill first of the spring, its blackness made tender by the lilac wash of the afterglow, lay upon the high, open stretches of the stump lots. The winter-whitened stumps, the sparse patches of juniper and bay just budding, the rough-mossed hillocks, the harsh boulders here and there up-thrusting from the soil, the swampy hollows wherein a coarse grass began to show green, all seemed anointed, as it were, to an ecstasy of peace by the chrism of that paradisal colour. Against the lucid immensity of the April sky the thin tops of five or six ram-pikes aspired like violet flames. Along the skirts of the stump lots a fir wood reared a ragged-crested wall of black against the red amber of the horizon.

Late that afternoon, beside a juniper thicket not far from the centre of the stump lots, a young black and white cow had given birth to her first calf. The little animal had been licked assiduously by the mother's caressing tongue till its colour began to show of a rich dark red. Now it had struggled to its feet, and, with its disproportionately long, thick legs braced wide apart, was beginning to nurse. Its blunt wet muzzle and thick lips tugged eagerly, but somewhat blunderingly as yet, at the unaccustomed teats; and its tail lifted, twitching with delight, as the first warm streams of mother milk went down its throat. It was a pathetically awkward, unlovely little figure, not yet advanced to that youngling winsomeness which is the heritage, to some degree and at some period, of the infancy of all the kindreds that breathe upon the earth. But to the young mother's eyes it was the most beautiful of things. With her head twisted far around, she nosed and licked its heaving flanks as it nursed; and between deep, ecstatic breathings she uttered in her throat low murmurs, unspeakably tender, of encouragement and caress. The delicate but pervading flood of sunset colour had the effect of blending the ruddy-hued calf into the tones of the landscape; but the cow's insistent blotches of black and white stood out sharply, refusing to harmonise. The drench of violet light was of no avail to soften their staring contrasts. They made her vividly conspicuous across the whole breadth of the stump lots, to eyes that watched her from the forest coverts.

The eyes that watched her—long, fixedly, hungrily—were small and red. They belonged to a lank she-bear, whose gaunt flanks and rusty coat proclaimed a season of famine in the wilderness. She could not see the calf, which was hidden by a hillock and some juniper scrub; but its presence was very legibly conveyed to her by the mother's solicitous watchfulness. After a motionless scrutiny from behind the screen of fir branches, the lean bear stole noiselessly forth from the shadows into the great wash of violet light. Step by step, and very slowly, with the patience that endures because confident of its object, she crept toward that oasis of mothering joy in the vast emptiness of the stump lots. Now crouching, now crawling, turning to this side and to that, taking advantage of every hollow, every thicket, every hillock, every aggressive stump, her craft succeeded in eluding even the wild and menacing watchfulness of the young mother's eyes.

The spring had been a trying one for the lank she-bear. Her den, in a dry tract of hemlock wood some furlongs back from the stump lots, was a snug little cave under the uprooted base of a lone pine, which had somehow grown up among the alien hemlocks only to draw down upon itself at last, by its superior height, the fury of a passing hurricane. The winter had contributed but scanty snowfall to cover the bear in her sleep; and the March thaws, unseasonably early and ardent, had called her forth to activity weeks too soon. Then frosts had come with belated severity, sealing away the budding tubers, which are the bear's chief dependence for spring diet; and worst of all, a long stretch of intervale meadow by the neighbouring river, which had once been rich in ground-nuts, had been ploughed up the previous spring and subjected to the producing of oats and corn. When she was feeling the pinch of meagre rations, and when the fat which a liberal autumn of blueberries had laid up about her ribs was getting as shrunken as the last snow in the thickets, she gave birth to two hairless and hungry little cubs. They were very blind, and ridiculously small to be born of so big a mother; and having so much growth to make during the next few months, their appetites were immeasurable. They tumbled, and squealed, and tugged at their mother's teats, and grew astonishingly, and made huge haste to cover their bodies with fur of a soft and silken black; and all this vitality of theirs made a strenuous demand upon their mother's milk. There were no more bee-trees left in the neighbourhood. The long wanderings which she was forced to take in her search for roots and tubers were in themselves a drain upon her nursing powers. At last, reluctant though she was to attract the hostile notice of the settlement, she found herself forced to hunt on the borders of the sheep pastures. Before all else in life was it important to her that these two tumbling little ones in the den should not go hungry. Their eyes were open now—small and dark and whimsical, their ears quaintly large and inquiring for their roguish little faces. Had she not been driven by the unkind season to so much hunting and foraging, she would have passed near all her time rapturously in the den under the pine root, fondling those two soft miracles of her world.

With the killing of three lambs—at widely scattered points, so as to mislead retaliation—things grew a little easier for the harassed bear; and presently she grew bolder in tampering with the creatures under man's protection. With one swift, secret blow of her mighty paw she struck down a young ewe which had strayed within reach of her hiding-place. Dragging her prey deep into the woods, she fared well upon it for some days, and was happy with her growing cubs. It was just when she had begun to feel the fasting which came upon the exhaustion of this store that, in a hungry hour, she sighted the conspicuous markings of the black and white cow.

It is altogether unusual for the black bear of the eastern woods to attack any quarry so large as a cow, unless under the spur of fierce hunger or fierce rage. The she-bear was powerful beyond her fellows. She had the strongest possible incentive to bold hunting, and she had lately grown confident beyond her wont. Nevertheless, when she began her careful stalking of this big game which she coveted, she had no definite intention of forcing a battle with the cow. She had observed that cows, accustomed to the protection of man, would at times leave their calves asleep and stray off some distance in their pasturing. She had even seen calves left all by themselves in a field, from morning till night, and had wondered at such negligence in their mothers. Now she had a confident idea that sooner or later the calf would lie down to sleep, and the young mother roam a little wide in search of the scant young grass. Very softly, very self-effacingly, she crept nearer step by step, following up the wind, till at last, undiscovered, she was crouching behind a thick patch of juniper, on the slope of a little hollow not ten paces distant from the cow and the calf.

By this time the tender violet light was fading to a greyness over hillock and hollow; and with the deepening of the twilight the faint breeze, which had been breathing from the northward, shifted suddenly and came in slow, warm pulsations out of the south. At the same time the calf, having nursed sufficiently, and feeling his baby legs tired of the weight they had not yet learned to carry, laid himself down. On this the cow shifted her position. She turned half round, and lifted her head *"tropological enslavement"* (Margot Norris) silly but memorable term — means their use as metaphor — animals have (the vast majority) have been used as met. for humans & not given credit for a life of their own.

high. As she did so a scent of peril was borne in upon her fine nostrils. She recognised it instantly. With a snort of anger she sniffed again; then stamped a challenge with her fore hoofs, and levelled the lance-points of her horns toward the menace. The next moment her eyes, made keen by the fear of love, detected the black outline of the bear's head through the coarse screen of the juniper. Without a second's hesitation, she flung up her tail, gave a short bellow, and charged.

The moment she saw herself detected, the bear rose upon her hindquarters; nevertheless she was in a measure surprised by the sudden blind fury of the attack. Nimbly she swerved to avoid it, aiming at the same time a stroke with her mighty forearm, which, if it had found its mark, would have smashed her adversary's neck. But as she struck out, in the act of shifting her position, a depression of the ground threw her off her balance. The next instant one sharp horn caught her slantingly in the flank, ripping its way upward and inward, while the mad impact threw her upon her back.

Grappling, she had her assailant's head and shoulders in a trap, and her gigantic claws cut through the flesh and sinew like knives; but at the desperate disadvantage of her position she could inflict no disabling blow. The cow, on the other hand, though mutilated and streaming with blood, kept pounding with her whole massive weight, and with short tremendous shocks crushing the breath from her foe's ribs.

Presently, wrenching herself free, the cow drew off for another battering charge; and as she did so the bear hurled herself violently down the slope, and gained her feet behind a dense thicket of bay shrub. The cow, with one eye blinded and the other obscured by blood, glared around for her in vain, then, in a panic of mother terror, plunged back to her calf.

Snatching at the respite, the bear crouched down, craving that invisibility which is the most faithful shield of the furtive kindred. Painfully, and leaving a drenched red trail behind her, she crept off from the disastrous neighbourhood. Soon the deepening twilight sheltered her. But she could not make haste; and she knew that death was close upon her.

Once within the woods, she struggled straight toward the

den that held her young. She hungered to die licking them. But destiny is as implacable as iron to the wilderness people, and even this was denied her. Just a half score of paces from the lair in the pine root, her hour descended upon her. There was a sudden redder and fuller gush upon the trail; the last light of longing faded out of her eyes; and she lay down upon her side.

The merry little cubs within the den were beginning to expect her, and getting restless. As the night wore on, and no mother came, they ceased to be merry. By morning they were shivering with hunger and desolate fear. But the doom of the ancient wood was less harsh than its wont, and spared them some days of starving anguish; for about noon a pair of foxes discovered the dead mother, astutely estimated the situation, and then, with the boldness of good appetite, made their way into the unguarded den.

As for the red calf, its fortune was ordinary. Its mother, for all her wounds, was able to nurse and cherish it through the night; and with morning came a searcher from the farm and took it, with the bleeding mother, safely back to the settlement. There it was tended and fattened, and within a few weeks found its way to the cool marble slabs of a city market.

Sara Jeannette Duncan (1861-1922)

Duncan began her career as a journalist, writing reviews, columns and sketches for *The Week*, the Toronto *Globe* and the *Montreal Star*. A trip around the world to gather 'material' for her first novel resulted in her marriage to Everard Cotes, a British civil servant living in India, in 1891. She wrote twenty-two books including one collection of short stories and one of personal essays; *The Imperialist* (1904), a novel which draws on her childhood memories of Brantford, Ontario, is a staple of Canadian literature courses. Her circumlocutory style (especially in her short stories) is influenced by Henry James, and critics note the characteristic ironic tone of her first-person narrators, her interest in social manners and distinctions, and her inclusion of realistic detail.

"A Mother In India" is a long short story (or perhaps a novella) which was originally published in *Scribners Monthly* in two parts: 33 (June 1903): 747-56 and 34 (July 1903): 107-16). This version is taken from its first book publication in *The Pool in the Desert* (New York: D. Appleton, 1903).

A Mother in India

I

There were times when we had to go without puddings to pay John's uniform bills, and always I did the facings myself with a cloth-ball to save getting new ones. I would have polished his sword, too, if I had been allowed; I adored his sword. And once, I remember, we painted and varnished our own dog-cart, and very smart it looked, to save fifty rupees. We had nothing but our pay—John had his company when we were married, but what is that?—and life was made up of small knowing economies, much more amusing in recollection than in practice. We were sodden poor, and that is a fact, poor and conscientious, which was worse. A big fat spider of a money-lender came one day into the veranda and tempted us—we lived in a hut, but it had a veranda—and John threatened to report him to the police. Poor when everybody else had enough to live in the open-handed Indian fashion, that was what made it so hard; we were alone in our sordid little ways. When the expectation of Cecily came to us we made out to be delighted, knowing that the whole station pitied us, and when Cecily came herself, with a swamping burst of expense, we kept up the pretense splendidly. She was peevish, poor little thing, and she threatened convulsions from the beginning, but we both knew that it was abnormal not to love her a great deal, more than life, immediately and increasingly; and we applied ourselves honestly to do it, with the thermometer at a hundred and two, and the nurse leaving at the end of a fortnight because she discovered that I had only six of everything for the table. To find out a husband's virtues, you must marry a poor man. The regiment was under-officered as usual, and John had to take parade at daylight quite three times a week; but he walked up and down the veranda with Cecily constantly till two in the morning, when a little coolness came. I usually lay awake the rest of the night in fear that a scorpion would drop from the ceiling on her. Nevertheless, we were of excellent mind toward Cecily; we were in such terror, not so much of failing in our duty toward her as toward the ideal standard of mankind. We were very anxious indeed not to come short. To be found too small for one's place in nature would have been odious. We would talk about her for an hour at a time, even when John's charger was threatening glanders and I could see his mind perpetually wandering to the stable. I would say to John that she had brought a new element into our lives—she had indeed!—and John would reply, "I know what you mean," and go on to prophesy that she would "bind us together." We didn't need binding together; we were more to each other, there in the desolation of that arid frontier outpost, than most husbands and wives; but it seemed a proper and hopeful thing to believe, so we believed it. Of course, the real experience would have come, we weren't monsters; but fate curtailed the opportunity. She was just five weeks old when the doctor told us that we must either pack her home immediately or lose her, and the very next day John went down with enteric. So Cecily was sent to England with a sergeant's wife who had lost her twins, and I settled down under the direction of a native doctor, to fight for my husband's life, without ice or proper food, or sickroom comforts of any sort. Ah! Fort Samila, with the sun glaring up from the sand!—however, it is a long time ago now. I trusted the baby willingly to Mrs. Berry and to Providence, and did not fret; my capacity for worry, I suppose, was completely absorbed. Mrs. Berry's letter, describing the child's improvement on the voyage and safe arrival came, I remember, the day on which John was allowed his first solid mouthful; it had been long siege. "Poor little wretch!" he said when I read it aloud; and after that Cecily became an episode.

She had gone to my husband's people; it was the best arrangement. We were lucky that it was possible; so many children had to be sent to strangers and hirelings. Since an unfortunate infant must be brought into the world and set adrift, the haven of its grandmother and its Aunt Emma and its Aunt Alice certainly seemed providential. I had absolutely no cause for anxiety, as I often told people, wondering that I did not feel a little all the same. Nothing, I knew, could exceed the conscientious devotion of all three Farnham ladies to the child. She would appear upon their somewhat barren horizon as a new and interesting duty, and the small additional income she also represented would be almost nominal compensation for the care she would receive. They were excellent persons of the kind that talk about matins and vespers, and attend both. They helped little charities and gave little teas, and wrote little notes, and made deprecating allowance for the eccentricities of their titled or moneyed acquaintances. They were the subdued, smiling, unimaginatively dressed women on a small definite income that you meet at every rectory garden-party in the country, a little snobbish, a little priggish, wholly conventional, but apart from these weaknesses, sound and simple and dignified, managing their two small servants with a display of the most exact traditions, and keeping a somewhat vague and belated but constant eye upon the doings of their country as chronicled in a biweekly paper. They were all immensely interested in royalty, and would read paragraphs aloud to each other about how the Princess Beatrice or the Princess Maud had opened a fancy bazaar, looking remarkably well in plain grey poplin trimmed with Irish lace—an industry which, as is well known, the Royal Family has set its heart on rehabilitating. Upon which Mrs. Farnham's comment invariably would be, "How thoughtful of them, dear!" and Alice would usually say, "Well, if I were a princess, I should like something nicer than plain grey poplin." Alice, being the youngest, was not always expected to think before she spoke. Alice painted in water-colours, but Emma was supposed to have the most common sense.

They took turns in writing to us with the greatest regularity about Cecily; only once, I think, did they miss the weekly mail, and that was when she threatened diphtheria and they thought we had better be kept in ignorance. The kind and affectionate terms of these letters never altered except with the facts they described—teething, creeping, measles, cheeks growing round and rosy, all were conveyed in the same smooth, pat, and proper phrases, so absolutely empty of any glimpse of the child's personality that after the first few months it was like reading about a somewhat uninteresting infant in a book. I was sure Cecily was not uninteresting, but her chroniclers were. We used to wade through the long, thin sheets and saw how much more satisfactory it would be when Cecily could write to us herself. Meanwhile we noted her weekly progress with much the feeling one would have about a far-away little bit of property that was giving no trouble and coming on exceedingly well. We would take possession of Cecily at our convenience; till then, it was gratifying to hear of our unearned increment in dear little dimples and sweet little curls.

She was nearly four when I saw her again. We were home on three months' leave. John had just got his first brevet for doing something which he does not allow me to talk about in the Black Mountain country; and we were fearfully pleased with ourselves. I remember that excitement lasted well up to Port Said. As far as the Canal, Cecily was only one of the pleasures and interests we were going home to: John's majority was the thing that really gave savor to life. But the first faint line of

Europe brought my child to my horizon; and all the rest of the way she kept her place, holding out her little arms to me, beckoning me on. Her four motherless years brought compunction to my heart and tears to my eyes; she should have all the compensation that could be. I suddenly realized how ready I was— how ready!—to have her back. I rebelled fiercely against John's decision that we must not take her with us on our return to the frontier; privately, I resolved to dispute and, if necessary, I saw myself abducting the child—my own child. My days and nights as the ship crept on were full of a long ache to possess her; defrauded tenderness of the last four years rose in me and sometimes caught at my throat. I could think and talk and dream of nothing else. John indulged me as much as was reasonable, and only once betrayed by a yawn that the subject was not for him endlessly absorbing. Then I cried and apologized. "You know," he said, "it isn't exactly the same thing. I'm not her mother." At which I dried my tears and expanded, proud and pacified. I was her mother!

Then the rainy little station and Alice, all-embracing in a damp waterproof, and the drive in the fly, and John's mother at the gate and a necessary pause while I kissed John's mother. Dear thing, she wanted to hold our hands and look in our faces and tell us how little we had changed for all our hardships; and on the way to the house she actually stopped to point out some alteration in the flower-borders. At last the drawing-room door and the smiling housemaid turning the handle and the unforgettable picture of a little girl, a little girl unlike anything we had imagined, starting bravely to trot across the room with the little speech that had been taught her. Half-way she came; suppose our regards were too fixed, too absorbed, for there she stopped with a wail of terror at the strange faces, and ran straight back to the outstretched arms of her Aunt Emma. The most natural thing in the world, no doubt. I walked over to a chair opposite with my hand-bag and umbrella and sat down— a spectator, aloof and silent. Aunt Emma fondled and quieted the child, apologizing for her to me, coaxing her to look up, but the little figure still shook with sobs, hiding its face in the bosom that it knew. I smiled politely, like any other stranger, at

Emma's deprecations, and sat impassive, looking at my alleged baby breaking her heart at the sight of her mother. It is not amusing even now to remember the anger that I felt. I did not touch her or speak to her; I simply sat observing my alien possession, in the frock I had not made and the sash I had not chosen, being coaxed and kissed and protected and petted by its Aunt Emma. Presently I asked to be taken to my room, and there I locked myself in for two atrocious hours. Just once my heart beat high, when a tiny knock came and a timid, docile little voice said that tea was ready. But I heard the rustle of a skirt, and guessed the directing angel in Aunt Emma, and responded, "Thank you, dear, run away and say that I am coming," with a pleasant visitor's inflection which I was able to sustain for the rest of the afternoon.

"She goes to bed at seven," said Emma.

"Oh, does she?" said I. "A very good hour, I should think."

"She sleeps in my room," said Mrs. Farnham.

"We give her mutton broth very often, but seldom stock soup," said Aunt Emma. "Mamma thinks it is too stimulating."

"Indeed?" said I, to all of it.

They took me up to see her in her crib, and pointed out, as she lay asleep, that though she has "a general look" of me, her features were distinctively Farnham.

"Won't you kiss her?" asked Alice. "You haven't kissed her yet, and she is used to so much affection."

"I don't think I could take such an advantage of her," I said.

They looked at each other, and Mrs. Farnham said that I was plainly worn out. I mustn't sit up to prayers.

If I had been given anything like reasonable time I might have made a fight for it, but four weeks—it took a month each way in those days—was too absurdly little; I could do nothing. But I would not stay at mamma's. It was more than I would ask of myself, that daily disappointment under the mask of gratified discovery, for long.

I spent an approving, unnatural week, in my farcical character, bridling my resentment and hiding my mortification with pretty phrases; and then I went up to town and drowned my sorrows in the summer sales. I took John with me. I may have been Cecily's mother in theory, but I was John's wife in fact.

We went back to the frontier, and the regiment saw a lot of service. That meant medals and fun for my husband, but economy and anxiety for me, though I managed to be allowed as close to the firing line as any woman.

Once the Colonel's wife and I, sitting in Fort Samila, actually heard the rifles of a punitive expedition cracking on the other side of the river—that was a bad moment. My man came in after fifteen hours' fighting, and went sound asleep, sitting before his food with his knife and fork in his hands. But service makes heavy demands besides those on your wife's nerves. We had saved two thousand rupees, I remember, against another run home, and it all went like powder, in the Mirzai expedition; and the run home diminished to a month in a boarding-house in the hills.

Meanwhile, however, we had begun to correspond with our daughter, in large round words of one syllable, behind which, of course, was plain the patient guiding hand of Aunt Emma. One could hear Aunt Emma suggesting what would be nice to say, trying to instil a little pale affection for the far-off papa and mamma. There was so little Cecily and so much Emma—of course, it could not be otherwise—that I used to take, I fear, but a perfunctory joy in those letters. When we went home again I stipulated absolutely that she was to write to us without any sort of supervision—the child was ten.

"But the spelling!" cried Aunt Emma, with lifted eyebrows.

"Her letters aren't exercises," I was obliged to retort; "she will do the best she can."

We found her a docile little girl, with nice manners, a thoroughly unobjectionable child. I saw quite clearly that I could not have brought her up so well; indeed, there were moments when I fancied that Cecily, contrasting me with her aunts, wondered a little what my bringing up could have been like. With this reserve of criticism on Cecily's part, however, we got on very tolerably, largely because I found it impossible to assume any responsibility toward her, and in moments of doubt or discipline referred her to her aunts. We spent a pleasant summer with a little girl in the house whose interest in us was amusing, and whose outings it was gratifying to arrange; but when we went back, I had no desire to take her with us. I thought her very much better where she was.

Then came the period which is filled, in a subordinate degree, with Cecily's letters. I do not wish to claim more than I ought; they were not my only or even my principal interest in life. It was a long period; it lasted till she was twenty-one. John had had promotion in the meantime, and there was rather more money, but he had earned his second brevet with a bullet through one lung, and the doctors ordered our leave to be spent in South Africa. We had photographs, we knew she had grown tall and athletic and comely, and the letters were always very creditable. I had the unusual and qualified privilege of watching my daughter's development from ten to twenty-one, at a distance of four thousand miles, by means of the written word. I wrote myself as provocatively as possible; I sought for every string, but the vibration that came back across the seas to me was always other than the one I looked for, and sometimes there was none. Nevertheless, Mrs. Farnham wrote me that Cecily very much valued my communications. Once when I had described an unusual excursion in a native state, I learned that she had read my letter aloud to the sewing circle. After that I abandoned description, and confined myself to such intimate personal details as no sewing circle could find amusing. The child's own letters were simply a mirror of the ideas of the Farnham ladies; that must have been so, it was not altogether my jaundiced eye. Alice and Emma and grandmamma paraded the pages in turn. I very early gave up hope of discoveries in my daughter, though as much of the original as I could detect was satisfactorily simple and sturdy. I found little things to criticize, of course, tendencies to correct; and by return post I criticized and corrected, but the distance and the deliberation seemed to touch my maxims with a kind of arid frivolity, and sometimes I tore them up. One quick, warm-blooded scolding would have been worth a sheaf of them. My studied little phrases could only inoculate her with a dislike for me without protecting her from anything under the sun.

However, I found she didn't dislike me, when John and I went home at last to bring her out. She received me with just a hint of kindness, perhaps, but on the whole very well.

II

John was recalled, of course, before the end of our furlough, which knocked various things on the head; but that is the sort of thing one learned to take with philosophy in any lengthened term of Her Majesty's service. Besides, there is usually sugar for the pill; and in this case it was a Staff command bigger than anything we expected for at least five years to come. The excitement of it when it was explained to her gave Cecily a charming colour. She took a good deal of interest in the General, her papa; I think she had an idea that his distinction would alleviate the situation in India, however it might present itself. She accepted that prospective situation calmly; it had been placed before her all her life. There would always be a time when she should go and live with papa and mamma in India, and so long as she was of an age to receive the idea with rebel tears she was assured that papa and mamma would give her a pony. The pony was no longer added to the prospect; it was absorbed no doubt in the general list of attractions calculated to reconcile a young lady to a parental roof with which she had no practical acquaintance. At all events, when I feared the embarrassment and dismay of a pathetic parting with darling grandmamma and the aunties, and the sweet cat and the dear vicar and all the other objects of affection, I found an agreeable unexpected philosophy.

I may add that while I anticipated such broken-hearted farewells I was quite prepared to take them easily. Time, I imagined, had brought philosophy to me also, equally agreeable and equally unexpected.

It was a Bombay ship, full of returning Anglo-Indians. I looked up and down the long saloon tables with a sense of relief and of solace; I was again among my own people. They belonged to Bengal and to Burma, to Madras and to the Punjab, but they were all my people. I could pick out a score that

I knew in fact, and there were none that in imagination I didn't know. The look of wider seas and skies, the casual experienced glance, the touch of irony and of tolerance, how well I knew it and how well I liked it! Dear old England, sitting in our wake, seemed to hold by comparison a great many soft, unsophisticated people, immensely occupied about very particular trifles. How difficult it had been, all the summer, to be interested! These of my long acquaintance belonged to my country's Executive, acute, alert, with the marks of travail on them. Gladly I went in and out of the women's cabins and listened to the argot of the men; my own ruling, administering, soldiering little lot.

Cecily looked at them askance. To her the atmosphere was alien, and I perceived that gently and privately she registered objections. She cast a disapproving eye upon the wife of a Conservator of Forests, who scanned with interest a distant funnel and laid a small wager that it belonged to the Messageries Maritimes. She looked with a straightened lip at the crisply stepping women who walked the deck in short and rather shabby skirts with their hands in their jacket-pockets talking transfers and promotions; and having got up at six to make a water-colour sketch of the sunrise, she came to me in profound indignation to say that she had met a man in his pajamas; no doubt, poor wretch, on his way to be shaved. I was unable to convince her that he was not expected to visit the barber in all his clothes.

At the end of the third day she told me that she wished these people wouldn't talk to her; she didn't like them. I had turned in the hour we left the Channel and had not left my berth since, so possibly I was not in the most amiable mood to receive a douche of cold water. "I must try to remember, dear," I said, "that you have been brought up altogether in the society of pussies and vicars and elderly ladies, and of course you miss them. But you must have a little patience. I shall be up tomorrow, if this beastly sea continues to go down; and then we will try to find somebody suitable to introduce to you."

"Thank you, mamma," said my daughter, without a ray of suspicion. Then she added consideringly, "Aunt Emma and

Aunt Alice do seem quite elderly ladies beside you, and yet you are older than either of them, aren't you? I wonder how that is."

It was so innocent, so admirable, that I laughed at my own expense; while Cecily, doing her hair, considered me gravely. "I wish you would tell me why you laugh, mamma," quoth she; "you laugh so often."

We had not to wait after all for my good offices of the next morning. Cecily came down at ten o'clock that night quite happy and excited; she had been talking to a bishop, such a dear bishop. The bishop had been showing her his collection of photographs, and she had promised to play the harmonium for him at the eleven-o'clock service in the morning. "Bless me!" said I, "is it Sunday?" It seemed she had got on very well indeed with the bishop, who knew the married sister, at Tunbridge, of her very greatest friend. Cecily herself did not know the married sister, but that didn't matter—it was a link. The bishop was charming. "Well, my love," said I—I was teaching myself to use these forms of address for fear she would feel an unkind lack of them, but it was difficult— "I am glad that somebody from my part of the world has impressed you favourably at last. I wish we had more bishops."

"Oh, but my bishop doesn't belong to your part of the world," responded my daughter sleepily. "He is travelling for his health."

It was the most unexpected and delightful thing to be packed into one's chair next morning by Dacres Tottenham. As I emerged from the music saloon after breakfast—Cecily had stayed below to look over her hymns and consider with her bishop the possibility of an anthem—Dacres's face was the first I saw; it simply illuminated, for me, that portion of the deck. I noticed with pleasure the quick toss of the cigar overboard as he recognized and bore down upon me. We were immense friends; John liked him too. He was one of those people who make a tremendous difference; in all our three hundred passengers there could be no one like him, certainly no one whom I could be more glad to see. We plunged at once into immediate personal affairs, we would get at the heart of them later. He gave his vivid word to everything he had seen and done; we laughed and exclaimed and were silent in a concert of admirable understanding. We were still unravelling, still demanding and explaining when the ship's bell began to ring for church, and almost simultaneously Cecily advanced toward us. She had a proper Sunday hat on, with flowers under the brim, and a church-going frock; she wore gloves and clasped a prayer-book. Most of the women who filed past to the summons of the bell were going down as they were, in cotton blouses and serge skirts, in tweed caps or anything, as to a kind of family prayers. I knew exactly how they would lean against the pillars of the saloon during the psalms. This young lady would be little less than a rebuke to them. I surveyed her approach; she positively walked as if it were Sunday.

"My dear," I said, "how *endimanchée* you look! The bishop will be very pleased with you. This gentleman is Mr. Tottenham, who administers Her Majesty's pleasure in parts of India about Allahabad. My daughter, Dacres." She was certainly looking very fresh, and her calm grey eyes had the repose in them that has never known itself to be disturbed about anything. I wondered whether she bowed so distantly also because it was Sunday, and then I remembered that Dacres was a young man, and that the Farnham ladies had probably taught her that it was right to be very distant with young men.

"It is almost eleven, mamma."

"Yes, dear. I see you are going to church."

"Are you not coming, mamma?"

I was well wrapped up in an extremely comfortable corner. I had *La Duchesse Bleue* uncut in my lap, and an agreeable person to talk to. I fear that in any case I should not have been inclined to attend the service, but there was something in my daughter's intonation that made me distinctly hostile to the idea. I am putting things down as they were, extenuating nothing.

"I think not, dear."

"I've turned up two such nice seats."

"Stay, Miss Farnham, and keep us in countenance," said Dacres, with his charming smile. The smile displaced a look of discreet and amused observation. Dacres had an eye always for a situation, and this one was even newer to him than to me.

"No, no. She must run away and not bully her mamma," I said. "When she comes back we will see how much she remembers of the sermon;" and as the flat tinkle from the companion began to show signs of diminishing, Cecily, with one grieved glance, hastened down.

"You amazing lady!" said Dacres. "A daughter—and such a tall daughter! I somehow never—"

"You knew we had one?"

"There was theory of that kind, I remember, about ten years ago. Since then—excuse me—I don't think you've mentioned her."

"You talk as if she were a skeleton in the closet!"

"You *didn't* talk—as if she were."

"I think she was, in a way, poor child. But the resurrection day hasn't confounded me as I deserved. She's a very good girl."

"If you had asked me to pick out your daughter—"

"She would have been the last you would indicate! Quite so," I said. "She is like her father's people. I can't help that."

"I shouldn't think you would if you could," Dacres remarked absently; but the sea air, perhaps, enabled me to digest his thoughtlessness with a smile.

"No," I said, "I am just as well pleased. I think a resemblance to me would confuse me, often."

There was a trace of scrutiny in Dacres's glance. "Don't you find yourself in sympathy with her?" he asked.

"My dear boy, I have seen her just twice in twenty-one years! You see, I've always stuck to John."

"But between mother and daughter—I may be old-fashioned, but I had an idea that there was an instinct that might be depended on."

"I am depending on it," I said, and let my eyes follow the little blue waves that chased past the handrail. "We are making very good speed, aren't we? Thirty-five knots since last night at ten. Are you in the sweep?"

"I never bet on the way out—can't afford it. Am I old-fashioned?" he insisted.

"Probably. Men are very slow in changing their philosophy about women. I fancy their idea of the maternal relation is firmest fixed of all."

"We see it a beatitude!" he cried.

"I know," I said wearily, "and you never modify the view."

Dacres contemplated the portion of the deck that lay between us. His eyes were discreetly lowered, but I saw embarrassment and speculation and a hint of criticism in them.

"Tell me more about it," said he.

"Oh, for heaven's sake don't be sympathetic!" I exclaimed. "Lend me a little philosophy instead. There is nothing to tell. There she is and there I am, in the most intimate relation in the world, constituted when she is twenty-one and I am forty." Dacres started slightly at the ominous word; so little do men realize that the women they like can ever pass out of the constated years of attraction. "I find the young lady very tolerable, very creditable, very nice. I find the relation atrocious. There you have it. I would like to break the relation into pieces," I went on recklessly, "and throw it into the sea. Such things should be tempered to one. I should feel it much less if she occupied another cabin, and would consent to call me Elizabeth or Jane. It is not as if I had been her mother always. One grows fastidious at forty—new intimacies are only possible then on a basis of temperament—"

I paused; it seemed to me that I was making excuses, and I had not the least desire in the world to do that.

"How awfully rough on the girl!" said Dacres Tottenham.

"That consideration has also occurred to me," I said candidly, "though I have perhaps been even more struck by its converse."

"You had no earthly business to be her mother," said my friend, with irritation.

I shrugged my shoulders—what would you have done?— and opened *La Duchesse Bleue*.

III

Mrs. Morgan, wife of a judge of the High Court of Bombay, and I sat amidships on the cool side in the Suez Canal. She was outlining "Soiled Linen" in chain-stitch on a green canvas bag; I was admiring the Egyptian sands. "How charming," said I, "is this solitary desert in the endless oasis we are compelled to cross!"

"Oasis in the desert, you mean," said Mrs. Morgan; "I haven't noticed any, but I happened to look up this morning as I was putting on my stockings, and I saw through my port-hole the most lovely mirage."

I had been at school with Mrs. Morgan more than twenty years agone, but she had come to the special enjoyment of the dignities of life while I still liked doing things. Mrs. Morgan was the kind of person to make one realize how distressing a medium is middle age. Contemplating her precipitous lap, to which conventional attitudes were certainly more becoming, I crossed my own knees with energy, and once more resolved to be young until I was old.

"How perfectly delightful for you to be taking Cecily out!" said Mrs. Morgan placidly.

"Isn't it?" I responded, watching the gliding sands.

"But she was born in sixty-nine—that makes her twenty-one. Quite time, I should say."

"Oh, we couldn't put it off any longer. I mean—her father has such a horror of early débuts. He simply would not hear of her coming before."

"Doesn't want her to marry in India, I dare say—the only one," purred Mrs. Morgan.

"Oh, I don't know. It isn't such a bad place. I was brought out there to marry, and I married. I've found it very satisfactory."

"You always did say exactly what you thought, Helena," said Mrs. Morgan excusingly.

"I haven't much patience with people who bring their daughters out to give them the chance they never would have in England, and then go about devoutly hoping they won't marry in India," I said. "I shall be very pleased if Cecily does as well as your girls have done."

"Mary in the Indian Civil and Jessie in the Imperial Service Troops," sighed Mrs. Morgan complacently. "And both, my dear, within a year. It *was* a blow."

"Oh, it must have been!" I said civilly.

There was no use in bandying words with Emily Morgan.

"There is nothing in the world like the satisfaction and pleasure one takes in one's daughters," Mrs. Morgan went on limpidly. "And one can be in such *close* sympathy with one's girls. I have never regretted having no sons."

"Dear me, yes. To watch oneself growing up again—call back the lovely April of one's prime, etcetera—to read every thought and anticipate every wish—there is no more golden privilege in life, dear Emily. Such a direct and natural avenue for affection, such a wide field for interest!"

I paused, lost in the volume of my admirable sentiments.

"How beautifully you talk, Helena! I wish I had the gift."

"It doesn't mean very much," I said truthfully.

"Oh, I think it's everything! And how companionable a girl is! I quite envy you, this season, having Cecily constantly with you and taking her about everywhere. Something quite new for you, isn't it?"

"Absolutely," said I; "I am looking forward to it immensely. But it is likely she will make her own friends, don't you think?" I added anxiously.

"Hardly the first season. My girls didn't. I was practically their only intimate for months. Don't be afraid; you won't be obliged to go shares in Cecily with anybody for a good long while," added Mrs. Morgan kindly. "I know just how you feel about *that*."

The muddy water of the Ditch chafed up from under us against its banks with a smell that enabled me to hide the emotions Mrs. Morgan evoked behind my handkerchief. The pale desert was pictorial with the drifting, deepening purple shadows of clouds, and in the midst a blue glimmer of the Bitter Lakes, with a white sail on them. A little frantic Arab boy ran alongside keeping pace with the ship. Except for the smell, it was like a dream, we moved so quietly; on, gently on and on between the ridgy clay banks and the rows of piles. Peace was on the ship; you could hear what the Fourth in his white ducks said to the quartermaster in his blue denims; you could count the strokes of the electric bell in the wheel-house; peace was on the ship as she pushed on, an ever-venturing, double-funneled impertinence, through the sands of the ages. My eyes wandered along a plank-line in the deck till they were arrested by a petticoat I knew, when they returned of their own accord. I seemed to be always seeing that petticoat.

"I think," resumed Mrs. Morgan, whose glance had wandered in the same direction, "that Cecily is a very fine type of our English girls. With those dark grey eyes, a *little* prominent possibly, and that good colour—it's rather high now perhaps, but she will lose quite enough of it in India—and those regular features, she would make a splendid Britannia. Do you know, I fancy she must have a great deal of character. Has she?"

"Any amount. And all of it good," I responded, with private dejection.

"No faults at all?" chaffed Mrs. Morgan.

I shook my head. "Nothing," I said sadly, "that I can put my finger on. But I hope to discover a few later. The sun may bring them out."

"Like freckles. Well, you are a lucky woman. Mine had plenty, I assure you. Untidiness was no name for Jessie, and Mary—I'm *sorry* to say that Mary sometimes fibbed."

"How lovable of her! Cecily's neatness is a painful example to me, and I don't believe she would tell a fib to save my life."

"Tell me," said Mrs. Morgan, as the lunch-bell rang and she gathered her occupation into her workbasket, "who is that talking to her?"

"Oh, an old friend," I replied easily; "Dacres Tottenham, a dear fellow, and most benevolent. He is trying on my behalf to reconcile her to the life she'll have to lead in India."

"She won't need much reconciling, if she's like most girls," observed Mrs. Morgan, "but he seems to be trying very hard."

That was quite the way I took it—on my behalf—for several days. When people have understood you very adequately for ten years you do not expect them to boggle at any problem you may present at the end of the decade. I thought Dacres was moved by a fine sense of compassion. I thought that with his admirable perception he had put a finger on the little comedy of fruitfulness in my life that laughed so bitterly at the tragedy of the barren woman, and was attempting, by delicate manipulation, to make it easier. I really thought so. Then I observed that myself had preposterously deceived me, that it wasn't like that at all. When Mr. Tottenham joined us, Cecily and me, I saw that he listened more than he talked, with an ear specially cocked to register any small irony which might appear in my remarks to my daughter. Naturally he registered more than there were, to make up perhaps for dear Cecily's obviously not registering any. I could see, too, that he was suspicious of any flavour of kindness; finally, to avoid the strictures of his upper lip, which really, dear fellow, began to bore me, I talked exclusively about the distant sails and the Red Sea littoral. When he no longer joined us as we sat or walked together, I perceived that his hostility was fixed and his *parti pris*. He was brimful of compassion, but it was all for Cecily, none for the situation or for me. (She would have marvelled, placidly, why he pitied her. I am glad I can say that.) The primitive man in him rose up as Pope of nature and excommunicated me as a creature recusant to her functions. Then deliberately Dacres undertook an office of consolation; and I fell to wondering, while Mrs. Morgan spoke her convictions plainly out, how far an impulse of reparation for a misfortune with which he had nothing to do might carry a man.

I began to watch the affair with an interest which even to me seemed queer. It was not detached, but it was semi-detached, and, of course, on the side for which I seem, in this history, to be perpetually apologizing. With certain limitations it didn't matter an atom whom Cecily married. So that he was sound and decent, with reasonable prospects, her simple requirements and ours for her would be quite met. There was the ghost of a consolation in that; one needn't be anxious or exacting.

I could predict with a certain amount of confidence that in her first season she would probably receive three or four proposals, any one of which she might accept with as much propriety and satisfaction as any other one. For Cecily it was so simple; prearranged by nature like her digestion, one could not see any logical basis for difficulties. A nice upstanding sapper, a dashing Bengal Lancer—oh, I could think of half a dozen types that would answer excellently. She was the kind of young person, and that was the summing up of it, to marry a type and be typically happy. I hoped and expected that she would. But Dacres!

Dacres should exercise the greatest possible discretion. He was not a person who could throw the dice indifferently with fate. He could respond to so much, and he would inevitably, sooner or later, demand so much response! He was governed by a preposterously exacting temperament, and he wore his nerves outside. And what vision he had! How he explored the world he lived in and drew out of it all there was, all there was! I could see him in the years to come ranging alone the fields that were sweet and the horizons that lifted for him, and ever returning to pace the common dusty mortal road by the side of a purblind wife. On general principles, as a case to point at, it would be a conspicuous pity. Nor would it lack the aspect of a particular, a personal misfortune. Dacres was occupied in quite the natural normal degree with his charming self; he would pass his misery on, and who would deserve to escape it less than his mother-in-law?

I listened to Emily Morgan, who gleaned in the ship more information about Dacres Tottenham's people, pay, and prospects than I had ever acquired, and I kept an eye upon the pair which was, I flattered myself, quite maternal. I watched them without acute anxiety, deploring the threatening destiny, but hardly nearer to it than one is in the stalls to the stage. My moments of real concern for Dacres were mingled more with anger than with sorrow—it seemed inexcusable that he, with his infallible divining-rod for temperament, should be on the point of making such an ass of himself. Though I talk of the stage there was nothing at all dramatic to reward my attention, mine and Emily Morgan's. To my imagination, excited by its idea of what Dacres Tottenham's courtship ought to be, the attentions he paid to Cecily were most humdrum. He threw rings into buckets with her—she was good at that—and quoits upon the "bull" board; he found her chair after the decks were swabbed in the morning and established her in it; he paced the deck with her at convenient times and seasons. They were humdrum, but they were constant and cumulative. Cecily took them with an even breath that perfectly matched. There was hardly anything, on her part, to note—a little discreet observation of his comings and goings, eyes scarcely lifted from her book, and later just a hint of proprietorship, as the evening she came up to me on deck, our first night in the Indian Ocean. I was lying in my long chair looking at the thick, low stars and thinking it was a long time since I had seen John.

"Dearest mamma, out here and nothing over your shoulders! You *are* imprudent. Where is your wrap? Mr. Tottenham, will you please fetch mamma's wrap for her?"

"If mamma so instructs me," he said audaciously.

"Do as Cecily tells you," I laughed, and he went and did it, while I by the light of a quartermaster's lantern distinctly saw my daughter blush.

Another time, when Cecily came down to undress, she bent over me as I lay in the lower berth with unusual solicitude. I had been dozing, and I jumped.

"What is it, child?" I said. "Is the ship on fire?"

"No, mamma, the ship is not on fire. There is nothing wrong. I'm so sorry I startled you. But Mr. Tottenham has been telling me all about what you did for the soldiers the time plague broke out in the lines at Mian-Mir. I think it was splendid, mamma, and so does he."

"Oh, *Lord!*" I groaned. "Good night."

IV

It remained in my mind, that little thing that Dacres had taken the trouble to tell my daughter; I thought about it a good deal. It seemed to me the most serious and convincing circumstances that had yet offered itself to my consideration. Dacres was no longer content to bring solace and support to the more appealing figure of the situation; he must set to work, bless him! to improve the situation itself. He must try to induce Miss Farnham, by telling her everything he could remember to my credit, to think as well of her mother as possible, in spite of the strange and secret blows which that mother might be supposed to sit up at night to deliver to her. Cecily thought very well of me already; indeed, with private reservations as to my manners and—no, *not* my morals, I believe I exceeded her expectations of what a perfectly new and untrained mother would be likely to prove. It was my theory that she found me all she could understand me to be. The maternal virtues of the outside were certainly mine; I put them on with care every morning and wore them with patience all day. Dacres, I assured myself, must have allowed his preconception to lead him absurdly by the nose not to see that the girl was satisfied, that my impatience, my impotence, did not at all make her miserable. Evidently, however, he had created our relations differently; evidently he had set himself to their amelioration. There was portent in it; things seemed to be closing in. I bit off a quarter of an inch of wooden pen-handle in considering whether or not I should mention it in my letter to John, and decided that it would be better just perhaps to drop a hint. Though I could not expect John to receive it with any sort of perturbation. Men are different; he would probably think Tottenham well enough able to look after himself.

I had embarked on my letter, there at the end of a cornertable of the saloon, when I saw Dacres saunter through. He wore a very conscious and elaborately purposeless air; and it jumped with my mood that he had nothing less than the crisis of his life in his pocket, and was looking for me. As he advanced toward me between the long tables doubt left me and alarm assailed me. "I'm glad to find you in a quiet corner," said he, seating himself, and confirmed my worst anticipations.

"I'm writing to John," I said, and again applied myself to my pen-handle. It is a trick Cecily has since done her best in vain to cure me of.

"I am going to interrupt you," he said. "I have not had an opportunity of talking to you for some time."

"I like that!" I exclaimed derisively.

"And I want to tell you that I am very much charmed with Cecily."

"Well," I said, "I am not going to gratify you by saying anything against her."

"You don't deserve her, you know."

"I won't dispute that. But, if you don't mind—I'm not sure

that I'll stand being abused, dear boy."

"I quite see it isn't any use. Though one spoke with the tongues of men and of angels—"

"And had not charity," I continued for him. "Precisely. I won't go on, but your quotation is very apt."

"I so bow down before her simplicity. It makes a wide and beautiful margin for the rest of her character. She is a girl Ruskin would have loved."

"I wonder," said I. "He did seem fond of the simple type, didn't he?"

"Her mind is so clear, so transparent. The motive spring of everything she says and does is so direct. Don't you find you can most completely depend upon her?"

"Oh yes," I said; "certainly. I nearly always know what she is going to say before she says it, and under given circumstances I can tell precisely what she will do."

"I fancy her sense of duty is very beautifully developed."

"It is," I said. "There is hardly a day when I do not come in contact with it."

"Well, that is surely a good thing. And I find that calm poise of hers very restful."

"I would not have believed that so many virtues could reside in one young lady," I said, taking refuge in flippancy, "and to think that she should be my daughter!"

"As I believe you know, that seems to me rather a cruel stroke of destiny, Mrs. Farnham."

"Oh yes, I know! You have a constructive imagination, Dacres. You don't seem to see that the girl is protected by her limitations, like a tortoise. She lives within them quite secure and happy and content. How determined you are to be sorry for her!"

Mr. Tottenham looked at the end of this lively exchange as though he sought for a polite way of conveying to me that I rather was the limited person. He looked as if he wished he could say things. The first of them would be, I saw, that he had quite a different conception of Cecily, that it was illuminated by many trifles, nuances of feeling and expression, which he had noticed in his talks with her whenever they had skirted the subject of her adoption by her mother. He knew her, he was longing to say, better than I did; when it would have been natural to reply that one could not hope to compete in such a direction with an intelligent young man, and we should at once have been upon delicate and difficult ground. So it was as well perhaps that he kept silence until he said, as he had come prepared to say, "Well, I want to put that beyond a doubt—her happiness—if I'm good enough. I want her, please, and I only hope that she will be half as willing to come as you are likely to be to let her go."

It was a shock when it came, plump, like that; and I was horrified to feel how completely every other consideration was lost for the instant in the immense relief that it prefigured. To be my whole complete self again, without the feeling that a fraction of me was masquerading about in Cecily! To be freed at once, or almost, from an exacting condition and an impossible ideal! "Oh!" I exclaimed, and my eyes positively filled. "You *are* good, Dacres, but I couldn't let you do that."

His undisguised stare brought me back to a sense of the proportion of things. I saw that in the combination of influences that had brought Mr. Tottenham to the point of proposing to marry my daughter consideration for me, if it had a place, would be fantastic. Inwardly I laughed at the egotism of raw nerves that had conjured it up, even for an instant, as a reason for gratitude. The situation was not so peculiar, not so interesting, as that. But I answered his stare with a smile; what I had said might very well stand.

"Do you imagine," he said, seeing that I did not mean to amplify it, "that I want to marry her out of any sort of *good*ness?"

"Benevolence is your weakness, Dacres."

"I see. You think one's motive is to withdraw her from a relation which ought to be the most natural in the world, but which is, in her particular and painful case, the most equivocal."

"Well, come," I remonstrated. "You have dropped one or two things, you know, in the heat of your indignation, not badly calculated to give one that idea. The eloquent statement you have just made, for instance—it carries all the patness of old conviction. How often have you rehearsed it?"

I am a fairly long-suffering person, but I began to feel a little annoyed with my would-be son-in-law. If the relation were achieved it would give him no prescriptive right to bully me; and we were still in very early anticipation of that.

"Ah!" he said disarmingly. "Don't let us quarrel. I'm sorry you think that; because it isn't likely to bring your favour to my project, and I want you friendly and helpful. Oh, confound it!" he exclaimed, with sudden temper. "You ought to be. I don't understand this aloofness. I half suspect it's pose. You undervalue Cecily—well, you have no business to undervalue me. You know me better than anybody in the world. Now are you going to help me to marry your daughter?"

"I don't think so," I said slowly, after a moment's silence, which he sat through like a mutinous schoolboy. "I might tell you that I don't care a button whom you marry, but that would not be true. I do care more or less. As you say, I know you pretty well. I'd a little rather you didn't make a mess of it; and if you must I should distinctly prefer not to have the spectacle under my nose for the rest of my life. I can't hinder you, but I won't help you."

"And what possesses you to imagine that in marrying Cecily I should make a mess of it? Shouldn't your first consideration be whether *she* would?"

"Perhaps it should, but, you see, it isn't. Cecily would be happy with anybody who made her comfortable. You would ask a good deal more than that, you know."

Dacres, at this, took me up promptly. Life, he said, the heart of life, had particularly little to say to temperament. By the heart of life I suppose he meant married love. He explained that its roots asked other sustenance, and that it throve best of all on simple elemental goodness. So long as a man sought in women mere casual companionship, perhaps the most exquisite thing to be experienced was the stimulus of some spiritual feminine counterpart; but when he desired of one woman that she should be always and intimately with him, the background of his life, the mother of his children, he was better advised to avoid nerves and sensibilities, and try for the repose of the common—the uncommon—domestic virtues. Ah, he said, they were sweet, like lavender. (Already, I told him, he smelled the housekeeper's linen-chest.) But I did not interrupt him much; I couldn't, he was too absorbed. To temperamental pairing, he declared, the century owed its breed of decadents. I asked him if he had ever really recognized one; and he retorted that if he hadn't he didn't wish to make a beginning in his own family. In a quarter of an hour he repudiated the theories of a lifetime, a gratifying triumph for simple elemental goodness. Having denied the value of the subtler pretensions to charm in woman as you marry her, he went artlessly on to endow Cecily with as many of them as could possibly be desirable. He actually persuaded himself to say that it was lovely to see the reflections of life in her tranquil spirit; and when I looked at him incredulously he grew angry, and hinted that Cecily's sensitiveness to reflections and other things might be a trifle beyond her mother's ken. "She responds instantly, intimately, to the beautiful everywhere," he declared.

"Aren't the opportunities of life on board ship rather limited to demonstrate that?" I inquired. "I know—you mean sunsets. Cecily is very fond of sunsets. She is always asking me to come and look at them."

"I was thinking of last night's sunset," he confessed. "We looked at it together."

"What did she say?" I asked idly.

"Nothing very much. That's just the point. Another girl would have raved and gushed."

"Oh, well, Cecily never does that," I responded. "Nevertheless she is a very ordinary human instrument. I hope I shall have no temptation ten years hence to remind you that I warned you of her quality."

"I wish, not in the least for my own profit, for I am well convinced already, but simply to win your cordiality and your approval—never did an unexceptional wooer receive such niggard encouragement!—I wish there were some sort of test for her quality. I would be proud to stand by it, and you would be convinced. I can't find words to describe my objection to your state of mind."

The thing seemed to me to be a foregone conclusion. I saw

it accomplished, with all its possibilities of disastrous commonplace. I saw all that I have here taken the trouble to foreshadow. So far as I was concerned, Dacres's burden would add itself to my philosophies, *voilà tout*. I should always be a little uncomfortable about it, because it had been taken from my back; but it would not be a matter for the wringing of hands. And yet—the hatefulness of the mistake! Dacres's bold talk of a test made no suggestion. Should my invention be more fertile? I thought of something.

"You have said nothing to her yet?" I asked.

"Nothing. I don't think she suspects for a moment. She treats me as if no such fell design were possible. I'm none too confident, you know," he added, with a longer face.

"We go straight to Agra. Could you come to Agra?"

"Ideal!" he cried. "The memory of Mumtaz! The garden of the Taj! I've always wanted to love under the same moon as Shah Jehan. How thoughtful of you!"

"You must spend a few days with us in Agra," I continued. "And as you say, it is the very place to shrine your happiness, if it comes to pass there."

"Well, I am glad to have extracted a word of kindness from you at last," said Dacres, as the stewards came to lay the table. "But I wish," he added regretfully, "you could have thought of a test."

V

Four days later we were in Agra. A time there was when the name would have been the key of dreams to me; now it stood for John's headquarters. I was rejoiced to think I would look again upon the Taj; and the prospect of living with it was a real enchantment; but I pondered most the kind of house that would be provided for the General Commanding the District, how many the dining-room would seat, and whether it would have a roof of thatch or of corrugated iron—I prayed against corrugated iron. I confess these my preoccupations. I was forty, and at forty the practical considerations of life hold their own even against domes of marble, world-renowned, and set about with gardens where the bulbul sings to the rose. I smiled across the years at the raptures of my first vision of the place at twenty-one, just Cecily's age. Would I now sit under Arjamand's cypresses till two o'clock in the morning to see the wonder of her tomb at a particular angle of the moon? Would I climb one of her tall white ministering minarets to see anything whatever? I very greatly feared that I would not. Alas for the aging of sentiment, of interest! Keep your touch with life and your seat in the saddle as long as you will, the world is no new toy at forty. But Cecily was twenty-one, Cecily who sat stolidly finishing her lunch while Dacres Tottenham talked about Akbar and his philosophy. "The sort of man," he said, "that Carlyle might have smoked a pipe with."

"But surely," said Cecily reflectively, "tobacco was not discovered in England then. Akbar came to the throne in 1526."

"Nor Carlyle either for that matter," I hastened to observe. "Nevertheless, I think Mr. Tottenham's proposition must stand."

"Thanks, Mrs. Farnham," said Dacres. "But imagine Miss Farnham's remembering Akbar's date! I'm sure you didn't!"

"Let us hope she doesn't know too much about him," I cried gaily, "or there will be nothing to tell!"

"Oh, really and truly very little!" said Cecily, "but as soon as we heard papa would be stationed here Aunt Emma made me read up about those old Moguls and people. I think I remember the dynasty. Baber, wasn't he the first? and then Humayon, and after him Akbar, and then Jehangir, and then Shah Jehan. But I've forgotten every date but Akbar's."

She smiled her smile of brilliant health and even spirits as she made the damaging admission, and she was so good to look at, sitting there simple and wholesome and fresh, peeling her banana with her well-shaped fingers, that we swallowed the dynasty as it were whole, and smiled back upon her. John, I may say, was extremely pleased with Cecily; he said she was a very satisfactory human accomplishment. One would have thought, positively, the way he plumed himself over his handsome daughter, that he alone was responsible for her. But John, having received his family, straightway set off with his Staff on a tour of inspection, and thereby takes himself out of this history. I sometimes think that if he had stayed—but there has never been the lightest recrimination between us about it, and I am not going to hint one now.

"Did you read," asked Dacres, "what he and the Court poet wrote over the entrance gate to the big mosque at Fattehpur-Sikri? It's rather nice. 'The world is a looking-glass, wherein the image has come and is gone—take as thine own nothing more than what thou lookest upon.'"

My daughter's thoughtful gaze was, of course, fixed upon the speaker, and in his own glance I saw a sudden ray of consciousness; but Cecily transferred her eyes to the opposite wall, deeply considering, and while Dacres and I smiled across the table, I saw that she had perceived no reason for blushing. It was a singularly narrow escape.

"No," she said, "I didn't; what a curious proverb for an emperor to make! He couldn't possibly have been able to see all his possessions at once."

"If you have finished," Dacres addressed her, "do let me show you what your plain and immediate duty is to the garden. The garden waits for you—all the roses expectant—"

"Why, there isn't one!" cried Cecily, pinning on her hat. It was pleasing, and just a trifle pathetic, the way he hurried her out of the scope of any little dart; he would not have her even within range of amused observation. Would he continue, I wondered vaguely, as, with my elbows on the table, I tore into strips the lemon-leaf that floated in my finger-bowl—would he continue, through life, to shelter her from his other clever friends as now he attempted to shelter her from her mother? In that case he would have to domicile her, poor dear, behind the curtain, like the native ladies—a good price to pay for a protection of which, bless her heart! she would be all unaware. I had quite stopped bemoaning the affair; perhaps the comments of my husband, who treated it with broad approval and satisfaction, did something to soothe my sensibilities. At all events, I had gradually come to occupy a high fatalistic ground toward the pair. If it was written upon their foreheads that they should marry, the inscription was none of mine; and, of course, it was true, as John had indignantly stated, that Dacres might do very much worse. One's interest in Dacres Tottenham's problematical future had in no way diminished; but the young man was so positive, so full of intention, so disinclined to discussion—he had not reopened the subject since that morning in the saloon of the Caledonia—that one's feeling about it rather took the attenuated form of a shrug. I am afraid, too, that the pleasurable excitement of such an impending event had a little supervened; even at forty there is no disallowing the natural interests of one's sex. As I sat there pulling my lemon-leaf to pieces, I should not have been surprised or in the least put about if the two had returned radiant from the lawn to demand my blessing. As to the test of quality that I had obligingly invented for Dacres on the spur of the moment without his knowledge or connivance, it had some time ago faded into what he apprehended it to be—a mere idyllic opportunity, a charming background, a frame for his project, of prettier sentiment than the funnels and the handrails of a ship.

Mr. Tottenham had ten days to spend with us. He knew the place well; it belonged to the province to whose service he was dedicated, and he claimed with impressive authority the privilege of showing it to Cecily by degrees—the Hall of Audience to-day, the Jessamine Tower to-morrow, the tomb of Akbar another, and the Deserted City yet another day. We arranged the expeditions in conference, Dacres insisting only upon the order of them, which I saw was to be cumulative, with the Taj at the very end, on the night precisely of the full of the moon, with a better chance of roses. I had no special views, but Cecily contributed some; that we should do the Hall of Audience in the morning, so as not to interfere with the club tennis in the afternoon, that we should bicycle to Akbar's tomb and take a cold luncheon—if we were sure there would be no snakes—to the Deserted City, to all of which Dacres gave loyal assent. I indorsed everything; I was the encouraging chorus, only stipulating that my number should be swelled from day to day by the addition of such persons as I should approve. Cecily, for instance, wanted to invite the Bakewells because we had come out in the same ship with them; but I could not endure the Bakewells, and it seemed to me that our having made the voyage with them was the best possible reason for declining to lay eyes on them for the rest of our natural lives. "Mamma has such strong prejudices," Cecily remarked, as she reluctantly gave up the idea; and I waited to see whether the graceless Tottenham would unmurmuringly take down the Bakewells. How strong must be the sentiment that turns a man into a boa-constrictor without a pang of transmigration! But no, this time he was faithful to the principles of his pre-Cecilian existence. "They are rather Boojums," he declared. "You would think so, too, if you knew them better. It is that kind of excellent person that makes the real burden of India." I could have patted him on the back.

Thanks to the rest of the chorus, which proved abundantly available, I was no immediate witness to Cecily's introduction to the glorious fragments which sustain in Agra the memory of the Moguls. I may as well say that I arranged with care that if anybody must be standing by when Dacres disclosed them, it should not be I. If Cecily had squinted, I should have been sorry, but I would have found in it no personal humiliation. There were other imperfections of vision, however, for which I felt responsible and ashamed; and with Dacres, though the situation, Heaven knows, was none of my seeking, I had a little the feeling of a dealer who offers a defective *bibelot* to a connoisseur. My charming daughter—I was fifty times congratulated upon her appearance and her manners—had many excellent qualities and capacities which she never inherited from me; but she could see no more than the bulk, no further than the perspective; she could register exactly as much as a camera.

This was a curious thing, perhaps, to displease my maternal vanity, but it did; I had really rather she squinted; and when there was anything to look at I kept out of the way. I can not tell precisely, therefore, what the incidents were that contributed to make Mr. Tottenham, on our return from these expeditions, so thoughtful, with a thoughtfulness which increased, toward the end of them, to a positive gravity. This would disappear during dinner under the influence of food and drink. He would talk nightly with new enthusiasm and fresh hope—or did I imagine it?—of the loveliness he had arranged to reveal on the following day. If again my imagination did not lead me astray, I fancied this occurred later and later in the course of the meal as the week went on; as if his state required more stimulus as time progressed. One evening, when I expected it to flag altogether, I had a whim to order champagne and observe the effect; but I am glad to say that I reproved myself, and refrained.

Cecily, meanwhile, was conducting herself in a manner which left nothing to be desired. If, as I sometimes thought, she took Dacres very much for granted, she took him calmly for granted; she seemed a prey to none of those fluttering uncertainties, those suspended judgments and elaborate indifferences which translate themselves so plainly in a young lady receiving addresses. She turned herself out very freshly and very well; she was always ready for everything, and I am sure that no glance of Dacres Tottenham's found aught but direct and decorous response. His society on these occasions gave her solid pleasure; so did the drive and the lunch; the satisfactions were apparently upon the same plane. She was aware of the plum, if I may be permitted a brusque but irresistible simile; and with her mouth open, her eyes modestly closed, and her head in a convenient position, she waited, placidly, until it should fall in. The Farnham ladies would have been delighted with the result of their labours in the sweet reason and eminent propriety of this attitude. Thinking of my idiotic sufferings when John began to fix himself upon my horizon, I pondered profoundly the power of nature in differentiation.

One evening, the last, I think, but one, I had occasion to go to my daughter's room, and found her writing in her commonplace-book. She had a commonplace-book, as well as a Where Is It? an engagement-book, an account-book, a diary, a Daily Sunshine, and others with purposes too various to remember. "Dearest mamma," she said, as I was departing, "there is only one 'p' in 'opulence,' isn't there?"

"Yes," I replied, with my hand on the door handle, and added curiously, for it was an odd word in Cecily's mouth, "Why?"

She hardly hesitated. "Oh," she said, "I am just writing down one or two things Mr. Tottenham said about Agra before

I forget them. They seemed so true."

"He has a descriptive touch," I remarked.

"I think he describes beautifully. Would you like to hear what he said to-day?"

"I would," I replied, sincerely.

"'Agra,'" read this astonishing young lady, "'is India's one pure idyl. Elsewhere she offers other things, foolish opulence, tawdry pageant, treachery of eunuchs and jealousies of harems, thefts of kings' jewels and barbaric retributions; but they are all actual, visualized, or part of a past that shows to the backward glance hardly more relief and vitality than a Persian painting'— I should like to see a Persian painting—'but here the immortal tombs and pleasure-houses rise out of colour delicate and subtle; the vision holds across three hundred years; the print of the court is still in the dust of the city.'"

"Did you really let him go on like that?" I exclaimed. "It has the license of a lecture!"

"I encouraged him to. Of course he didn't say it straight off. He said it naturally; he stopped now and then to cough. I didn't understand it all; but I think I have remembered every word."

"You have a remarkable memory. I'm glad he stopped to cough. Is there any more?"

"One little bit. 'Here the Moguls wrought their passions into marble, and held them up with great refrains from their religion, and set them about with gardens; and here they stand in the twilight of the glory of those kings and the noonday splendour of their own.'"

"How clever of you!" I exclaimed. "How wonderfully clever of you to remember!"

"I had to ask him to repeat one or two sentences. He didn't like that. But this is nothing. I used to learn pages letter-perfect for Aunt Emma. She was very particular. I think it is worth preserving, don't you?"

"Dear Cecily," I responded, "you have a frugal mind."

There was nothing else to respond. I could not tell her just how practical I thought her pathetic little book.

VI

We drove together, after dinner, to the Taj. The moonlight lay in an empty splendour over the broad sandy road, with the acacias pricking up on each side of it and the gardens of the station bungalows stretching back into clusters of crisp shadows. It was an exquisite February night, very still. Nothing seemed abroad but two or three pariah dogs, upon vague and errant business, and the Executive Engineer going swiftly home from the club on his bicycle. Even the little shops of the bazaar were dark and empty; only here and there a light showed barred behind the carved balconies of the upper rooms, and there was hardly any tom-tomming. The last long slope of the road showed us the river curving to the left, through a silent white waste that stretched indefinitely into the moonlight on one side, and was crowned by Akbar's fort on the other. His long high line of turrets and battlements still guarded a hint of their evening rose, and dim and exquisite above them hovered the three dome-bubbles of the Pearl Mosque. It was a night of perfect illusion, and the illusion was mysterious, delicate, and faint. I sat silent as we rolled along, twenty years nearer to the original joy of things when John and I drove through the same old dream.

Dacres, too, seemed preoccupied; only Cecily was, as they say, herself. Cecily was really more than herself, she exhibited an unusual flow of spirits. She talked continually, she pointed out this and that, she asked who lived here and who lived there. At regular intervals of about four minutes she demanded if it wasn't simply too lovely. She sat straight up with her vigorous profile and her smart hat; and the silhouette of her personality sharply refused to mingle with the dust of any dynasty. She was a contrast, a protest; positively she was an indignity. "Do lean back, dear child," I exclaimed at last. "You interfere with the landscape."

She leaned back, but she went on interfering with it in terms of sincerest enthusiasm.

When we stopped at the great archway of entrance I begged to be left in the carriage. What else could one do, when the golden moment had come, but sit in the carriage and measure it? They climbed the broad stone steps together and passed under the lofty gravures into the garden, and I waited. I waited and remembered. I am not, as perhaps by this time is evident, a person of overwhelming sentiment, but I think the smile upon my lips was gentle. So plainly I could see, beyond the massive archway and across a score of years, all that they saw at that moment—Arjamand's garden, and the long straight tank of marble cleaving it full of sleeping water and the shadows of the marshalling cypresses; her wide dark garden of roses and of pomegranates, and at the end the Vision, marvellous, aerial, the soul of something—is it beauty? is it sorrow?—that great white pride of love in mourning such as only here in all the round of our little world lifts itself to the stars, the unpaintable, indescribable Taj Mahal. A gentle breath stole out with a scent of jessamine and such a memory! I closed my eyes and felt the warm luxury of a tear.

Thinking of the two in the garden, my mood was very kind, very conniving. How foolish after all were my cherry-stone theories of taste and temperament before that uncalculating thing which sways a world and builds a Taj Mahal! Was it probable that Arjamand and her Emperor had loved fastidiously, and yet how they had loved! I wandered away into consideration of the blind forces which move the world, in which comely young persons like my daughter Cecily had such a place; I speculated vaguely upon the value of the subtler gifts of sympathy and insight which seemed indeed, at that enveloping moment, to be mere flowers strewn upon the tide of deeper emotions. The garden sent me a fragrance of roses; the moon sailed higher and picked out the little kiosks set along the wall. It was a charming, charming thing to wait, there at the portal of the silvered, scented garden, for an idyl to come forth.

When they reappeared, Dacres and my daughter, they came with casual steps and cheerful voices. They might have been a couple of tourists. The moonlight fell full upon them on the platform under the arch. It showed Dacres measuring with his stick the length of the Sanscrit letters which declared the stately texts, and Cecily's expression of polite, perfunctory interest. They looked up at the height above them; they looked back at the vision behind. Then they sauntered toward the carriage, he offering a formal hand to help her down the uncertain steps, she gracefully accepting it.

"You—you have not been long," said I. "I hope you didn't hurry on my account."

"Miss Farnham found the marble a little cold under foot," replied Dacres, putting Miss Farnham in.

"You see," explained Cecily, "I stupidly forgot to change into thicker soles. I have only my slippers. But, mamma, how lovely it is! Do let us come again in the daytime. I am dying to make a sketch of it."

Mr. Tottenham was to leave us on the following day. In the morning, after "little breakfast," as we say in India, he sought me in the room I had set aside to be particularly my own.

Again I was writing to John, but this time I waited for precisely his interruption. I had got no further than "My dearest husband," and my penhandle was a fringe.

"Another fine day," I said, as if the old, old Indian joke could give him ease, poor man!

"Yes," said he, "we are having lovely weather."

He had forgotten that it was a joke. Then he lapsed into silence while I renewed my attentions to my pen.

"I say," he said at last, with so strained a look about his mouth that it was almost a contortion, "I haven't done it, you know."

"No," I responded, cheerfully, "and you're not going to. Is that it? Well!"

"Frankly—" said he.

"Dear me, yes! Anything else between you and me would be grotesque," I interrupted, "after all these years."

"I don't think it would be a success," he said, looking at me resolutely with his clear blue eyes, in which still lay, alas! the possibility of many delusions.

"No," I said, "I never did, you know. But the prospect had begun to impose upon me."

"To say how right you were would seem, under the circumstances, the most hateful form of flattery."

"Yes," I said, "I think I can dispense with your verbal indorsement." I felt a little bitter. It was, of course, better that the connoisseur should have discovered the flaw before concluding the transaction; but although I had pointed it out myself I was not entirely pleased to have the article returned.

"I am infinitely ashamed that it should have taken me all these days—day after day and each contributory—to discover what you saw so easily and so completely."

"You forget that I am her mother," I could not resist the temptation of saying.

"Oh, for God's sake don't jeer! Please be absolutely direct, and tell me if you have reason to believe that to the extent of a thought, of a breath—to any extent at all—she cares."

He was, I could see, very deeply moved; he had not arrived at this point without trouble and disorder not lightly to be put on or off. Yet I did not hurry to his relief, I was still possessed by a vague feeling of offense. I reflected that any mother would be, and I quite plumed myself upon my annoyance. It was so satisfactory, when one had a daughter, to know the sensations of even any mother. Nor was it soothing to remember that the young man's whole attitude toward Cecily had been based upon criticism of me, even though he sat before me whipped with his own lash. His temerity had been stupid and obstinate; I could not regret his punishment.

I kept him waiting long enough to think all this, and then I replied, "I have not the least means of knowing."

I can not say what he expected, but he squared his shoulders as if he had received a blow and might receive another. Then he looked at me with a flash of the old indignation. "You are not near enough to her for that!" he exclaimed.

"I am not near enough to her for that."

Silence fell between us. A crow perched upon an opened venetian and cawed lustily. For years afterward I never heard a crow caw without a sense of vain, distressing experiment. Dacres got up and began to walk about the room. I very soon put a stop to that. "I can't talk to a pendulum," I said, but I could not persuade him to sit down again.

"Candidly," he said at length, "do you think she would have me?"

"I regret to say that I think she would. But you would not dream of asking her."

"Why not? She is a dear girl," he responded, inconsequently.

"You could not possibly stand it."

Then Mr. Tottenham delivered himself of this remarkable phrase: "I could stand it," he said, "as well as you can."

There was far from being any joy in the irony with which I regarded him and under which I saw him gather up his resolution to go; nevertheless I did nothing to make it easy for him. I refrained from imparting my private conviction that Cecily would accept the first presentable substitute that appeared, although it was strong. I made no reference to my daughter's large fund of philosophy and small balance of sentiment. I did not even—though this was reprehensible—confess the test, the test of quality in these ten days with the marble archives of the Moguls, which I had almost wantonly suggested, which he had so unconsciously accepted, so disastrously applied. I gave him quite fifteen minutes of his bad quarter of an hour, and when it was over I wrote truthfully but furiously to John....

That was ten years ago. We have since attained the shades of retirement, and our daughter is still with us when she is not with Aunt Emma and Aunt Alice—grandmamma has passed away. Mr. Tottenham's dumb departure that day in February—it was the year John got his C.B.—was followed, I am thankful to say, by none of the symptoms of unrequited affection on Cecily's part. Not for ten minutes, so far as I was aware, was she the maid forlorn. I think her self-respect was of too robust a character, thanks to the Misses Farnham. Still less, of course, had she any reproaches to serve upon her mother, although for a long time I thought I detected—or was it my guilty conscience?—a spark of shrewdness in the glance she bent upon me when the talk was of Mr. Tottenham and the probabilities of his return to Agra. So well did she sustain her experience, or so little did she feel it, that I believe the impression went abroad that Dacres had been sent disconsolate away. One astonishing conversation I had with her some six months later, which turned upon the point of a particularly desirable offer. She told me something then, without any sort of embarrassment, but quite lucidly and directly, that edified me much to hear. She said that while she was quite sure that Mr. Tottenham thought of her only as a friend—she had never had the least reason for any other impression—he had done her a service for which she could not thank him enough—in showing her what a husband might be. He had given her a standard; it might be high, but it was unalterable. She didn't know whether she could describe it, but Mr. Tottenham was different from the kind of man you seemed to meet in India. He had his own ways of looking at things, and he talked so well. He had given her an ideal, and she intended to profit by it. To know that men like Mr. Tottenham existed, and to marry any other kind would be an act of folly which she did not intend to commit. No, Major the Hon. Hugh Taverel did not come near it—very far short, indeed! He had talked to her during the whole of dinner the night before about jackal-hunting with a bobbery pack—not at all an elevated mind. Yes, he might be a very good fellow, but as a companion for life she was sure he would not be at all suitable. She would wait.

And she has waited. I never thought she would, but she has. From time to time men have wished to take her from us, but the standard has been inexorable, and none of them have reached it. When Dacres married the charming American whom he caught like a butterfly upon her Eastern tour, Cecily sent them as a wedding present an alabaster model of the Taj, and I let her do it—the gift was so exquisitely appropriate. I suppose he never looks at it without being reminded that he didn't marry Miss Farnham, and I hope that he remembers that he owes it to Miss Farnham's mother. So much I think I might claim; it is really very little considering what it stands for. Cecily is permanently with us—I believe she considers herself an intimate. I am very reasonable about lending her to her aunts, but she takes no sort of advantage of my liberality; she says she knows her duty is at home. She is growing into a firm and solid English maiden lady, with a good colour and great decision of character. That she always had.

I point out to John, when she takes our crumpets away from us, that she gets it from him. I could never take away anybody's crumpets, merely because they were indigestible, least of all my own parents'. She has acquired a distinct affection for us, by some means best known to herself; but I should have no objection to that if she would not rearrange my bonnet-strings. That is a fond liberty to which I take exception; but it is one thing to take exception and another to express it.

Our daughter is with us, permanently with us. She declares that she intends to be the prop of our declining years; she makes the statement often, and always as if it were humorous. Nevertheless I sometimes notice a spirit of inquiry, a note of investigation in her encounters with the opposite sex that suggests an expectation not yet extinct that another and perhaps a more appreciative Dacres Tottenham may flash across her field of vision—alas, how improbable! Myself I can not imagine why she should wish it; I have grown in my old age into a perfect horror of cultivated young men; but if such a person should by a miracle at any time appear, I think it is extremely improbable that I will interfere on his behalf.

Duncan Campbell Scott (1862-1947)

The son of a Methodist minister, Duncan Campbell Scott was a career civil servant in the Department of Indian Affairs as well as a poet, short story writer and an accomplished musician. The central interest in his poetry is the relationship of form to content; while his early poems were dominated by traditional and European models, his later work used innovations in poetic form and rhythm to represent his experience as a treaty commissioner and his love of Northern and Western Canada. Much of the contemporary criticism of his work has been concerned with reconciling his legacy as a public official (he was responsible for the notorious residential schools policy, for example) with the aesthetic appeal and human sympathy of his literary work.

"Charcoal" is based on a real court case; its realism is typical of Scott's technique in representing northern or Aboriginal peoples. It was first published (as "Star Blanket") in *Canadian Magazine* 23:3 (July 1904) 251-256. This version is taken from the collection *The Circle of Affection* (Toronto: McClelland and Stewart, 1947).

Charcoal

Pretty-face had promised to behave herself once more. But this time she promised in a different way, and her husband, Charcoal, was satisfied, which he had not always been before. Charcoal wanted to be what his agent called "a good Indian." He wanted to have a new cooking stove, and a looking-glass. He already had cattle on loan, and was one of the best workers in the hay-fields. But it was disturbing that he should so often come back from his work to find his wife talking to Bad-young-man, who never did a stroke of work, who ranged off the reserve into Montana or Kootenay scorning permits, and who made trouble wherever he came. Pretty-face would promise solemnly never to have a word with Bad-young-man again, but many times had she broken her promise, and Charcoal would return to meet the rover on his pony, and hear his impudent hail as he passed him in his barbaric trappings, his hair full of brass pistol cartridges and the tin trademarks from tobacco plugs. But this last promise of Pretty-face was in something different, and Charcoal was satisfied. So satisfied was he that he bought for her the medicine-pole-bag, which made her, without any question, the first lady on the reserve.

And Pretty-face kept her promise. It was true that Bad-young-man was away, no one knew where; but Charcoal was infinitely satisfied to come home and find her looking after the children, or preparing his supper herself, instead of leaving it to her mother, whose cookery his soul hated. He took a great satisfaction now in the prospect of his small shanty and his larger stable, with three tepees grouped around them, and his verdant garden patches fenced to keep out the cattle. He took a greater pleasure out of his wife's social position than she did, and viewed the medicine-pole-bag with a sort of awe. With an infantile curiosity he wondered what were the sacred mysteries of the "Mow-to-kee" when the centre pole was raised. Pretty-face allowed him to see the contents of the parfleche bag, which had cost him so many good dollars; the snake-skin head-band into which the feathers were stuck; the little sacks of paint, red earth and grease; the shells in which the paint is mixed; the sweet grass to burn as incense during prayer-making; and the whistle to mark the rhythm for dancing.

More and more evident were the results of his toil and his obedience to his agent and his instructor. He began to see clearly that what they had told him was truth. He could trace every dollar of the twenty-five he had paid for the medicine-pole-bag to some good stroke of work he had done in the hay-fields. He did not know it, but the agent had asked the Department for lumber to build him a new house, and his chief ambitions were forming solidly in the future. Verily, the white man's ways were the best.

So his feeling was all the more intense when he returned home one evening in October and found that Bad-young-man had been there. He did not see him, but there was no need of such crude evidence. There was no visible trace in the demeanour of Pretty-face nor in the bearing of the mother-in-law. His wife had even prepared his favourite dish for supper. But another date had been written down. Bad-young-man had come back.

Charcoal ate his meal in silence, and Pretty-face was so frightened that she went away when he began to fill his pipe. But he did not really care just then what she did. He wrapped a blanket around his shirt and went out to see his paternal grandfather, who lived in one of the tepees. He had been a mighty warrior in his day but now he was old, and could only remember the time of his prowess which had gone by. He could talk, but he could not see, and his chief delight was in smoking and sleeping in the sun. That night when he smelt Charcoal's tobacco, his tongue was loosened, and he told many a story of violent deed and desperate death; of how he had killed Crees as if they were coyotes; of how he had shot and scalped whitemen who now seemed to own the prairies, and he had scalps to prove his valour. Charcoal was convinced that the old way was a good way, and he went out into the moonlight, unhobbled one of his ponies and rode away furiously, yelling every little while at the moon. When he came back he pulled Pretty-face out of one of the tepees where she was hiding. She thought he was going to kill her, but he only warned her that he would kill her and Bad-young-man if he ever heard of them being together again. Then he let her go, and went and got the medicine-pole-bag and gave it to his grandfather.

After a night's sleep he had forgotten his lapse to paganism, and again found himself wanting to be a "good" Indian. It was the end of October, and a ration day, and Charcoal went up to the ration house himself, instead of sending one of his women. He rode his best pony, and took his rifle with him. The farther he got from home the more restless he felt, and he went down to his brother-in-law's camp and had dinner.

It was late in the afternoon when he returned to his own place taking a shortcut over an unused trail. As he neared his camp he saw fresh marks of a pony's hoofs. They ran into the bushes beside the trail. He knew they were made by Bad-young-man's pony. He seemed to be only thinking as he rode along, but he was keenly watching, and when he saw a slight movement, hardly the tremble of leaves, he fired. His pony stopped. Something fell out from the bushes, half way across the trail. It was Bad-young-man's body. The pony sniffed, then plunged and dashed by; but Charcoal never dropped his eyes. When he reached the house he went into the tepee to talk with his grandfather, and the women who had heard the shot rushed off to find Pretty-face.

After Charcoal had heard what his grandfather had to say, he declared that the old way was the best, that he had done well, and he went out and made his "mark" to kill a white man. But he would take his time over that; no one would miss Bad-young-man for a long while. Pretty-face, remembering his warning, expected to be shot, and she kept out of sight for two days; but when he saw her he only scolded and called her the worst name he could in his own language, and nearly the worst he could in English, and because he had had nothing to eat all that time except her mother's odious bannocks fried in rancid grease. Charcoal's settlement was some distance from the main trail to Macleod, and there was little likelihood of any one coming up to his hill; so, for a week, Bad-young-man lay as he had fallen. No one went near him. For a day and a night his pony stood by him, but, wandering away looking for grass he was taken by one of the women and hobbled at night with the others.

Suddenly Charcoal became restless. Watching from a small hill near his house, he saw the agent stop and look up at his place as if debating whether to visit him or not. He went on, but the next time he might come. That night it was dark, and a heavy cloud in the east threatened snow. Charcoal deemed that this was a good time to do a little shooting, so when one of the farm instructors, moving about his house, came between the lamp and a window, he heard the sharp crack of a rifle, and saw a flower-pot jump off the window sill. He did not believe he was hit until the doctor, tracing the bullet from the point of his hip backward, produced it from somewhere near his spine. Another inch and he would not have seen the flower-pot jump off the window sill. Up came the cloud carrying and scattering snow, and away went Charcoal with it.

In the morning the reserve was alive with excitement. The Northwest Mounted Police patrols were out scouring the country, but safely were the marks of Charcoal's pony hidden in the obscurity of the snow. Charcoal kept close to his place all day, but one of his women brought him up the news. The instructor was not even badly hurt; in a day or two he would be as well as ever. Charcoal did not care very much; all white men were alike to him; only he made his mark to kill one, the Agent this time. He would have done so had not Bad-young-man's pony broken away and gone straight to the lower camp. His appearance caused a commotion, and soon it was known everywhere that Bad-young-man's pony had come back without Bad-young-man, and the question naturally arose—what had become of that celebrated gambler and lady-killer. Every possible and probable cause of his disappearance was canvassed, when Medicine-pipe-crane-turning declared that he had been murdered. He had no evidence to offer, but he looked the pony all over and declared that he had been murdered.

Charcoal was uneasy when he found that Bad-young-man's pony had strayed off, and later in the morning he saw a girl of Wolf-bull's band come out of the bushes near his trail. Something in the way this girl hurried along made him know that she had found Bad-young-man. Toward evening, when the police rode up with tramp and jangle, they found only Charcoal's blind grandfather huddled up in his tepee. Hours before Charcoal and his whole menage, ponies, women, kids, kettles, blankets and all, had taken to the brush.

That night it was known over the whole reserve that Charcoal had shot Bad-young-man and had tried to kill an instructor. The word went out by runners to the farthest police posts, and while the fugitives were hidden in the bottom of some coulee under the stars and out of the wind, his fame had travelled from Macleod half-way round the world. No one could understand how Charcoal, who wanted to be a "good" Indian, had done this thing. He was a mild, big fellow, with sad eyes in a face rather emaciated. But whatever reasons he had had, he was now to be caught and punished. It was once more civilization against savagery. Against this one Indian who had dared to follow the old tradition was arrayed all organized law. The Mounted Police, the Indian agent, and the Bloods, the people of his own clan and totem, who had learned well the white man's treachery, were banded together to hunt him down.

Charcoal resolved that, so far as he was able, he would make it a long and merry chase. To that end he began by discarding all the comforts of home; and one evening, about sundown, a squad of police were surprised to stumble on his women with the paraphernalia of his camp scurrying along the main trail. They gathered them in, but from them they could gain no clue to the whereabouts of the murderer. Now that he was free of his impediments Charcoal began a flitting to and fro that puzzled the most cunning scouts and unsettled the most phlegmatic brave on the reserve. Knowing all the fleetest ponies he stole them by night and used each one until it was played out. In vain the scouts followed tracks in the snow. Reports came in that he had been seen, mounted on a white horse, in the Belly River bottom; but it was found to be one of Cochrane's cowboys. Three-bull's piebald racer, the fastest pony on the reserve, was stolen, although his owner was watching all night, and the next morning he was found forty miles away completely exhausted. The Indians fell into a panic; no one did a stroke of work. Reports came in, which, if true, would mean that he had been seen on the same night in two different places thirty miles apart. The Indians believed that he had some "medicine," and that he would never be caught. Three weeks had been lost in the chase, and even the police were beginning to chaff one another. It looked probable that Charcoal had retired to the wilds of the Kootenay, or had flitted over the line to Montana.

He could have done either of these things readily enough, but, with a sort of bravado he chose to circle like a hawk about his own reserve. He well knew what an excitement his escapade was causing, and his gratified vanity bore him through perils and hardships which he might have shunned. All the nights of the late October were cold; he sometimes lay next his pony in the bottom of a coulee, sheltered from the wind, with his single blanket for a covering, or riding in the teeth of a storm of snow or sleet to appear or disappear like a spirit. Hunger pursued him. The white man, with his cunning, had locked up his women, and they could not cache food for him. He distrusted his relatives, he knew that they would be bribed to hunt him down or lay a trap for him. Sometimes he stood under the stars so near their tepees that he could hear their breathing. Once he stole two days' rations from a Mounted Policeman who was sleeping by his hobbled horse. But always he was hungry. His face grew more emaciated and his eyes took on the glitter of ice under starlight. He called on his gods to strike his enemies. They had taken his country from him, his manners and his garb, and when he rebelled against them, their hands were upon him. Sometimes he felt as if his head was on fire, and he held his hands up in the dark to see the reflection of the flames. Sometimes he reeled in his saddle when he looked off towards the foothills of the Rockies, shining silvery in the distance, like an uplifted land of promise.

 He was getting tired of it all. A sort of contempt for his pursuers, for the hundreds of them that could not catch him, crept upon him. He grew more careless and more daring. They found his trail mingled with their own. One day after a storm, in which three inches of snow had fallen, he struck the trail boldly at Bentley's, crossed the ford there without any attempt at concealment, worked his way down the river. Again he forded; then doubling on his tracks through thick brush, recrossed his own trail at Bentley's, and then followed the river bank up stream. Then, after a mile or so, he came out into the open. It was a clear morning after the storm; above, a lofty blue sky; below, the plain stretching away covered with the gleaming snow. He was riding leisurely, when suddenly, without turning around, he knew he was followed. Urging his horse and glancing over his shoulder, he saw three mounted men on his trail about a mile away. He dashed ahead, at first without eagerness, with an air of reckless contempt. The next time he looked he noticed that one of the horsemen had begun to draw away from his companions.

 Charcoal's pony was not fresh, he had ridden him many a mile in the night, and the beast showed signs of fatigue. He urged him to the top of his speed, but the next time he looked behind him his pursuer had gained. He could see that he was mounted on a spirited horse which was perfectly fresh. He calculated that before he had gone another mile his enemy would be abreast of him. His own beast, instead of responding to his cries, seemed to lag. When Charcoal looked over his shoulder again he could almost distinguish the features of his pursuer. He had long, blonde moustaches and a ruddy face. Charcoal knew who it was. It was Sergeant Wales of the Pincher Creek detachment. He was rapidly overhauling him. Charcoal could hear him shout now and then. Glancing once more behind him, he saw that Wales had drawn his pistol and he would soon be within its range. Again he urged his tired beast. He kept his eyes fixed for a while on the snow which the hoofs of his pony were tramping. Over the light, uneven sound of his hoofs and the movements of his trappings, he began to hear the pounding of the approaching feet, regular and strong, and the jingle and rattle of accoutrements. Every moment he expected to hear the whistle of a bullet past his ears.

Suddenly the thought flashed through him that Wales intended to take him alive and lead him back to barracks a captive. No, he would never do that. Once more, and for the last time, he looked behind him. Rushing splendidly, horse and rider moving as one, they thundered down upon him. Sun flashing from red tunic, from points of brass and steel, foam springing from nostril white as the snow into which it fell, on they came to overwhelm irresistibly this rickety pony with its starved rider. Charcoal gazed for a moment; he could see the eye-balls of his captor gleam. He did not utter a sound; he merely smiled with the glorious excitement and triumph. I will make him shoot me, the Indian thought. His rifle lay in the hollow of his arm; he turned away, and fired. Now he will shoot me in the back, he thought. No. Thirty yards they went. The Indian heard a cry behind him. He turned in time to see the towering frame of Wales swerve in his saddle, bend backwards, swing from his horse. In a flash Charcoal wheeled his pony. The horse, dragging its master's weight, rushed on for twenty yards, then stopped. Quickly, so quickly that the words of the story seem leaden, Charcoal dismounted. A couple of bullets whistled far over his head from his other pursuers half a mile away. Then he did something inconceivably brave for an Indian. He ran close to the dead man, fired into him, grabbed his horse, leaped into the saddle and was off. From a mile distant he saw his pursuers stooping over the body of the sergeant. Slowly he raised his arm and turned from them, making for Stand-Off and the mouth of the Kootenay.

Wolf-plume was Charcoal's brother-in-law. He had a house with two stories, and one bed in which he never slept. Following the agent's directions, by day his house wore an inviting appearance; by night it was lighted as if prepared for feasting and tea drinking. The third night after the shooting of Wales, the snow had begun to fall near sundown, and fell silently, unmoved by wind, as the night deepened. Through the snow, an Indian, leading his horse, his face hidden in his blanket, approached Wolf-plume's house. He tapped softly at the door. When Wolf-plume came, the covering dropped a little from the face. It was Charcoal. At first he would not come nearer. But, reassured by the words of his brother-in-law, and drawn powerfully by the odor of a stew that came out strongly into the snow, he threw the rein off his arm, left his horse standing, and entered. There was no danger in sight. A bench was placed for him. The stew tasted like nothing which had ever passed his lips before; and weariness overcame him, weariness and sleep. After weeks of privation, starved, frozen, jaded with the saddle, hunted for his life, he lay down in the house of his friends and slept.

He slept. Then Wolf-plume took the lamp out of the east window and from miles away started the policemen who had waited only for that signal. Soon they had surrounded the little house. They let him sleep as a free man, sleep as the snow fell and the clouds cleared off, and stars came out piercingly bright in the sky. He woke toward morning, and all about him was the stamping of horses and the movement of red tunics.

Many days after that, just before they hanged him, he thought of the medicine-pole-bag. He had often thought of Pretty-face, but he did not want to see her. He had thought of many things which he did not understand. He was to be killed in the white man's manner; to his mind it was only vengeance, death for deaths, which the warriors of his own race dealt to their foes in the old days, and in a braver fashion. They had driven away the buffalo, and made the Indian sad with flour and beef, and had put his muscles into harness. He had only shot a bad Indian, and they rose upon him. His gun had shot a big policeman, and when they had taught his brother-in-law their own idea of fair dealing he was taken in sleep, and now there was to be an end. He did not know what Père Pauquette meant by his prayers, and the presentation of the little crucifix worn bright with many salutations. It was all involved in mystery.

Groping about for some solace he sent for the medicine-pole-bag, and when they brought it and he was left alone, he placed it in a corner of his cell and gazed for a long time upon the parfleche covering with its magical markings. When they had left him for his last sleep he gathered it to his breast, and all night he slept contentedly. Early the next morning they took it away. It was very cold for early spring. He did not hear or understand what Père Pauquette murmured in his ear. His was the calm of a stoic. He breathed deeply the scent of the sweet grass with which the medicine-pole-bag was filled, which clung to his shirt and rose like incense about his face. And so Charcoal died.

Robert Barr (1850-1912)

Born in Scotland and raised in Windsor, Ontario, Barr trained as a teacher and was principal of Windsor Central School when one of his free-lance submissions caught the eye of the editor of the *Detroit Free Press*. In 1876 he became a reporter, and later moved to England to edit a weekly edition of the paper. A prolific and commercially successful writer, Barr published fifteen collections of sketches and short stories as well as twenty novels, all designed to appeal to popular taste and all out-of-print today.

"Dinner for Seven in the Temple" is taken from *The Triumphs of Eugène Valmont* (New York: Appleton, 1906), a book of detective stories featuring the fastidious French detective who is often seen as a precursor to Agatha Christie's Hercule Poirot.

The Dinner for Seven in the Temple

When the card was brought in to me, I looked upon it with some misgiving, for I scented a commercial transaction, and, although such cases are lucrative enough, nevertheless I, Eugène Valmont, formerly high in the service of the French Government, do not care to be connected with them. They usually pertain to sordid business affairs, presenting little that is of interest to a man who, in his time, has dealt with subtle questions of diplomacy upon which the welfare of nations sometimes turned.

The name of Bentham Gibbes is familiar to everyone, connected as it is with the much-advertised pickles, whose glaring announcements in crude crimson and green strike the eye throughout Great Britain, and shock the artistic sense wherever seen. Me! I have never tasted them, and shall not so long as a French restaurant remains open in London. But I doubt not they are as pronounced to the palate as their advertisement is distressing to the eye. If, then, this gross pickle manufacturer expected me to track down those who were infringing upon the recipes for making his so-called sauces, chutneys, and the like, he would find himself mistaken, for I was now in a position to pick and choose my cases, and a case of pickles did not allure me. "Beware of imitations," said the advertisement; "none genuine without a facsimile of the signature of Bentham Gibbes." Ah, well, not for me were either the pickles or the tracking of imitators. A forged check! yes, if you like, but the forged signature of Mr. Gibbes on a pickle bottle was out of my line. Nevertheless, I said to Armand:

"Show the gentleman in," and he did so.

To my astonishment there entered a young man, quite correctly dressed in the dark frock coat, faultless waistcoat and trousers that proclaimed a Bond Street tailor. When he spoke his voice and language were those of a gentleman.

"Monsieur Valmont?" he inquired.

"At your service," I replied, bowing and waving my hand as Armand placed a chair for him, and withdrew.

"I am a barrister with chambers in the Temple," began Mr. Gibbes, "and for some days a matter has been troubling me about which I have now come to seek your advice, your name having been suggested by a friend in whom I confided."

"Am I acquainted with him?" I asked.

"I think not," replied Mr. Gibbes; "he also is a barrister with chambers in the same building as my own. Lionel Dacre is his name."

"I never heard of him."

"Very likely not. Nevertheless, he recommended you as a man who could keep his own counsel, and if you take up this case I desire the utmost secrecy preserved, whatever may be the outcome."

I bowed, but made no protestation. Secrecy is a matter of course with me.

The Englishman paused for a few moments as if he expected fervent assurances; then went on with no trace of disappointment on his countenance at not receiving them.

"On the night of the twenty-third, I gave a little dinner to six friends of mine in my own rooms. I may say that so far as I am aware they are all gentlemen of unimpeachable character. On the night of the dinner I was detained later than I expected at a reception, and in driving to the Temple was still further delayed by a block of traffic in Piccadilly, so that when I arrived at my chambers there was barely time for me to dress and receive my guests. My man Johnson had everything laid out ready for me in my dressing room, and as I passed through to it I hurriedly flung off the coat I was wearing and carelessly left it hanging over the back of a chair in the dining room, where neither Johnson nor myself noticed it until my attention was called to it after the dinner was over, and everyone rather jolly with wine.

"This coat contains an inside pocket. Usually any frock coat I wear at an afternoon reception has not an inside pocket, but I had been rather on the rush all day. My father is a manufacturer whose name may be familiar to you, and I am on the directors' board of his company. On this occasion I took a cab from the city to the reception I spoke of, and had no time to go and change at my rooms. The reception was a somewhat bohemian affair, extremely interesting, of course, but not too particular as to costume, so I went as I was. In this inside pocket rested a thin package, composed of two pieces of cardboard, and between them rested five twenty-pound Bank of England notes, folded lengthwise, held in place by an elastic rubber band. I had thrown the coat across the chair back in such a way that the inside pocket was exposed, leaving the ends of the notes plainly recognizable.

"Over the coffee and cigars one of my guests laughingly called attention to what he termed my vulgar display of wealth, and Johnson, in some confusion at having neglected to put away the coat, now picked it up, and took it to the reception room where the wraps of my guests lay about promiscuously. He should, of course, have hung it up in my wardrobe, but he said afterwards he thought it belonged to the guest who had spoken. You see, Johnson was in my dressing room when I threw my coat on the chair in the corner while making my way thither, and I suppose he had not noticed the coat in the hurry of arriving guests, otherwise he would have put it where it belonged. After everybody had gone Johnson came to me and said the coat was there, but the package was missing, nor has any trace of it been found since that night."

"The dinner was fetched in from outside, I suppose?"

"Yes."

"How many waiters served it?"

"Two. They are men who have often been in my employ on similar occasions, but, apart from that, they had left my chambers before the incident of the coat happened."

"Neither of them went into the reception room, I take it?"

"No. I am certain that not even suspicion can attach to either of the waiters."

"Your man Johnson—?"

"Has been with me for years. He could easily have stolen much more than the hundred pounds if he had wished to do so, but I have never known him to take a penny that did not belong to him."

"Will you favour me with the names of your guests, Mr. Gibbes?"

"Viscount Stern sat at my right hand, and at my left Lord Templemere; Sir John Sanclere next to him, and Angus McKeller next to Sanclere. After Viscount Stern was Lionel Dacre, and at his right, Vincent Innis."

On a sheet of paper I had written the names of the guests, and noted their places at the table.

"Which guest drew your attention to the money?"

"Lionel Dacre."

"Is there a window looking out from the reception room?"

"Two of them."

"Were they fastened on the night of the dinner party?"

"I could not be sure; very likely Johnson would know. You are hinting at the possibility of a thief coming in through a reception-room window while we were somewhat noisy over our wine. I think such a solution highly improbable. My rooms are on the third floor, and a thief would scarcely venture to make an entrance when he could not but know there was company being entertained. Besides this, the coat was there less than an hour, and it appears to me that whoever stole those notes knew where they were."

"That seems reasonable," I had to admit. "Have you spoken to anyone of your loss?"

"To no one but Dacre, who recommended me to see you. Oh, yes, and to Johnson, of course."

I could not help noting that this was the fourth or fifth time Dacre's name had come up during our conversation.

"What of Dacre?" I asked.

"Oh, well, you see, he occupies chambers in the same building on the ground floor. He is a very good fellow, and we are by way of being firm friends. Then it was he who had called attention to the money, so I thought he should know the sequel."

"How did he take your news?"

"Now that you call attention to the fact, he seemed slightly troubled. I should like to say, however, that you must not be misled by that. Lionel Dacre could no more steal than he could lie."

"Did he show any surprise when you mentioned the theft?"

Bentham Gibbes paused a moment before replying, knitting his brows in thought.

"No," he said at last; "and, come to think of it, it appeared as if he had been expecting my announcement."

"Doesn't that strike you as rather strange, Mr. Gibbes?"

"Really, my mind is in such a whirl, I don't know what to think. But it's perfectly absurd to suspect Dacre. If you knew the man you would understand what I mean. He comes of an excellent family, and he is—oh! he is Lionel Dacre, and when you have said that you have made any suspicion absurd."

"I suppose you caused the rooms to be thoroughly searched. The packet didn't drop out and remain unnoticed in some corner?"

"No; Johnson and myself examined every inch of the premises."

"Have you the numbers of the notes?"

"Yes; I got them from the bank next morning. Payment was stopped, and so far not one of the five has been presented. Of course, one or more may have been cashed at some shop, but none have been offered to any of the banks."

"A twenty-pound note is not accepted without scrutiny, so the chances are the thief may find some difficulty in disposing of them."

"As I told you, I don't mind the loss of the money at all. It is the uncertainty, the uneasiness caused by the incident which troubles me. You will comprehend how little I care about the notes when I say that if you are good enough to interest yourself in this case, I shall be disappointed if your fee does not exceed the amount I have lost."

Mr. Gibbes rose as he said this, and I accompanied him to the door assuring him that I should do my best to solve the mystery. Whether he sprang from pickles or not, I realized he was a polished and generous gentleman, who estimated the services of a professional expert like myself at their true value.

I shall not set down the details of my researches during the following few days, because the trend of them must be gone over in the account of that remarkable interview in which I took part somewhat later. Suffice it to say that an examination of the rooms and a close cross-questioning of Johnson satisfied me he and the two waiters were innocent. I became certain no thief had made his way through the window, and finally I arrived at the conclusion that the notes were stolen by one of the guests. Further investigation convinced me that the thief was no other than Lionel Dacre, the only one of the six in pressing need of money at this time. I caused Dacre to be shadowed, and during one of his absences made the acquaintance of his man Hopper, a surly, impolite brute, who accepted my golden sovereign quickly enough, but gave me little in exchange for it. While I conversed with him, there arrived in the passage where we were talking together a huge case of champagne, bearing one of the best known names in the trade, and branded as being of the vintage of '78. Now I knew that the product of Camelot Frères is not bought as cheaply as British beer, and I also had learned that two short weeks before Mr. Lionel Dacre was at his wits' end for money. Yet he was still the same briefless barrister he had ever been.

On the morning after my unsatisfactory conversation with his man Hopper, I was astonished to receive the following note, written on a dainty correspondence card:

> 3 and 4, Vellum Buildings,
> Inner Temple, E.C.
> Mr. Lionel Dacre presents his compliments to Monsieur Eugène Valmont, and would be obliged if Monsieur Valmont could make it convenient to call upon him in his chambers to-morrow morning at eleven.

Had the young man become aware that he was being shadowed, or had the surly servant informed him of the inquiries made? I was soon to know. I called punctually at eleven next morning, and was received with charming urbanity by Mr. Dacre himself. The taciturn Hopper had evidently been sent away for the occasion.

"My dear Monsieur Valmont, I am delighted to meet you," began the young man with more of effusiveness than I had ever noticed in an Englishman before, although his very next words supplied an explanation that did not occur to me until afterwards as somewhat farfetched. "I believe we are by way of being country-men, and, therefore, although the hour is early, I hope you will allow me to offer you some of this bottled sunshine of the year '78 from *la belle France*, to whose prosperity and honour we shall drink together. For such a toast any hour is propitious," and to my amazement he brought forth from the case I had seen arrive two days before a bottle of that superb Camelot Frères' '78.

"Now," said I to myself, "it is going to be difficult to keep a clear head if the aroma of this nectar rises to the brain. But tempting as is the cup, I shall drink sparingly, and hope he may not be so judicious."

Sensitive, I already experienced the charm of his personality, and well understood the friendship Mr. Bentham Gibbes felt for him. But I saw the trap spread before me. He expected, under the influence of champagne and courtesy, to extract a promise from me which I must find myself unable to give.

"Sir, you interest me by claiming kinship with France. I had understood that you belonged to one of the oldest families of England."

"Ah, England!" he cried, with an expressive gesture of outspreading hands truly Parisian in its significance. "The trunk belongs to England, of course, but the root—ah! the root—Monsieur Valmont, penetrated the soil from which this wine of the gods has been drawn."

Then filling my glass and his own he cried:

"To France, which my family left in the year 1066!"

I could not help laughing at his fervent ejaculation.

"1066! With William the Conqueror! That is a long time ago, Mr. Dacre."

"In years perhaps; in feelings but a day. My forefathers came over to steal, and, Lord! how well they accomplished it. They stole the whole country—something like a theft, say I—under that prince of robbers whom you have well named the Conqueror. In our secret hearts we all admire a great thief, and if not a great one, then an expert one, who covers his tracks so perfectly that the hounds of justice are baffled in attempting to follow them. Now even you, Monsieur Valmont (I can see you are the most generous of men, with a lively sympathy found to perfection only in France), even you must suffer a pang of regret when you lay a thief by the heels who has done his task deftly."

"I fear, Mr. Dacre, you credit me with a magnanimity to which I dare not lay claim. The criminal is a danger to society."

"True, true, you are in the right, Monsieur Valmont. Still, admit there are cases that would touch you tenderly. For example, a man ordinarily honest; a great need; a sudden opportunity. He takes that of which another has abundance, and he, nothing. What then Monsieur Valmont? Is the man to be sent to perdition for a momentary weakness?"

His words astonished me. Was I on the verge of hearing a confession? It almost amounted to that already.

"Mr. Dacre," I said, "I cannot enter into the subtleties you pursue. My duty is to find the criminal."

"Again I say you are in the right, Monsieur Valmont, and I am enchanted to find so sensible a head on French shoulders. Although you are a more recent arrival, if I may say so, than myself, you nevertheless already give utterance to sentiments which do honour to England. It is your duty to hunt down the criminal. Very well. In that I think I can aid you, and thus have taken the liberty of requesting your attendance here this morning. Let me fill your glass again, Monsieur Valmont."

"No more, I beg of you, Mr. Dacre."

"What, do you think the receiver is as bad as the thief?"

I was so taken aback by this remark that I suppose my face showed the amazement within me. But the young man merely laughed with apparently free-hearted enjoyment, poured more wine into his own glass, and tossed it off. Not knowing what to say, I changed the current of conversation.

"Mr. Gibbes said you had been kind enough to recommend me to his attention. May I ask how you came to hear of me?"

"Ah! who has not heard of the renowned Monsieur Valmont," and as he said this, for the first time there began to grow a suspicion in my mind that he was chaffing me, as it is called in England—a procedure which I cannot endure. Indeed, if this gentleman practiced such a barbarism in my own country he would find himself with a duel on his hands before he had gone far. However, the next instant his voice resumed its original fascination, and I listened to it as to some delicious melody.

"I need only mention my cousin, Lady Gladys Dacre, and you will at once understand why I recommended you to my friend. The case of Lady Gladys, you will remember, required a delicate touch which is not always to be had in this land of England, except when those who possess the gift do us the honour to sojourn with us."

I noticed that my glass was again filled, and bowing an acknowledgment of his compliment, I indulged in another sip of the delicious wine. I sighed, for I began to realize it was going to be very difficult for me, in spite of my disclaimer, to tell this man's friend he had stolen the money. All this time he had been sitting on the edge of the table, while I occupied a chair at its end. He sat there in a careless fashion, swinging a foot to and fro. Now he sprang to the floor, and drew up a chair, placing on the table a blank sheet of paper. Then he took from the mantelshelf a packet of letters, and I was astonished to see they were held together by two bits of cardboard and a rubber band similar to the combination that had contained the folded bank notes. With great nonchalance he slipped off the rubber band, threw it and the pieces of cardboard on the table before me, leaving the documents loose to his hand.

"Now, Monsieur Valmont," he cried jauntily, "you have been occupied for several days on this case, the case of my dear friend Bentham Gibbes, who is one of the best fellows in the world."

"He said the same of you, Mr. Dacre."

"I am gratified to hear it. Would you mind letting me know to what point your researches have led you?"

"They have led me in a direction rather than to a point."

"Ah! In the direction of a man, of course?"

"Certainly."

"Who is he?"

"Will you pardon me if I decline to answer this question at the present moment?"

"That means you are not sure."

"It may mean, Mr. Dacre, that I am employed by Mr. Gibbes, and do not feel at liberty to disclose the results of my quest without his permission."

"But Mr. Bentham Gibbes and I are entirely at one in this matter. Perhaps you are aware that I am the only person with whom he has discussed the case besides yourself."

"That is undoubtedly true, Mr. Dacre; still, you see the difficulty of my position."

"Yes, I do, and so shall press you no farther. But I also have been studying the problem in a purely amateurish way, of course. You will perhaps express no disinclination to learn whether or not my deductions agree with yours."

"None in the least. I should be very glad to know the conclusion at which you have arrived. May I ask if you suspect anyone in particular?"

"Yes, I do."

"Will you name him?"

"No; I shall copy the admirable reticence you yourself have shown. And now let us attack this mystery in a sane and businesslike manner. You have already examined the room. Well, here is a rough sketch of it. There is the table; in this corner stood the chair on which the coat was flung. Here sat Gibbes at the head of the table. Those on the left-hand side had their backs to the chair. I, being on the centre to the right, saw the chair, the coat, and the notes and called attention to them. Now our first duty is to find a motive. If it were a murder our motive might be hatred, revenge, robbery—what you like. As it is simply the stealing of money, the man must have been either a born thief or else some hitherto innocent person pressed to the crime by great necessity. Do you agree with me, Monsieur Valmont?"

"Perfectly. You follow exactly the line of my own reasoning."

"Very well. It is unlikely that a born thief was one of Mr. Gibbes's guests. Therefore we are reduced to look for a man under the spur of necessity; a man who has no money of his own, but who must raise a certain amount, let us say, by a certain date. If we can find such a man in that company, do you not agree with me that he is likely to be the thief?"

"Yes, I do."

"Then let us start our process of elimination. Out goes Viscount Stern, a lucky individual with twenty thousand acres of land, and God only knows what income. I mark off the name of Lord Templemere, one of his Majesty's judges, entirely above suspicion. Next, Sir John Sanclere; he also is rich, but Vincent Innis is still richer, so the pencil obliterates both names. Now we arrive at Angus McKeller, an author of some note, as you are well aware, deriving a good income from his books and a better one from his plays; a canny Scot, so we may rub his name from our paper and our memory. How do my erasures correspond with yours, Monsieur Valmont?"

"They correspond exactly, Mr. Dacre."

"I am flattered to hear it. There remains one man untouched, Mr. Lionel Dacre, the descendant, as I have said, of robbers."

"I have not said so, Mr. Dacre."

"Ah! my dear Valmont, the politeness of your country asserts itself. Let us not be deluded, but follow our inquiry wherever it leads. I suspect Lionel Dacre. What do you know of his circumstances before the dinner of the twenty-third?"

As I made no reply he looked up at me with his frank, boyish face illumined by a winning smile.

"You know nothing of his circumstances?" he asked.

"It grieves me to state that I do. Mr. Lionel Dacre was penniless on the night of the dinner."

"Oh, don't exaggerate, Monsieur Valmont," cried Dacre, with a gesture of pathetic protest; "his pocket held one sixpence, two pennies, and a half-penny. How came you to suspect he was penniless?"

"I knew he ordered a case of champagne from the London representative of Camelot Frères, and was refused unless he paid the money down."

"Quite right, and then when you were talking to Hopper you saw that case of champagne delivered. Excellent! excellent! Monsieur Valmont. But will a man steal, think you, even to supply himself with so delicious a wine as this we have been tasting?—and, by the way, forgive my neglect. Allow me to fill your glass, Monsieur Valmont."

"Not another drop, if you will excuse me, Mr. Dacre."

"Ah, yes, champagne should not be mixed with evidence. When we have finished, perhaps. What further proof have you discovered, monsieur?"

"I hold proof that Mr. Dacre was threatened with bankruptcy if, on the twenty-fourth, he did not pay a bill of seventy-eight pounds that had been long outstanding. I hold proof that this was paid, not on the twenty-fourth, but on the twenty-sixth. Mr. Dacre had gone to the solicitor and assured him he would pay the money on that date, whereupon he was given two days' grace."

"Ah, well, he was entitled to three, you know, in law. Yes, there, Monsieur Valmont, you touch the fatal point. The threat of bankruptcy will drive a man in Dacre's position to almost any crime. Bankruptcy to a barrister means ruin. It means a career blighted; it means a life buried, with little chance of resurrection. I see, you grasp the supreme importance of that bit of evidence. The case of champagne is as nothing compared with it, and this reminds me that in the crisis now upon us I shall take another sip, with your permission. Sure you won't join me?"

"Not at this juncture, Mr. Dacre."

"I envy your moderation. Here's to the success of our search, Monsieur Valmont."

I felt sorry for the gay young fellow as with smiling face he drank the champagne.

"Now, monsieur," he went on, "I am amazed to learn how much you have discovered. Really, I think tradespeople, solicitors, and all such should keep better guard on their tongues than they do. Nevertheless, these documents at my elbow, which I expected would surprise you, are merely the letters and receipts. Here is the communication from the solicitor threatening me with bankruptcy; here is his receipt dated the twenty-sixth; here is the refusal of the wine merchant, and here is his receipt for the money. Here are smaller bills liquidated. With my pencil we will add them up. Seventy-eight pounds—the principal debt—bulks large. We add the smaller items and it reaches a total of ninety-three pounds seven shillings and fourpence. Let us now examine my purse. Here is a five-pound note; there is a golden sovereign. I now count out and place on the table twelve and sixpence in silver and twopence in coppers. The purse thus becomes empty. Let us add the silver and copper to the amount on the paper. Do my eyes deceive me, or is the sum exactly a hundred pounds? There is your money fully accounted for."

"Pardon me, Mr. Dacre," I said, "but I observe a sovereign resting on the mantelpiece."

Dacre threw back his head and laughed with greater heartiness than I had yet known him to indulge in during our short acquaintance.

"By Jove!" he cried; "you've got me there. I'd forgotten entirely about that pound on the mantelpiece, which belongs to you."

"To me? Impossible!"

"It does, and cannot interfere in the least with our century calculation. That is the sovereign you gave to my man Hopper, who, knowing me to be hard pressed, took it and shamefacedly presented it to me, that I might enjoy the spending of it. Hopper belongs to our family, or the family belongs to him. I am never sure which. You must have missed in him the deferential bearing of a manservant in Paris, yet he is true gold, like the sovereign you bestowed upon him, and he bestowed upon me. Now here, monsieur, is the evidence of the theft, together with the rubber band and two pieces of cardboard. Ask my friend Gibbes to examine them minutely. They are all at your disposition, monsieur, and thus you learn how much easier it is to deal with the master than with the servant. All the gold you possess would not have wrung these incriminating documents from old Hopper. I was compelled to send him away to the West End an hour ago, fearing that in his brutal British way he might assault you if he got an inkling of your mission."

"Mr. Dacre," said I slowly, "you have thoroughly convinced me—"

"I thought I would," he interrupted with a laugh.

"—that you did *not* take the money."

"Oho, this is a change of wind, surely. Many a man has been hanged on a chain of circumstantial evidence much weaker than this which I have exhibited to you. Don't you see the subtlety of my action? Ninety-nine persons in a hundred would say: 'No man could be such a fool as to put Valmont on his own track, and then place in Valmont's hands such striking evidence.' But there comes in my craftiness. Of course, the rock you run up against will be Gibbes's incredulity. The first question he will ask you may be this: 'Why did not Dacre come and borrow the money from me?' Now there you find a certain weakness in your chain of evidence. I knew perfectly well that Gibbes would lend me the money, and he knew perfectly well that if I were pressed to the wall I should ask him."

"Mr. Dacre," said I, "you have been playing with me. I should resent that with most men, but whether it is your own genial manner or the effect of this excellent champagne, or both together, I forgive you. But I am convinced of another thing. You know who took the money."

"I don't know, but I suspect."

"Will you tell me whom you suspect?"

"That would not be fair, but I shall now take the liberty of filling your glass with champagne."

"I am your guest, Mr. Dacre."

"Admirably answered, monsieur," he replied, pouring out the wine, "and now I offer you a clew. Find out all about the story of the silver spoons."

"The story of the silver spoons! What silver spoons?"

"Ah! That is the point. Step out of the Temple into Fleet Street, seize the first man you meet by the shoulder, and ask him to tell you about the silver spoons. There are but two men and two spoons concerned. When you learn who those two men are, you will know that one of them did not take the money, and I give you my assurance that the other did."

"You speak in mystery, Mr. Dacre."

"But certainly, for I am speaking to Monsieur Eugène Valmont."

"I echo your words, sir. Admirably answered. You put me on my mettle, and I flatter myself that I see your kindly drift. You wish me to solve the mystery of this stolen money. Sir, you do me honour, and I drink to your health."

"To yours, monsieur," said Lionel Dacre, and thus we drank and parted.

On leaving Mr. Dacre I took a hansom to a *café* in Regent Street, which is a passable imitation of similar places of refreshment in Paris. There, calling for a cup of black coffee, I sat down to think. The clew of the silver spoons! He had laughingly suggested that I should take by the shoulders the first man I met, and ask him what the story of the silver spoons was. This course naturally struck me as absurd, and he doubtless intended it to seem absurd. Nevertheless, it contained a hint. I must ask somebody, and that the right person, to tell me the tale of the silver spoons.

Under the influence of the black coffee I reasoned it out in this way. On the night of the twenty-third one of the six guests there present stole a hundred pounds, but Dacre had said that an actor in the silver-spoon episode was the actual thief. That person, then, must have been one of Mr. Gibbes's guests at the dinner of the twenty-third. Probably two of the guests were the participators in the silver-spoon comedy, but, be that as it may, it followed that one, at least, of the men around Mr. Gibbes's table knew the episode of the silver spoons. Perhaps Bentham

Gibbes himself was cognizant of it. It followed, therefore, that the easiest plan was to question each of the men who partook of that dinner. Yet if only one knew about the spoons, that one must also have some idea that these spoons formed the clew which attached him to the crime of the twenty-third, in which case he was little likely to divulge what he knew to an entire stranger.

Of course, I might go to Dacre himself and demand the story of the silver spoons, but this would be a confession of failure on my part, and I rather dreaded Lionel Dacre's hearty laughter when I admitted that the mystery was too much for me. Besides this I was very well aware of the young man's kindly intentions toward me. He wished me to unravel the coil myself, and so I determined not to go to him except as a last resource.

I resolved to begin with Mr. Gibbes, and, finishing my coffee, I got again into a hansom, and drove back to the Temple. I found Bentham Gibbes in his room, and after greeting me, his first inquiry was about the case.

"How are you getting on?" he asked.

"I think I'm getting on fairly well," I replied, "and expect to finish in a day or two, if you will kindly tell me the story of the silver spoons."

"The silver spoons?" he echoed, quite evidently not understanding me.

"There happened an incident in which two men were engaged, and this incident related to a pair of silver spoons. I want to get the particulars of that."

"I haven't the slightest idea of what you are talking about," replied Gibbes, thoroughly bewildered. "You will need to be more definite, I fear, if you are to get any help from me."

"I cannot be more definite, because I have already told you all I know."

"What bearing has all this on our own case?"

"I was informed that if I got hold of the clew of the silver spoons I should be in a fair way of settling your case."

"Who told you that?"

"Mr. Lionel Dacre."

"Oh, does Dacre refer to his own conjuring?"

"I don't know, I'm sure. What was his conjuring?"

"A very clever trick he did one night at dinner here about two months ago."

"Had it anything to do with silver spoons?"

"Well, it was silver spoons or silver forks, or something of that kind. I had entirely forgotten the incident. So far as I recollect at the moment there was a sleight-of-hand man of great expertness in one of the music halls, and the talk turned upon him. Then Dacre said the tricks he did were easy, and holding up a spoon or a fork, I don't remember which, he professed his ability to make it disappear before our eyes, to be found afterwards in the clothing of some one there present. Several offered to bet that he could do nothing of the kind, but he said he would bet with no one but Innis, who sat opposite him. Innis, with some reluctance, accepted the bet, and then Dacre, with a great show of the usual conjurer's gesticulations, spread forth his empty hands, and said we should find the spoon in Innis's pocket, and there, sure enough, it was. It seemed a proper sleight-of-hand trick, but we were never able to get him to repeat it."

"Thank you very much, Mr. Gibbes; I think I see daylight now."

"If you do you are cleverer than I by a long chalk," cried Bentham Gibbes as I took my departure.

I went directly downstairs, and knocked at Mr. Dacre's door once more. He opened the door himself, his man not yet having returned.

"Ah, monsieur," he cried, "back already? You don't mean to tell me you have so soon got to the bottom of the silver-spoon entanglement?"

"I think I have, Mr. Dacre. You were sitting at dinner opposite Mr. Vincent Innis. You saw him conceal a silver spoon in his pocket. You probably waited for some time to understand what he meant by this, and as he did not return the spoon to its place, you proposed a conjuring trick, made the bet with him, and thus the spoon was returned to the table."

"Excellent! excellent, monsieur! that is very nearly what occurred, except that I acted at once. I had had experiences with Mr. Vincent Innis before. Never did he enter these rooms of mine without my missing some little trinket after he was gone. Although Mr. Innis is a very rich person, I am not a man of many possessions, so if anything is taken, I meet little difficulty in coming to a knowledge of my loss. Of course, I never mentioned these abstractions to him. They were all trivial, as I have said, and so far as the silver spoon was concerned, it was of no great value either. But I thought the bet and the recovery of the spoon would teach him a lesson; it apparently has not done so. On the night of the twenty-third he sat at my right hand, as you will see by consulting your diagram of the table and the guests. I asked him a question twice, to which he did not reply, and looking at him I was startled by the expression in his eyes. They were fixed on a distant corner of the room, and following his gaze I saw what he was staring at with such hypnotizing concentration. So absorbed was he in contemplation of the packet there so plainly exposed, now my attention was turned to it, that he seemed to be entirely oblivious of what was going on around him. I roused him from his trance by jocularly calling Gibbes's attention to the display of money. I expected in this way to save Innis from committing the act which he seemingly did commit. Imagine then the dilemma in which I was placed when Gibbes confided to me the morning after what had occurred the night before. I was positive Innis had taken the money, yet I possessed no proof of it. I could not tell Gibbes, and I dared not speak to Innis. Of course, monsieur, you do not need to be told that Innis is not a thief in the ordinary sense of the word. He had no need to steal, and yet apparently cannot help doing so. I am sure that no attempt has been made to pass those notes. They are doubtless resting securely in his house at Kensington. He is, in fact, a kleptomaniac, or a maniac of some sort. And now, monsieur, was my hint regarding the silver spoons of any value to you?"

"Of the most infinite value, Mr. Dacre."

"Then let me make another suggestion. I leave it entirely to your bravery; a bravery which, I confess, I do not myself possess. Will you take a hansom, drive to Mr. Innis's house on the Cromwell Road, confront him quietly, and ask for the return of the packet? I am anxious to know what will happen. If he hands it to you, as I expect he will, then you must tell Mr. Gibbes the whole story."

"Mr. Dacre, your suggestion shall be immediately acted upon, and I thank you for your compliment to my courage."

I found that Mr. Innis inhabited a very grand house. After a time he entered the study on the ground floor, to which I had been conducted. He held my card in his hand, and was looking at it with some surprise.

"I think I have not the pleasure of knowing you, Monsieur Valmont," he said courteously enough.

"No. I ventured to call on a matter of business. I was once investigator for the French Government, and now am doing private detective work here in London."

"Ah! And how is that supposed to interest me? There is nothing that I wish investigated. I did not send for you, did I?"

"No, Mr. Innis, I merely took the liberty of calling to ask you to let me have the package you took from Mr. Bentham Gibbes's frock-coat pocket on the night of the twenty-third."

"He wishes it returned, does he?"

"Yes."

Mr. Innis calmly walked to a desk, which he unlocked and opened, displaying a veritable museum of trinkets of one sort and another. Pulling out a small drawer he took from it the packet containing the five twenty-pound notes. Apparently it had never been opened. With a smile he handed it to me.

"You will make my apologies to Mr. Gibbes for not returning it before. Tell him I have been unusually busy of late."

"I shall not fail to do so," said I, with a bow.

"Thanks so much. Good morning, Monsieur Valmont."

"Good morning, Mr. Innis."

And so I returned the packet to Mr. Bentham Gibbes, who pulled the notes from between their pasteboard protection, and begged me to accept them.

— Didactic — moral lesson — but readable.
—

Nellie McClung (1873-1951)

Nellie McClung was born in rural Ontario and moved with her family to a homestead in Manitoba in 1880. She trained as a teacher, and after her marriage to Wes McClung in 1896 began to write stories. "Sowing Seeds in Danny" was first published in *Canadian Magazine 26* (December 1905): 116-22. A sympathetic editor encouraged her to expand it into a book, and *Sowing Seeds in Danny* (Toronto: William Briggs, 1908) became her first commercial success, selling over 100,000 copies.

McClung's writing is imbued with the values of the Christian social gospel movement; she was a member of the WCTU and toured Canada and the United States giving speeches in support of women's suffrage. Her political activism and her writing were mutually reinforcing, as "Sowing Seeds in Danny" demonstrates; in it, McClung promotes temperance, the amelioration of poverty through hard work and social welfare, a recognition of women's contribution to society, and the power of Christian charity, rightly directed.

Sowing Seeds in Danny

In her comfortable sitting room Mrs. J. Burton Francis sat, at peace with herself and all mankind. The glory of the short winter afternoon streamed into the room and touched with new warmth and tenderness the face of a Madonna on the wall.

The whole room suggested peace. The quiet elegance of its furnishings, the soft leather-bound books on the table, the dreamy face of the occupant, who sat with folded hands looking out of the window, were all in strange contrast to the dreariness of the scene below, where the one long street of the little Manitoba town, piled high with snow, stretched away into the level, white, never-ending prairie. A farmer tried to force his tired horses through the drifts; a little boy with a milk-pail plodded bravely from door to door, sometimes laying down his burden to blow his breath on his stinging fingers.

The only sound that disturbed the quiet of the afternoon in Mrs. Francis's sitting room was the regular rub-rub of the wash-board in the kitchen below.

"Mrs. Watson is slow with the washing to-day," Mrs. Francis murmured with a look of concern on her usually placid face. "Possibly she is not well. I will call her and see."

"Mrs. Watson, will you come upstairs, please?" she called from the stairway.

Mrs. Watson, slow and shambling, came up the stairs, and stood in the doorway wiping her face on her apron.

"Is it me ye want ma'am?" she asked when she had recovered her breath.

"Yes, Mrs. Watson," Mrs. Francis said sweetly. "I thought perhaps you were not feeling well to-day. I have not heard you singing at your work, and the washing seems to have gone slowly. You must be very careful of your health, and not overdo your strength."

While she was speaking, Mrs. Watson's eyes were busy with the room, the pictures on the wall, the cosey window-seat with its numerous cushions; the warmth and brightness of it all brought a glow to her tired face.

"Yes, ma'am," she said, "thank ye kindly, ma'am. It is very kind of ye to be thinkin' o' the likes of me."

"Oh, we should always think of others, you know," Mrs. Francis replied quickly with her most winning smile, as she seated herself in a rocking-chair. "Are the children all well? Dear little Danny, how is he?"

"Indade, ma'am, that same Danny is the upsettinest one of the nine, and him only four come March. It was only this morn's mornin' that he sez to me, sez he, as I was comin' away, 'Ma, d' ye think she'll give ye pie for your dinner? Thry and remember the taste of it, won't ye ma, and tell us when ye come home,' sez he."

"Oh, the sweet prattle of childhood," said Mrs. Francis, clasping her shapely white hands. "How very interesting it must be to watch their young minds unfolding as the flower! Is it nine little ones you have, Mrs. Watson?"

"Yes, nine it is, ma'am. God save us. Teddy will be fourteen on St. Patrick's Day, and all the rest are younger."

"It is a great responsibility to be a mother, and yet how few there be that think of it," added Mrs. Francis, dreamily.

"Thrue for ye ma'am," Mrs. Watson broke in. "There's my own man, John Watson. That man knows no more of what it manes than you do yerself that hasn't one at all at all, the Lord be praised; and him the father of nine."

"I have just been reading a great book by Dr. Ernestus Parker, on 'Motherhood.' It would be a great benefit to both you and your husband."

"Och, ma'am," Mrs. Watson broke in, hastily, "John is no hand for books and has always had his suspicions o' them since his own mother's great-uncle William Mulcahey got himself transported durin' life or good behaviour for havin' one found on him no bigger 'n an almanac, at the time of the riots in Ireland. No, ma'am, John wouldn't rade it at all at all, and he don't know one letther from another, what's more."

"Then if you would read it and explain it to him, it would be so helpful to you both, and so inspiring. It deals so ably with the problems of child-training. You must be puzzled many times in the training of so many little minds, and Dr. Parker really does throw wonderful light on all the problems that confront mothers. And I am sure the mother of nine must have a great many perplexities."

Yes, Mrs. Watson had a great many perplexities—how to make trousers for four boys out of the one old pair the minister's wife had given her; how to make the memory of the rice-pudding they had on Sunday last all the week; how to work all day and sew at night, and still be brave and patient; how to make little Danny and Bugsey forget they were cold and hungry. Yes, Mrs. Watson had her problems; but they were not the kind that Dr. Ernestus Parker had dealt with in his book on "Motherhood."

"But I must not keep you, Mrs. Watson," Mrs. Francis said, as she remembered the washing. "When you go downstairs will you kindly bring me up a small red notebook that you will find on the desk in the library?"

"Yes ma'am," said Mrs. Watson, and went heavily down the stairs. She found the book and brought it up.

While she was making the second laborious journey down the softly padded stairs, Mrs. Francis was making an entry in the little red book.

> Dec. 7, 1903. Talked with one woman to-day *re* Beauty of Motherhood. Recommended Dr. Parker's book. Believe good done.

Then she closed the book with a satisfied feeling. She was going to have a very full report for her department at the next Annual Convention of the Society for Propagation of Lofty Ideals.

In another part of the same Manitoba town lived John Watson, unregenerate hater of books, his wife and their family of nine. Their first dwelling when they had come to Manitoba from the Ottawa Valley, thirteen years ago, had been C.P.R. box-car No. 722, but this had soon to be enlarged, which was done by adding to it other car-roofed shanties. One of these was painted a bright yellow and was a little larger than the others. It had been the caboose of a threshing outfit that John had worked for in '96. John was the fireman and when the boiler blew up and John was carried home insensible the "boys" felt that they should do something for the widow and orphans. They raised one hundred and sixty dollars forthwith, every man contributing his wages for the last four days. The owner of the outfit, Sam Motherwell, in a strange fit of generosity, donated the caboose.

The next fall Sam found that he needed the caboose himself, and came with his trucks to take it back. He claims that he had given it with the understanding that John was going to die. John had not fulfilled his share of the contract, and Sam felt that his generosity had been misplaced.

John was cutting wood beside his dwelling when Sam arrived with his trucks, and accused him of obtaining goods under false pretences. John was a man of few words and listened attentively to Sam's reasoning. From the little window of the caboose came the discordant wail of a very young infant, and Old Sam felt his claims growing more and more shadowy.

John took the pipe from his mouth and spat once at the woodpile. Then, jerking his thumb toward the little window, he said briefly:

"Twins. Last night."

Sam Motherwell mounted his trucks and drove away. He knew when he was beaten.

The house had received additions on every side, until it seemed to threaten to run over the edge of the lot, and looked like a section of a wrecked freight train, with its yellow refrigerator car.

The snow had drifted up to the windows, and entirely over the little lean-to that had been erected at the time that little Danny had added his feeble wail to the general family chorus.

But the smoke curled bravely up from the chimney into the frosty air, and a snug pile of wood by the "cheek of the dure" gave evidence of John's industry, notwithstanding his dislike of the world's best literature.

Inside the floor was swept and the stove was clean, and an air of comfort was over all, in spite of the evidence of poverty. A great variety of calendars hung on the wall. Every store in town it seems had sent one this year, last year and the year before. A large poster of the Winnipeg Industrial Exhibition hung in the parlour, and a Massey-Harris self-binder, in full swing, propelled by three maroon horses, swept through a waving field of golden grain, driven by an adipose individual in blue shirt and grass-green overalls. An enlarged picture of John himself glared grimly from a very heavy frame, on the opposite wall, the grimness of it somewhat relieved by the row of Sunday-school "big cards" that were stuck in around the frame.

On the afternoon that Mrs. Watson had received the uplifting talk on motherhood, and Mrs. Francis had entered it in the little red book, Pearlie Watson, aged twelve, was keeping the house, as she did six days in the week. The day was too cold for even Jimmy to be out, and so all except the three eldest boys were in the kitchen variously engaged. Danny under promise of a story was in the high chair submitting to a thorough going over with soap and water. Patsey, looking up from his self-appointed task of brushing the legs of the stove with the hair-brush, loudly demanded that the story should begin at once.

"Story, is it?" cried Pearlie in her wrath, as she took the hair-brush from Patsey. "What time have I to be thinkin' of stories and you that full of badness. My heart is bruck wid ye."

"I'll be good now," Patsey said, penitently, sitting on the wood-box, and tenderly feeling his skinned nose. "I got hurt to-day, mind that, Pearlie."

"So ye did, poor bye," said Pearlie, her wrath all gone, "and what will I tell yez about, my beauties?"

"The pink lady where Jimmy brings the milk," said Patsey promptly.

"But it's me that's gettin' combed," wailed Danny. "I should say what ye'r to tell, Pearlie."

"True for ye," said Pearlie. "Howld ye'r tongue, Patsey. What will I tell about, honey?"

"What Patsey said'll do" said Danny with an injured air, "and don't forget the chockalut drops she had the day ma was there and say she sent three o' them to me, and you can have one o' them, Pearlie."

"And don't forget the big plate o' potatoes and gravy and mate she gave the dog, and the cake she threw in the fire to get red of it," said Mary, who was knitting a sock for Teddy.

"No, don't tell that," said Jimmy, "it always makes wee Bugsey cry."

"Well," began Pearlie, as she had done many times before. "Once upon a time not very long ago, there lived a lovely pink lady in a big house painted red, with windies in ivery side of it, and a bell on the front dure, and a velvet carpet on the stair and—"

"What's a stair?" asked Bugsey.

"It's a lot of boxes piled up higher and higher, and nailed down tight so that ye can walk on them, and when ye get away up high, there is another house right farninst ye—well anyway, there was a lovely pianny in the parlow, and flowers in the windies, and two yalla burds that sing as if their hearts wud break, and the windies had a border of coloured glass all around them, and long white curtings full of holes, but they like them all the better o' that, for it shows they are owld and must ha' been good to ha' stood it so long. Well, annyway, there was a little boy called Jimmie Watson"—here all eyes were turned on Jimmy, who was sitting on the floor mending his moccasin with a piece of sinew. "There was a little boy called Jimmy Watson who used to carry milk to the lady's back dure, and a girl with black eyes and white teeth all smiley used to take it from him, and put it in a lovely pitcher with birds flying all over it. But one day the lady, herself, was there all dressed in lovely pink velvet and lace, and a train as long as from me to you, and she sez to Jimmy, sez she, 'Have you any sisters or brothers at home,' and Jim speaks up real proud-like, 'Just nine,' he sez, and sez she, swate as you please, 'Oh, that's lovely! Are they all as purty as you?' she sez, and Jimmy sez, 'Purtier if anything,' and she sez, 'I'll be steppin' over to-day to see yer ma,' and Jim ran home and told them all, and they all got brushed and combed and actin' good, and in she comes, laving her carriage at the dure, and her in a long pink velvet cape draggin' behind her on the flure, and wide white fer all around it, her silk skirts creakin' like a bag of cabbage and the eyes of her just dancin' out of her head, and she says, 'These are fine purty childer ye have here, Mrs. Watson. This is a rale purty girl, this oldest one. What's her name?' and ma ups and tells her it is Rebecca Jane Pearl, named for her two grandmothers, and Pearl just for short. She says, 'I'll be for taking you home wid me, Pearlie, to play the pianny for me,' and then she asks all around what the children's names is, and then she brings out a big box, from under her cape, all tied wid store string, and she planks it on the table and tearin' off the string, she sez, 'Now, Pearlie, it's ladies first, tibby sure. What would you like to see in here?' And I says up quick—'A long coat wid fer on it, and a handkerchief smellin' strong of satchel powder,' and she whipped them out of the box and threw them on my knee, and a new pair of red mitts too. And then she says, 'Mary, acushla, it's your turn now.' And Mary says, 'A doll with a real head on it,' and there it was as big as Danny, all dressed in green satin, opening its eyes, if you plaze."

"Now, me!" roared Danny, squirming in his chair.

"'Daniel Mulcahey Watson, what wud you like?' she says, and Danny ups and says, 'Chockaluts and candy men and 'taffy and curren' buns and ginger bread,' and she had every wan of them."

"'Robert Roblin Watson, him as they call Bugsey, what would you like?' and 'Patrick Healy Watson, as is called Patsey, what is your choice?' says she, and—"

In the confusion that ensued while these two young gentlemen thus referred to stated their modest wishes, their mother came in, tired and pale, from her hard day's work.

"How is the pink lady to-day, ma?" asked Pearlie, setting Danny down and beginning operations on Bugsey.

"Oh, she's as swate as ever, an' can talk that soft and kind about children as to melt the heart in ye."

Danny crept up on his mother's knee, "Ma, did she give ye pie?" he asked, wistfully.

"Yes, me beauty, and she sent this to you wid her love," and Mrs. Watson took a small piece out of a newspaper from under her cape. It was the piece that had been set on the kitchen table for Mrs. Watson's dinner. Danny called them all to have a bite.

"Sure it's the first bite that's always the best, a body might not like it so well on the second," said Jimmy as he took his, but Bugsey refused to have any at all. "Wan bite's no good," he said, "it just lets yer see what yer missin."

"D'ye think she'll ever come to see us, ma?" asked Pearlie, as she set Danny in the chair to give him his supper. The family was fed in divisions. Danny was always in Division A.

"Her? Is it?" said Mrs. Watson and they all listened, for Pearlie's story to-day had far surpassed all her former efforts, and it seemed as if there must be some hope of its coming true. "Why och! chiler dear, d'ye think a foine lady like her would be bothered with the likes of us? She is r'adin' her book, and writin' letthers, and thinkin' great thoughts, all the time. When she was speakin' to me to-day, she looked at me so wonderin' and faraway I could see that she thought I wasn't there at all at all, and me farninst her all the time—no childer, dear, don't be thinkin' of it, and Pearlie, I think ye'd better not be puttin' notions inter their heads. Yer father wouldn't like it. Well Danny, me man, how goes it?" went on Mrs. Watson, as her latest born was eating his rather scanty supper. "It's not skim milk and dhry bread ye'd be havin', if you were her child this night, but taffy candy filled wid nuts and chunks o' cake as big as yer head." Whereupon Danny wailed dismally, and had to be taken from his chair and have the "Little Boy Blue" sung to him, before he could be induced to go on with his supper.

The next morning when Jimmy brought the milk to Mrs. Francis's back door the dark-eyed girl with the "smiley" teeth let him in, and set a chair beside the kitchen stove for him to warm his little blue hands. While she was emptying the milk into the pitcher with the birds on it, Mrs. Francis, with a wonderful pink kimono on, came into the kitchen.

"Who is this boy, Camilla?" she asked, regarding Jimmy with a critical gaze.

"This is Master James Watson, Mrs. Francis," answered Camilla with her pleasant smile. "He brings the milk every morning."

"Oh yes; of course, I remember now," said Mrs. Francis, adjusting her glasses. "How old is the baby, James?"

"Danny is it?" said Jim. "He's four come March."

"Is he very sweet and cunning James, and do you love him very much?"

"Oh, he's all right," Jim answered sheepishly.

"It is a great privilege to have a little brother like Daniel. You must be careful to set before him a good example of honesty and sobriety. He will be a man some day, and if properly trained he may be a useful factor in the uplifting and refining of the world. I love little children," she went on rapturously, looking at Jimmy as if he wasn't there at all, "and I would love to train one, for service in the world to uplift and refine."

"Yes ma'am," said Jimmy. He felt that something was expected of him, but he was not sure what.

"Will you bring Daniel to see me to-morrow, James?" she said, as Camilla handed him his pail. "I would like to speak to his young mind and endeavour to plant the seeds of virtue and honesty in that fertile soil."

When Jimmy got home he told Pearlie of his interview with the pink lady, as much as he could remember. The only thing that he was sure of was that she wanted to see Danny, and that she had said something about planting seeds in him.

Jimmy and Pearlie thought it best not to mention Danny's proposed visit to their mother, for they knew that she would be fretting about his clothes, and would be sitting up mending and sewing for him when she should be sleeping. So they resolved to say "nothin' to nobody."

The next day their mother went away early to wash for the Methodist minister's wife, and that was always a long day's work.

Then the work of preparation began on Danny. A washbasin full of snow was put on the stove to melt, and Danny was put in the high chair which was always the place of his ablutions.

Pearlie began to think aloud. "Bugsey, your stockin's are the best. Off wid them, Mary, and mend the hole in the knees of them, and, Bugsey, hop into bed for we'll be needin' your pants anyway. It's awful stylish for a little lad like Danny to be wearin' pants under his dresses, and now what about boots? Let's see yours, Patsey. They're all gone in the uppers, and Billy's are too big, even if they were here, but they're off to school on him. I'll tell you what Mary, hurry up wid that sock o' Ted's and we'll draw them on him over Bugsey's boots and purtind they're overstockin's, and I'll carry him all the way so's not to dirty them."

Mary stopped her dish-washing, and drying her hands on the thin towel that hung over the looking glass, found her knitting and began to knit at the top of her speed.

"Isn't it good we have that dress o' his, so good yet, that he got when we had all of yez christened. Put the irons on there Mary; never mind, don't stop your knittin'. I'll do it myself. We'll press it out a bit, and we can put ma's handkerchief, the one pa gev her for Christmas, around his neck, sort o' sailor collar style, to show he's a boy. And now the snow is melted, I'll go at him. Don't cry now Danny, man, yer goin' up to the big house where the lovely pink lady lives that has the chockalut drops on her stand and chunks of cake on the table wid nuts in them as big as marbles. There now," continued Pearlie, putting the towel over her finger and penetrating Danny's ear, "she'll not say she can plant seeds in you. Yer ears are as clean as hers," and Pearlie stood back and took a critical view of Danny's ears front and back.

"Chockaluts?" asked Danny to be sure that he hadn't been mistaken.

"Yes," went on Pearlie to keep him still while she fixed his shock of red hair into stubborn little curls, and she told again with ever growing enthusiasm the story of the pink lady, and the wonderful things she had in the box tied up with store string.

At last Danny was completed and stood on a chair for inspection. But here a digression from the main issue occurred, for Bugsey had grown tired of his temporary confinement and complained that Patsey had not contributed one thing to Danny's wardrobe while he had had to give up both his stockings and his pants.

Pearlie stopped in the work of combing her own hair to see what could be done.

"Patsey, where's your gum?" she asked. "Git it for me this minute," and Patsey went to the "fallen leaf" of the table and found it on the inside where he had put it for safe keeping. "Now you give that to Bugsey," she said, "and that'll make it kind o' even though it does look as if you wuz gettin' off pretty light."

Pearlie struggled with her hair to make it lie down and "act dacint," but the image that looked back at her from the cracked glass was not encouraging, even after making allowance for the crack, but she comforted herself by saying, "Sure it's Danny she wants to see, and she won't be lookin' much at me anyway."

Then the question arose, and for a while looked serious— What was Danny to wear on his head? Danny had no cap, nor ever had one. There was one little red toque in the house that Patsey wore, but by an unfortunate accident, it had that very morning fallen into the milk pail and was now drying on the oven door. For a while it seemed as if the visit would have to be postponed until it dried, when Mary had an inspiration.

"Wrap yer cloud around his head and say you wuz feart of the earache, the day is so cold."

This was done and a blanket off one of the beds was pressed into service as an outer wrap for Danny. He was in such very bad humour at being wrapped up so tight that Pearlie had to set him down on the bed again to get a fresh grip on him.

"It's just as well I have no mitts," she said as she lifted her heavy burden. "I couldn't howld him at all if I was bothered with mitts. Open the dure, Patsey, and mind you shut it tight again. Keep up the fire, Mary. Bugsey, lie still and chew your gum, and don't fight any of yez."

When Pearlie and her heavy burden arrived at Mrs. Francis's back door they were admitted by the dark-haired Camilla, who set a rocking-chair beside the kitchen stove for Pearlie to sit in while she unrolled Danny, and when Danny in his rather remarkable costume stood up on Pearlie's knee, Camilla laughed so good humouredly that Danny felt the necessity of showing her all his accomplishments and so made the face that Patsey had taught him by drawing down his eyes, and putting his fingers in his mouth. Danny thought she liked it very much, for she went hurriedly into the pantry and brought back a cookie for him.

The savoury smell of fried salmon, for it was near lunch time, increased Danny's interest in his surroundings, and his eyes were big with wonder when Mrs. Francis herself came in. "And is this little Daniel!" she cried rapturously. "So sweet; so innocent; so pure! Did Big Sister carry him all the way? Kind Big Sister. Does oo love Big Sister?"

"Nope," Danny spoke up quickly, "just like chockaluts."

"How sweet of him, isn't it, really?" she said, "with the world all before him, the great untried future lying vast and prophetic waiting for his baby feet to enter. Well as Dr. Parker said: 'A little child is a bundle of possibilities and responsibilities.'"

"If ye please, ma'am," Pearlie said timidly, not wishing to contradict the lady, but still anxious to set her right, "it was just this blanket I had him rolled in."

At which Camilla again retired to the pantry with precipitate haste.

"Did you see the blue, blue sky, Daniel, and the white, white snow, and did you see the little snow-birds, whirling by like brown leaves?" Mrs. Francis asked with an air of great childishness.

"Nope," said Danny shortly, "didn't see nothin'."

"Please, ma'am," began Pearlie again, "it was the cloud around his head on account of the earache that done it."

"It is sweet to look into his innocent young eyes and wonder what visions they will some day see," went on Mrs. Francis, dreamily, but there she stopped with a look of horror frozen on her face, for at the mention of his eyes Danny remembered his best trick and how well it had worked on Camilla, and in a flash his eyes were drawn down and his mouth stretched to its utmost limit.

"What ails the child?" Mrs. Francis cried in alarm. "Camilla, come here."

Camilla came out of the pantry and gazed at Danny with sparkling eyes, while Pearlie, on the verge of tears, vainly tried to awaken in him some sense of the shame he was bringing on her. Camilla hurried to the pantry again, and brought another cookie. "I believe, Mrs. Francis, that Danny is hungry," she said. "Children sometimes act that way," she added, laughing.

"Really, how very interesting; I must see if Dr. Parker mentions this strange phenomenon in his book."

"Please, ma'am, I think I had better take him home now," said Pearlie. She knew what Danny was, and was afraid that greater disgrace might await her. But when she tried to get him back into the blanket he lost every joint in his body and slipped to the floor. This is what she had feared—Danny had gone limber.

"I don't want to go home" he wailed dismally. "I want to stay with her, and her; want to see the yalla burds, want a chockalut."

"Come Danny, that's a man," pleaded Pearlie, "and I'll tell you all about the lovely pink lady when we go home, and I'll get Bugsey's gum for ye and I'll—"

"No," Danny roared, "tell me now about the pink lady, tell her, and her."

"Wait till we get home, Danny man." Pearlie's grief flowed afresh. Disgrace had fallen on the Watsons, and Pearlie knew it.

"It would be interesting to know what mental food this little mind has been receiving. Please do tell him the story, Pearlie."

Thus admonished, Pearlie, with flaming cheeks began the story. She tried to make it less personal, but at every change Danny screamed his disapproval, and held her to the original version, and when it was done, he looked up with his sweet little smile, and said to Mrs. Francis nodding his head. "You're it! You're the lovely pink lady." There was a strange flush on Mrs. Francis's face, and a strange feeling stirring her heart, as she hurriedly rose from her chair and clasped Danny in her arms.

"Danny! Danny!" she cried, "you shall see the yellow birds, and the stairs, and the chocolates on the dresser, and the pink lady will come to-morrow with the big parcel."

Danny's little arms tightened around her neck.

"It's her," he shouted. "It's her."

When Mrs. Burton Francis went up to her sitting-room, a few hours later to get the "satchel" powder to put in the box that was to be tied with the store string, the sun was shining on the face of the Madonna on the wall, and it seemed to smile at her as she passed.

The little red book lay on the table forgotten. She tossed it into the waste-paper basket.

Edith Eaton (Sui Sin Far) (1865-1914)

Born in England to a Chinese mother and a British father, Edith Eaton embraced her identity as "Sui Sin Far, the half-Chinese writer." She was raised in Montreal as part of a large family (her sister Winnifred published stories as Onoto Watanna, and her sister Grace married American journalist Walter Blackburn Harte). While making her living as a typist and stenographer, Eaton began a career as a journalist writing about the Chinese-Canadian community; her work appeared in the *Montreal Daily Witness, Dominion Illustrated* and many other Canadian and US periodicals. In 1896 she published a forthright attack on federal government measures to discourage Chinese immigration in the *Montreal Daily Star*. Seeking wider opportunities for publication, she moved to the United States where she wrote about Chinatowns in Los Angeles, San Francisco and Seattle, finally publishing her book of stories, *Mrs. Spring Fragrance*, in 1912.

Eaton's stories often address the interaction between white and Chinese North Americans in domestic situations. 'Interracial' marriages and mixed race children are common subjects of her stories, as are recent immigrants and their victimization by immigration bureaucracies. "Its Wavering Image" appeared in *Mrs. Spring Fragrance* (Chicago: McClurg, 1912).

Its Wavering Image

Pan was a half white, half Chinese girl. Her mother was dead, and Pan lived with her father who kept an Oriental Bazaar on Dupont Street. All her life had Pan lived in Chinatown, and if she were different in any sense from those around her, she gave little thought to it. It was only after the coming of Mark Carson that the mystery of her nature began to trouble her.

They met at the time of the boycott of the Sam Yups by the See Yups. After the heat and dust and unsavoriness of the highways and byways of Chinatown, the young reporter who had been sent to find a story, had stepped across the threshold of a cool, deep room, fragrant with the odor of dried lilies and sandalwood, and found Pan.

She did not speak to him, nor he to her. His business was with the spectacled merchant, who, with a pointed brush, was making up accounts in brown paper books and rolling balls in an abacus box. As to Pan, she always turned from whites. With her father's people she was natural and at home; but in the presence of her mother's she felt strange and constrained, shrinking from their curious scrutiny as she would from the sharp edge of a sword.

When Mark Carson returned to the office, he asked some questions concerning the girl who had puzzled him. What was she? Chinese or white? The city editor answered him, adding: "She is an unusually bright girl, and could tell more stories about the Chinese than any other person in this city—if she would."

Mark Carson had a determined chin, clever eyes, and a tone to his voice which easily won for him the confidence of the unwary. In the reporter's room he was spoken of as "a man who would sell his soul for a story."

After Pan's first shyness had worn off, he found her bewilderingly frank and free with him; but he had all the instincts of a gentleman save one, and made no ordinary mistake about her. He was Pan's first white friend. She was born a Bohemian, exempt from the conventional restrictions imposed upon either the white or Chinese woman; and the Oriental who was her father mingled with his affection for his child so great a respect for and trust in the daughter of the dead white woman, that everything she did or said was right to him. And Pan herself! A white woman might pass over an insult; a Chinese woman fail to see one. But Pan! He would be a brave man indeed who offered one to childish little Pan.

All this Mark Carson's clear eyes perceived, and with delicate tact and subtlety he taught the young girl that, all unconscious until his coming, she had lived her life alone. So well did she learn this lesson that it seemed at times as if her white self must entirely dominate and trample under foot her Chinese.

Meanwhile, in full trust and confidence, she led him about Chinatown, initiating him into the simple mystery and history of many things, for which she, being of her father's race, had a tender regard and pride. For her sake he was received as a brother by the yellow-robed priest in the joss house, the Astrologer of Prospect Place, and other conservative Chinese. The Water Lily Club opened its doors to him when she knocked, and the Sublimely Pure Brothers' organization admitted him as one of its honorary members, thereby enabling him not only to see but to take part in a ceremony in which no American had ever before participated. With her by his side, he was welcomed wherever he went. Even the little Chinese women in the midst of their babies, received him with gentle smiles, and the children solemnly munched his candies and repeated nursery rhymes for his edification.

He enjoyed it all, and so did Pan. They were both young and light-hearted. And when the afternoon was spent, there was always that high room open to the stars, with its China bowls full of flowers and its big coloured lanterns, shedding a mellow light.

Sometimes there was music. A Chinese band played three evenings a week in the gilded restaurant beneath them, and the louder the gongs sounded and the fiddlers fiddled, the more delighted was Pan. Just below the restaurant was her father's bazaar. Occasionally Man You would stroll upstairs and inquire of the young couple if there was anything needed to complete their felicity, and Pan would answer: "Thou only." Pan was very proud of her Chinese father. "I would rather have a Chinese for a father than a white man," she often told Mark Carson. The last time she had said that he had asked whom she would prefer for a husband, a white man or a Chinese. And Pan, for the first time since he had known her, had no answer for him.

II

It was a cool, quiet evening, after a hot day. A new moon was in the sky.

"How beautiful above! How unbeautiful below!" exclaimed Mark Carson involuntarily.

He and Pan had been gazing down from their open retreat into the lantern-lighted, motley-thronged street beneath them.

"Perhaps it isn't very beautiful," replied Pan, "but it is here I live. It is my home." Her voice quivered a little.

He leaned towards her suddenly and grasped her hands.

"Pan," he cried, "you do not belong here. You are white—white."

"No! no!" protested Pan.

"You are," he asserted. "You have no right to be here."

"I was born here," she answered, "and the Chinese people look upon me as their own."

"But they do not understand you," he went on. "Your real self is alien to them. What interest have they in the books you read—the thoughts you think?"

"They have an interest in me," answered faithful Pan. "Oh, do not speak in that way any more."

"But I must," the young man persisted. "Pan, don't you see that you have got to decide what you will be—Chinese or white? You cannot be both."

"Hush! Hush!" bade Pan. "I do not love you when you talk to me like that."

A little Chinese boy brought tea and saffron cakes. He was a picturesque little fellow with a quaint manner of speech. Mark Carson jested merrily with him, while Pan holding a teabowl between her two small hands laughed and sipped.

When they were alone again, the silver stream and the crescent moon became the objects of their study. It was a very beautiful evening.

After a while Mark Carson, his hand on Pan's shoulder, sang:

> "And forever, and forever,
> As long as the river flows,
> As long as the heart has passions,
> As long as life has woes,
> The moon and its broken reflection,
> And its shadows shall appear,
> As the symbol of love in heaven,
> And its wavering image here."

Listening to that irresistible voice singing her heart away, the girl broke down and wept. She was so young and so happy.

"Look up at me," bade Mark Carson. "Oh, Pan! Pan! Those tears prove that you are white."

Pan lifted her wet face.

"Kiss me, Pan," said he. It was the first time.

Next morning Mark Carson began work on the special-feature article which he had been promising his paper for some weeks.

III

"Cursed be his ancestors," bayed Man You.

He cast a paper at his daughter's feet and left the room.

Startled by her father's unwonted passion, Pan picked up the paper, and in the clear passionless light of the afternoon read that which forever after was blotted upon her memory.

"Betrayed! Betrayed! Betrayed to be a betrayer!"

It burnt red hot; agony unrelieved by words, unassuaged by tears.

So till evening fell. Then she stumbled up the dark stairs which led to the high room open to the stars and tried to think it out. Someone had hurt her. Who was it? She raised her eyes. There shone: "Its Wavering Image." It helped her to lucidity. He had done it. Was it unconsciously dealt—that cruel blow? Ah, well did he know that the sword which pierced her through others, would carry with it to her own heart, the pain of all those others. None knew better than he that she, whom he had called "a white girl, a white woman," would rather that her own naked body and soul had been exposed, than that things, sacred and secret to those who loved her, should be cruelly unveiled and ruthlessly spread before the ridiculing and uncomprehending foreigner. And knowing all this so well, so well, he had carelessly sung her heart away, and with her kiss upon his lips, had smilingly turned and stabbed her. She, who was of the race that remembers.

IV

Mark Carson, back in the city after an absence of two months, thought of Pan. He would see her that very evening. Dear little Pan, pretty Pan, clever Pan, amusing Pan; Pan, who was always so frankly glad to have him come to her; so eager to hear all that he was doing; so appreciative, so inspiring, so loving. She would have forgotten that article by now. Why should a white woman care about such things? Her true self was above it all. Had he not taught her *that* during the weeks in which they had seen so much of one another? True, his last lesson had been a little harsh, and as yet he knew not how she had taken it; but even if its roughness had hurt and irritated, there was a healing balm, a wizard's oil which none knew so well as he how to apply.

But for all these soothing reflections, there was an undercurrent of feeling which caused his steps to falter on his way to Pan. He turned into Portsmouth Square and took a seat on one of the benches facing the fountain erected in memory of Robert Louis Stevenson. Why had Pan failed to answer the note he had written telling her of the assignment which would keep him out of town for a couple of months and giving her his address? Would Robert Louis Stevenson have known why? Yes—and so did Mark Carson. But though Robert Louis Stevenson would have boldly answered himself the question, Mark Carson thrust it aside, arose, and pressed up the hill.

"I knew they would not blame you, Pan!"

"Yes."

"And there was no word of you, dear. I was careful about that, not only for your sake, but for mine."

Silence.

"It is mere superstition anyway. These things have got to be exposed and done away with."

Still silence.

Mark Carson felt strangely chilled. Pan was not herself tonight. She did not even look herself. He had been accustomed to seeing her in American dress. Tonight she wore the Chinese costume. But for her clear-cut features she might have been a Chinese girl. He shivered.

"Pan," he asked, "why do you wear that dress?"

Within her sleeves Pan's small hands struggled together; but her face and voice were calm.

"Because I am a Chinese woman," she answered.

"You are not," cried Mark Carson, fiercely. "You cannot say that now, Pan. You are a white woman—white. Did your kiss not promise me that?"

"A white woman!" echoed Pan her voice rising high and clear to the stars above them. "I would not be a white woman for all the world. *You* are a white man. And *what* is a promise to a white man!"

* * *

When she was lying low, the element of Fire having raged so fiercely within her that it had almost shrivelled up the childish frame, there came to the house of Man You a little toddler who could scarcely speak. Climbing upon Pan's couch, she pressed her head upon the sick girl's bosom. The feel of that little head brought tears.

"Lo!" said the mother of the toddler. "Thou wilt bear a child thyself some day, and all the bitterness of this will pass away."

And Pan, being a Chinese woman, was comforted.

Stephen Leacock (1869-1944)

Stephen Leacock was born in England and raised in Ontario, where his father farmed, unsuccessfully. He studied Political Economy at the University of Chicago with Thorstein Veblen, obtaining a PhD. in 1903, and soon afterward he became a lecturer in the department of Economics and Political Science at McGill. Though he became famous in Canada, the United States and England as a writer of humorous sketches and stories, his first book (published in 1906) was a textbook on Political Science.

Leacock's Mariposa, the setting of *Sunshine Sketches of a Little Town* was based on Orillia, Ontario, the site of his summer home. The sketches initially appeared serially in the *Montreal Star* in 1912, and were published in book form later that year by Bell and Cockburn of Toronto. "The Marine Excursion" parodies the ubiquitous conventions of the (still) popular 'disaster' narrative, creating in contrast a portrait of a uniquely local and humane community.

The Marine Excursion of the Knights of Pythias

Half-past six on a July morning! The Mariposa Belle is at the wharf, decked in flags, with steam up ready to start.

Excursion day!

Half-past six on a July morning, and Lake Wissanotti lying in the sun as calm as glass. The opal colours of the morning light are shot from the surface of the water.

Out on the lake the last thin threads of the mist are clearing away like flecks of cotton wool.

The long call of the loon echoes over the lake. The air is cool and fresh. There is in it all the new life of the land of the silent pine and the moving waters. Lake Wissanotti in the morning sunlight! Don't talk to me of the Italian lakes, or the Tyrol or the Swiss Alps. Take them away. Move them somewhere else. I don't want them.

Excursion Day, at half-past six of a summer morning! With

the boat all decked in flags and all the people in Mariposa on the wharf, and the band in peaked caps with big cornets tied to their bodies ready to play at any minute! I say! Don't tell me about the Carnival of Venice and the Delhi Durbar. Don't! I wouldn't look at them. I'd shut my eyes! For light and colour give me every time an excursion out of Mariposa down the lake to the Indian's Island out of sight in the morning mist. Talk of your Papal Zouaves and your Buckingham Palace Guard! I want to see the Mariposa band in uniform and the Mariposa Knights of Pythias with their aprons and their insignia and their picnic baskets and their five-cent cigars!

Half-past six in the morning, and all the crowd on the wharf and the boat due to leave in half an hour. Notice it!—in half an hour. Already she's whistled twice (at six, and at six fifteen), and at any minute now, Christie Johnson will step into the pilot house and pull the string for the warning whistle that the boat will leave in half an hour. So keep ready. Don't think of running back to Smith's Hotel for the sandwiches. Don't be fool enough to try to go up to the Greek Store, next to Netley's, and buy fruit. You'll be left behind for sure if you do. Never mind the sandwiches and the fruit! Anyway, here comes Mr. Smith himself with a huge basket of provender that would feed a factory. There must be sandwiches in that. I think I can hear them clinking. And behind Mr. Smith is the German waiter from the caff with another basket—indubitably lager beer; and behind him, the bar-tender of the hotel, carrying nothing, as far as one can see. But of course if you know Mariposa you will understand that why he looks so nonchalant and empty-handed is because he has two bottles of rye whiskey under his linen duster. You know, I think, the peculiar walk of a man with two bottles of whiskey in the inside pockets of a linen coat. In Mariposa, you see, to bring beer to an excursion is quite in keeping with public opinion. But, whiskey,—well, one has to be a little careful.

Do I say that Mr. Smith is here? Why, everybody's here. There's Hussell the editor of the Newspacket, wearing a blue ribbon on his coat, for the Mariposa Knights of Pythias are, by their constitution, dedicated to temperance; and there's Henry Mullins, the manager of the Exchange Bank, also a Knight of

Pythias, with a small flask of Pogram's Special in his hip pocket as a sort of amendment to the constitution. And there's Dean Drone, the Chaplain of the Order, with a fishing-rod (you never saw such green bass as lie among the rocks at Indian's Island), and with a trolling line in case of maskinonge, and a landing net in case of pickerel, and with his eldest daughter, Lilian Drone, in case of young men. There never was such a fisherman as the Rev. Rupert Drone.

Perhaps I ought to explain that when I speak of the excursion as being of the Knights of Pythias, the thing must not be understood in any narrow sense. In Mariposa practically everybody belongs to the Knights of Pythias just as they do to everything else. That's the great thing about the town and that's what makes it so different from the city. Everybody is in everything.

You should see them on the seventeenth of March, for example, when everybody wears a green ribbon and they're all laughing and glad,—you know what the Celtic nature is,—and talking about Home Rule.

On St. Andrew's Day every man in town wears a thistle and shakes hands with everybody else, and you see the fine old Scotch honesty beaming out of their eyes.

And on St. George's Day!—well, there's no heartiness like the good old English spirit, after all; why shouldn't a man feel glad that he's an Englishman?

Then on the Fourth of July there are stars and stripes flying over half the stores in town, and suddenly all the men are seen to smoke cigars, and to know all about Roosevelt and Bryan and the Philippine Islands. Then you learn for the first time that Jeff Thorpe's people came from Massachusetts and that his uncle fought at Bunker Hill (it must have been Bunker Hill,—anyway Jefferson will swear it was in Dakota all right enough); and you find that George Duff has a married sister in Rochester and that her husband is all right; in fact, George was down there as recently as eight years ago. Oh, it's the most American town imaginable is Mariposa,—on the fourth of July.

But wait, just wait, if you feel anxious about the solidity of the British connection, till the twelfth of the month, when everybody is wearing an orange streamer in his coat and the Orangemen (every man in town) walk in the big procession. Allegiance! Well, perhaps you remember the address they gave to the Prince of Wales on the platform of the Mariposa station as he went through on his tour to the west. I think that pretty well settled that question.

So you will easily understand that of course everybody belongs to the Knights of Pythias and the Masons and Oddfellows, just as they all belong to the Snow Shoe Club and the Girls' Friendly Society.

And meanwhile the whistle of the steamer has blown again for a quarter to seven:—loud and long this time, for any one not here now is late for certain, unless he should happen to come down in the last fifteen minutes.

What a crowd upon the wharf and how they pile on to the steamer! It's a wonder that the boat can hold them all. But that's just the marvellous thing about the Mariposa Belle.

I don't know,—I have never known,—where the steamers like the Mariposa Belle come from. Whether they are built by Harland and Wolff of Belfast, or whether, on the other hand, they are not built by Harland and Wolff of Belfast, is more than one would like to say offhand.

The Mariposa Belle always seems to me to have some of those strange properties that distinguish Mariposa itself. I mean, her size seems to vary so. If you see her there in the winter, frozen in the ice beside the wharf with a snowdrift against the windows of the pilot house, she looks a pathetic little thing the size of a butternut. But in the summer time, especially after you've been in Mariposa for a month or two, and have paddled alongside of her in a canoe, she gets larger and taller, and with a great sweep of black sides, till you see no difference between the Mariposa Belle and the Lusitania. Each one is a big steamer and that's all you can say.

Nor do her measurements help you much. She draws about eighteen inches forward, and more than that,—at least half an inch more, astern, and when she's loaded down with an excursion crowd she draws a good two inches more. And above the water,—why, look at all the decks on her! There's the deck you walk on to, from the wharf, all shut in, with windows along it, and the after cabin with the long table, and above that the deck with all the chairs piled upon it, and the deck in front where the band stand round in a circle, and the pilot house is higher than that, and above the pilot house is the board with the gold name and the flag pole and the steel ropes and the flags; and fixed in somewhere on the different levels is the lunch counter where they sell the sandwiches, and the engine room, and down below the deck level, beneath the water line, is the place where the crew sleep. What with steps and stairs and passages and piles of cordwood for the engine,—oh no, I guess Harland and Wolff didn't build her. They couldn't have.

Yet even with a huge boat like the Mariposa Belle, it would be impossible for her to carry all of the crowd that you see in the boat and on the wharf. In reality, the crowd is made up of two classes,—all of the people in Mariposa who are going on the excursion and all those who are not. Some come for the one reason and some for the other.

The two tellers of the Exchange Bank are both there standing side by side. But one of them,—the one with the cameo pin and the long face like a horse,—is going, and the other,—with the other cameo pin and the face like another horse,—is not. In the same way, Hussell of the Newspacket is going, but his brother, beside him, isn't. Lilian Drone is going, but her sister can't; and so on all through the crowd.

And to think that things should look like that on the morning of a steamboat accident.

How strange life is!

To think of all these people so eager and anxious to catch the steamer, and some of them running to catch it, and so fearful that they might miss it,—the morning of a steamboat accident. And the captain blowing his whistle, and warning them so severely that he would leave them behind,—leave them out of the accident! And everybody crowding so eagerly to be in the accident.

Perhaps life is like that all through.

Strangest of all to think, in a case like this, of the people who were left behind, or in some way or other prevented from going, and always afterwards told of how they had escaped being on board the Mariposa Belle that day!

Some of the instances were certainly extraordinary.

Nivens, the lawyer, escaped from being there merely by the fact that he was away in the city.

Towers, the tailor, only escaped owing to the fact that, not intending to go on the excursion he had stayed in bed till eight o'clock and so had not gone. He narrated afterwards that waking up that morning at half-past five, he had thought of the excursion and for some unaccountable reason had felt glad that he was not going.

The case of Yodel, the auctioneer, was even more inscrutable. He had been to the Oddfellows' excursion on the train the week before and to the Conservative picnic the week before that, and had decided not to go on this trip. In fact, he had not the least intention of going. He narrated afterwards how the night before someone had stopped him on the corner of Nippewa and Tecumseh Streets (he indicated the very spot) and asked: "Are you going to take in the excursion to-morrow?" and he had said, just as simply as he was talking when narrating it: "No." And ten minutes after that, at the corner of Dalhousie and Brock Streets (he offered to lead a party of verification to the precise place) somebody else had stopped him and asked: "Well, are you going on the steamer trip to-morrow?" Again he had answered: "No," apparently almost in the same tone as before.

He said afterwards that when he heard the rumour of the accident it seemed like the finger of Providence, and he fell on his knees in thankfulness.

There was the similar case of Morison (I mean the one in Glover's hardware store that married one of the Thompsons). He said afterwards that he had read so much in the papers about accidents lately,—mining accidents, and aeroplanes and gasoline,—that he had grown nervous. The night before his wife had asked him at supper: "Are you going on the excursion?" He had answered: "No, I don't think I feel like it," and had added: "Perhaps your mother might like to go." And the next evening just at dusk, when the news ran through the town, he said the first thought that flashed through his head was: "Mrs. Thompson's on that boat."

He told this right as I say it—without the least doubt or confusion. He never for a moment imagined she was on the Lusitania or the Olympic or any other boat. He knew she was on this one. He said you could have knocked him down where he stood. But no one had. Not even when he got half-way down,—on his knees, and it would have been easier still to knock him down or kick him. People do miss a lot of chances.

Still, as I say, neither Yodel nor Morison nor anyone thought about there being an accident until just after sundown when they—

Well, have you ever heard the long booming whistle of a steamboat two miles out on the lake in the dusk, and while you listen and count and wonder, seen the crimson rockets going up against the sky and then heard the fire bell ringing right there beside you in the town, and seen the people running to the town wharf?

That's what the people of Mariposa saw and felt that summer evening as they watched the Mackinaw life-boat go plunging out into the lake with seven sweeps to a side and the foam clear to the gunwale with the lifting stroke of fourteen men!

But, dear me, I am afraid that this is no way to tell a story. I suppose the true art would have been to have said nothing about the accident till it happened. But when you write about Mariposa, or hear of it, if you know the place, it's all so vivid and real that a thing like the contrast between the excursion crowd in the morning and the scene at night leaps into your mind and you must think of it.

But never mind about the accident,—let us turn back again to the morning.

The boat was due to leave at seven. There was no doubt about the hour,—not only seven, but seven sharp. The notice in the Newspacket said: "The boat will leave sharp at seven;" and the advertising posters on the telegraph poles on Missinaba Street that began "Ho, for Indian's Island!" ended up with the words: "Boat leaves at seven sharp." There was a big notice on the wharf that said: "Boat leaves sharp on time."

So at seven, right on the hour, the whistle blew loud and long, and then at seven fifteen three short peremptory blasts, and at seven thirty one quick angry call,—just one,—and very soon after that they cast off the last of the ropes and the Mariposa Belle sailed off in her cloud of flags, and the band of the Knights of Pythias, timing it to a nicety, broke into the "Maple Leaf for Ever!"

I suppose that all excursions when they start are much the same. Anyway, on the Mariposa Belle everybody went running up and down all over the boat with deck chairs and camp stools and baskets, and found places, splendid places to sit, and then got scared that there might be better ones and chased off again. People hunted for places out of the sun and when they got them swore that they weren't going to freeze to please anybody; and the people in the sun said that they hadn't paid fifty cents to be roasted. Others said that they hadn't paid fifty cents to get covered with cinders, and there were still others who hadn't paid fifty cents to get shaken to death with the propeller.

Still, it was all right presently. The people seemed to get sorted out into the places on the boat where they belonged. The women, the older ones, all gravitated into the cabin on the lower deck and by getting round the table with needlework, and with all the windows shut, they soon had it, as they said themselves, just like being at home.

All the young boys and the toughs and the men in the band got down on the lower deck forward, where the boat was dirtiest and where the anchor was and the coils of rope.

And upstairs on the after deck there were Lilian Drone and Miss Lawson, the high school teacher, with a book of German poetry,—Gothey I think it was,—and the bank teller and the younger men.

In the centre, standing beside the rail, were Dean Drone and Dr. Gallagher, looking through binocular glasses at the shore.

Up in front on the little deck forward of the pilot house was a group of the older men, Mullins and Duff and Mr. Smith in a deck chair, and beside him Mr. Golgotha Gingham, the undertaker of Mariposa, on a stool. It was part of Mr. Gingham's principles to take in an outing of this sort, a business matter, more or less,—for you never know what may happen at these water parties. At any rate, he was there in a neat suit of black, not, of course, his heavier or professional suit, but a soft clinging effect as of burnt paper that combined gaiety and decorum to a nicety.

"Yes," said Mr. Gingham, waving his black glove in a general way towards the shore, "I know the lake well, very well. I've been pretty much all over it in my time."

"Canoeing?" asked somebody.

"No," said Mr. Gingham, "not in a canoe." There seemed a peculiar and quiet meaning in his tone.

"Sailing, I suppose," said somebody else.

"No," said Mr. Gingham. "I don't understand it."

"I never knowed that you went on to the water at all, Gol," said Mr. Smith, breaking in.

"Ah, not now," explained Mr. Gingham; "it was years ago, the first summer I came to Mariposa. I was on the water practically all day. Nothing like it to give a man an appetite and keep him in shape."

"Was you camping?" asked Mr. Smith.

"We camped at night," assented the undertaker, "but we put in practically the whole day on the water. You see we were after a party that had come up here from the city on his vacation and gone out in a sailing canoe. We were dragging. We were up every morning at sunrise, lit a fire on the beach and cooked breakfast, and then we'd light our pipes and be off with the net for a whole day. It's a great life," concluded Mr. Gingham wistfully.

"Did you get him?" asked two or three together.

There was a pause before Mr. Gingham answered.

"We did," he said,— "down in the reeds past Horseshoe Point. But it was no use. He turned blue on me right away."

After which Mr. Gingham fell into such a deep reverie that the boat had steamed another half-mile down the lake before anybody broke the silence again.

Talk of this sort,—and after all what more suitable for a day on the water?—beguiled the way.

Down the lake, mile by mile over the calm water, steamed the Mariposa Belle. They passed Poplar Point where the high sandbanks are with all the swallows' nests in them, and Dean Drone and Dr. Gallagher looked at them alternately through the binocular glasses, and it was wonderful how plainly one could see the swallows and the banks and the shrubs,—just as plainly as with the naked eye.

And a little further down they passed the Shingle Beach, and Dr. Gallagher, who knew Canadian history, said to Dean Drone that it was strange to think that Champlain had landed there with his French explorers three hundred years ago; and Dean Drone, who didn't know Canadian history, said it was stranger still to think that the hand of the Almighty had piled up the hills and rocks long before that; and Dr. Gallagher said it was wonderful how the French had found their way through such a pathless wilderness; and Dean Drone said that it was wonderful also to think that the Almighty had placed even the smallest shrub in its appointed place. Dr. Gallagher said it filled him with admiration. Dean Drone said it filled him with awe. Dr. Gallagher said he'd been full of it ever since he was a boy; and Dean Drone said so had he.

Then a little further, as the Mariposa Belle steamed on down the lake, they passed the Old Indian Portage where the great grey rocks are; and Dr. Gallagher drew Dean Drone's attention to the place where the narrow canoe track wound up from the shore to the woods, and Dean Drone said he could see it perfectly well without the glasses.

Dr. Gallagher said that it was just here that a party of five hundred French had made their way with all their baggage and accoutrements across the rocks of the divide and down to the Great Bay. And Dean Drone said that it reminded him of Xenophon leading his ten thousand Greeks over the hill passes of Armenia down to the sea. Dr. Gallagher said that he had often wished he could have seen and spoken to Champlain, and Dean Drone said how much he regretted to have never known Xenophon.

And then after that they fell to talking of relics and traces of the past, and Dr. Gallagher said that if Dean Drone would come round to his house some night he would show him some Indian arrow heads that he had dug up in his garden. And Dean Drone said that if Dr. Gallagher would come round to the rectory any afternoon he would show him a map of Xerxes' invasion of Greece. Only he must come some time between the Infant Class and the Mothers' Auxiliary.

So presently they both knew that they were blocked out of one another's houses for some time to come, and Dr. Gallagher walked forward and told Mr. Smith, who had never studied Greek, about Champlain crossing the rock divide.

Mr. Smith turned his head and looked at the divide for half a second and then said he had crossed a worse one up north back of the Wahnipitae and that the flies were Hades,—and then went on playing freezeout poker with the two juniors in Duff's bank.

So Dr. Gallagher realized that that's always the way when you try to tell people things, and that as far as gratitude and appreciation goes one might as well never read books or travel anywhere or do anything.

In fact, it was at this very moment that he made up his mind to give the arrows to the Mariposa Mechanics' Institute,—they afterwards became, as you know, the Gallagher Collection. But, for the time being, the doctor was sick of them and wandered off round the boat and watched Henry Mullins showing George Duff how to make a John Collins without lemons, and finally went and sat down among the Mariposa band and wished that he hadn't come.

So the boat steamed on and the sun rose higher and higher, and the freshness of the morning changed into the full glare of noon, and they went on to where the lake began to narrow in at its foot, just where the Indian's Island is,—all grass and trees and with a log wharf running into the water. Below it the Lower Ossawippi runs out of the lake, and quite near are the rapids, and you can see down among the trees the red brick of the power house and hear the roar of the leaping water.

The Indian's Island itself is all covered with trees and tangled vines, and the water about it is so still that it's all reflected double and looks the same either way up. Then when the steamer's whistle blows as it comes into the wharf, you hear it echo among the trees of the island, and reverberate back from the shores of the lake.

The scene is all so quiet and still and unbroken, that Miss Cleghorn,—the sallow girl in the telephone exchange, that I spoke of—said she'd like to be buried there. But all the people were so busy getting their baskets and gathering up their things that no one had time to attend to it.

I mustn't even try to describe the landing and the boat crunching against the wooden wharf and all the people running to the same side of the deck and Christie Johnson calling out to the crowd to keep to the starboard and nobody being able to find it. Everyone who has been on a Mariposa excursion knows all about that.

Nor can I describe the day itself and the picnic under the trees. There were speeches afterwards, and Judge Pepperleigh gave such offence by bringing in Conservative politics that a man called Patriotus Canadiensis wrote and asked for some of the invaluable space of the Mariposa Times-Herald and exposed it.

I should say that there were races too, on the grass on the open side of the island, graded mostly according to ages,—races for boys under thirteen and girls over nineteen and all that sort of thing. Sports are generally conducted on that plan in Mariposa. It is realized that a woman of sixty has an unfair advantage over a mere child.

Dean Drone managed the races and decided the ages and gave out the prizes; the Wesleyan minister helped, and he and the young student, who was relieving in the Presbyterian Church, held the string at the winning point.

They had to get mostly clergymen for the races because all the men had wandered off, somehow, to where they were drinking lager beer out of two kegs stuck on pine logs among the trees.

But if you've ever been on a Mariposa excursion you know all about these details anyway.

So the day wore on and presently the sun came through the trees on a slant and the steamer whistle blew with a great puff of white steam and all the people came straggling down to the wharf and pretty soon the Mariposa Belle had floated out on to the lake again and headed for the town, twenty miles away.

I suppose you have often noticed the contrast there is between an excursion on its way out in the morning and what it looks like on the way home.

In the morning everybody is so restless and animated and moves to and fro all over the boat and asks questions. But coming home, as the afternoon gets later and later and the sun sinks beyond the hills, all the people seem to get so still and quiet and drowsy.

So it was with the people on the Mariposa Belle. They sat there on the benches and the deck chairs in little clusters, and listened to the regular beat of the propeller and almost dozed off asleep as they sat. Then when the sun set and the dusk drew on, it grew almost dark on the deck and so still that you could hardly tell there was anyone on board.

And if you had looked at the steamer from the shore or from one of the islands, you'd have seen the row of lights from the cabin windows shining on the water and the red glare of the burning hemlock from the funnel, and you'd have heard the soft thud of the propeller miles away over the lake.

Now and then, too, you could have heard them singing on the steamer,—the voices of the girls and the men blended into unison by the distance, rising and falling in long-drawn melody: "*O—Can-a-da—O—Can-a-da.*"

You may talk as you will about the intoning choirs of your European cathedrals, but the sound of "O Can-a-da," borne across the waters of a silent lake at evening is good enough for those of us who know Mariposa.

I think that it was just as they were singing like this: "*O—Can-a-da,*" that word went round that the boat was sinking.

If you have ever been in any sudden emergency on the water, you will understand the strange psychology of it,—the way in which what is happening seems to become known all in a moment without a word being said. The news is transmitted from one to the other by some mysterious process.

At any rate, on the Mariposa Belle first one and then the other heard that the steamer was sinking. As far as I could ever learn the first of it was that George Duff, the bank manager, came very quietly to Dr. Gallagher and asked him if he thought that the boat was sinking. The doctor said no, that he had thought so earlier in the day but that he didn't now think that she was.

After that Duff, according to his own account, had said to Macartney, the lawyer, that the boat was sinking, and Macartney said that he doubted it very much.

Then somebody came to Judge Pepperleigh and woke him up and said that there was six inches of water in the steamer and that she was sinking. And Pepperleigh said it was perfect scandal and passed the news on to his wife and she said that they had no business to allow it and that if the steamer sank that was the last excursion she'd go on.

So the news went all round the boat and everywhere the people gathered in groups and talked about it in the angry and excited way that people have when a steamer is sinking on one of the lakes like Lake Wissanotti.

Dean Drone, of course, and some others were quieter about it, and said that one must make allowances and that naturally there were two sides to everything. But most of them wouldn't listen to reason at all. I think, perhaps, that some of them were frightened. You see the last time but one that the steamer had sunk, there had been a man drowned and it made them nervous.

What? Hadn't I explained about the depth of Lake Wissanotti? I had taken it for granted that you knew; and in any case parts of it are deep enough, though I don't suppose in this stretch of it from the big reed beds up to within a mile of the town wharf, you could find six feet of water in it if you tried. Oh, pshaw! I was not talking about a steamer sinking in the ocean and carrying down its screaming crowds of people into the hideous depths of green water. Oh, dear me, no! That kind of thing never happens on Lake Wissanotti.

But what does happen is that the Mariposa Belle sinks every now and then, and sticks there on the bottom till they get things straightened up.

On the lakes round Mariposa, if a person arrives late anywhere and explains that the steamer sank, everybody understands the situation.

You see when Harland and Wolff built the Mariposa Belle, they left some cracks in between the timbers that you fill up with cotton waste every Sunday. If this is not attended to, the boat sinks. In fact, it is part of the law of the province that all the steamers like the Mariposa Belle must be properly corked,—I think that is the word,—every season. There are inspectors who visit all the hotels in the province to see that it is done.

So you can imagine now that I've explained it a little straighter, the indignation of the people when they knew that the boat had come uncorked and that they might be stuck out there on a shoal or a mud-bank half the night.

I don't say either that there wasn't any danger; anyway, it doesn't feel very safe when you realise that the boat is settling down with every hundred yards that she goes, and you look over the side and see only the black water in the gathering night.

Safe! I'm not sure now that I come to think of it that it isn't worse than sinking in the Atlantic. After all, in the Atlantic there is wireless telegraphy, and a lot of trained sailors and stewards. But out on Lake Wissanotti,—far out, so that you can only just see the lights of the town away off to the south,—when the propeller comes to a stop,—and you can hear the hiss of steam as they start to rake out the engine fires to prevent an explosion,—and when you turn from the red glare that comes from the furnace doors as they open them, to the black dark that is gathering over the lake,—and there's a night wind beginning to run among the rushes,—and you see the men going forward to the roof of the pilot house to send up the rockets to rouse the town,—safe? Safe yourself, if you like; as for me, let me once get back into Mariposa again, under the night shadow of the maple trees, and this shall be the last, last time I'll go on Lake Wissanotti.

Safe! Oh yes! Isn't it strange how safe other people's adventures seem after they happen. But you'd have been scared, too, if you'd been there just before the steamer sank, and seen them bringing up all the women on to the top deck.

I don't see how some of the people took it so calmly; how Mr. Smith, for instance, could have gone on smoking and telling how he'd had a steamer "sink on him" on Lake Nipissing and a still bigger one, a side-wheeler, sink on him in Lake Abbitibbi.

Then, quite suddenly, with a quiver, down she went. You could feel the boat sink, sink,—down, down,—would it never get to the bottom? The water came flush up to the lower deck, and then—thank heaven,—the sinking stopped and there was the Mariposa Belle safe and tight on a reed bank.

Really, it made one positively laugh! It seemed so queer and, anyway, if a man has a sort of natural courage, danger makes him laugh. Danger? pshaw! fiddlesticks! everybody scouted the idea. Why, it is just the little things like this that give zest to a day on the water.

Within half a minute they were all running round looking for sandwiches and cracking jokes and talking of making coffee over the remains of the engine fires.

I don't need to tell at length how it all happened after that.

I suppose the people on the Mariposa Belle would have had to settle down there all night or till help came from the town, but some of the men who had gone forward and were peering out into the dark said that it couldn't be more than a mile across the water to Miller's Point. You could almost see it over there to the left,—some of them, I think, said "off on the port bow," because you know when you get mixed up in these marine disasters, you soon catch the atmosphere of the thing.

So pretty soon they had the davits swung out over the side and were lowering the old lifeboat from the top deck into the water.

There were men leaning out over the rail of the Mariposa Belle with lanterns that threw the light as they let her down, and the glare fell on the water and the reeds. But when they got the boat lowered, it looked such a frail, clumsy thing as one saw it from the rail above, that the cry was raised: "Women and children first!" For what was the sense, if it should turn out that the boat wouldn't even hold women and children, of trying to jam a lot of heavy men into it?

So they put in mostly women and children and the boat pushed out into the darkness so freighted down it would hardly float.

In the bow of it was the Presbyterian student who was relieving the minister, and he called out that they were in the hands of Providence. But he was crouched and ready to spring out of them at the first moment.

So the boat went and was lost in the darkness except for the lantern in the bow that you could see bobbing on the water. Then presently it came back and they sent another load, till pretty soon the decks began to thin out and everybody got impatient to be gone.

It was about the time that the third boat-load put off that Mr. Smith took a bet with Mullins for twenty-five dollars, that he'd be home in Mariposa before the people in the boats had walked round the shore.

No one knew just what he meant, but pretty soon they saw Mr. Smith disappear down below into the lowest part of the steamer with a mallet in one hand and a big bundle of marline in the other.

They might have wondered more about it, but it was just at this time that they heard the shouts from the rescue boat—the big Mackinaw lifeboat—that had put out from the town with fourteen men at the sweeps, when they saw the first rockets go up.

I suppose there is always something inspiring about a rescue at sea, or on the water.

After all, the bravery of the lifeboat man is the true bravery,—expended to save life, not to destroy it.

Certainly they told for months after of how the rescue boat came out to the Mariposa Belle.

I suppose that when they put her in the water the lifeboat touched it for the first time since the old Macdonald Government placed her on Lake Wissanotti.

Anyway, the water poured in at every seam. But not for a moment,—even with two miles of water between them and the steamer,—did the rowers pause for that.

By the time they were half-way there the water was almost up to the thwarts, but they drove her on. Panting and exhausted (for mind you, if you haven't been in a fool boat like that for years, rowing takes it out of you), the rowers stuck to their task. They threw the ballast over and chucked into the water the heavy cork jackets and lifebelts that encumbered their movements. There was no thought of turning back. They were nearer to the steamer than the shore.

"Hang to it, boys," called the crowd from the steamer's deck, and hang they did.

They were almost exhausted when they got them; men leaning from the steamer threw them ropes and one by one every man was hauled aboard just as the lifeboat sank under their feet.

Saved! by Heaven, saved, by one of the smartest pieces of rescue work ever seen on the lake.

There's no use describing it; you need to see rescue work of this kind by lifeboats to understand it.

Nor were the lifeboat crew the only ones that distinguished themselves.

Boat after boat and canoe after canoe had put out from Mariposa to the help of the steamer. They got them all.

Pupkin, the other bank teller, with a face like a horse, who hadn't gone on the excursion,—as soon as he knew that the boat was signalling for help and that Miss Lawson was sending up rockets,—rushed for a row boat, grabbed an oar (two would have hampered him), and paddled madly out into the lake. He struck right out into the dark with the crazy skiff almost sinking beneath his feet. But they got him. They rescued him. They watched him, almost dead with exhaustion, make his way to the steamer, where he was hauled up with ropes. Saved! Saved!!

They might have gone on that way half the night, picking up the rescuers, only, at the very moment when the tenth load of people left for the shore,—just as suddenly and saucily as you please, up came the Mariposa Belle from the mud bottom and floated.

FLOATED?

Why, of course she did. If you take a hundred and fifty people off a steamer that has sunk, and if you get a man as shrewd as Mr. Smith to plug the timber seams with mallet and marline, and if you turn ten bandsmen of the Mariposa band on to your hand pump on the bow of the lower decks—float? why, what else can she do?

Then, if you stuff in hemlock into the embers of the fire that you were raking out, till it hums and crackles under the boiler, it won't be long before you hear the propeller thud-thudding at the stern again, and before the long roar of the steam whistle echoes over to the town.

And so the Mariposa Belle, with all steam up again and with the long train of sparks careering from the funnel, is heading for the town.

But no Christie Johnson at the wheel in the pilot house this time.

"Smith! Get Smith!" is the cry.

Can he take her in? Well, now! Ask a man who has had steamers sink on him in half the lakes from Temiscaming to the Bay, if he can take her in? Ask a man who has run a York boat down the rapids of the Moose when the ice is moving, if he can grip the steering wheel of the Mariposa Belle? So there she steams safe and sound to the town wharf!

Look at the lights and the crowd! If only the federal census taker could count us now! Hear them calling and shouting back and forward from the deck to the shore! Listen! There is the rattle of the shore ropes as they get them ready, and there's the Mariposa band,—actually forming in a circle on the upper deck just as she docks, and the leader with his baton,—one—two—ready now,—

"O CAN-A-DA!"

a bit of all {
- sensationalist gothic tale
- ghost story / gothic tale
- historical story
}

effective evocation of the dangers of the wilderness

<u>Gothic lit</u> — location based
— sensational lit.
"The Monk" so over the top.
— power of nature — to show that human nature has the ability to be powerless.

- The indian represents an ironic portrait of the Indian Guide.
  - inversion of the white man in the wilderness story
  - gothic danger

Marjorie Pickthall (1883-1922)

Born in England, Pickthall was educated at Bishop Strachan School in Toronto and became an assistant librarian at Victoria College at the University of Toronto. Precociously successful, she published her first poems at the age of sixteen.

Pickthall's poetry was celebrated during her lifetime for its use of mythological subjects, but her stories unabashedly catered to the public taste for daring tales of adventure. "The Third Generation" takes place in the ideologically charged 'contact zone' of civilization and indigenous culture. It appeared originally in *The Bellman* 25 (December 14, 1918) 659-62; this version is taken from the posthumous collection, *Angels' Shoes* (London: Hodder and Stoughton, 1923).

The Third Generation

No shanty fires shall cheer them,
No comrades march beside,
But the northern lights shall beckon
And the wandering winds shall guide.
They shall cross the silent waters
By a trail that is wild and far,
To the place of the lonely lodges
Under a lonely star.
La Longue Traverse.

"Bob, is this Lake Lemaire?"

Bob Lemaire, leaning against a wind-twisted tamarack on the ridge above the portage, looked long and very long at the desolate country spread out beneath them. Then he looked at a map, drawn on parchment in faded ink, which he had just unfolded from a waterproof case. "I can't identify it," he confessed at last, "but I think—"

"If you say another word," groaned Barrett, "about the reliability of your grandfather, I —I'll heave rocks at you." Lemaire smiled slowly, and the smile transfigured his lean, serious face; he folded the map and replaced it in the little case. "Well," he answered, comfortingly, "we can't mistake

P'tite Babiche, anyway, when we come to it."

"If the thing exists... Oh, I know your grandfather said he found it, and stuck it on his map. But no one else has ever found it since."

"No one else," said Lemaire, quietly, "has been so far west from the Gran' Babiche."

He looked again at the land, one of the most desolate in the world, across which they must go. Lake, rapid, river; rock, scrub, pine, and caribou moss—here the world held only these things, repeated to infinity. But as Lemaire's grave eyes rested on them, those eyes showed nothing but stillness and a strange content. And Barrett, who had been watching his friend and not the new chain of lakes ahead, cried suddenly, "Bob, I believe you like it!"

"Yes, I like it—if like is the word."

"O gosh! And you never saw it till five years ago?"

"No."

"And your father never saw it at all?"

"No. He married young, you know, and had no money. He worked in an office all his life. My mother said he used to talk in his sleep of—all this—which he had never seen. And when I saw it, it just seemed to—come natural." He smiled again. "We've three—four—more portages," he went on, "before we camp."

"And it's along of having Forbes Lemaire for a grandfather," groaned Barrett, as he limped after Lemaire's light stride, down the rocky slope to the little beach where they had left their canoe.

They launched the canoe, thigh deep in the rush of the ice-clear water, and put out into yet another of that endless chain of unknown and uncharted lakes whose course they were following. Only one map in the world showed these lakes, those low iron hills, that swamp–the map made by Bob Lemaire's grandfather fifty years before; as far as was known, only one white man before themselves had ever tried the journey from the Gran' Babiche due west to the P'tite Babiche, that mythical river, and that had been Forbes Lemaire. As Barrett said, it was a tour personally conducted by the ghost of a grandfather.

The Third Generation

Another wet portage—tripping and sliding under a low cliff among fallen shale and willow bushes—another lake, as wide, as lonely, as the former one. So for three hours. And then the afternoon shut down in drive on drive of damp gray mist; and they edged the canoe inshore, and beached it at last upon a dun ridge of sand, the shadows of dwarfed bullpines promising firing.

Too tired to speak, they made their camp, deftly, as long practice had taught them. Tinned beef, flapjacks and coffee had power, however, to change the very aspect of the weather. And Barrett, smoking the pipe of repletion, under a wisp of tent, had time to admire the Japanese effect of the writhed pines in the fog, to hear a sort of wild music in the voices of rain and water, and to meditate on the chances of an ouananiche for the morning's meal.

The shadows of the fog were changing to the shadows of night, and the silent Lemaire rose and flung wood on the fire. It sent out a warm glow; and as if it had been a signal, a living shadow crept from the shadow of the rocks, and very timidly approached the light.

Both men rose with an exclamation; for they had not seen a human being for nearly a month. Barrett said, "An Indian," and sank back on his blanket, leaving Lemaire to ask questions. Lemaire went round the fire, and stooped over the queer huddled shadow on the ground.

"Well?" Barrett called after him at last.

"A Montagnais," Lemaire answered after a pause, some trouble in his voice. "About the oldest old Indian I've ever seen; they aren't long-lived.... He seems a bit wrong in the head. He doesn't seem to know his name or where he comes from. But— he says he's going to a big encampment many day's journey west. He says he's been following us. He says he's a friend of mine."

"Is he?"

"I never saw him before... That's all I can get out of him. He's probably been cast off by his tribe. Why? Oh, too old to be useful."

"Cruel brutes."

"Not so cruel as some white men," said Lemaire, half to himself. He had come back to the firelight, and was rummaging among their stores, none too plentiful. He returned to the old Indian, carrying food; and presently Barrett heard snapping sounds, as of a hungry dog feeding. Lemaire came again to his nook under the tent; and Barrett smoked out his pipe in silence. Then, as he knocked the ashes, fizzling, into a little pool of rain, he said gently, "Bob, what makes you so uncommonly good to the Indians?"

Quiet Lemaire did not attempt to evade the direct question. But a rather shy flush rose to his dark, lean cheeks as he said diffidently, "I suppose—because I feel my family—any one of my name—owes 'em something."

"The grandfather again, eh?"

"Yes... Men had no souls in those days, Barrett. I think the tremendous loneliness—the newness—the lack of responsibility—something killed their souls.... Wait."

Leaning forward, he flung more wood on the fire. And the red light flickered on his strong and gentle face. He glanced at his friend, and went on abruptly. "I've my grandfather's maps and journals, you know—what my father called the shameful records of his fame. He was absolutely explicit in 'em. I never saw them in father's lifetime, but he left them to me, saying I could read them or not, as I liked. I was very proud of them. I read them. And upon my word—though from them I got the hints that may lead us to the rediscovery of the Lost Babiche—I'm almost sorry I did. It leaves a bad taste in the mind, if you know what I mean, to think that one's father's father was such a heroic scoundrel."

"A bad record, Bobby?"

"Bad even for those days. Listen to me. While he was on this very expedition we're on now, he was taken sick. He was very sick, and going to be worse. He knew what it was. He was near the big summer camp of a tribe of Indians that had been very kind to him, coast Indians, come inland for the caribou hunting; he went to them. He was sick, and they took him in, and nursed him. And all the time he knew what it was he had. It was the smallpox.

"You know what La Picotte is in the wilds. They've a song about it still, down along the Lamennais... For of all that tribe, only one family, they say, escaped. All the others died; they died as if the Angel of Destruction had come among them with his sword— they died like flies, they died in heaps. And over the bones of the dead the tepees stood for years, ragged, blowing in the winds. And then the skins rotted, and the bare poles stood, gleaming white, over the rotting bones that covered an acre of ground, they say. No one ever went to that place any more. It was cursed... because of my grandfather."

"Monsieur Forbes made his get-away?"

"Yes, or I shouldn't be telling you about it." Lemaire summoned a smile, but his eyes were sombre. "And so I guess— that's one reason why. One among many."

"You're a likeable old freak," murmured Barrett affectionately, "but—*you* ain't responsible, you know!"

"As I look at it, we're all responsible."

"Well—anyway, I wouldn't give that old scarecrow too much of our grubstake, old man. We've none too much, if the Babiche doesn't turn up according to schedule."

"Probably we won't see any more of him. He'll be gone by the morning."

He was gone with the morning. But as day followed weary day, and there was still no sign of the lakes narrowing to the long-sought river, Barrett was increasingly conscious that the old man was close upon their trail. Sometimes, in the brief radiance of the September dawns, he would see, far and far behind on the wrinkled silver water, a warped canoe paddling feebly. They always hauled away, by miles, from that decrepit canoe. But always, some time in the dark hours, it crept up again. Sometimes, he would see, in the sunset, a wavering thread of smoke arising from the site of their last-camp-but-one. It irritated him at last; the thought of that ragged, cranky canoe, paddled by the ragged, dirty, old imbecile, forever following them—creeping, creeping, under the great gaunt stars, creeping, creeping, under the flying dawns, the stormy moons; when he found Lemaire leaving little scraps of precious tobacco, a pinch of flour in a screw of paper, or a fresh-caught fish beside the trodden ashes of their cooking-place, he exploded.

"I can't help it," Lemaire apologized, "I *know* I'm all kinds of a fool, Barrett. But the poor old wretch is nearly blind—from long-ago smallpox, I should think. He can't catch things for himself much."

Barrett, aware that wisdom was on his side, yet felt sorry for his explosion. He said nothing more. Soon he forgot the matter, having much else to think about.

For the Lost Babiche, the once-discovered river, did not "turn up according to schedule." The chain of lakes they had been following turned due south. They left them, and, after a terrible portage, launched the canoe in a stream that ran west. Here their progress was very slow, for there were rapids, and consequent portages, every mile or so. This stream, instead of feeding another lake, died out in impassable quaking mosses. They saw a range of low hills some four or five miles ahead; so again they left the canoe and struck out for them on foot, half-wading, half-walking. It was exhausting work. At last they climbed the barren spurs and saw beyond, under a flaring yellow sunset, a world of interlacing waterways, unvisited and unknown, that seemed then as if they smoked under the vast clouds and spirals of wildfowl settling homeward to the reeds. The two men watched that wonderful sight in silence.

At last, "They're gathering to go south," said Lemaire briefly. And Barrett answered, "D'you know what date it is? It's the day on which we said we'd turn back if we hadn't found the Lost Babiche. It's the fifteenth of September."

"Well... are we going back?"

"Not until we've found our river," cried Barrett, with half a laugh and half a curse. They gripped hands, smiling rather grimly. They made a miserable, fireless camp, and went back the next day, carrying canoe and supplies, in four toilsome trips, across the hills; repacking and relaunching the second day on a new lake, where in all probability no white man—but one—had ever before dipped paddle.

They had been in the wilderness so long that they had fallen into the habit of carrying on conversations as if the lapse of two or three days had been as many minutes. Barrett knew to what Lemaire referred when he said abruptly, "After all, it isn't as if you were ignorant of the risks."

"I guess I know just as much about them as you," said Barrett, cheerily. "We're taking chances on the grub, aren't we? If we find the Lost Babiche before the game moves, we'll be alright, though our own supplies won't take us there. Once there, Bob, we're pretty sure to find friendly Indians when we link up with the Silver Fork—which we do seventy miles down the P'tit Babiche if your grandpa's map's correct. Well there are a good many 'ifs' in the programme, but don't you worry. We'll get through or out, somehow. There's always fish. I've a feeling that this country *can't* go back on a Lemaire!"

They went on to a pleasant camp that night on a sandy islet overgrown with dwarf willow, and a wild-duck supper. The current of these new lakes went west with such increasing strength that Lemaire thought they were feeling the "pull" of some big river into which the system drained; and if so, it could be no river but the lost Babiche. They slept, all a-tingle with the fever of discovery and re-made maps in their dreams.

Behind them many miles, a wandering smoke arose from the ashes of their last camp. The old Indian, about whom they had almost forgotten, had gained on them while they packed their supplies over the hills. Now he was close upon them again.

The life of that old savage seemed thin and wavering as the smoke of the fire he made. All night he sat in the ashes, motionless as a stone. Only once, just before the fierce dawn, he rose to his feet with an inarticulate cry, stirred to some instinctive excitement. For in a moment the vast, chill dusk was filled with a musical thrill, a tremendous clamour and rush of life, as thousand by thousand after their kinds, teal and widgeon, mallard and sheldrake, lifted from the reeds and fled before the coming cold. As the old man dimly watched, two delicate things fell and touched his face; one was a feather, the second was a flake of snow.

In those few delicate flakes, Lemaire and Barrett seemed to feel for the first time the ever-present hostility of nature; with such a brief, exquisite touch were they first made aware of the powers against which they strove. The new waterways seemed to stretch interminably. Each time they cleared one of the deep-cut channels which linked lake with lake as regularly as a thread links beads, they looked ahead with the same question. Each time they saw the same expanse of gray water, low islets, barren shores; the country passed them changing and unchanging as a dream. They seemed to be moving in a dream, conscious of nothing but the pressure of the current on their paddles.

Then came the mist.

It shut them into a circle ten feet wide, a pearl-white prison. Outside the circle were shadows, wandering voices, trees as men walking. For two days they felt their way westward through this fog; two nights they shivered over a damp-wood fire, hearing nothing but water beading and dripping everywhere with a sound of grief. It strangely broke Lemaire's steel nerve. On the second night he said, restlessly, "We must turn back to-morrow."

"Bob!"

He flung out a tanned hand passionately. "I know.... But can't you feel it? Things have turned against us. These things." He pointed at the veiled sky, the milky water. "I daren't go on. If we don't find the river tomorrow, we'll go back. And then... the land will have done for me what it never did for my grandfather."

"What, Bob, old fellow?"

"Beaten me," said Lemaire, and rolled into his blankets without another word.

He woke next morning with the touch of clear sunlight on his eyelids. He leaped to his feet silently, without waking Barrett, and as he did so, ice broke and tinkled like glass where the edge of the blankets had lain in a little pool of moisture. The last of the fog was draining in golden smoke from the low, dark hills. He strode to the edge of the water, and stopped, shaking suddenly as if he were cold. Then he went to Barrett, and stooped over him.

"Hullo, Bob is it morning?" Then, as he saw Lemaire's face, "My God what is it?"

Twice Lemaire tried to speak. Then he pointed eastward to three high rocky islands which lay across the water, exactly spaced, like the ruined spans of a great bridge which once had stretched from shore to shore.

"Barrett," he said huskily, "We entered the Lost Babiche yesterday in the fog, and never knew. Those islands are ten miles down the river on Forbes Lemaire's map."

They faced each other in silence, too much moved to speak. Their hands met in a long grip. Then Barrett said suddenly, "Anything else."

"Yes. It's freezing hard."

"But... we've won, Bob, we've won!"

"Not yet," said the man whose fathers had been bred in the wilderness, and wed to it. "Not yet. It's still against us."

But there was no talk now of turning back.

The Lost Babiche—lost no more—was a noble river; a gray and ice-clear stream winding in generous curves between high cliffs of slate-coloured rock. These cliffs were much cut into ravines and gullies, where grew timber of fine size for that country. But as their tense excitement lessened a little, they were struck by the absence of all life; even in the deep rock-shadows they saw no fish. Of human life there was not a sign; though in Forbes Lemaire's days the country had supported many Indians. And now— "Not a soul but ourselves," said Barrett, in an awed voice; "not a living soul..."

Yes. One soul yet living. Far behind them, in the staggering old canoe, the old Indian paddled valiantly on their trail. But he had forgotten them now, as they had long forgotten him. He stopped no more for the offal of their camps. A stronger instinct even than that of hunger was drawing him on the way they also went; down the Lost Babiche. Had they looked, they would not have seen him. And soon, between him and them, the clouds which had been gathering all day dropped a curtain of fine snow.

The first sting of the tiny balled flakes on his knuckles was to Lemaire like the thunder of guns, the opening of a battle.

He had no need to speak to Barrett. They bent over the paddles and the canoe surged forward. It was a race; a race between the early winter and themselves. If the cold weather set in so soon, if they found no Indians on the little-known Silver

Fork—there were a dozen "ifs" in their minds as, mile after mile, they fled down the P'tite Babiche. Even as they fled from the winter, so that other white man long ago had fled from the sickness; seen those stark bluffs unrolling; viewed perhaps those very trees.

They made a record distance that day. "We're winning, Bob, we're winning," said Barrett over the fire that night. Lemaire had not the heart to contradict him; but Lemaire's instincts, inherited from generations, told him that the wilderness was still mysteriously their enemy. He sat smoking, silent, hearing nothing but the faint, innumerable hiss of the snowflakes falling into the flames.

The snow was thickening in the morning, and by noon a bitter wind arose, blowing in their faces and against the stream. Soon the canoe was smack-smack-smacking on the waves, and the snow was driving almost level. The continual pressure of wind and snow drugged their senses. They never heard the voice of the rapids until, rounding an abrupt bend, the ravelled water seemed to leap at them from under the very bow of the canoe.

There was only one thing to be done, and— "Let her go!" yelled Lemaire, crouching tense as a spring above the steering paddle.

Now for the trained eye, the strong hand—the eye to see the momentary chance, the hand to obey without a falter.

Now for the sleeping instincts of a brain inherited from far generations of wanderers and voyageurs. Flash on flash of leaping water, the drive of spray and snow, the canoe staggering and checking like a thing hurt, but always recovering.

Barrett, in the bows, paddled blindly. His life lay in Bob Lemaire's hands, and he was content to leave it there during those roaring moments. But those hands failed—by an inch.

They were in smooth water. Barrett would have paused to take breath, but Lemaire's voice barked at him from the stern. He obeyed. The canoe drove forward again—forward in great leaps, towards the point of a small island ahead, dimly seen through the snow—something wrong, though, thought Barrett, grunting; he could get no "beef" on the thing—it dragged; you'd have thought Bob was paddling against him.

Then, suddenly, he understood. He called up the last of his strength, drove the paddle in, once, twice—again—heard a shout, flung himself overside into water waist-deep, and just as the canoe was sinking under them, he and Lemaire caught it and ran it ashore. Then, dripping, they looked each other in the face, and each seemed to see the face of disaster.

"It was a rock," said Lemaire at last, very quietly, "a few inches below the surface. It has almost cut the canoe in two."

"What's to be done?"

"Find shelter, I suppose."

They were very quiet about it. There was no shelter on their islet but a few rocks and a dead spruce in the middle. Here they set up their tent as a wind-break. It was bitterly cold; the island was sheathed with white ice, for the spray from the rough water froze now as it fell; everything in the canoe was wet; they were wet to their waists. They tried to induce the dead tree to burn, but the wood was so rotted with wet it only smouldered and went out. They had a little cooking-lamp and a few squares of compressed fuel for it; they lighted this, and Lemaire made tea with numbed hands. It renewed the life in them, but could not dry them. They huddled against the little lamp in silence, waiting—waiting.

After some time Lemaire heard a curious sound from Barrett; his teeth were chattering. Lemaire saw that his face had taken a waxy white hue. He spoke to him, and Barrett looked up, but his eyes were dim and glazed. "It'll be all right," he said, thickly, "we'll get through, somehow. I've a feeling that this country can't go back on a Lemaire."

They were the first symptoms of collapse. Lemaire groaned. He got to his feet, and staggered across the slippery rocks. He shook his fist in the implacable face of the desolation. He shouted, foolish rage and defiance, caught back at his sanity; shouted again... This time he thought he heard a faint cry in the snow. It whipped him back to self-control. He splashed out into the curdling shallows, shouting desperately.

Out of the gray drive of snow loomed the ghost of a canoe, paddled, as it seemed, by a ghost. It was the old Indian, whom Lemaire had long forgotten; the weather had not hindered him, the rapids had not wrecked him. At Lemaire's cry he raised his head, and the canoe put inshore, waveringly. Lemaire splashed to meet it, met the incurious gaze of the half-blind old eyes under the scarred lids, and read into the wrinkled, foul old face, a sort of animal kindness.

Five minutes later he was desperately trying to rouse Barrett. Barrett looked at him at last, and Lemaire saw that the brief delirium was past. "What is it, Bob?" he asked, weakly. And Lemaire broke into a torrent of words.

"The old Indian—the old Indian you said was a hoodoo—don't you remember? He's here. He has caught us up, God knows how. He says his canoe'll hold three. He says that a very little way on there's a big camp, and that he'll take us there—in a very little while. He says his tribe is always kind to strangers, to white men.... I can't make out all he says, he's queer in his head. But he's dead sure of the encampment. He says it's always there."

Still talking eagerly, Lemaire snatched together a few things, got an arm round Barrett, lifted him up to his feet, got him reeling to the canoe, laid him in the bottom, and helped the old Indian push off. There was no second paddle. There was no need of it. The current took them at once.

The cold was increasing, as the wind died and the snow thinned. Lemaire ceased to be conscious of the passing of time, but within himself the stubborn life burned; he was strongly curious to know the end, to discover what it was the wilderness had in store for him after five years, to read the riddle of that relationship with himself which had called him from the cities to this.

He was aware, at last, of a vast, golden light. The clouds were parting behind the snow, and the sunset was gleaming through. It turned the snow into a mist of rose and molten gold. The old Indian feebly turned the canoe. It crept toward the shore.

"The lodges of my people," muttered the old Indian. He stood erect, and pointed with his bleached paddle. "They are very many—a very strong tribe."

Lemaire also looked, and saw.

Silently, the canoe took the half-frozen sand. Silently, very slowly, Lemaire stepped out. The old Indian waited for him. It seemed that the whole world was waiting for him.

He, like a man in a dream, moved slowly into the midst of a level stretch of sand, and stood there. All about him, covering the whole level, were the ridgepoles of wigwams, but the coverings had long fallen away and rotted, and the sunset glowed through the gaunt poles. Lemaire stretched out his hand, and touched the nearest; they fell into dust and rot.... Under his feet he crushed the bones of the dead—the dead, who had died fifty years before, and had waited for him here ever since, under the blown sand and the ground willows.... "They've a song about it, down along the Lamennais. For of all that tribe, only one family, they say, escaped. All the others died... they died like flies, they died in heaps. And over the bones of the dead the tepees stood for years.... No one ever went to that place any more. It was cursed... because of my grandfather...."

He went back to the canoe. Whining like an old animal, the old Indian was busied above Barrett. "The lodges of my people," he muttered, "a very strong tribe, and kind to the white men."

Very gently, Lemaire put aside the blind old hands that touched Barrett's unconscious face. "Don't wake him," he said.

Documents

Sara Jeannette Duncan
The Heroine of Old-Time

Has it occurred to nobody, in his struggles to keep abreast of the tide of new activity that sets in fiction, as in every other department of modern thought, to cast one deploring glance over his shoulder at the lovely form of the heroine of old-time, drifting fast and far into oblivion? It would be strange indeed if we did not regret her, this daughter of the lively imagination of a bygone day. By long familiarity, how dear her features grew! Having heard of her blue eyes, with what zestful anticipation we foreknew the golden hair, the rosebud mouth, the faintly flushed, ethereal cheek, and the pink sea-shell that was privileged to do auricular duty in catching the never ceasing murmur of adoration that beat about the feet of the blonde maiden! Wotting of her ebon locks, with what subtle prescience we guessed the dark and flashing optics, the alabaster forehead, the lips curved in fine scorn, the regal height, and the very unapproachable demeanour of the brunette! The fact that these startling differences were purely physical, that the lines of their psychical construction ran sweetly parallel, never interfered with our joyous interest in them as we breathlessly followed their varying fortunes from an auspicious beginning, through harrowing vicissitudes, to a blissful close. So that her ringlets were long enough, and her woes deep enough, and her conduct under them marked by a beautiful resignation and the more becoming forms of grief, it never occurred to us to cavil at the object of Algernon's passion, because her capabilities were strictly limited to making love and Oriental landscapes in Berlin wool. Her very feminine attributes were invariably forthcoming; and if the author by any chance forgot to particularize the sweetness of her disposition, the neatness of her *boudoir*—they all had *boudoirs*—or the twining nature of her affections, we unconsciously supplied the deficiency, and thought no less respectfully of Araminta. She was very wooden, this person for whom gallant youths attained remarkable heights of self-sacrifice, and villains intrigued in vain; her virtues and her faults alike might form part of the intricate and expensive interior of a Paris doll; and we loved her perhaps with the unmeaning love of infancy for its toys. She was the painted pivot of the merry-go-round—it could not possibly revolve, with its exciting episodes, without her; yet her humble presence bore no striking relation to the mimic pageant that went on about her. She vanished with the last page, ceased utterly with the sound of her wedding-bells; and we remembered for a little space, not the maiden, but the duels in her honour, the designs upon her fortune, and the poetic justice that overtook her calumniators.

But extinction in time overtook this amiable damsel. Mere complexion began to be considered an insufficient basis upon which to erect a character worthy of public attention in the capacity of a heroine. So we were introduced to the young creature of "parts"—the parts consisting of an immoderate desire to investigate the wisdom of the ancients, as Plato has expressed it, an insatiable appetite for metaphysical conversation, and a lofty contempt for the frivolities of her sex. To keep the balance between these somewhat laudable peculiarities and proper womanly accomplishments, she was usually invested with a powerful and melodious vocal organ, whose minor notes frequently depressed her frivolous associates of the drawing room to tears, and reduced the hitherto invincible heart of the interesting woman-hater of the volume to instant and abject submission. To preserve the unities, charms of feature and philosophical tendencies being somewhat incompatible, she was given a rather wide mouth, and a forehead too high and thoughtful for beauty's strict requirements; while her dark expressive eyes and straight nose sufficed to secure our regard from an aesthetic standpoint. Then came that daring innovator who gave us a countenance all out of line, with freckles on it, a look of restless intellectuality, and a vague charm that was beyond his power to analyse or ours to conceive. The conduct of this young person was usually characterized by the wildest vagaries. She held communings with herself, which she reluctantly imparted to the interesting youth in whom she recognised her mental superior, and therefore her fate; and the sole end of her existence appeared to be to make his as wretched as possible. The plot, of which this ingenuous maid was the centre, usually turned upon a mood of hers—the various chapters, indeed, were chiefly given over to the elucidation of her moods, and their effect upon her unfortunate admirers.

Just about here, in the development of the heroine, do we begin to see that she is not a fixed quantity in the problem of the novelist, but varies with his day and generation. Araminta was the product of an age that demanded no more of femininity than unlimited affection and embroidery. The advent of the blue-stocking suggested the introduction of brains into her composition, though her personality was not seriously affected by them, as the blue-stocking was but a creature of report in the mind of the story-teller, the feminine intelligence not being popularly cultivated beyond the seminary limit. As dissatisfaction with her opportunities infected the modern young lady, her appearance in fiction with a turned-up nose and freckles, solely relying upon her yearnings after the infinite for popular appreciation, followed as a matter of course.

We are not talking, O captious soul—with a dozen notable heroines of the past at your fingers' ends!—of the great people in the world of fiction, but of the democracy of that populous literary sphere. We are discussing those short-lived Ethels and Irenes who have long since gone over, with their devoted Arthurs and Adolphuses, to that great majority whose fortunes are to be traced only at the second-hand book-stalls now; but whose afflictions formed the solace of many an hour in the dusty seclusion of the garret, while the rain pattered on the roof, and the mice adventured over the floor, and the garments of other days swayed to and fro in dishevelled remembrance of their departed possessors. Ah, Genevieve and Rosabel, Vivien and Belinda, how fare ye now whose yellow-bound vicissitudes were treasured so carefully from the fiery fate that awaited them at the hands of stern authorities diametrically opposed to "light reading!" By what black ingratitude are ye reduced, alas! to the pulp of the base material economy of the age on which, perhaps, the fortunes of damsels less worthy and less fair are typographically set forth for the fickle amusement of later generation!

Hardly less complete is the evanishment of Rosabel and Belinda than that of their successors in fiction, and the time-honoured functions they performed. A novel without a heroine used to be as absurd an idea as the play of Hamlet with Hamlet left out. But the heroine of to-day's fiction is the exception, not the rule. The levelling process the age is undergoing has reduced women with their own knowledge and consent to very much the same plane of thought and action as men. It has also raised them to it, paradoxical though the statement be. The woman of to-day is no longer an exceptional being surrounded by exceptional circumstances. She bears a translatable relation to the world; and the novelists who translate it correctly have ceased to mark it by unduly exalting one woman by virtue of her sex to a position of interest in their books which dwarfs all the other characters. It has been found that successful novels can be written without her. The woman of to-day understands herself, and is understood in her present and possible worth. The novel of to-day is a reflection of our present social state. The women who enter into its composition are but intelligent agents in this reflection and show themselves as they are, not as a false ideal would have them.

The Week, October 28, 1886.

J. Macdonald Oxley
Periodical Literature in Canada

The simple fact of the matter is that Canada possesses no magazine of her own, because she has such an unceasing flood of English and American periodicals poured upon her that any domestic enterprise must infallibly be drowned beneath its waves. So far as my observation enables me to judge, I would hazard the assertion that as many copies of the leading American periodicals are sold in the larger Canadian cities as in cities of corresponding size in the United States. The *North American*

Review, Century, Harper's, Scribner's, Lippincott's, may be had at any first-class book-store, and one or more will be found in every home where there is the least pretension to culture. This being the case, upon what could the domestic magazine build its hopes of success in competing with so many formidable rivals? Upon superiority of contents? That were hardly possible, even though a syndicate of Croesuses should put their purses at its editor's command, for the literary genius of both the Old and New Worlds is already under tribute to supply the "great monthlies," and how would surpassing or even corresponding attractions be secured? Then might the magazine depend upon the loyalty of Canadians to patronize the home product in preference to the imported article? The state of affairs in England does not give much encouragement in this direction, for it may with truth be said that there, at the present time, while the home periodicals sell by thousands, the American monthlies, ay, and weeklies too, go off by the tens of thousands, and if this be the case amongst the most sturdily loyal nation in the world, what may be expected of a people admittedly lacking in true national life and sentiment? The conclusion seems to be inevitable that there are only two ways in which a distinctively Canadian periodical can be established. Either the policy of protection must be extended to it, as it has been with success to the sugar and cotton industries, and outside competition made impracticable, or some one of the millionaires, whose numbers are pleasantly increasing in our midst, shall have to adopt the establishment of a magazine as his form of benefaction in preference to endowing a hospital or founding a college for women. The first method would be suicidal to the intellectual interests of Canada, the second is eminently Utopian; and so the summing up of the whole matter seems to be that there is slight prospect of Canada having a representative national periodical within the near future.

The Week, October 4th, 1888.

Pauline Johnson
A Strong Race Opinion: On the Indian Girl in Modern Fiction

E. Pauline Johnson of The Iroquois Makes Some Remarks – The One Distressful Type – Winona – Her Suicidal Tendency – Mair's "Tecumseh" – "The Algonquin Maiden" – Chance for Writers.

Every race in the world enjoys its own peculiar characteristics, but it scarcely follows that every individual of a nation must possess these prescribed singularities, or otherwise forfeit in the eyes of the world their nationality. Individual personality is one of the most charming things to be met with, either in the flesh and blood existence, or upon the pages of fiction, and it matters little to what race an author's heroine belongs, if he makes her character distinct, unique and natural.

The American book heroine of to-day is vari-coloured as to personality and action. The author does not consider it necessary to the development of her character, and the plot of the story to insist upon her having American-coloured eyes, an American carriage, an American voice, American motives, and an American mode of dying; he allows her to evolve an individuality ungoverned by nationalisms–but the outcome of impulse and nature and a general womanishness.

Not so the Indian girl in modern fiction, the author permits her character no such spontaneity, she must not be one of womankind at large, neither must she have an originality, a singularity that is not definitely "Indian." I quote "Indian" as there seems to be an impression amongst authors that such a thing as tribal distinction does not exist amongst the North American aborigines.

Tribal Distinctions

The term "Indians" signifies about as much as the term "European," but I cannot recall ever having read a story where the heroine was described as "a European." The Indian girl we meet in cold type [print], however, is rarely distressed by having to belong to any tribe, or to reflect any tribal characteristics. She is merely a wholesale sort of admixture of any band existing between the Mic Macs of Gaspé and the Kwaw-Kewiths of British Columbia, yet strange to say, that notwithstanding the numerous tribes, with their aggregate numbers reaching more than 122,000 souls in Canada alone, our Canadian authors can cull from this huge revenue of character, but one Indian girl, and stranger still that this lonely little heroine never had a prototype [model] in breathing flesh-and-blood existence!

It is a deplorable fact, but there is only one of her. The story-writer who can create a new kind of Indian girl, or better still portray a "real live" Indian girl will do something in Canadian literature that has never been done, but once. The general author gives the reader the impression that he has concocted the plot, created his characters, arranged his action, and at the last moment has been seized with the idea that the regulation Indian maiden will make a very harmonious background whereon to paint his pen picture that he, never having, met this interesting individual, stretches forth his hand to his library shelves, grasps the first Canadian novelist he sees, reads up his subject, and duplicates it in his own work.

After a half dozen writers have done this, the reader might as well leave the tale unread as far as the interest touches upon the Indian character, for an unvarying experience tells him that this convenient personage will repeat herself with monotonous accuracy. He knows what she did and how she died in other romances by other romancers, and she will do and die likewise in this, (she always does die, and one feels relieved that it is so, for she is too unhealthy and too unnatural to live).

The Inevitable "Winona"

The rendition of herself and her doings gains no variety in the pens of manifold authors, and the last thing that they will ever think of will be to study "The Indian Girl" from life, for the being we read of is the offspring of the writer's imagination and never existed outside the book covers that her name decorates.

Yes, there is only one of her, and her name is "Winona." Once or twice she has borne another appellation, but it always has a "Winona" sound about it. Even Charles Mair, in that masterpiece of Canadian-Indian romances, "Tecumseh," could not resist "Winona." We meet her as a Shawnee, as a Sioux, as a Huron, and then, her tribe unnamed, in the vicinity of Brockville.

She is never dignified by being permitted to own a surname, although, extraordinary to note, her father is always a chief, and, had he ever existed, would doubtless have been as conservative as his contemporaries about the usual significance that his people attach to family name and lineage.

In addition to this most glaring error this surnameless creation is possessed with a suicidal mania. Her unhappy, self-sacrificing life becomes such a burden, both to herself and the author that this is the only means by which they can extricate themselves from a lamentable tangle, though, as a matter of fact suicide is an evil positively unknown among Indians. Today there may be rare instances where a man crazed by liquor might destroy his own life, but in the periods from whence "Winona's" character is sketched self-destruction was unheard of. This seems to be a fallacy which the best American writers have fallen a prey to. Even Helen Hunt Jackson, in her powerful and beautiful romance of "Ramona," has weakened her work deplorably by having no less than three Indians suicide while maddened by their national wrongs and personal grief.

To Be Crossed in Love Her Lot

But the hardest fortune that the Indian girl in fiction meets with is the inevitable doom that shadows her love affairs. She is always desperately in love with the young white hero, who in turn is grateful to her for services rendered the garrison in general and himself in particular during red days of war. In short, she is so much wrapped up in him that she is treacherous to her own people, tells falsehoods to her father and the other chiefs of her tribe, and otherwise makes herself detestable and dishonourable. Of course, this white hero never marries her! Will some critic who understands human nature, and particularly the nature of authors, please tell the reading public why marriage with the Indian girl is so despised in books and so general in real life! Will this good far-seeing critic also tell us why the book-made Indian makes all the love advances to the white gentleman, though the real wild Indian girl (by the way, we are never given any stories of educated girls, though there are many such throughout Canada) is the most retiring, reticent, noncommittal being in existence!

Captain [John] Richardson, in that inimitable novel, "Wacousta," scarcely goes as far in this particular as his followers. To be sure he has his Indian heroine madly in love with young de Haldimar, a passion which it goes without saying he does not reciprocate, but which he plays upon to the extent of making her a traitor to Pontiac inasmuch as she betrays the secret of one of the cleverest intrigues of war known in the history of America, namely, the scheme to capture Fort Detroit through the means of an exhibition game of lacrosse. In addition to this de Haldimar makes a cat's paw of the girl, using her as a means of communication between his fiancee and himself, and so the excellent author permits his Indian girl to get herself despised by her own nation and disliked by the reader. Unnecessary to state, that as usual the gallant white marries his fair lady, who the poor little red girl has assisted hero to recover.

G. Mercer Adam's Algonquin Maiden

Then comes another era in Canadian-Indian fiction, wherein G. Mercer Adam and A. Ethelwyn Wetherald have given us the semi-historic novel, "An Algonquin Maiden." The former's masterly touch can be recognized on every page he has written; but the outcome of the combined pens is the same old story. We find "Wanda" violently in love with Edward MacLeod; she makes all the overtures, conducts herself disgracefully, assists him to a reunion with his fair-skinned love, Helene; then betakes herself to a boat, rows out into the lake in a thunderstorm, chants her own death-song, and is drowned.

But notwithstanding all this, the authors have given us something exceedingly unique and novel as regards their red heroine. They have sketched us a wild Indian girl who kisses. They, however, forgot to tell us where she learned this pleasant fashion of emotional expression; though two such prominent authors who have given so much time to the study of Indian customs and character, most certainly have noticed the entire ignorance of kissing that is universal among the Aborigines.

A wild Indian never kisses; mothers never kiss their children even, nor lovers their sweethearts, husbands their wives. It is something absolutely unknown, unpractised.

But "Wanda" was one of the few book Indian girls who had an individuality and was not hampered with being obliged to continually be national first and natural afterwards. No, she was not national; she did things and said things about as un-Indian-like as Bret Harte's "M'liss;" in fact, her action generally resembles M'liss" more than anything else; for "Wanda's" character has the peculiarity of being created more by the dramatis personae in the play than by the authors themselves. For example: Helene speaks of her as a "low, untutored savage," and Rose is guilty of remarking that she is "a coarse, ignorant woman, whom you cannot admire, whom it would be impossible for you to respect;" and these comments are both sadly truthful, one cannot love or admire a heroine that grubs in the mud like a turtle, climbs trees like a raccoon, and tears and soils her gowns like a mad woman.

The "Beautiful Little Brute"

Then the young hero describes her upon two occasions as a "beautiful little brute." Poor little Wanda! Not only is she nondescript and ill starred, but as usual the authors take away her love, her life, and last and most terrible of all, her reputation; for they permit a crowd of men-friends of the hero to call her a "squaw" and neither hero nor authors deny that she is a "squaw." It is almost too sad when so much prejudice exists against the Indians, that any one should write up an Indian heroine with such glaring accusations against her virtue, and no contradictory statements either from writer, hero or circumstance, "Wanda" had without doubt the saddest, unsunniest, unequal life ever given to Canadian readers.

Jessie M. Freeland has written a pretty tale published in *The Week;* it is called "Winona's Tryst," but oh! Grim fatality! here again our Indian girl duplicates her former self. "Winona" is the unhappy victim of violent love for Hugh Gordon, which he does not appreciate or return. She assists him, serves him, saves him in the usual "dumb animal" style of book Indians. She manages by self abnegation, danger, and many heart-aches to restore him to the arms of Rose McTavish, who of course he has loved and longed for all through the story. Then "Winona" secures the time-honoured canoe, paddles out into the lake and drowns herself.

But Miss Freeland closes this pathetic little story with one of the simplest, truest, strongest paragraphs that a Canadian pen has ever written, it is the salvation of the, otherwise threadbare development of plot. Hugh Gordon speaks, "I solemnly pledge myself in memory of Winona to do something to help her unfortunate nation. The rightful owners of the soil, dispossessed and driven back inch by inch over their native prairies by their French and English conquerors; and he kept his word."

Mair's Drama "Tecumseh"

Charles Mair has enriched Canadian-Indian literature perhaps more than any of our authors, in his magnificent drama, "Tecumseh." The character of the grand old chief himself is most powerfully and accurately, drawn. Mair has not fallen into that unattractive fashion of making his Indians "assent with a grunt"—or look with "eyes of dog-like fidelity" or to appear "very grave very dignified, and not very immaculately clean." Mair avoids the usual commonplaces used in describing Indians by those who have never met or mixed with them. His drama bears upon every page evidence of long study and life with the people whom he has written of so carefully, so truthfully.

As for his heroine, what portrayal of Indian character has ever been more faithful than that of "Iena." Oh! Happy inspiration vouchsafed the author of "Tecumseh" he has invented a novelty in fiction—a white man who deserves, wins and reciprocates the Indian maiden's love—who says, as she dies on his bosom, while the bullet meant for him stills and tears her heart.

> "Silent forever. Oh! My girl! My girl!
> Those rich eyes melt; those lips are sunwarm still—
> They look like life, yet have no semblant voice.
> Millions of creatures throng and multitudes
> Of heartless beings, flaunt upon the earth,
> There's room enough for them, but thou, dull fate—
> Thou cold and partial tender of life's field,
> That pluck'st the flower, and leav'st the weed to thrive—
> Thou had'st not room for her! Oh, I must seek
> A way out of the rack—I need not live, but she is dead—
> And love is left upon the earth to starve,
> My object's gone, and I am but a shell,
> A husk, an empty case, or anything what may be kicked
>   about the world."

After perusing this refreshing white-Indian drama the reader has but one regret, that Mair did not let "Iena" live. She is the one "book" Indian girl that has Indian life, Indian character, Indian beauty, but the inevitable doom of death could not be stayed even by Mair's sensitive Indian-loving pen. No, the Indian girl must die, and with the exception of "Iena" her heart's blood must stain every page of fiction whereon she appears. One learns to love Lefroy, the poet painter; he never abuses by coarse language and derisive epithets his little Indian love, "Iena" accepts delicately and sweetly his overtures, Lefroy prizes nobly and honourably her devotion. Oh! Lefroy, where is your fellowman in fiction? "Iena," where your prototype? Alas, for all the other pale-faced lovers, they are indifferent, almost brutal creations, and as for the red skin girls that love them, they are all fawn eyed, unnatural, unmaidenly idiots and both are merely imaginary make-shifts to help out romances, that would be immeasurably improved by their absence.

A Chance for Canadian Writers

Perhaps, sometimes an Indian romance may be written by someone who will be clever enough to portray national character without ever having come in contact with it. Such things have been done, for are we not told that Tom Moore had never set foot in Persia before he wrote Lalla Rookh? And those who best know what they affirm declare that remarkable poem as a faithful and accurate delineation of Oriental scenery, life and character. But such things are rare, half of our authors who write up Indian stuff have never been on an Indian reserve in their lives, have never met a "real live" Redman, have never even read Parkman, Schoolcraft or Catten; what wonder that their conception of a people they are ignorant of, save by hearsay, is dwarfed, erroneous and delusive.

And here follows the thought—do authors who write Indian romances love the nation they endeavour successfully or unsuccessfully to describe? Do they, like Tecumseh, say, "And I, who love your nation, which is just, when deeds deserve it," or is the Indian introduced into literature but to lend a dash of vivid colouring to an otherwise tame and sombre picture of colonial life: it looks suspiciously like the latter reason, or why should the Indian always get beaten in the battles of romance, or the Indian girl get inevitably the cold shoulder in the wars of love?

Surely the Redman has lost enough, has suffered enough without additional losses and sorrows being heaped upon him in romance. There are many combats he has won in history from the extinction of the Jesuit Fathers at Lake Simcoe to Cut Knife Creek. There are many girls who have placed dainty red feet figuratively upon the white man's neck from the days of Pocahontas to those of little "Bright Eyes," who captured all Washington a few seasons ago. Let us not only hear, but read something of the North American Indian "besting" some one at least once in a decade, and above all things let the Indian girl of fiction develop from the "doglike," "fawnlike," "deerfooted," "fire-eyed," "crouching,""submissive" book heroine into something of the quiet, sweet womanly woman she is, if wild, or the everyday, natural, laughing girl she is, if cultivated and educated, let her be *natural,* even if the author is not competent to give her tribal characteristics.

Toronto: May 22, 1892
[source: newspaper clipping in the McMaster University Pauline Johnson Collection]

Lily Dougall
The Leaven of the Pharisees

It is a curious fact, illustrative of much, that in Christian sermons we often hear the indifferent and the vicious—those who are called "the world" in contradistinction to the religious class—condemned as the murderers of Jesus, whereas the guilt of the deed belonged wholly to men who firmly believed that morality and the worship of the true God would be swept from the earth if his teaching were accepted. Other men, less concerned for religion, might have hindered the crime and did not, but theirs was not the guilt of initiation. From this it surely follows that the chief task suggested by the Gospel drama is to find wherein the Christ-life seemed to the true pietist subversive of good.

It requires no deep research to perceive wherein the religion of Jesus chiefly differed from that of the pious Jew. His God was the father of sinners; his practice was friendship with sinners.

Now let us consider first his practice, for through that his conception of God's perfection as consisting in blessing equally the just and the unjust is clearly seen.

Jesus feasted with sinners. Some, of course, of his companions at these feasts were sinners only in the legal sense, but some were also vicious. They were all undoubtedly sinners in our sense, not doing what they believed they ought to do, and doing that which they believed they ought not to do. There is no record—not one—that in social converse Jesus interfered with their habits of life by didactic gravity or reproach. Whenever we have incidents of reform, the reform is distinctly voluntary. Before his ministry he grew in favour with men, and during that ministry with men who knew themselves sinners, and we know that men are so constituted that he who habitually finds fault does not grow in favour with them. It may be urged that there was about him a supernatural grace which disarmed the sinner of his natural dislike for reproof. Why, then, did not this supernatural grace operate with the separatists, whom he certainly did constantly reprove? It cannot have been by accident that the Gospel incidents are selected. If there is no record of Jesus publicly finding fault with men of vicious habits, it is because he did not do it. That he preached and lived a life as far above outward righteousness as it was above sin, does not alter the obvious fact that there could not have been reproach in the sunny serenity of his behaviour when he fraternised with publicans and sinners. These loved to have him with them, while the righteous looking on cried out in disgust that his manner was convivial. His behaviour gave to the cursory spectator the impression of self-indulgence, and those righteous persons who watched him with critical zeal were confounded and fell back upon a blacker interpretation.

When we consider all of friendliness that it involves to eat a man's bread, the behaviour of Jesus concerning sinners was very remarkable. If our neighbour makes his money by corrupt practice, and we accept his invitation to dinner, it means, if we have any sense of honour at all, that we will stand by him when others condemn; that we are prepared to justify his dishonesty with at any rate the plea that he is no worse than other men. This last, at least, was what the behaviour of the Christ said—that the faults of the immoral were no worse than the faults of the moral. Let us again entirely disabuse our minds of the idea that the religious Jews led corrupt lives: they did not. Under their absurd casuistry stood the Ten Commandments, which, according to their light, they kept. "All these have I kept from my youth up," said the young ruler; but Jesus, even in the impulse of love for this beautiful personation of morality, said, "How hardly!" Rich in morals, in respectability, in self-control, in orthodox opinions, in all things that make men able to acquire and keep material goods (the knave is never your typical rich man; his inheritance is but transient), and yet the kingdom of heaven is nearer the sinners. Yes, when he ate the bread of the sinners, an action in those days of tithing more suggestive of comradeship in disobedience to God than it is today, Jesus began by saying to the righteous, "They are no worse than you," and he ended by saying, "They are better; they go into the kingdom before you." Thus the teaching of his practice, added to and filled out by the teaching of his words, appeared to the moralists of that day inimical to the righteousness of their nation.

Take, as an example of this, those seemingly gratuitous defiances of ordinary Sabbath observance, such as telling the impotent man to carry his bed, and allowing his disciples to eat the ears of corn. Absurd as were scribal definitions of the main Sabbath laws, without much definition it would have been impossible to apply those laws to the life of the day. The Jews alone among the nations stood for the Sabbath. Foreign influences were pressing against it on every side. In this the Lord appeared to side with heathen influence against the faithful Jew.

If we look at the behaviour of Jesus in his friendly intercourse with the Pharisees, we shall see how this attitude was emphasized. The washing of hands before meat was as sacred a symbol to them as is any religious rite to us. Had not Moses prepared the nation by the washing of their persons and garments for the great first covenant? All those frequent baptisms for which Jesus derided the then accepted tradition of God's will were to its devotees the outward recognition of their belief that human defilement must be washed away ere the simplest blessing could be received, the simplest action performed in the presence of God. The Pharisees did not believe that washings were of avail except as a fulfilment of the divine command. If this same Jesus should come to earth now, and pass through our churches without removing his hat, or should extinguish altar candles, or pray in a sitting posture, he would affect the mind of the reverent ritualist as he affected the mind of the earnest Pharisee by refusing to wash his hands before meat. If he should dwell in some evangelical household and confess that he did not carry a copy of the Scriptures, or refuse to attend at family prayer, the same effect would be produced. I am not saying here that the rules and customs of our Christendom may not be expressly ordered by God, as the washings of the Pharisees may not have been, but merely that if some great teacher should repudiate them we should not be more hurt and annoyed than was the Pharisee at this conduct of Jesus.

Even yet we are astonished that our Lord should have refused so beautiful and simple a rite. Even if he saw it to be unnecessary, reverence for his brother's faith, good taste, kindness of heart—all these would have prompted gentle compliance. The thing itself was not wrong; wherein lay the virtue of his uncompromising nonconformity?

Jesus would have no share in any outward act which was set up as a test of spiritual condition. The sin which he is often supposed thus to have rebuked is separation of the observance from its spiritual significance, but on looking nearer this is seen to be a false view. The sin he detested was not the separation of truth from observance, but the spiritual pride that could not separate them. "God, we thank thee that we know the way of salvation, and that we walk in it; that we are not as the people who know not the will and are condemned." Even when the ceremony was harmless he replied, "I take my stand outside your way, with those who, you say, know not the law and are cursed. I neglect your rite, despise your interpretations of Scripture, and make my friends among those who ignore them. See now if you can recognise God's inspiration in another form." And those Pharisees could not. Let us remember that the devout among them thanked God for their privileges, that they coupled this gratitude with an unresting zeal for converts, and with a sense also that there was something of redeeming force for the many in the faithfulness of the few. Had they lived nowadays we might have defended them, saying how very good they were— "very narrow, bigoted, in fact, but that is almost a necessary consequence of intensity." Jesus Christ called them "children of hell."

From *Pro Christo et Ecclesia*.

Charles G.D. Roberts
The Animal Story

Alike in matter and in method, the animal story, as we have it to-day, may be regarded as a culmination. The animal story, of course, in one form or another, is as old as the beginnings of literature. Perhaps the most engrossing part in the life-drama of primitive man was that played by the beasts which he hunted, and by those which hunted him. They pressed incessantly upon his perceptions. They furnished both material and impulse for his first gropings toward pictorial art. When he acquired the kindred art of telling a story, they supplied his earliest themes; and they suggested the hieroglyphs by means of which, on carved bone or painted rock, he first gave his narrative a form to outlast the spoken breath. We may not unreasonably infer that the first animal story—the remote but authentic ancestor of "Mowgli" and "Lobo" and "Krag"—was a story of some successful hunt, when success meant life to the starving family; or of some desperate escape, when the truth of the narrative was attested, to the hearers squatted trembling about their fire, by the sniffings of the baffled bear or tiger at the rock-barred mouth of the cave. Such first animal stories had at least one merit of prime literary importance. They were convincing. The first critic, however supercilious, would be little likely to cavil at their verisimilitude.

Somewhat later, when men had begun to harass their souls, and their neighbours, with problems of life and conduct, then these same animals, hourly and in every aspect thrust beneath the eyes of their observation, served to point the moral of their tales. The beasts, not being in a position to resent the ignoble office thrust upon them, were compelled to do duty as concrete types of those obvious virtues and vices of which alone the unsophisticated ethical sense was ready to take cognisance. In this way, as soon as a composition became a *métier*, was born the fable; and in this way the ingenuity of the first author enabled him to avoid a perilous unpopularity among those whose weaknesses and defects his art held up to the scorn of all the caves.

These earliest observers of animal life were compelled by the necessities of the case to observe truly, if not deeply. Pitting their wits against those of their four-foot rivals, they had to know their antagonists, and respect them, in order to overcome them. But it was only the most salient characteristics of each species that concerned the practical observer. It was simple to remember that the tiger was cruel, the fox cunning, the wolf rapacious. And so, as advancing civilization drew an ever widening line between man and the animals, and men became more and more engrossed in the interests of their own kind, the personalities of the wild creatures which they had once known so well became obscured to them, and the creatures themselves came to be regarded, for the purposes of literature, as types or symbols merely,—except in those cases, equally obstructive to exact observation, where they were revered as temporary tenements of the spirits of departed kinsfolk. The characters in that great beast-epic of the middle ages, "Reynard the Fox," though far more elaborately limned than those which play their succinct roles in the fables of Aesop, are at the same time in their elaboration far more alien to the truths of wild nature. Reynard, Isegrim, Bruin, and Greybeard have little resemblance to the fox, the wolf, the bear, and the badger, as patience, sympathy, and the camera reveal them to us to-day.

The advent of Christianity, strange as it may seem at first glance, did not make for a closer understanding between man and the lower animals. While it was militant, fighting for its life against the forces of paganism, its effort was to set man at odds with the natural world, and fill his eyes with the wonders of the spiritual. Man was the only thing of consequence on earth, and of man, not his body, but his soul. Nature was the ally of the enemy. The way of nature was the way of death. In man alone was the seed of the divine. Of what concern could be the joy or pain of creatures of no soul, to-morrow returning to the dust? To strenuous spirits, their eyes fixed upon the fear of hell for themselves, and the certainty of it for their neighbours, it smacked of sin to take thought of the feelings of such evanescent products of corruption. Hence it came that, in spite of the gentle understanding of such sweet saints as Francis of Assisi,

Anthony of Padua, and Colomb of the Bees, the inarticulate kindred for a long time reaped small comfort from the Dispensation of Love.

With the spread of freedom and the broadening out of all intellectual interests which characterize these modern days, the lower kindreds began to regain their old place in the concern of man. The revival of interest in the animals found literary expression (to classify roughly) in two forms, which necessarily overlap each other now and then, viz., the story of adventure and the anecdote of observation. Hunting as a recreation, pursued with zest from pole to tropics by restless seekers after the new, supplied a species of narrative singularly akin to what the first animal stories must have been,—narratives of desperate encounter, strange peril, and hairbreadth escape. Such hunters' stories and travellers' tales are rarely conspicuous for the exactitude of their observation; but that was not the quality at first demanded of them by fireside readers. The attention of the writer was focussed, not upon the peculiarities or the emotions of the beast protagonist in each fierce, brief drama, but upon the thrill of the action, the final triumph of the human actor. The inevitable tendency of these stories of adventure with beasts was to awaken interest in animals, and to excite a desire for exact knowledge of their traits and habits. The interest and the desire evoked the natural historian, the inheritor of the half-forgotten mantle of Pliny. Precise and patient scientists made the animals their care, observing with microscope and measure, comparing bones, assorting families, subdividing subdivisions, till at length all the beasts of significance to man were ticketed neatly, and laid bare, as far as the inmost fibre of their material substance was concerned, to the eye of popular information.

Altogether admirable and necessary as was this development at large, another, of richer or at least more spiritual significance, was going on at home. Folk who loved their animal comrades—their dogs, horses, cats, parrots, elephants—were observing, with the wonder and interest of discoverers, the astonishing fashion in which the mere instincts of these so-called irrational creatures were able to simulate the operations of reason. The results of this observation were written down, till "anecdotes of animals" came to form a not inconsiderable body of literature. The drift of all these data was overwhelmingly toward one conclusion. The mental processes of the animals observed were seen to be far more complex than the observers had supposed. Where instinct was called in to account for the elaborate ingenuity with which a dog would plan and accomplish the outwitting of a rival, or the nice judgment with which an elephant, with no nest-building ancestors behind him to instruct his brain, would choose and adjust the teak-logs which he was set to pile, it began to seem as if that faithful faculty was being overworked. To explain yet other cases, which no accepted theory seemed to fit, coincidence was invoked, till that rare and elusive phenomenon threatened to become as customary as buttercups. But when instinct and coincidence had done all that could be asked of them, there remained a great unaccounted-for body of facts; and men were forced at last to accept the proposition that, within their varying limitations, animals can and do reason. As far, at least, as the mental intelligence is concerned, the gulf dividing the lowest of the human species from the highest of the animals has in these latter days been reduced to a very narrow psychological fissure.

Whether avowedly or not, it is with the psychology of animal life that the representative animal stories of to-day are first of all concerned. Looking deep into the eyes of certain of the four-footed kindred, we have been startled to see therein a something, before unrecognised, that answered to our inner and intellectual, if not spiritual selves. We have suddenly attained a new and clearer vision. We have come face to face with personality, where we were blindly wont to predicate mere instinct and automatism. It is as if one should step carelessly out of one's back door, and marvel to see unrolling before his new-awakened eyes the peaks and seas and misty valleys of an unknown world. Our chief writers of animal stories at the present day may be regarded as explorers of this unknown world, absorbed in charting its topography. They work, indeed, upon a substantial foundation of known facts. They are minutely scrupulous as to their natural history, and assiduous contributors to that science. But above all are they diligent in their search for the motive beneath the action. Their care is to catch the varying, elusive personalities which dwell back of the luminous brain windows of the dog, the horse, the deer, or wrap themselves in reserve behind the inscrutable eyes of all the cats, or sit aloof in the gaze of the hawk and the eagle. The animal story at its highest point of development is a psychological romance constructed on a framework of natural science.

The real psychology of the animals, so far as we are able to grope our way toward it by deduction and induction combined, is a very different thing from the psychology of certain stories of animals which paved the way for the present vogue. Of these, such books as "Beautiful Joe" and "Black Beauty" are deservedly conspicuous examples. It is no detraction from the merit of these books, which have done great service in awakening a sympathetic understanding of the animals and sharpening our sense of kinship with all that breathe, to say that their psychology is human. Their animal characters think and feel as human beings would think and feel under like conditions. This marks the stage which these works occupy in the development of the animal story.

The next stage must be regarded as, in literature, a climax indeed, but not the climax in this genre. I refer to the "Mowgli" stories of Mr. Kipling. In these tales the animals are frankly humanized. Their individualization is distinctly human, as are also their mental and emotional processes, and their highly elaborate powers of expression. Their notions are complex; whereas the motives of real animals, so far as we have hitherto been able to judge them, seem to be essentially simple, in the sense that the motive dominant at a given moment quite obliterates, for the time, all secondary motives. Their reasoning powers and their constructive imagination are far beyond anything which present knowledge justifies us in ascribing to the inarticulate kindreds. To say this is in no way to depreciate such work, but merely to classify it. There are stories being written now which, for interest and artistic value, are not to be mentioned in the same breath with the "Mowgli" tales, but which nevertheless occupy a more advanced stage in the evolution of this genre.

It seems to me fairly safe to say that this evolution is not likely to go beyond the point to which it has been carried today. In such a story, for instance, as that of "Krag, the Kootenay Ram," by Mr. Ernest Seton, the interest centres about the personality, individuality, mentality, of an animal, as well as its purely physical characteristics. The field of animal psychology so admirably opened is an inexhaustible world of wonder. Sympathetic exploration may advance its boundaries to a degree of which we hardly dare to dream; but such expansion cannot be called evolution. There would seem to be no further evolution possible, unless based upon a hypothesis that animals have souls. As souls are apt to elude exact observation, to forecast any such development would seem to be at best merely fanciful.

The animal story, as we now have it, is a potent emancipator. It frees us for a little from the world of shop-worn utilities, and from the mean tenement of self of which we do well to grow weary. It helps us to return to nature, without requiring that we at the same time return to barbarism. It leads us back to the old kinship of earth, without asking us to relinquish by way of toll any part of the wisdom of the ages, any fine essential of the "large result of time." The clear and candid life to which it re-initiates us, far behind though it lies in the long upward march of being, holds for us this quality. It has ever the more significance, it has ever the richer gift of refreshment and renewal, the more humane the heart and spiritual the understanding which we bring to the intimacy of it.

Kindred of the Wild

Edith Eaton (Sui Sin Far)
Leaves from the Mental Portfolio of an Eurasian

When I look back over the years I see myself, a little child of scarcely four years of age, walking in front of my nurse, in a green English lane, and listening to her tell another of her kind that my mother is Chinese. "Oh, Lord!" exclaims the informed.

She turns around and scans me curiously from head to foot. Then the two women whisper together. Tho the word "Chinese" conveys very little meaning to my mind, I feel that they are talking about my father and mother and my heart swells with indignation. When we reach home I rush to my mother and try to tell her what I have heard. I am a young child. I fail to make myself intelligible. My mother does not understand, and when the nurse declares to her, "Little Miss Sui is a storyteller," my mother slaps me.

Many a long year has past over my head since that day—the day on which I first learned that I was something different and apart from other children, but tho my mother has forgotten it, I have not.

I see myself again, a few years older. I am playing with another child in a garden. A girl passes by outside the gate. "Mamie," she cries to my companion. "I wouldn't speak to Sui if I were you. Her mamma is Chinese."

"I don't care," answers the little one beside me. And then to me, "Even if your mamma is Chinese, I like you better than I like Annie."

"But I don't like you," I answer, turning my back on her. It is my first conscious lie.

I am at a children's party, given by the wife of an Indian officer whose children were schoolfellows of mine. I am only six years of age, but have attended a private school for over a year, and have already learned that China is a heathen country, being civilized by England. However, for the time being, I am a merry romping child. There are quite a number of grown people present. One, a white haired old man, has his attention called to me by the hostess. He adjusts his eyeglasses and surveys me critically. "Ah, indeed!" he exclaims. "Who would have thought it at first glance. Yet now I see the difference between her and other children. What a peculiar colouring! Her mother's eyes and hair and her father's features, I presume. Very interesting little creature!"

I had been called from my play for the purpose of inspection. I do not return to it. For the rest of the evening I hide myself behind a hall door and refuse to show myself until it is time to go home.

My parents have come to America. We are in Hudson City, N.Y., and we are very poor. I am out with my brother, who is ten months older than myself. We pass a Chinese store, the door of which is open. "Look!" says Charlie. "Those men in there are Chinese!" Eagerly I gaze into the long low room. With the exception of my mother, who is English bred with English ways and manner of dress, I have never seen a Chinese person. The two men within the store are uncouth specimens of their race, drest in working blouses and pantaloons with queues hanging down their backs. I recoil with a sense of shock.

"Oh, Charlie," I cry. "Are we like that?"

"Well, we're Chinese, and they're Chinese, too, so we must be!" returns my seven-year-old brother.

"Of course you are," puts in a boy who has followed us down the street, and who lives near us and has seen my mother: "Chinky, Chinky, Chinaman, yellow-face, pig-tail, rat-eater." A number of other boys and several little girls join in with him.

"Better than you," shouts my brother, facing the crowd. He is younger and smaller than any there, and I am even more insignificant than he; but my spirit revives.

"I'd rather be Chinese than anything else in the world," I scream.

They pull my hair, they tear my clothes, they scratch my face, and all but lame my brother; but the white blood in our veins fights valiantly for the Chinese half of us. When it is all over, exhausted and bedraggled, we crawl home, and report to our mother that we have "won the battle."

"Are you sure?" asks my mother doubtfully.

"Of course. They ran from us. They were frightened," returns my brother.

My mother smiles with satisfaction.

"Do you hear?" she asks my father.

"Umm," he observes, raising his eyes from his paper for an instant. My childish instinct, however, tells me that he is more interested than he appears to be.

It is tea time, but I cannot eat. Unobserved I crawl away. I

do not sleep that night. I am too excited and I ache all over. Our opponents had been so very much stronger and bigger than we. Toward morning, however, I fall into a doze from which I awake myself, shouting:
"Sound the battle cry;
See the foe is nigh."

My mother believes in sending us to Sunday school. She has been brought up in a Presbyterian college.

The scene of my life shifts to Eastern Canada. The sleigh which has carried us from the station stops in front of a little French Canadian hotel. Immediately we are surrounded by a number of villagers, who stare curiously at my mother as my father assists her to alight from the sleigh. Their curiosity, however, is tempered with kindness, as they watch, one after another, the little black heads of my brothers and sisters and myself emerge out of the buffalo robe, which is part of the sleigh's outfit. There are six of us, four girls and two boys; the eldest, my brother, being only seven years of age. My father and mother are still in their twenties. "Les pauvres enfants," the inhabitants murmur, as they help to carry us into the hotel. Then in lower tones: "Chinoise, Chinoise."

For some time after our arrival, whenever we children are sent for a walk, our footsteps are dogged by a number of young French and English Canadians, who amuse themselves with speculations as to whether, we being Chinese, are susceptible to pinches and hair pulling, while older persons pause and gaze upon us, very much in the same way that I have seen people gaze upon strange animals in a menagerie. Now and then we are stopt and plied with questions as to what we eat and drink, how we go to sleep, if my mother understands what my father says to her, if we sit on chairs or squat on floors, etc., etc., etc.

There are many pitched battles, of course, and we seldom leave the house without being armed for conflict. My mother takes a great interest in our battles, and usually cheers us on, tho I doubt whether she understands the depth of the troubled waters thru which her little children wade. As to my father, peace is his motto, and he deems it wisest to be blind and deaf to many things.

School days are short, but memorable. I am in the same class with my brother, my sister next to me in the class below. The little girl whose desk my sister shares shrinks close against the wall as my sister takes her place. In a little while she raises her hand.

"Please, teacher!"

"Yes, Annie."

"May I change my seat?"

"No, you may not!"

The little girl sobs. "Why should she have to sit beside a—"

Happily my sister does not seem to hear, and before long the two little girls become great friends. I have many such experiences.

My brother is remarkably bright; my sister next to me has a wonderful head for figures, and when only eight years of age helps my father with his night work accounts. My parents compare her with me. She is of sturdier build than I, and, as my father says, "Always has her wits about her." He thinks her more like my mother, who is very bright and interested in every little detail of practical life. My father tells me that I will never make half the woman that my mother is or that my sister will be. I am not as strong as my sisters, which makes me feel somewhat ashamed, for I am the eldest little girl, and more is expected of me. I have no organic disease, but the strength of my feelings seems to take from me the strength of my body. I am prostrated at times with attacks of nervous sickness. The doctor says that my heart is unusually large; but in the light of the present I know that the cross of the Eurasian bore too heavily upon my childish shoulders. I usually hide my weakness from the family until I cannot stand. I do not understand myself, and I have an idea that the others will despise me for not being as strong as they. Therefore, I like to wander away alone, either by the river or in the bush. The green fields and flowing water have a charm for me. At the age of seven, as it is today, a bird on the wing is my emblem of happiness.

I have come from a race on my mother's side which is said to be the most stolid and insensible to feeling of all races, yet I look back over the years and see myself so keenly alive to every shade of sorrow and suffering that it is almost a pain to live.

If there is any trouble in the house in the way of a difference between my father and mother, or if any child is punished, how I suffer! And when harmony is restored, heaven seems to be around me. I can be sad, but I can also be glad. My mother's screams of agony when a baby is born almost drive me wild, and long after her pangs have subsided I feel them in my own body. Sometimes it is a week before I can get to sleep after such an experience.

A debt owing by my father fills me with shame. I feel like a criminal when I pass the creditor's door. I am only ten years old. And all the while the question of nationality perplexes my little brain. Why are we what we are? I and my brothers and sisters. Why did God make us to be hooted and stared at? Papa is English, mamma is Chinese. Why couldn't we have been either one thing or the other? Why is my mother's race despised? I look into the faces of my father and mother. Is she not every bit as dear and good as he? Why? Why? She sings us the songs she learned at her English school. She tells us tales of China. Tho a child when she left her native land she remembers it well, and I am never tired of listening to the story of how she was stolen from her home. She tells us over and over again of her meeting with my father in Shanghai and the romance of their marriage. Why? Why?

I do not confide in my father and mother. They would not understand. How could they? He is English, she is Chinese. I am different to both of them—a stranger, tho their own child. "What are we?" I ask my brother. "It doesn't matter, sissy," he responds. But it does. I love poetry, particularly heroic pieces. I also love fairy tales. Stories of everyday life do not appeal to me. I dream dreams of being great and noble; my sisters and brothers also. I glory in the idea of dying at the stake and a great genie arising from the flames and declaring to those who have scorned us: "Behold, how great and glorious and noble are the Chinese people!"

My sisters are apprenticed to a dressmaker; my brother is entered in an office. I tramp around and sell my father's pictures, also some lace which I make myself. My nationality, if I had only known it at that time, helps to make sales. The ladies who are my customers call me "The Little Chinese Lace Girl." But it is a dangerous life for a very young girl. I come near to "mysteriously disappearing" many a time. The greatest temptation was in the thought of getting far away from where I was known, to where no mocking cries of "Chinese!" "Chinese!" could reach.

Whenever I have the opportunity I steal away to the library and read every book I can find on China and the Chinese. I learn that China is the oldest civilized nation on the face of the earth and a few other things. At eighteen years of age what troubles me is not that I am what I am, but that others are ignorant of my superiority. I am small, but my feelings are big—and great is my vanity.

My sisters attend dancing classes, for which they pay their own fees. In spite of covert smiles and sneers, they are glad to meet and mingle with other young folk. They are not sensitive in the sense that I am. And yet they understand. One of them tells me that she overheard a young man say to another that he would rather marry a pig than a girl with Chinese blood in her veins.

In course of time I too learn shorthand and take a position in an office. Like my sister, I teach myself, but, unlike my sister, I have neither the perseverance nor the ability to perfect myself. Besides, to a temperament like mine, it is torture to spend the hours in transcribing other people's thoughts. Therefore, altho I can always earn a moderately good salary, I do not distinguish myself in the business world as does she.

When I have been working for some years I open an office of my own. The local papers patronize me and give me a number of assignments, including most of the local Chinese reporting. I meet many Chinese persons, and when they get into trouble am often called upon to fight their battles in the papers. This I enjoy. My heart leaps for joy when I read one day an article by a New York Chinese in which he declares, "The Chinese in America owe an everlasting debt of gratitude to Sui Sin Far for the bold stand she has taken in their defense."

The Chinaman who wrote the article seeks me out and calls upon me. He is a clever and witty man, a graduate of one of the American colleges and as well a Chinese scholar. I learn that he has an American wife and several children. I am very much interested in these children, and when I meet them my heart throbs in sympathetic tune with the tales they relate of their experiences as Eurasians. "Why did papa and mamma born us?" asks one. Why?

I also meet other Chinese men who compare favourably with the white men of my acquaintance in mind and heart qualities. Some of them are quite handsome. They have not as finely cut noses and as well developed chins as the white men, but they have smoother skins and their expression is more serene; their hands are better shaped and their voices softer.

Some little Chinese women whom I interview are very anxious to know whether I would marry a Chinaman. I do not answer No. They clap their hands delightedly, and assure me that the Chinese are much the finest and best of all men. They are, however, a little doubtful as to whether one could be persuaded to care for me, full-blooded Chinese people having a prejudice against the half white.

Fundamentally, I muse, all people are the same. My mother's race is as prejudiced as my father's. Only when the whole world becomes as one family will human beings be able to see clearly and hear distinctly. I believe that some day a great part of the world will be Eurasian. I cheer myself with the thought that I am but a pioneer. A pioneer should glory in suffering.

"You were walking with a Chinaman yesterday," accuses an acquaintance.

"Yes, what of it?"

"You ought not to. It isn't right."

"Not right to walk with one of my mother's people? Oh, indeed!"

I cannot reconcile his notion of righteousness with my own.

* * *

I am living in a little town away off on the north shore of a big lake. Next to me at the dinner table is the man for whom I work as a stenographer. There are also a couple of business men, a young girl and her mother.

Some one makes a remark about the cars full of Chinamen that past that morning. A transcontinental railway runs thru the town.

My employer shakes his rugged head. "Somehow or other," says he, "I cannot reconcile myself to the thought that the Chinese are humans like ourselves. They may have immortal souls, but their faces seem to be so utterly devoid of expression that I cannot help but doubt."

"Souls," echoes the town clerk. "Their bodies are enough for me. A Chinaman is, in my eyes, more repulsive than a nigger."

"They always give me such a creepy feeling," puts in the young girl with a laugh.

"I wouldn't have one in my house," declares my landlady.

"Now, the Japanese are different altogether. There is something bright and likeable about those men," continues Mr. K.

A miserable, cowardly feeling keeps me silent. I am in a Middle West town. If I declare what I am, every person in the place will hear about it the next day. The population is in the main made up of working folks with strong prejudices against my mother's countrymen. The prospect before me is not an enviable one—if I speak. I have no longer an ambition to die at the stake for the sake of demonstrating the greatness and nobleness of the Chinese people.

Mr. K. turns to me with a kindly smile.

"What makes Miss Far so quiet?" he asks.

"I don't suppose she finds the 'washee washee men' particularly interesting subjects of conversation," volunteers the young manager of the local bank.

With a great effort I raise my eyes from my plate. "Mr. K.," I say, addressing my employer, "the Chinese people may have no souls, no expression on their faces, be altogether beyond the pale of civilization, but whatever they are, I want you to understand that I am—I am a Chinese."

There is silence in the room for a few minutes. Then Mr. K. pushes back his plate and standing up beside me, says:

"I should not have spoken as I did. I know nothing whatever about the Chinese. It was pure prejudice. Forgive me!"

I admire Mr. K.'s moral courage in apologizing to me; he is a conscientious Christian man, but I do not remain much longer in the little town.

* * *

I am under a tropic sky, meeting frequently and conversing with persons who are almost as high up in the world as birth, education and money can set them. The environment is peculiar, for I am also surrounded by a race of people, the reputed descendants of Ham, the son of Noah, whose offspring, it was prophesied, should be the servants of the sons of Shem and Japheth. As I am a descendant, according to the Bible, of both Shem and Japheth, I have a perfect right to set my heel upon the Ham people; but tho I see others around me following out the Bible suggestion, it is not in my nature to be arrogant to any but those who seek to impress me with their superiority, which the poor black maid who has been assigned to me by the hotel certainly does not. My employer's wife takes me to task for this. "It is unnecessary," she says, "to thank a black person for service."

The novelty of life in the West Indian island is not without its charm. The surroundings, people, manner of living, are so entirely different from what I have been accustomed to up North that I feel as if I were "born again." Mixing with people of fashion, and yet not of them, I am not of sufficient importance to create comment or curiosity. I am busy nearly all day and often well into the night. It is not monotonous work, but it is certainly strenuous. The planters and business men of the island take me as a matter of course and treat me with kindly courtesy. Occasionally an Englishman will warn me against the "brown boys" of the island, little dreaming that I too am of the "brown people" of the earth.

When it begins to be whispered about the place that I am not all white, some of the "sporty" people seek my acquaintance.

I am small and look much younger than my years. When, however, they discover that I am a very serious and sober-minded spinster indeed, they retire quite gracefully, leaving me a few amusing reflections.

One evening a card is brought to my room. It bears the name of some naval officer. I go down to my visitor, thinking he is probably some one who, having been told that I am a reporter for the local paper, has brought me an item of news. I find him lounging in an easy chair on the veranda of the hotel—a big, blond, handsome fellow, several years younger than I.

"You are Lieutenant———?" I inquire.

He bows and laughs a little. The laugh doesn't suit him somehow—and it doesn't suit me, either.

"If you have anything to tell me, please tell it quickly, because I'm very busy."

"Oh, you don't really mean that," he answers, with another silly and offensive laugh. "There's always plenty of time for good times. That's what I am here for. I saw you at the races the other day and twice at King's House. My ship will be here for ——— weeks."

"Do you wish that noted?" I ask.

"Oh, no! Why—I came just because I had an idea that you might like to know me. I would like to know you. You look such a nice little body. Say, wouldn't you like to go for a sail this lovely night? I will tell you all about the sweet little Chinese girls I met when we were at Hong Kong. They're not so shy!"

* * *

I leave Eastern Canada for the Far West, so reduced by another attack of rheumatic fever that I only weigh eighty-four pounds. I travel on an advertising contract. It is presumed by the railway company that in some way or other I will give them full value for their transportation across the continent. I have been ordered beyond the Rockies by the doctor, who declares that I will never regain my strength in the East. Nevertheless, I am but two days in San Francisco when I start out in search of work. It is the first time that I have sought work as a stranger in a strange town. Both of the other positions away from home were secured for me by home influence. I am quite surprised to find that there is no demand for my services in San Francisco and that no one is particularly interested in me. The best I can do is to accept an offer from a railway agency to typewrite their correspondence for $5 a month. I stipulate, however, that I shall have the privilege of taking in outside work and that my hours shall be light. I am hopeful that the sale of a story or newspaper article may add to my income, and I console myself with the reflection that, considering that I still limp and bear traces of sickness, I am fortunate to secure any work at all.

The proprietor of one of the San Francisco papers, to whom I have a letter of introduction, suggests that I obtain some subscriptions from the people of China town, that district of the city having never been canvassed. This suggestion I carry out with enthusiasm, tho I find that the Chinese merchants and people generally are inclined to regard me with suspicion. They have been imposed upon so many times by unscrupulous white people. Another drawback—save for a few phrases, I am unacquainted with my mother tongue. How, then, can I expect these people to accept me as their own countrywoman? The Americanized Chinamen actually laugh in my face when I tell them that I am of their race. However, they are not all "doubting Thomases." Some little women discover that I have Chinese hair, colour of eyes and complexion, also that I love rice and tea. This settles the matter for them—and for their husbands.

My Chinese instincts develop. I am no longer the little girl who shrunk against my brother at the first sight of a Chinaman. Many and many a time, when alone in a strange place, has the appearance of even a humble laundryman given me a sense of protection and made me feel quite at home. This fact of itself proves to me that prejudice can be eradicated by association.

I meet a half Chinese, half white girl. Her face is plastered with a thick white coat of paint and her eyelids and eyebrows are blackened so that the shape of her eyes and the whole expression of her face is changed. She was born in the East, and at the age of eighteen came West in answer to an advertisement. Living for many years among the working class, she had heard little but abuse of the Chinese. It is not difficult, in a land like California, for a half Chinese, half white girl to pass as one of Spanish or Mexican origin. This poor child does, tho she lives in nervous dread of being "discovered." She becomes engaged to a young man, but fears to tell him what she is, and only does so when compelled by a fearless American girl friend. This girl, who knows her origin, realizing that the truth sooner or later must be told, and better soon than late, advises the Eurasian to confide in the young man, assuring her that he loves her well enough not to allow her nationality to stand, a bar sinister, between them. But the Eurasian prefers to keep her secret, and only reveals it to the man who is to be her husband when driven to bay by the American girl, who declares that if the half-breed will not tell the truth she will. When the young man hears that the girl he is engaged to has Chinese blood in her veins, he exclaims: "Oh, what will my folks say?" But that is all. Love is stronger than prejudice with him, and neither he nor she deems it necessary to inform his "folks."

The Americans, having for many years manifested a much higher regard for the Japanese than for the Chinese, several half Chinese young men and women, thinking to advance themselves, both in a social and business sense, pass as Japanese. They continue to be known as Eurasians; but a Japanese Eurasian does not appear in the same light as a Chinese Eurasian. The unfortunate Chinese Eurasians! Are not those who compel them to thus cringe more to be blamed than they?

People, however, are not all alike. I meet white men, and women, too, who are proud to mate with those who have Chinese blood in their veins, and think it a great honour to be distinguished by the friendship of such. There are also Eurasians and Eurasians. I know of one who allowed herself to become engaged to a white man after refusing him nine times. She had discouraged him in every way possible, had warned him that she was half Chinese; that her people were poor, that every week or month she sent home a certain amount of her earnings, and that the man she married would have to do as much, if not more; also, most uncompromising truth of all, that she did not love him and never would. But the resolute and undaunted lover swore that it was a matter of indifference to him whether she was a Chinese or a Hottentot, that it would be his pleasure and privilege to allow her relations double what it was in her power to bestow, and as to not loving him—that did not matter at all. He loved her. So, because the young woman had a married mother and married sisters, who were always picking at her and gossiping over her independent manner of living, she finally consented to marry him, recording the agreement in her diary thus:

> "I have promised to become the wife of ———— on ————, 189—,because the world is so cruel and sneering to a single woman—and for no other reason."

Everything went smoothly until one day. The young man was driving a pair of beautiful horses and she was seated by his side, trying very hard to imagine herself in love with him, when a Chinese vegetable gardener's cart came rumbling along. The Chinaman was a jolly-looking individual in blue cotton blouse and pantaloons, his rakish looking hat being kept in place by a long queue which was pulled upward from his neck and wound around it. The young woman was suddenly possest with the spirit of mischief. "Look!"she cried, indicating the Chinaman, "there's my brother. Why don't you salute him?"

The man's face fell a little. He sank into a pensive mood. The wicked one by his side read him like an open book.

"When we are married,"said she, "I intend to give a Chinese party every month."

No answer.

"As there are very few aristocratic Chinese in this city, I shall fill up with the laundrymen and vegetable farmers. I don't believe in being exclusive in democratic America, do you?"

He hadn't a grain of humour in his composition, but a sickly smile contorted his features as he replied:

"You shall do just as you please, my darling. But—but—consider a moment. Wouldn't it be just a little pleasanter for us if, after we are married, we allowed it to be presumed that you were—er—Japanese? So many of my friends have inquired of me if that is not your nationality. They would be so charmed to meet a little Japanese lady."

"Hadn't you better oblige them by finding one?"

"Why—er—what do you mean?"

"Nothing much in particular. Only—I am getting a little tired of this," taking off his ring.

"You don't mean what you say! Oh, put it back, dearest! You know I would not hurt your feelings for the world!"

"You haven't. I'm more than pleased. But I do mean what I say."

That evening the "ungrateful" Chinese Eurasian diaried, among other things, the following:

> "Joy, oh, joy! I'm free once more. Never again shall I be untrue to my own heart. Never again will I allow any one to 'hound' or 'sneer' me into matrimony."

I secure transportation to many California points. I meet some literary people, chief among whom is the editor of the magazine who took my first Chinese stories. He and his wife give me a warm welcome to their ranch. They are broadminded people, whose interest in me is sincere and intelligent, not affected and vulgar. I also meet some funny people who advise me to "trade" upon my nationality. They tell me that if I wish to succeed in literature in America I should dress in Chinese costume, carry a fan in my hand, wear a pair of scarlet beaded slippers, live in New York, and come of high birth. Instead of making myself familiar with the Chinese Americans around me, I should discourse on my spirit acquaintance with Chinese ancestors and quote in between the "Good mornings" and "How d'ye dos" of editors.

> *"Confucius, Confucius, how great is Confucius, Before Confucius, there never was Confucius. After Confucius, there never came Confucius,"* etc., etc., etc.,

or something like that, both illuminating and obscuring, don't you know. They forget, or perhaps they are not aware that the old Chinese sage taught "The way of sincerity is the way of heaven."

My experiences as an Eurasian never cease; but people are not now as prejudiced as they have been. In the West, too, my friends are more advanced in all lines of thought than those whom I knew in Eastern Canada—more genuine, more sincere, with less of the form of religion, but more of its spirit.

So I roam backward and forward across the continent. When I am East, my heart is West. When I am West, my heart is East. Before long I hope to be in China. As my life began in my father's country it may end in my mother's.

After all I have no nationality and am not anxious to claim any. Individuality is more than nationality. "You are you and I am I," says Confucius. I give my right hand to the Occidentals and my left to the Orientals, hoping that between them they will not utterly destroy the insignificant "connecting link." And that's all.

Independent, January 21, 1909.

Criticism

James Doyle
Canadian Women Writers and the American Literary Milieu of the 1890s

"The market for Canadian literary wares," wrote Sara Jeannette Duncan in 1887, "is New York, where the intellectual life of the continent is rapidly centralizing" (41). American magazines, agreed Archibald Lampman in 1892, "are attracting to them most of our literary and artistic effort" (Davies, 96). Margaret Marshall Saunders, reminiscing in 1921 about the beginning of her literary career in the 1890s, explains: "When I started writing I met with so little encouragement in Canada that I went to [the United States]—but without the slightest resentment. My publishers knew I was a Canadian, they knew I loved my own country best, but it never made any difference to them" (Saunders Papers). Robert Barr, who left Canada for the United States and subsequently for England, exhorted young Canadian literary aspirants in 1899: "Get over the border as soon as you can; come to London or go to New York; shake the dust of Canada from your feet" (10).

    It is one of the ironies of Canadian cultural history that, at a time when artistic activity was feeling the impetus of a revitalized nationalism, most of the anglophone writers in the country were looking abroad for publishing outlets and critical recognition. It is rather surprising, furthermore, that historians of Canadian literature have shown little interest in this phenomenon. The circumstances and consequences of this widespread cultural dependency need to be thoroughly researched. Research is particularly needed in the subject of women writers, whose situation, in this generally neglected aspect of Canadian literary history, has been almost completely overlooked.

    As Robert Barr indicated in his account of his own youthful employment on the Detroit *Free Press,* one means to literary success in the United States was a staff job with a metropolitan newspaper or magazine. American newspapers, especially in the 1880s and 1890s, provided abundant opportunities for would-be writers, including many enterprising and independent women. Sara Jeannette Duncan, hired by the Washington *Post* in 1885 to write book reviews and cultural articles, is the most prominent Canadian woman writer to achieve success in this direction.... Marjory Lang cites several other examples of Canadian women journalists who succeeded in the United States in the late nineteenth century. But for writers primarily committed to *belles-lettres,* the hectic demands and stylistic debasement of writing for newspaper deadlines were sometimes regarded as an impediment to creative achievement. "The man [and, presumably, the woman too] who innocently goes into journalism under the hallucination that it has some sort of intermittent relation to literature, sells his soul to the Devil" (170), was the angry complaint of Walter Blackburn Harte, an English-born essayist and critic who began his career writing for Canadian newspapers before moving on to the United States in 1890. Not all Canadian writers would go quite so far in expressing their distaste for journalism, but many would agree that the better opportunities for literary success lay with the magazines. "The literature of the day in America, as far as fiction, poetry, and criticism are concerned," wrote Archibald Lampman, "is concentrated in the magazines" (Davies, 96).

Most Canadian writers of Lampman's generation were not only submitting their work regularly to the American magazines; many of them had gone south to find work in the editorial offices, to be an active part of what were considered the main source and medium of modern literature. In 1891 Walter Blackburn Harte became an assistant editor for *New England Magazine* of Boston, and subsequently worked for *Arena* and several smaller periodicals. Bliss Carman worked for various New York and Boston publications, including *The Chap-Book, The Independent,* and *Current Literature.* Charles G. D. Roberts was briefly with *Illustrated American* in 1897, while his brother William Carman Roberts edited *Literary Digest.* E. W. Thomson was on the staff of the Boston family magazine

Youth's Companion, and Peter McArthur was editor of *Truth* in New York.

In spite of the proliferation of American literary magazines in the 1890s, however, and in spite of the remarkable success of male Canadian expatriates, no female Canadian writers seem to have been able to land similar editorial jobs. This failure is not easy to explain, or even to document conclusively, but a few factors seem relevant. The North American bourgeois attitude of protectiveness towards women may have been a consideration: many periodical offices were unsavory places where men worked in their shirt sleeves, chomped cigars, used slang and profanity. Even William Dean Howells' rather antiseptic account of this kind of environment in his novel *A Hazard of New Fortunes* (1890) excludes women except as occasional visitors. Jack London's fuller-blooded picture of a typical shoestring literary magazine in *Martin Eden* (1908) includes fistfights between editors and unpaid contributors.

But even if such dens were more unattractive than the newspaper offices where Canadian women were making inroads, there should have been a more receptive atmosphere in the burgeoning women's magazines, such as *Harper's Bazaar* (established in 1867), *Ladies' Home Journal* (1883), *McCall's* (1885), and *Vogue* (1892), all of which had predominantly female editorial staffs (Mott 1938, 388; 1957, 536, 580, 756). By 1890, furthermore, a few American women had moved into influential editorial positions in other magazines. The most famous was probably Jeannette Gilder, editor of *Critic* for over twenty years. Also worth noting are Susan Ward, literary editor of *The Independent,* and Helen Gardner, co-editor of *Arena* in 1895-96, along with Walter Blackburn Harte.

Perhaps the exclusion of expatriate Canadian women from the editorial offices of American literary periodicals merely reflects the fact that fewer Canadian women than men went job-hunting in the United States. Young Canadian men, with no need of green cards or chaperones, could head for New York to seek their fortune or to live a hand-to-mouth bohemian existence if necessary, as Toronto-born Harvey O'Higgins' 1906 novel *Don-A-Dreams* describes. For a young, middle-class

Canadian woman, however, several months of living in a rooming house in an ethnically mixed New York neighbourhood while making the rounds of editorial offices might have raised eyebrows back home. The 1890s was the era of the New Woman in the United States, and the independent cigarette-smoking female writer or artist living on a par with men was a titillating idea, as Arthur Stringer, another Canadian expatriate in New York, indicated in his 1903 novel *The Silver Poppy.* But Stringer's heroine is an American, and American women might be capable of any outrage, even plagiarism, as Stringer's prim provincial hero observes with consternation.

But if few Canadian women followed the men into exile, they did try as eagerly as their male compatriots to break into print with the American magazines and book publishers. Sara Jeannette Duncan's work appeared in *Harper's Bazaar, Scribner's, Century,* and *Atheneum,* and most of her novels were published by Appleton of New York. Ethelwyn Wetherald was in *Scribner's, Harper's, New England Magazine,* and *Youth's Companion,* and her book, *House of Trees,* was issued in 1895 by Lamson, Wolffe, a small Boston firm which was also Bliss Carman's publisher. Susan Frances Harrison had poems in *New England Magazine* and *Littel's Living Age;* Agnes Maule Machar appeared in *Century,* although the bulk of her output was placed with Canadian periodicals.

It is impossible, however, to avoid the conclusion that, in their efforts to seek the international prominence and substantial remuneration available in American magazine and book publication, Canadian women writers encountered discrimination—a discrimination compounded perhaps by nationality as well as by sex. American magazines in the 1890s were paying increasing critical attention to Canadian literature through reviews and survey articles, although American critics tended to impose on English-Canadian writers certain stereotyped expectations. Canadian literature was supposed to be a celebration of nature, as established by the Tantramar poems of Charles G. D. Roberts, the lake lyrics of Wilfred Campbell, the wilderness poems of Duncan Campbell Scott. Canadian women writers, it appears, were expected to produce a more delicate version of these stereotypes. The influence of American editors and critics was probably strong enough to make these women conform to their expectations willingly, perhaps even with unquestioning acceptance of the literary assumptions involved. Still, one wonders what individualistic tendencies were suppressed in this authoritarian cultural climate—especially when the authorities were foreign.

This is not to say that American editors and critics paid a lot of attention to Canadian women writers, comparatively speaking. Three survey articles on Canadian literature, which appeared in American magazines of the 1890s, provide a suggestive indication of American responses. An article by a journalist named Joseph Dana Miller, "The Singers of Canada," published in *Munsey's* in May 1895, effused at length over Roberts, Lampman, Carman, and other male writers and then devoted a concluding half-page to Pauline Johnson, Isabella Valancy Crawford, Susan Frances Harrison, and Agnes Maule Machar. A female critic for the New York *Bookman*, Winifred Lee Wendell, mentioned Lily Dougall, Marjory McMurchy, and Margaret Marshall Saunders as well as Johnson and Harrison in her 1900 article "The Modern School of Canadian Writers," but the references were very brief in comparison to her treatment of Carman, Roberts, and other male writers. Walter Blackburn Harte included more detailed appreciations of Duncan, Machar, Wetherald, and Harrison in his "Some Canadian Writers of To-Day" for *New England Magazine* in 1895, but these four are overshadowed by the male writers surveyed in the article.

This kind of discrimination is evident too in the infrequent inclusion of Canadians in American anthologies of the period. A substantial section on Canadian poetry was included in the influential *Victorian Anthology 1837-1895*, edited in 1895 by the New York littérateur E. C. Stedman. But among the generous representations of Roberts, Carman, Lampman, Campbell, and Scott were one poem by Susanna Moodie, two by Isabella Valancy Crawford, two by Susan Frances Harrison, three by Pauline Johnson, four by Ethelwyn Wetherald, and one by Elizabeth G. Roberts. The inclusion of Charles G. D. Roberts' sister was not perhaps an exclusively literary decision:

Roberts himself had edited the Canadian section at Stedman's invitation, as correspondence between the two men reveals (Stedman, 1910, II, 199-200). Roberts' editorial policies raise another possibility: that the male Canadians active in the American literary scene tended, albeit without malevolence, to exclude or discourage their female compatriots. Bliss Carman, for instance, as editor of *The Chap-Book,* established in Cambridge, Massachusetts, in 1894, ignored Canadian women writers except for publishing two poems by Ethelwyn Wetherald in 1896. Roberts and Carman were the centre of a rather clubby and bohemian circle of Canadian literary expatriates, where lunches and late night get-togethers in Greenwich Village restaurants became part of some legendary and predominantly masculine exploits.

But if Canadian women writers had trouble with mainline editors, even among their own countrymen, they could and did seek American publication in the eccentric but innovative little magazines that emerged in the United States by the dozen around the turn of the century. Flimsy in format, limited in circulation and in funds to pay contributors, these pocket-sized ephemeral periodicals, like *Yellow Book* in England, provided outlets for iconoclastic literary and social movements. Bliss Carman's *Chap-Book* is sometimes described as the first of the American little magazines, although it soon lapsed into the conventionalities of the mass-circulation periodicals, leaving the iconoclasm to its imitators. Women writers were not inordinately represented in such publications, although one magazine, *Ebell* of Los Angeles (1898-99), was edited and written entirely by women, and some editors included feminism among the modern causes their publications advocated (Faxon, 72-74, 92, 106-107, 125-126; Heyl, 21-26).

Carman did publish in *The Chap-Book* two poems by Ethelwyn Wetherald, whose work also appeared in *Lotus*, edited in 1895-96 by Walter Blackburn Harte. Harte published the work of another Canadian, Edith Eaton, whose short stories appeared in *Lotus* and in a second short-lived venture of Harte's, *Fly-Leaf* (1896), as well as in a magazine called *Chautauquan* (1905). Harte and Eaton had begun their literary careers together in Montreal, publishing short stories and prose sketches in John-Talon Lesperance's *The Dominion Illustrated News* in 1888. Eaton, the Eurasian daughter of a silk merchant who lived for several years in China, adopted the pen name Sui Sin Far, and went on to publish short stories in a variety of American periodicals until her death in 1914 at the age of forty-seven. Edith Eaton is overshadowed in reputation by her younger sister Winnifred, who in the first quarter of the twentieth century published a series of sentimental novels about Japan under the pen name Onoto Watanna. But Eaton's one book, a collection of stories entitled *Mrs. Spring Fragrance* (1912), reveals a remarkably bold commitment to urban realism and controversial social themes, involving the problems of Chinese and Eurasians in the United States and Canada.

The example of Edith Eaton points up the need for more research in a specialized but vital area of Canadian literary history. The work of other obscure writers, and of better-known ones, needs to be sought out and identified in the back issues of late nineteenth-century American magazines. Many of the more ephemeral publications, in brief and unindexed runs, are housed in the rare periodicals collections of the New York and Boston public libraries and in Princeton University library. Not nearly enough research is done by Canadian literary historians, biographers, and critics in the field of late nineteenth-century American publishing outlets, partly because of an underestimation of the literary importance of periodicals in that era and of the extent and significance of the Canadian involvement with publications in the United States.

The manuscript collections of magazines, editors, and publishing companies also need to be thoroughly searched. The archives of the Century Company in the New York public library contain letters from many Canadian authors, including Agnes Deans Cameron, Sara Jeannette Duncan, Agnes Laut, and Agnes Maule Machar. Much of this correspondence is of considerable biographical and critical interest, since the authors are often writing to introduce themselves to editors and to describe work in progress. One letter from Duncan to the Century editors, for instance, contains an outline of an untitled work-in-progress that is obviously an early version of *The Imperialist*. Such research should, of course, be part of a comprehensive scrutiny of the whole literary history of late nineteenth-century Canada, including the lives and careers of writers of both sexes, and the editing and publishing milieux on both sides of the Canadian-American border. So little work has been done in this direction that all historical and biographical investigation is to be welcomed. But a concentration on the experience of women writers is especially urgent, for it may lead to important revisions of perceptions of late nineteenth century Canadian literature. The most widely held notions about this period tend to resolve into two familiar cliches: almost all the work of enduring value was done by three or four male poets, and the prevailing literary medium was a genteel romanticism harking back to Wordsworth, Shelley, and Keats. In fact, the English-Canadian literary milieu from 1867 to the early twentieth century was a turmoil of activity involving the distinctive talents of many now forgotten individuals, as well as various internal and external influences, always and especially including the monolithic and seductive influence of the United States. At the least, research along the lines indicated here should lead to a clearer picture of what it was like to be a Canadian writer in the late nineteenth century. In addition, such research could lead to the rediscovery of important writers and to a better understanding of the social and cultural forces which form part of the explanation as to why Canadian writers wrote as they did at that time.

Re(Dis)covering Our Foremothers ed. McMullen.

W.H. New
from Back to the Future: The Short Story in Canada and the Writing of Literary History

My subject is threefold. I am concerned with the English-language short story in Canada, with the writing of literary history, and with the biases of time and critical expectation that have helped shape both story and history. I come to this topic from the work on which I have been recently engaged, trying to write literary history, and from my increasing awareness of the pressures of conformity and precedent that affect form, organization, judgment, and tone.... In particular I will look at attitudes to the short story, as a paradigm by which to estimate the processes of critical system.

I begin in retrospect in order to avoid the first pitfall of prospect: the temptation of predicting future practice in any art form. Existing volumes of literary history provide an illustration here. I can refer (as all commentators on Canadian short fiction now do) to a rash assertion Hugo McPherson made in 1965 in the "Fiction 1940-1960" chapter of the first edition of the *Literary History of Canada*. He simply announced that the short story in Canada was dying out. He wrote: "Compared with *belles-lettres* and humour, the record of the short story is good, but its importance in Canadian expression is declining.... [T]he short story has lost much of its prestige; a generation ago it was the recognized proving ground for aspiring novelists.... The short story... [used to be] a major form, and a form particularly suited to the needs of writers who could not find time for the extended effort demanded of the novel" (720-21). But with the advent of television, "magazines recognized that they could not compete with the 'instant' short fiction of television drama, and turned almost exclusively to educational or documentary essays.... Special pleas for the short story would be futile at this date" (720-21). He went on to mention Wilson, Raddall, Garner, Gallant, Ross, Reaney, Spettigue, Ludwig, and Alice Munro, but said that Canadian writers had now to compete in international markets and concluded: "In this difficult, exacting, and now declining genre, Morley Callaghan is still the unacknowledged master" (720-21). When the second edition of the *Literary History of Canada* appeared in 1976, these generalizations were excised, and some account was taken of 1960s activities in the genre. Since 1976, far from declining, the form has burgeoned.

This statement does not mean that television drama has therefore declined; the point is not to see genres as mutually exclusive, binary alternatives, but as multiple options. There have been scores of books and individual stories to appear; also some short story theory by Canadians (notably Mary Louise Pratt), and also several anthologies which (following on those by Pacey and Weaver—I am thinking of collections edited by Metcalf, Bowering, Wiebe, Phillips, Nichol, Blaise, and Hancock) have provided some commentary on short fiction in their introductions and in apparatuses designed for student readers. My first concern here, however, is not—at least directly—with these recent developments. I am concerned more with the paucity of commentary before they came into existence and with the fact of statements like those of McPherson. What presumptions underlie them? How do such presumptions affect critical judgments? To what degree do they express critical expectations of literary history rather than constitute anything more than superficial observations of aesthetic practice? And why?

In order to approach these questions—I say "approach" deliberately, rather than "answer"—I want to review the comments on short fiction made by three writers prior to 1930, and then to consider some of the implications they have for an understanding both of the genre and of its history (real or received) in Canada. The three writers are Allan Douglas Brodie, for "Canadian Short-Story Writers," published in February 1895; Archibald MacMechan, for his 1924 history *Head-Waters of Canadian Literature*; and B.K. Sandwell, for his review of Raymond Knister's 1928 anthology *Canadian Short Stories,* in the August 25, 1928 issue of *Saturday Night.* In some ways, all three of them lie behind the generic assessments that structure the first edition of the *Literary History of Canada.*

Brodie's ten-page profile of current short story writers of the 1890s appeared in *The Canadian Magazine*; it appealed to a general readership. The influence of the American critic Brander Matthews suggests itself in the hyphen between "short" and "story" in Brodie's title (Matthews had employed the term "short-story" to describe a particular kind of magazine-length fiction, with such characteristics as brevity and ingenuity; unity and compression; action; logical structure; and, if possible, fantasy). But the hyphen disappears between Brodie's title and

Brodie's text, so the influence may be illusory, an indication more of the copy editor's impulse than the critic's intention. Indeed, Brodie appears to be more concerned to celebrate a few national personalities (Macdonald Oxley, Marjory MacMurchy, Duncan Campbell Scott, Maud Ogilvy, Stuart Livingston, and a few others) than to reflect on the character of the art form.

His essay does open with a few justifications for the genre, but while these give lip service to verbal skill, they explain the art of the short story more fundamentally as a literary form that responds to laws of speed and demand. "In these days of excitement and confusion," Brodie writes, "caused by the general and all-absorbing pursuit of the elusive but ever mighty dollar, nothing plays so important a part in the delightful world of literature—even Canadian literature—as the 'short story.' The days of the three-volume novel are past and gone, it is earnestly hoped, never to return.... When [people now] wish to thoroughly enjoy themselves in a literary way, they crave, and must have, a terse, pithy, racy, and cleverly told short story, the writing of which is an art in itself" (334). Such comments then become his justification for whatever it is that Canadian magazine writers do. He continues: "It is a credit, rather than otherwise, to that little band of bright Canadian writers depicted in this article, that they have chosen, and have ably developed, this particular field of literature" (334). This assertion covertly declares a good deal about hierarchies in literary taste, hierarchies which themselves suggest that the criteria for judgment stem from outside the country. In Brodie's words, "Canadians are proud of the successes and triumphs of [those who have gone] abroad [meaning E.W. Thomson, Gilbert Parker, and Robert Barr]; but Canadians do not, or should not, forget that we still have some clever literary people among us" (334-35). For him there is, implicitly, a moral virtue in national enthusiasm, which "good" literature serves. The words of praise Brodie goes on to use begin after awhile to sound formulaic—D.C. Scott's works possess, he says, "both dramatic interest, and a certain poetic beauty all their own" (338); Livingston's are "possessed of power, brilliancy, and a certain poetic undercurrent"

(343); MacMurchy and William McLennan are praised respectively for "a touch of pathos... applied with a gentle and loving hand" (338), and for "dramatic interest" and "a pathos which is marvellously attractive" (340-41). It is never clear how these characteristics meet the demands for a clever, pithy, racy, terse literature. It suffices simply to name and praise; the nationality of the writers and the fact of their publishing magazine-length fiction constitute self-evident (and for Brodie interconnected) aesthetic values.

Some twenty-nine years later, Archibald MacMechan was less tolerant than Brodie of contemporary romance ("Parker," he wrote ironically, "has written many tales; and several are ostensibly Canadian in scene" [141]), but MacMechan was no less bound up than Brodie was in the unstated poetics of piety and received tradition. His title metaphor tells us something of his perspective: "Head-waters" is the term through which he conventionally implies a nation of source and flow, a single source and a linear flow, a notion of mainstream—like history itself (and the parallel is one which MacMechan's book argues). Indeed, MacMechan's main interest, in practice, is in history, for all his initial stated concerns about literature being the soul of a people. T.C. Haliburton, for example, is treated as a historian first and a satirist second, and such a set of priorities characterizes the drift of the book as a whole.

History for MacMechan is the fundament of culture rather than simply a context for it or a systematic rendering of it. History is deemed to be at once aesthetic and factual, a model for literary excellence. And then the idea of "factual" takes on a particular coloration. His primary criterion for assessing literature is its fidelity to empirical reality, an idea he narrows still further. Literary works are deemed to be Canadian insofar as they appear Canadian by setting. But while he tells us, as one manifestation of this criterion, that Sir Charles G.D. Roberts really found himself in his short stories of animal life and that journalism is important to literature in Canada, MacMechan does not pursue the ramifications of this belief. Instead, he constantly undermines it. For while he stresses the force of journalism and the relevance of the real to the subject and style of fiction—even referring to his own work as a "sketch," using that much-embraced nineteenth-century term of "objective" impressionism—he doesn't mention the sketch as an art form, nor treat journals as a place where a reader might look for "high" art.

Indeed, the relevance of MacMechan to short story history in Canada seems to lie in the degree to which he ignores the form. Poets were more important to him than short story writers. "In prose fiction... Canadians had never shown the ability so manifest in their poetry" (135), he declares. But his treatment of poetry reflects indirectly on his expectations of fiction. He focusses on single lyric poems and full-length prose books, praising "unity" but defining "unity" in two different ways. He gives aesthetic and moral precedence to poetry and demands empirical fidelity of prose. Further, by ignoring *short* fiction, except as an aside, he consigns it to an aesthetic periphery, characterizing it inferentially as the apprentice work of writers who demonstrate their substance in other, longer prose forms—in history, for example, or in the novel: long works that by implication have book-length unity and embody the linear principles of historical discourse.

Within four years of MacMechan's *Head-Waters*, Raymond Knister had published his minor revolution in Canadian fictional aesthetics, his anthology *Canadian Short Stories*. It was, in some sense, the first real survey of short fiction in Canada. Knister included writers from the nineteenth century, writers from the generation before his own, and writers of his own generation such as William Murtha and Morley Callaghan. The immediate critical response to the book was favourable, but in B.K. Sandwell's review in *Saturday Night* it took a particularly interesting form, which focusses our attention once again back on the taste that was shaping Canadian short fiction criticism. Sandwell located the anthology's strengths not in the moderns but in the work of Scott, Roberts, Thomson, and Parker, whom he called "those four princes of the last days of the century." The moderns, by contrast—Callaghan, for example—were "accomplished and earnest youngsters," whose "experiments" had "interest and value"; but of the extent of their value,

Sandwell was uncertain. Would their subjects, he asked—their "types," their "lively interest in futility"— "be as durable" as the material that "fell to the hand of Roberts and Thomson and Parker"? Would an interest in futility "be permanent"? And would the "revolt against style, or against everything that passed for style in the good old days," work towards a "permanent good"? That is, how could they match up against the "dignity and formality" of "a language based on Addison and tempered by Scott," a language of people who regarded themselves as "literary men, with a tradition to uphold and a law to follow" (7)?

The main criterion operating in this review is unstated, but it is scarcely concealed. It involves a belief in the fixity of normative judgment, the existence of some codifiable universal standard, in which the Canadian romance/realists of the turn of the century participated, but which somehow could not be extended to Callaghan. This standard had an ethical core, but it could not deal with class or language or place or gender except insofar as it classified them through anglo- and androcentric presumptions. Sandwell was simply resisting the kinds of change that by the 1920s were going on around him. Individual writers and the structures of society at large were challenging the presumptions on which his criticism rested in at least five ways: first of all by responding to shifts in ethnic and urban demography, and by attacking the existing structures of political power in the country; also by redefining the character of region and style, by resisting received notions of unity and logical sequence, and by using the idea of *parole* to combat the idea of dialect. In other words, the very indeterminacy of the short story form began to be both aesthetically and politically functional, reinforcing changes in social hierarchy and critical expectation.

We can take these three stances towards short fiction—the idea that it is an entertaining apprentice form, a peripheral form, and a normative vehicle of dignity and formality—and impose against them the several conventional theories, now currently in vogue, that attempt to explain what the short story in general, around the world, is and does. To do so is to begin to see how received notions of genre have shaped critical expectations and in turn, in Canada, shaped the design of literary tradition that people came, by the 1960s, to accept as their "natural" literary history. Canada was not alone, of course, in importing—or "receiving"—its conventions of critical estimation; I am using the Canadian experience as an example of a larger process, for which short fiction theory supplies a convenient paradigm.

Four standard ways of classifying the short story had come into existence by the 1920s; all of them to one degree or another were culturally biased. To generalize, British comment sought to find in short stories their link with other prose forms, and so to establish a tradition for the form: by seeing the story as a small history, moreover, such comment emphasized elements of narrative sequence and narrative consequence. American commentary, by contrast, considered the form to be both revolutionary and American, one that may have had some distant roots in other genres, but which was transformed by the power of the American speaking voice, which accorded "story" the legitimacy of cultural attitude. The practice of *conte* writers in France encouraged criticism there to pursue the patterns of folk culture. And from elsewhere—from Joyce in Ireland, Chekhov in Russia, Mansfield in New Zealand, for example—came the experiments in fragmentation which divided the new twentieth-century story from its nineteenth-century forebears. The new stories emphasized the passing moment, the flash of insight, the sudden epiphany, the character of absence: momentariness and interruption rather than eternals and continuity. Such categories—of sequence, orality, prototype, and fragmentation—inevitably fade into one another in literary practice, but in general terms these four critical concerns respectively suggest ways of justifying four forms of story: narrative history; anecdote; folktale and fable; and indirect narration. The trouble is, they have more characteristically been held to define the short story in toto, to describe the genre on the basis of one cultural practice and to claim it as a way of representing—or coding— "reality" as seen by all. Therein lies one of the main critical problems that colours analyses of the Canadian short story tradition. Up to 1965, English-Canadian critics, trained primarily to evaluate by means of British standards, were more receptive to versions of story as history than to versions of story as sketch or folk myth or fragment. Built into attitudes towards literary genres were particular cultural mindsets. And the systems of expectation determined declared value.

For example, any perception of the short story as merely a short version of a novel, or as an extended version of an illustrated parable, or as a simple written record of a vernacular entertainment, places it in an implied aesthetic hierarchy, codifies it as a "minor" form and establishes it "therefore" as a less-than-serious art. In parallel fashion, any identification of the "fragmentary" nature of the modern versions of the genre confirms to some critics that the short story lacks coherence or unity or "wholeness." By implication these criteria are themselves identifiable, their sacrosanct character not in question. The step from these underlying preconceptions to the critical history of the short story in Canada has interesting ramifications, which takes us back to Brodie, MacMechan, and Sandwell.

"Poetic charm"—that quality which Brodie found everywhere in Canadian magazine stories—is precisely what MacMechan would allow in poetry but reject in prose, insisting on historical argument instead; but, like Brodie, he identified the validity of a Canadian prose work by the documentary realism of its particular setting. The effect of the two impulses combined was to distort the way writers perceived landscape and society and the way they used language to artistic purpose. Subjects and settings carried more than their obvious resonance, feeding the hierarchical impulse. Consider, for example, stories of Quebec. To anglo-Canadian eyes, before 1930, the very word "Quebec" implied a whole set of attitudes, involving among other things Catholicism and provinciality. MacMechan, writing in *Head-Waters* a history of both English- and French-Canadian literature, nonetheless did so with a British-based historical bias. The folktales of Beaugrand and Fréchette go unremarked (except to note that some of Fréchette's prose presents such "oddities... as are fostered by a restricted provincial existence" [78]); moreover, what they represent goes unrecognized. These authors were not drawing on British patterns; they were attempting to adapt folk custom and local idiom to *conte* form and contemporary behaviour, sometimes with a political motive. But the ahistorical imagination of the surface narratives of their works apparently impedes for MacMechan any direct estimation of their fictional quality.

This pattern repeats itself even with MacMechan's treatment of the anglo-Canadian writer Duncan Campbell Scott, who from the 1890s to the 1920s was writing stories set in Quebec and poems about Indians. MacMechan acknowledges Scott for his biography of Governor Simcoe but mentions neither his fiction nor his verse. And while Brodie does acknowledge him, once again the version of Scott we get is one that has been skewed by expectation. Scott had attempted to use folktale form and sketch in order to probe the violence that lies beneath the more superficial realities of Quebec culture; but Brodie accepts these formal experiments as signs of poetic beauty and charm. Rather surprisingly, subsequent commentators have largely followed him, accepting Scott's stories as simple accounts of a quaint backwater. For the critics, a cultural stereotype about Quebec has become a fixed truth, governing the way they read. Though he ignored Scott, MacMechan still illustrates this attitude directly; his book goes so far as to give extended praise to the *patois* versifier William Henry Drummond—as poet and as national patriot. The fact that Drummond's voice was long accepted in English Canada as an authentic characterization of francophone speech and behaviour says a good deal about continuing presumptions concerning dialect and normative language, about cultural unfamiliarity and the misconceptions that stem from it. The case of D.C. Scott is the reverse side of Drummond's in stance: up to and including the treatment of Scott's books of short fiction, *In the Village of Viger* and *The Witching of Elspie*, in the 1965 version of the *Literary History of Canada*, to be quaint about Quebec was considered realistic, and to try to use the forms of Quebec in order to get past the stereotypes was regarded, in anglophone Canada, as mere "local colourism"—quaint, and perhaps even "escapist."

The animal stories of Roberts offer a parallel example of critical misreading. One of the things that characterizes these works is that they could be claimed equally by those who stood in demand of pathos and those who stood in need of real settings. As the opening of a sketch like "The Prisoners of the Pitcher-Plant" makes clear, the illusion of Roberts' objective realism inhered in his narrator's documentary stance and in the scientific terminology of the text. But the careful reader recognizes in word like "prisoner" a whole tradition of romance conventions, and in the story's adjectival subtext, a subjective impressionism that no rigorously objective documentary could sustain. But the ambivalence was less debilitating than it was productive. The effect of the double claim upon Roberts—as the master of reality and as the master of romance—was to legitimize a romantic illusion of wilderness as the record of true Canadian reality. This was paradoxically an illusion perpetrated by an urban critical community—by Sandwell, among others—who applied their borrowed expectations of literature to the evaluation of local literary practice. They used the conventional image of Canada to claim Canada's literary distinctiveness and yet at the same time situated this native cultural tradition inside a so-called "universal" mainstream, one that depended on closed form, linear sequence, and received notions of literary language.

By the time of the *Literary History of Canada*, this conventional sense of what constituted the Canadian tradition in the short story had solidified. Closer analysis, however, shows that a number of questions were being begged. The tradition was selective in its recognition of form; its assertion of realism was suspect; it was bound by its identification of Canada with wilderness, hence limited by subject and setting; it was implicitly centralist; and it was naive. These issues overlap. Some of them I have already noted at greater length: the centralist "mainstream" metaphors of MacMechan, for example; or the consignment of Haliburton's Atlantic Canada to a category called "history" (the "present" having somehow moved on and away); or the way Roberts was accepted as realistic and representative, although he was rural in subject, often impressionistic in language, hierarchical in stance, and immersed in a world of male norms. When such values are translated critically into the forms of the national tradition, something goes awry. There was in practice—among Canadian writers of short fiction before Callaghan—a substantial literary inventiveness that goes unnoticed if we accept as normative either Roberts's wilderness or Haliburton's satires.

There were other options being explored. There were options by place (there was a lively cultural activity in Victoria in the late nineteenth century, for example, and no-one has yet adequately recorded it). There were options by setting (there continues among anthologists a resistance to Canadian stories set outside Canada—Thomson wrote some lively Boston stories, for example, and Norman Duncan an instructive collection set in the Syrian quarter of New York: both of them urban as well as extraterritorial—but they seldom get read). There were options by race and culture, both of which had an impact on literary form (Quebec folktales and indigenous myth were both more sophisticated art forms than anglo-protestant rationalism was willing to admit). There were options by literary stance and design (there were mannered comedies as well as wilderness struggles, and to look closely at Haliburton is to discover a writer who deliberately experimented with literary genre, who worked with transformation tale as well as with history, with the conventions of sentimental romance as well as with those of the satiric dialogue). And there were options by gender. In all this discussion, where are the writers who were women? Brodie at least acknowledged their existence, though his terms of recognition are faintly patronizing: "In the realm of short story writing," he notes, "Canada has several clever lady writers whose work possesses a certain charm all its own" (337-38). Yet two of the most stylistically accomplished works of the later nineteenth and earlier twentieth centuries were Susan Frances Harrison's *Crowded Out! and Other Sketches* (1886) and Jessie Georgina Sime's *Sister Woman* (1919), neither book (and neither writer) recognized by Brodie or MacMechan. The problem was, neither book fit the critic's pattern. Harrison's sketches testily complained of British critical intransigence and wittily exposed the shallow mores of faddish urban American society; Sime's remarkable work adopted an interrupted narrative form in order to expose the inadequacies of a normative social pattern that consigned women to second-class status and abandoned them to penury, divorce, stillbirths, single parenthood, and domestic service.

The first point to make is that it is not subject alone but also the importance of the literary form to the subject that demands recognition, and that such recognition is the first step to re-evaluating the genre of short fiction in Canada and the tradition by which literary history has so far defined it. When Hugo McPherson in 1965 said that the short story was disappearing, he was in some sense right, if by what he said we understand a particular form of short story and a particular, closed notion of what the tradition was. New forms of story were on the way, resistant to then current narrative and social definitions. Such a need to redefine—and hence the need to re-evaluate individual works and their tradition—opens up the larger point to be made here. Any age, our own included, is subject to bias and preconception. What literary history valuably records is less a set of verifiable facts and universal principles than the perspective of the time and place in which it is written. To readers of literary history, such perspectives do not get in the way of knowledge; they are part of what is learned about literature. The "factuality" of data often changes. It is selective, and the very selectivity of design can shape both memory and expectations about the future. We have to remember that preconceptions, as well as the judgments to which they lead, illuminate for us the workings of a living culture.

New Contexts of Canadian Criticism.
Eds. Heble, Pennee and Struthers.

Mary Louise Pratt
from The Short Story: The Long and the Short of It

5. *Subject matter.* Just as it is used for formal experimentation, the short story is often the genre used to introduce new (and possibly stigmatized) subject matters into the literary arena. Bret Harte refers to this function, for example, in an 1899 retrospective on the origins of the American short story. Harte explains that he wrote "The Luck of Roaring Camp" because, as editor of *Overland Monthly*, he failed to find in all the materials submitted "anything of that wild and picturesque life which had impressed him, first as a truant schoolboy, and afterwards, as a youthful schoolmaster among the mining population" (Summers 1963: 8). For Harte the American short story signalled the end of the dominance of English models in American literature, the end of an era when "the literary man had little sympathy with the rough and half-civilized masses who were making his country's history: if he used them at all it was as a foil to bring into greater relief his hero of the unmistakable English pattern." In other parts of the world we similarly find the short story being used to introduce new regions or groups into an established national literature, or into an emerging national literature in the process of decolonization. In France, Maupassant through the short story breaks down taboos on matters of sexuality and class. In the establishment of a modern national literature in Ireland, the short story emerges as the central prose fiction genre, through which Joyce, O'Flaherty, O'Faolain, O'Connor, Moore, Lavin and so many others first document modern Irish life. Its role has been comparable in the emergence of the modern literature of the American South. In Canada, smalltown Ontario life was introduced, at an early stage of decolonization, in the comic stories of Stephen Leacock, and at a later stage, in the more serious work of Alice Munro. In Latin America, it is through the short story that Horacio Quiroga introduces the marginalized society of the Argentine jungle frontier into literature; in Peru Jose María

Arguedas first begins his exploration of modern indigenous life in the short story, before moving to the novel. It is in such regional (i.e. marginal with respect to some metropolis) writings that one sees most clearly the short story's relations to the sketch, a genre which it has now subsumed, and which was, as Ray West describes it, "a romantic means of catching the atmosphere of remote places" (Summers 1963: 28). On the other side, and perhaps moving toward the panoramic potential of the novel, it is also here on the regional periphery that the short story cycle has been most likely to make its appearance. Of the writers just mentioned, five wrote place-based short story cycles of the *Winesburg, Ohio* or *Dubliners* variety. (Joyce, *Dubliners*; Leacock, *Sunshine Sketches*; Munro, *Lives of Girls and Women*; Quiroga, *Los desterrados*; Arguedas, *El aylla*.) To some extent, such cycles do a kind of groundbreaking, establishing a basic literary identity for a region or group, laying out descriptive parameters, character types, social and economic settings, principal points of conflict for an audience unfamiliar either with the region itself or with seeing that region in print. But the short story cycle sometimes is used to convey a particular social perspective too. Speaking of Sherwood Anderson's use of the cycle in *Winesburg, Ohio*, Ian Reid remarks:

> The tight continuous structure of a novel is deliberately avoided: Anderson said he wanted 'a new looseness' of form to suit the particular quality of his material. His people are lonely, restless, cranky. Social cohesion is absent in their mid-western town. Even momentary communication seldom occurs between any two of them. Winesburg is undergoing a human erosion caused by the winds of change blowing from the cities, by the destabilizing of moral codes, and by the intrinsic thinness of small-town life. The 'new looseness' of Winesburg Ohio can convey with precision and pathos the duality that results: a superficial appearance (and indeed the ideal possibility) of communal wholeness, and an underlying actual separateness. (Reid 1977: 47-8)

Reid's comments also suggest why the short story cycle rather than the novel might be chosen to portray, for example, the disorder of frontier society, or of traditional societies disintegrating in the face of modernization.

Obviously, whether a given subject matter is central or peripheral, established or new in a literature has a great deal to do with what is central and peripheral in the community outside its literature, a great deal to do, that is, with values, and with socioeconomic, political and cultural realities. In some cases at least, there seem to develop dialectical correspondences between minor and marginal genres and what are evaluated as minor or marginal subjects. So for example, we find the short story used especially often for portraying childhood experience (illustrated by such classics, as Joyce's "Araby," Cortazar's "End of the Game," Lawrence's "Rocking Horse Winner," and so many by Faulkner). Novels dealing with childhood experience seem relatively rare on the other hand, except for the specialized (marked) categories of the picaresque and the bildungsroman. Such a tendency might be explained purely in terms of length and interest—a child's perspective is too naive, too thin, too unrevealing to sustain "full-length" novel treatment. But isn't this really a way of saying that childhood experience is not considered normative or authoritative in the society, or that it is considered an incomplete basis for the supposed totalizing vision of the novel? Similarly, the short story has a tradition of dealing with rural or peasant life. This is a long-standing trend in Russia. Speaking of the *conte* in late 19th century France, Ian Reid observes,

> Not the least important tendency of those latter writers [Daudet, Flaubert, Maupassant], was their predilection for rural subjects and simple folk. Mostly it could be left to the novel to delineate those large-scale social patterns which were so amply extended in urban life; the short story seemed especially suitable for the portrayal of regional life, or of individuals who, though situated in a city, lived there as aliens. (Reid 1977: 24)

Reid's comment suggests an explanation based on some kind of natural or intrinsic literary possibilities of the various subject matters—rural life is small and thus appropriate to small genres. But of course it is essential to see such a view simply as an expression of the values held by the particular class who had proprietorship over the two genres, and for whom the novel was the privileged vehicle for dealing with the areas of experience they cared about most. When it comes time for a dominant class to bring what Frank O'Connor likes to call "submerged population groups" to the surface, the short story often comes into play. One might offer a similar explanation for the fact that in the age of empiricism, the short story seems to have been the special domain for the fantastic and the supernatural—topics marginalized and stigmatized by a novel consolidating itself around realism.

The New Short Story Theories. Ed. Charles E. May.

Frank Davey
Genre Subversion in the English-Canadian Short Story

The title of this essay is more a problem than a title, because the question of whether genre is sufficiently substantial a concept to be subject to subversion, or whether what might be subverted is a critical illusion rather than some 'thing' called genre, is a difficult one, and not one I hope to resolve here—although obviously I have opinions, or perhaps illusions, about it. 'Subversion' or 'transgression' may well be usual operations in writing and reading, in which case the question arises of whether, being so usual, such operations can occur, there being perhaps no thing or praxis to be transgressed against. Not surprisingly, the possibility of subversion is most strongly embraced by those theorists intent on defending classical or pragmatic notions of genre.

Such puzzles, however, have not troubled most of the theorists of what they, and we for convenience here, call 'the short story.' The short story is both one of the most recent of literary genres and the most overdefined. I perhaps should have said the English-language short story because, of course, the term has no exact equivalent in other languages, but I hesitate because theorists of the short story, the English language short story, that is, have worked as much from the practice of Turgenev,

Gogol, Chekov and de Maupassant as from that of Poe, Harte, Joyce or Mansfield.

The brief history of the short story (the term is first used generically by Brander Matthews in 1885 and first appears in the *Oxford English Dictionary* in the supplement of 1933 [Reid 1]) is one mostly of defenders and apologists, who set out to establish it as a boundaried class of objects and to legitimize it as a form. In that landmark 1885 essay, Matthews established the goal of the enterprise in his attempt to define "the genuine Short-story"; in 1909 H.S. Canby followed Matthews by announcing a short story genre that was "sharply marked off from other forms"; in 1925 the Russian Formalist Boris Eichenbaum posited, in his influential essay on O. Henry, that the difference between the novel and the short story was "one of essence"; in 1965 Alberto Moravia declared that the short story was "a literary art which is unquestionably purer, more essential, more lyrical, more concentrated and more absolute than the novel" (in May 151). Throughout these writings there is a claim for the autonomy of the genre and an implication of timelessness that is curiously at odds with the brevity of its history. There is often an assumption of realism, often psychological realism, and a sharp insistence that the short story be marked off from earlier, and implicitly 'lower,' forms of short fiction; as Thomas Beachcroft wrote in 1964, "realistic stories [had] to be separated from religious teaching… from legends, monsters and fairies; then to develop from the merely grotesque or coarse anecdote, from the novella of astonishing events… and then to pass through the hands of the eighteenth-century essayists, who domesticated the short story but replaced religious teaching with moral advice" (7).

For the most part, the attributes claimed by these theorists for the short story have involved the notion of unity. Among the necessary characteristics of the story listed by Matthews were unity of impression, compression, a single action, and a form that is "logical, adequate and harmonious." Canby required a single mood or impression and described the genre as an "art of tone." F.L. Pattee in 1923 proposed that the story must have not only compression, unity and momentum but "culmination" — "a destination toward which it constantly moves" (366). In 1945 A.L. Bader wrote that the short story always possesses a structure of conflict, development, and final resolution, and moreover that even stories in which these elements are not readily apparent will reveal on close reading "the conventional dramatic pattern" (in May 107-15). Beachcroft argued that the story "must have an intense concentration of purpose" and "one or two vivid scenes" (15). As recently as 1981, Walter Allen declared that "the short story... deals with, dramatizes, a single incident" (7).

An even stronger attempt to establish the unity of the short story, and to valorize the story as an object of high art, was made by the New Critics, who used it, along with the lyric poem, as a pedagogical tool in the attempt to teach literature and taste to the newly large and democratized freshman classes that came to US universities following the Second World War. (I am extending here Terry Eagleton's analysis of the New Critics' view of the lyric as "a self-enclosed object, mysteriously intact in its own unique being" and their use of it in the American university curriculum [*Literary Theory* 47].) In their teaching of the short story, the New Critics built on the earlier Anglo-American theories of unity, and on the Russian Formalists' perception of the short story as a unified synchronic system, to postulate a genre that consisted of carefully crafted organic units, self-sufficient and self-contained, and consistent with the New Critics' larger theories of autotelic literary works. Brooks and Warren wrote in the notes to their college anthology *Understanding Fiction* that the power of a story depends "upon the total structure, upon a set of organic relationships, upon the logic of the whole," that a student "can best be brought to an appreciation of the more broadly human values implicit in fiction by... understanding the functions of the various elements which go to make up fiction and by understanding their relationships to each other in the whole construct" (xiii-xiv). The New Critics also insisted on a clear boundary, an important lesson for the new largely working-class students, between the literary and the popular. The literary story was timeless, uncontaminated by history or biography, and referred to its own symmetries, balances and tensions; it was also, however, through its symbolic operations, mimetic. (As Eagleton remarks, through its "unity, the work 'corresponded' in some sense to reality itself" [47].) The fetishizing bias of this period in North American education is reflected in the titles of its short-story anthologies: Day and Bauer's *Greatest American Short Stories* (1953), Havighurst's *Masters of the Modern Short Story* (1955), McLennan's *Masters and Masterpieces of the Short Story* (1960).

The canonic model for such a concept of the short story was provided by the stories of Joyce's *Dubliners*, taken out of their context in Irish history and the history of the production of literary forms. The model provided the necessary concentration on a single character and event, compression of a life into a single revealing segment, integration of effect, consistency of tone, as well as the necessary culminating moment, the Joycean epiphany. In this model, as well as in the writings of Matthews, Canby, Pattee, Brooks, Warren, Moravia and Allen, is an implicit short-story contract: that the text will produce a recognizable but independent world, include a single recognizable character, be brief, or at least entail only a single reading session, and that it will display some structural unity or logic, show its character in a situation about which the reader can experience concern, and resolve this situation in a manner which instructs the reader in how to interpret the preceding text, yet also leave a ponderable residue of irresolution.

Recent genre theory, of course, has argued persuasively the historicity of genre development, the semiotic character of genre attributes, and the interrelatedness of genres and subgenres. Genres here are not unchanging; as Todorov suggests, "*every* work modifies the sum of possible works, each new example alters the species" (6). "Genres are best not regarded... as classes, but types," Alastair Fowler advises, adding that "a literary genre changes with time, so that its boundaries cannot be defined by any single set of characteristics such as would determine a class" (37-38). For Heather Dubrow, as well as Fowler, genre characteristics constitute units of code through which authors can signal, falsely signal, assign, or allude; far from being classes which contain writers and writing, such attributes offer a cluster of signs with which writers can economically signal large amounts of information. Genres and genre attributes are subject to historical and ideological changes; Todorov again, in his 1976 essay "The Origin of Genres":

> a society chooses and codifies the acts that most closely correspond to its ideology; this is why the existence of certain genres in a society and their absence in another reveal a central ideology, and enable us to establish it with considerable certainty. It is not chance that the epic is possible during one era, the novel during another (the individual hero of the latter being opposed to the collective hero of the former): each of these choices depends upon the ideological framework in which it operates. (164)

Neither Todorov nor Fowler, however, here move past the notion that genre is single or unitary at any one moment of time. Todorov confuses space and time when he uses 'society' (*societé*) and 'era' (*époque*) as interchangeable terms; for a small, easily marginalized country like Canada, such a use of 'era' implies a world society and creates a potentially colonizing prescription of genre potentials. Fowler, when he employs the term 'boundaries'— "its [genre's] boundaries cannot be defined" mysteriously creates undefinable but nevertheless existent boundaries and implies a linear historical succession of undefinably boundaried genres.

It is with theorists like Derrida and Kristeva, for whom genre code may well be subsumable within a concept of *writing*, that we at last move away from unitary concepts of genre, and into the possibility that an indeterminate number of different acts of writing may exist at the same moment of history. With these theorists we enter the debate that rages throughout much of literary criticism today—over whether *writing* (or *text*) is, as Todorov proposes in the above essay, yet another genre within a human discourse that always defines itself generically and is aware of itself synchronically (161), or whether genres are pragmatic, and merely possibilities of temporal *writing acts*.

* * *

We indeed might debate. However, my proposal here moves in a somewhat different direction: that the development of the Canadian short story (the term used, for this occasion at least, along with terms denoting other genres, not as a class but as a location within a complex and mutable network of genre code) occurred almost entirely outside this early twentieth-century Anglo-American theory of the unified and autotelic story. My outline of that theory above is mainly to emphasize that this approach—despite many excellent recent books that take a pluralistic view of the short story (Ian Reid's *The Short Story*, Valerie Shaw's *The Short Story: A Critical Introduction*, 1983, Susan Lohafer's *Coming to Terms with the Short Story*, 1983) is still in many quarters the canonic view of the short story and its history—as Bates's *The Modern Short Story* and Walter Allen's *The Short Story in English* remind us. I propose that this view not only is irrelevant to most writing in the Canadian short story, but distorts any sense of its accomplishments, privileging a dubious set of 'international' conventions (which every major Anglo-American practitioner transgressed) over a locally produced praxis. Internationally this view had many interesting consequences, including the undervaluing of Stevenson, James, William Carlos Williams and Stein as short-fiction writers. In Canada it has been responsible for the notion that Callaghan is the first significant short-story practitioner, that Gallant is the outstanding contemporary practitioner, or that the significant history of the Canadian short story begins in the 1950s or 60s.

An examination of the Canadian short story requires a much more pluralistic and eclectic view of the story, and a more 'generous' sense of its generic language, than that which accompanied the development of the Anglo-American short story. It requires a non-hierarchical conception of story that, far from separating it, as Beachcroft argued for the Anglo-American story, from parable, fable, legend, anecdote and essay, sees it as continuously sharing unstable code-systems with them. Of nineteenth-century Canadian writers of short fiction, Haliburton works out of the practice of the English anecdotal essayists of the eighteenth century; Scott out of the German marchen codes of indeterminacy and enigmatic irony; Sara Jeannette Duncan out of the leisurely circumlocutory narrative, nearly devoid of external event, of Henry James. In this period, only Roberts's animal stories have a significant number of the literary features associated with the modern short story: brevity and economy of presentation, unity of action and setting, Poe's "unity of impression," and decisive, usually ironic, culmination. However, these features in Roberts may have a different source than they do in Joyce or Hemingway or Mansfield. Rather than being produced out of considerations about language or the morality of language, or out of a crisis in signification that leads to metonymy, symbolism and epiphany in Anglo-American fiction, they would appear to be—much like the seemingly 'imagist' features of some of Pratt's early poetry—the result of a specifically Canadian collision between a knowledge of Darwinian theory and an experience of a largely non-humanized environment. Further, these features that encode the perspective of modernist short fiction are themselves governed throughout in Roberts by the pervasive fact that these are animal stories, that the primary code invoked is that of the animal fable, and by the further modification of this code by the invocation of two additional genre codes, one of the empirical descriptions of science, and the other of romance. Roberts's interweaving of these codes can be seen in the opening sentences, as well as in the title, of "When Twilight Falls in the Stump Lots."

> The wet, chill first of the spring, its blackness made tender by the lilac wash of the afterglow, lay upon the high, open stretches of the stump lots. The winter-whitened stumps, the sparse patches of juniper and bay just budding, the rough-mossed hillocks, the harsh boulders here and there up-thrusting from the soil, the swampy hollows wherein a coarse grass began to show green, all seemed anointed, as it were, to an ecstasy of peace by the chrism of that paradisial colour. (*King of Beasts* 180)

The lexis of romance—*twilight, afterglow, anointed, ecstasy, chrism, paradisial*—which the story will ultimately render ironic, mingles with the pragmatic lexis of the Darwinian naturalist.

The next paragraph will introduce the main character, "not far from the centre of the stump lots, a young black and white cow," and call forth the fable mode.

* * *

In the first half of the twentieth century, the Anglo-American short story flourishes; in Canada there are relatively few writers who are changing its story: McClung, Leacock, Grove, Knister, Callaghan, Wilson, Garner and Ross. Of these, Callaghan is usually favoured by critics, not only because of his association with Hemingway and Fitzgerald but because of his practice of the canonic features of the modern story: extreme economy of language, directness of presentation, limitation of plot—often to a single hour—and focus on a single character. He is, however, occasionally faulted for repetitiveness of his narrative structures—by Victor Hoar for example (22-26) —or for adding to presumably realist stories conclusions that imply metaphysical presence. Such criticisms assume the modernist model: that most narratives will have a specific point-of-view character whose psychology declares itself in the narrative structure; that narratives should locate their culminations in psychological rather than theological vision. Again it is possible to find in Callaghan's stories a mixture of codes: his limited omniscient narrator and simplified diction encode the Christian parable as much as the modernist story, and prepare for the possibility of a visionary conclusion.

In the case of Sinclair Ross the assumption that his stories follow the modernist model appears to have led his critics to believe that no comment about their form is necessary. Margaret Laurence, for example, ascribes to Ross's style the desired modernist qualities "spare, lean, honest, no gimmicks," and passes on to focus on the quality of the marriages that occur between the characters (8). Yet these stories certainly cannot be accounted for as intense single actions that move toward brief epiphany. A structuralist reader would probably find, at the very least, a complex four-unit structure—man, woman, climate and animal, with woman indoors and man and animal outdoors, woman and climate acting in blocking roles, the animal filling a potentiating role, particularly in the area of sexuality and creativity.

Ethel Wilson is more often regarded as a writer of novels and novellas than as a short-story writer, and among her stories the most highly regarded are "We have to sit opposite," and "The Window," which most closely approach the ideals of unity and compression. The characteristic Wilson story, however, has two actions, only loosely linked by plot although closely linked symbolically. In "Hurry Hurry" a woman walking her dogs is unaware of a murdered woman behind her or of the grief of the murderer; in "Beware the Jabberwock" the marriage-story of the blind Mr. Olsen is nested inside the marriage-story of Tom and Dolly Krispin; in "A Drink with Adolphus" the narrative is split between Mrs. Gormley's benign account and Mr. Leaper's misanthropic diary-entry of the same events. The effect in the latter story is to subvert the hermeneutic and sememic aspects of the narrative act, and to undermine the reader's confidence that any narrative can serve as an adequate hypothesis about the world. Many of Wilson's stories begin with the marks of burlesque— "Mrs. Golightly," "Haply the Soul of My Grandmother," "Mr. Sleepwalker"; the author appears to mock her own characters—as she often does briefly in other stories. Again, the expected mimetic aspects of the narrative are subverted—are these characters versions of the pragmatic or are they literary constructions intended as part of the play of the writing?

In addition, Wilson gives us several texts of a kind which Beachcroft would likely consider too 'low' or fragmentary for the short story: "Hurry Hurry" lacks characterization and motivation, and could well be dismissed as a 'sketch' or 'vignette'; "God Help the Young Fisherman" is a brief dialogue that could be dismissed as 'anecdote'; "The Corner of X & Y Streets" has the marks of an 'informal essay,' much like Hugh Hood's stories much later in *Around the Mountain*. These texts do not warrant dismissal, which has been their fate to date; rather they call on the critic to speak to what occurs when they are read as 'short stories,' or read in the context of a book of short stories. A similar problem is posed by F.P. Grove's *Over Prairie Trails*, which usually must defer for critical attention to his novels. Once again we have texts that refuse to separate themselves from signs that mark writings allegedly 'lower' than the modern short story—specifically from the signs of the anecdote or the informal essay. Marked as informal essays, these texts also ask the reader to deal with the double fictionality created by the signs now posed by Grove's Canadian and German author-names.

* * *

In the texts of Canadian short-fiction writers of the 1960s and 70s, the kind of mixed genre code we encounter in Ethel Wilson's or Grove's or Callaghan's writing becomes commonplace. Certainly this generation of writers is the most energetic and talented in the Canadian short story to date. They have had one enormous advantage, however, over their predecessors: in this period the canonic Anglo-American short story is discredited, and in the writing of such international celebrities as Salinger, Updike, Barthelme, B.S. Johnson, Fowles, Borges, Marquez, Mailer (and later in the theory of Reid, Shaw and Lohafer) the concept of mixed, blended, blurred or interplaying genre signals receives considerable validation.

An interesting case in point are the stories of Alice Munro, which contain numerous non-modernist features which critics initially recuperated as signs of realism. To them, Munro was above all a writer who had grown up in rural Southern Ontario; her slow-paced, peripatetic narratives reflected the pace of rural life, or the confusions of growing up, or encoded a short-story version of the kunstlerroman, a young artistic girl growing up in a puzzlingly philistine society. James Polk included most of these observations in his review of *Lives of Girls and Women* before suggesting that "it works... because Munro hasn't forgotten a thing about lower-middle-class life in the drab and frugal forties." Later in the review, however, he says that the book consists of "basically unpruned short stories" and nostalgically recalls what he considers the "'conventional'" stories of her first collection *Dance of the Happy Shades* (102-04). More recent readings, including W.H. New's "Pronouns and Prepositions," Héliane Daziron's "The Preposterous Oxymoron," and some of the contributions to Louis McKendrick's collection *Probable Fictions*, however, have been considerably more sophisticated.

There is insufficient space here to explore in detail the genre play that occurs in the short fiction of Sheila Watson, Dave Godfrey, Norman Levine, Matt Cohen, Rudy Wiebe, George Bowering, Audrey Thomas, Margaret Atwood, bpNichol, Clark Blaise or Hugh Hood, or how this play in many cases obliges a reader to recognize in the text a distinct resistance to classical genre theory, reference and transparency. In Thomas's and Atwood's short fiction... this resistance encodes a refusal of a single authoritative (and consequently patriarchal) story in the preservation of which the canonic short story is implicated. In Godfrey and Bowering, as Walter Pache of the University of Augsburg has very recently observed in a slightly different context, it encodes a refusal of the monolithic story of US imperialism; i.e. the textuality of the Canadian story proclaims the play of Canadian culture. In Hood, the writing returns the story to both anecdote and parable, the former 'naturalizing' the latter and allowing art to masquerade as innocence. In Nichol the play of reference and self-reference has the effect of allowing the reader to enjoy her or his disappointment in the breaking of the expected generic contract. There may not be a single "true eventual story" of Billy the Kid, he may die, as most of us do without climax or epiphany, and without satisfactory psychoanalytic explanation— "god said billy why'd you do all those things and billy said god my dick was too short"— but the movement of the text—its joyful play of genre signals—acts as recompense for its absences.

In a sense, this story of not measuring up, of coming up short through excess (Nichol's 'story' is only four pages and won a Governor-General's Award for 'poetry')—is the story of Canadian short fiction (or perhaps the short sad book of Canadian short fiction); "god said Canadian short fiction why'd you do all those things?" Today we know this god, who probably doesn't want an answer, lived with Aristotle in New York or London, or taught at an American mid-western university, and was preoccupied with the unity of his empire. Perhaps someday someone will attempt to tell why, and begin another 'essay' or a Dave Godfrey 'story.'

Reading Canadian Reading

Stephen Scobie
from The Deconstruction of Writing

"A Mother in India" was published in Duncan's *The Pool in the Desert* (1903)... ; the republication of this volume by Penguin Books (1984), and the subsequent inclusion of "A Mother in India" in Rosemary Sullivan's anthology *Stories by Canadian Women* (Oxford, 1984), have brought the story back to attention. It is told by a first-person narrator, Helena Farnham (a narrator so modest that we learn her first name only from two stray references in reported dialogue), who is married to John, a career officer in the Indian army. Their first and only child, Cecily, has to be sent home to England, for reasons of health, and is brought up by John's family. Apart from occasional visits, the narrator does not see her daughter until she is twenty-one. Returning to India with her mother by ship, Cecily attracts the attention of Dacres Tottenham, a dashing and eligible young man. The narrator, however, has come to the conclusion that her daughter, brought up in an atmosphere of kindly but stultifying conventionality, is "a very ordinary human instrument" (26), and is appalled at the prospect of her marrying the lively and intelligent Dacres. Scheming quietly against the union, she arranges that Dacres be the guide for Cecily's first encounters with some of the most beautiful sites in India, culminating with the Taj Mahal. Properly disappointed by Cecily's platitudinous reactions, Dacres withdraws in mortification: but he has impressed Cecily with such a "standard" that all possible future husbands are found wanting. "Our daughter," the narrator concludes, "is with us, permanently with us" (40).

Even such a brief plot summary will indicate that "A Mother in India" depends upon gaps and absences, strange lacunae in the plot and in the reader's expectations. Much of the "action" consists of things that do not happen: Helena Farnham never develops the expected love and attachment of a mother for her child; Cecily never develops an interesting personality; Dacres never brings himself to propose marriage; Cecily never leaves home. Moreover, since Duncan observes the strict limitation of the first-person viewpoint, all the key scenes between Cecily and Dacres take place off-stage: we never hear what it is that Cecily says about the Taj Mahal that finally convinces Dacres of her mediocrity. Bound by the proprieties of polite society, the characters rarely express their feelings directly: contemplating her life-long annoyance with Cecily's tendency to rearrange her bonnet-strings, the narrator comments, "That is a fond liberty to which I take exception; but it is one thing to take exception and another to express it" (39-40).

Much of the wit and irony of the story, then, is of a type associated with Henry James: a delicate play around what is said and what is not said, the social understandings that pass wordlessly between the sophisticated characters (Dacres, the narrator), leaving the unsophisticated (Cecily) stranded. "A Mother in India" is a comedy of manners in the high Jamesian style, and as always in such a mode, a good deal of the wit depends on the ironic split between the awareness of the narrator and the stance of the implied author. While that author ("Duncan," for the sake of convenience) certainly is not identified with Helena,[1] there is a certain complicity between author and narrator in their sceptical interrogation of the word "natural." The opposition of nature and culture is problematic at every turn. It may well be argued, for instance, that, since "nature" has endowed human beings with intellect and manual dexterity, all the products of culture are thereby "natural." Between nature and culture falls the pejorative term "unnatural," which seems to argue that some forms of activity (of culture?) fall short of the standards of nature—yet it is only through culture that such standards are articulated and socially proclaimed. There is, in fact, an ideology of "nature," a socially produced coding and hierarchy of "natural" functions, used to validate political and economic structures. A class-based society will claim that its inherent inequalities are based on a "natural" order of things: that "nature" ordains there should be high and low, rich and poor, lord and peasant, white and black, man and woman. Far from being natural, "nature" is a society's culturally produced sanction for its own ideology.

In "A Mother in India," Duncan deals with the ideology of motherhood, that is, with her culture's formulation of what a mother "naturally" is. As Dacres begins to realise the narrator's low opinion of her daughter, and chivalrously to object to it, he states the ideology very clearly: "But between mother and daughter—I may be old-fashioned, but I had an idea that there was an instinct that might be depended on" (13). In her reply, Helena plays on two words in Dacres' speech: "depended" and "idea." "I am depending on it," she says, turning his sense of what is "depended" on (something invariable and not to be doubted) into her sense (something which she has not yet experienced, which she hopes for, but which may never in fact materialise). Similarly, she notes that "Men are very slow in changing their philosophy about women. I fancy their *idea* of the maternal relation is firmest fixed of all" (14, my emphasis). Dacres' casual use of "idea" ironically disclaims its status as an idea, trying instead to slip it in the back door of the natural, the given, the unchanging; but the narrator firmly returns it to the realm of "philosophy," of ideas, of things which can be changed.

A few pages later, Dacres' indignation boils over. "The primitive man in him rose up as Pope of nature and excommunicated me as a creature recusant to her functions" (18). Multiple ironies work to deconstruct the contraries in this sentence. Dacres is throughout portrayed as the most sophisticated, the most "cultural," and thus the most un-natural of men; but faced with the narrator's "unnatural" attitude towards her daughter, Dacres reverts to "the primitive man." This "primitivism," however, is expressed through the vocabulary of the most elaborately "cultural" of religions: Dacres becomes a "Pope," "excommunicating" a "recusant." This religion, moreover, is one that exalts motherhood (on the basis of a most unnatural instance of it) through the medium of an all-male priesthood. "Pope of nature" is an intensely paradoxical phrase: in itself a capsule deconstruction of "nature."

When the three-year-old Cecily first sees her mother, she is overcome by the occasion: "she stopped with a wail of terror at the strange faces, and ran straight back to the outstretched arms of her Aunt Emma." The narrator's comment underlines the irony: "The most natural thing in the world, no doubt" (5). From one point of view, it is "natural": the phenomenon of surrogate motherhood is well documented. But for the ideology of motherhood there is, no doubt, doubt. This incident is the turning-point in the narrator's attitudes towards her daughter. Approaching it, she had worked herself into the correct state of mind of a mother; rejected by her daughter, she retreats in confusion, and "locked myself in for two atrocious hours" (6). It would be possible to argue that the bitterness of this moment poisons the narrator's love for her daughter, and thus leads to a spiteful revenge in her later action of preventing Cecily's marriage. Such an interpretation (though I find it extreme) would only underline yet further the point that maternal feelings are learned (or in this case unlearned) rather than, in the way that Cecily is taught to think of courtship and marriage, "pre-arranged by nature like her digestion" (19). "A Mother in India" demonstrates that motherhood and digestion are not analogous.

Throughout the story, Duncan presents "the natural" as something which has to be learned, even if what you learn is that you're not supposed to have to learn it, it's supposed to come "naturally." When Cecily is born, "we both knew that it was abnormal not to love her a great deal, more than life, immediately and increasingly; and we applied ourselves honestly to do it" (2). "Abnormal" here aligns itself with "unnatural." The ideology of the natural states that the child should be loved both "immediately" (absolutely, "more than life," as a reflex action) and "increasingly" (somehow improving on the absolute, adding a supplement to what is already a plenitude). For Derrida, just such a "logic of the supplement" is the structure of writing itself, which produces "an infinite chain, ineluctably multiplying the supplementary mediations that produce the sense of the very thing they defer: the mirage of the thing itself, of immediate presence, of originary perception" (OG 157). Thus this contradiction of "the natural" —that its apparent plenitude must nevertheless be supplemented—is structurally built into the enunciation of the natural itself: "the natural" is *written*.

But for John and Helena, the natural is not something that comes naturally: they have to apply themselves to it, "honestly" but unsuccessfully. "We were," she continues, "of excellent mind toward Cecily: we were in such terror, not so much of failing in our duty toward her as toward the ideal standard of mankind. We were very anxious indeed not to come short. To be found too small for one's place in nature would have been odious" (2). Again, the natural can only be defined in terms of the cultural, of an "ideal standard" which belongs to mankind. The sanction of society, of other people's expectations, appears to supersede even the parents' responsibility to the child herself—not, surely, a very "natural" result of the desire to be natural. Duncan's narrator spends a good deal of time apologising for her failures to live up to that ideal standard, but these apologies are received by the reader with sceptical irony. The actual wording of the apologies, moreover, deconstructs their own assertions. "Of course, the real experience would have come, we weren't monsters; but fate curtailed the opportunity" (2). The "real" is equated with "the natural," and opposed to "monsters"—but "the real" would have had to come through "opportunity," that is, through time, exposure, and habituation. If Cecily hadn't been sent away at the age of five weeks... But the ideology of motherhood doesn't require even five weeks: the bond between mother and child is supposed to occur, "naturally," during pregnancy and childbirth. What is presented as a justification of "the real experience" in fact implies that the experience isn't real, but learned.

When mother and daughter do eventually meet, they have to learn how to relate to each other. Addressing her daughter as "my love," the narrator reflects: "I was teaching myself to use these forms of address for fear she [Cecily] would feel an unkind lack of them, but it was difficult" (11). Later she comments, "The maternal virtues of the outside were certainly mine; I put them on with care every morning and wore them with patience all day" (21). Duncan's language (the precision of "care," the irony of "patience") plays within the tensions and inbuilt contradictions of the ideology of motherhood. A mother should not have to teach herself to call her daughter "my love" —but this mother is "perfectly new and untrained" (21).

"It is not as if I had been her mother always," she complains to Dacres (14), and this is both true and untrue. No woman has "always" been a mother: yet the ideology sees all women as always potentially mothers, and assumes that there will be no need to "train" them. Helena has had, and continues to have, a strong emotional life of her own, with John. "I may have been Cecily's mother in theory," she says, "but I was John's wife in fact" (6).[2] When Cecily is born, John dutifully proclaims that she will "bind us together"; at the time, the narrator equally dutifully agrees, but now comments with hindsight, "We didn't need binding together; we were more to each other, there in the desolation of that arid frontier outpost, than most husbands and wives; but it seemed a proper and hopeful thing to believe, so we believed it" (2).

Cecily also is taught, but the results of her teaching lead to further speculations on what is or is not natural. In her relationship with Dacres, she "was conducting herself in a manner which left nothing to be desired" (31); the conventional phrase carries the ironic sting that there is nothing in Cecily worth desiring. She seems to have eliminated all the "natural" reactions of "fluttering uncertainties" (31) in a young girl being courted, and the narrator concludes that "The Farnham ladies would have been delighted with the result of their labours in the sweet reason and eminent propriety of this attitude." But, having noted this "labour," the narrator goes on to reflect, in the very next sentence, "Thinking of my idiotic sufferings when John began to fix himself upon my horizon, I pondered profoundly the power of nature in differentiation" (32). Are we then to attribute the differences between mother and daughter here to "the power of nature" or to the "labours" of the Farnham ladies? Again, culture and nature seem to infiltrate each other in ways which deny the absoluteness of the opposition between them, and which make their relationship quite indeterminate.

The whole question of natural vs. cultural attitudes towards mothers and children is further intertwined with a strain of materialism, even of commercialism. The ideology of motherhood is bound up with the ideologies of class and capitalism. "When the expectation of Cecily came to us," the narrator writes (itself a splendidly unnatural euphemism for a natural event), "we made out to be delighted, knowing that the whole station pitied us, and when Cecily came herself, with a swamping burst of expense, we kept up the pretense splendidly" (1). Again, motherhood is a "pretense," but the artifice here is directly related to the social and economic expectations of colonial society. Pity is not the "natural" response to the news that a young couple is expecting a child, but here that natural response is overridden by the social consideration of the couple's economic status. They are "sodden poor" —which turns out to mean, in colonial terms, that they had "only six of everything for the table" (2). So Cecily arrives in "a swamping burst," a phrase which seems for a moment to be a rather graphic metaphor of childbirth but which then resolves itself into "of expense." The following sentence is worth quoting in its entirety: I have already cited several parts of it, but it is important to note that it is all one sentence, and that the various levels of discourse are ironically equated, all run together into one quite breathless grammatical unit.

> She was peevish, poor little thing, and she threatened convulsions from the beginning, but we both knew that it was abnormal not to love her a great deal, more than life, immediately and increasingly; and we applied ourselves honestly to do it, with the thermometer at a hundred and two, and the nurse leaving at the end of a fortnight because she discovered that I had only six of everything for the table. (1-2)

The poor little thing continues, if not always "poor," often a "thing," especially an economic thing. While she is growing up in England, her parents "noted her weekly progress with much the feeling one would have about a far-away little bit of property that was giving no trouble and coming on exceedingly well. We would take possession of Cecily at our convenience; till then, it was gratifying to hear of our unearned increment in dear little dimples and sweet little curls" (4). The language of "the natural" (dimples, curls) is completely shot through with the cultural, in the form of colonial capitalism. Later, Cecily is referred to as "my alien possession" (5), and as "a very ordinary human instrument" (26). This possessiveness extends also to Dacres: there is a sense in which the narrator sees him as her creation and possession, and this in part accounts for her unwillingness to cede him to Cecily. Considering her attempts to discourage his suit, the narrator writes, "I had a little the feeling of a dealer who offers a defective bibelot to a connoisseur" (31); and when he comes to the same conclusion, she "felt a little bitter. It was, of course, better that the connoisseur should have discovered the flaw before concluding the transaction; but although I had pointed it out myself I was not entirely pleased to have the article returned" (36). Cecily as possession, instrument, trinket, article: when Dacres complains that the narrator "had no earthly business to be her mother" (14), the commercial implication of "business" is by no means unfounded.

Notes

[This extract presents the first half of Scobie's discussion of "A Mother In India." The second half goes on to discuss the treatment of writing in Duncan's story.]

[1] There are several points at which Duncan implies motives for Helena's actions of which Helena as narrator is only dimly, if at all, aware. At the end of the story, she complains to John that Cecily "Takes our crumpets away from us," and claims that she "could never take away anybody's crumpets" (39). Yet is this not exactly what she has just done to Dacres?

[2] Dacres later echoes the "theoretical" nature of Helena's motherhood, when he says, "there was theory of that kind, I remember, about ten years ago" (13). But Dacres goes on to hold the "theory" against her.

Daniel Francis
On Pauline Johnson

On a January evening in 1892, the overflowing crowd in the Gallery of Art at Toronto's Academy of Music was growing restive. Things had begun promisingly enough, with the poems of Agnes Machar and Wilfred Campbell. But then William Lighthall had droned on for far too long with his humourless reflections on nation-building. High-minded views on the future of Canada were expected at an event sponsored by the Young Men's Liberal Club, but this was supposed to be a literary get-together. Organizer Frank Yeigh had promised some of the leading writers of the day; but next on the program was a little known poetess from Brantford. It looked like it was going to be a long evening.[1]

Gathering her courage, Pauline Johnson emerged nervously from the wings and took her place on the platform. She was thirty years old, the daughter of a Mohawk chief, an uncelebrated writer of stories and poems who lived quietly with her mother in a provincial backwater. She knew Frank Yeigh as a classmate from school. He had seen a couple of her canoeing poems, and on the strength of them had asked her to appear at the Toronto recital. Neither of them realized that they were about to launch one of the most successful careers in Canadian entertainment history.

Above the rustling of the crowd and the murmur of whispered conversations, Pauline Johnson began to recite:

> My forest brave, my Red-skin love, farewell;
> We may not meet to-morrow; who can tell
> What mighty ills befall our little band,
> Or what you'll suffer from the white man's hand?

The poem was "A Cry from an Indian Wife," the lament of a Native woman whose husband is going off to fight alongside the Metis in the 1885 Northwest Rebellion.

> They but forget we Indians owned the land
> From ocean to ocean; that they stand

> Upon a soil that centuries agone
> Was our sole kingdom and our right alone.

Here was something different; the rebellion from the Native point of view, told dramatically, without apology, by a "daughter of the forest" herself. The audience was rivetted by the wild pathos of her words and when she finished it broke into enthusiastic applause, bringing her back for an encore.

Johnson chose another Indian poem, "As Red Men Die," a lurid story about a Mohawk captive who chooses death by hideous torture over life as a slave.

> Up the long trail of fire he boasting goes,
> Dancing a war dance to defy his foes.
> His flesh is scorched, his muscles burn and shrink,
> But still he dances to death's awful brink.
> ....
> Then loyal to his race,
> He bends to death—but *never* to disgrace.

Once again her audience responded with a long ovation. She had clearly taken literary Toronto by storm. "It was like the voice of the nations who once possessed this country, who have wasted away before our civilization," wrote the *Globe* reviewer, "speaking through this cultured, gifted, soft-voiced descendant."[2]

Frank Yeigh was elated. An enterprising promoter who knew when he was on to a good thing, he convinced Johnson that together they must take advantage of her sudden popularity. Hiring Toronto's Association Hall, he advertised an evening recital by "the Indian poetess." Once again the sold-out audience, and the critics, loved her. "Another triumph," enthused the *Globe*.[3]

Johnson was an instant celebrity. She embarked on a hectic, fifty-stop tour of Ontario, giving 125 recitals in just eight months. That autumn she teamed up with a British vaudeville performer, Owen Smiley, and following the Ontario tour they took their show to the Maritimes and into the northeastern United States. Boston, New York, Toronto, Halifax, Ottawa—everywhere the critics raved. "She is perhaps the most unique figure in the literary world on this continent," claimed the *New York Sun*.⁴ *Canadian Magazine* called her "the most popular figure in Canadian literature."⁵ To the poet, Charles G.D. Roberts, she was "the aboriginal voice of Canada." Critic Hector Charlesworth went so far as to call her "the greatest living poetess."

Her fame accompanied her to England in the spring of 1894 where she performed at house parties and found a publisher for a slim volume of her verse. Next year The Bodley Head released her first book, *The White Wampum*.

Johnson returned to Canada and resumed her whirlwind touring schedule, this time whistle-stopping all the way to the Pacific Coast aboard the Canadian Pacific Railway. For the next fifteen years, she was on the road almost constantly, enduring long, tiresome trips by rail, steamboat, stagecoach and wagon. Living out of a suitcase in hotels, rooming houses and police outposts, she performed wherever there was a hall to hold an audience, from the gaslit theatres of Toronto to the outports of Newfoundland to the backwoods camps of British Columbia. "There is hardly a town or settlement in Canada that we did not visit several times during those years," recalled her longtime partner, Walter McRaye.⁶ Once she even mounted a billiard table to recite to a roomful of miners, changing costume behind a Hudson's Bay blanket strung on a line. The discomfort of this routine was increased by recurring bouts of ill health which Johnson suffered all her life. Despite her hectic schedule, she was unable to save much money, and spent whatever spare time she had writing adventure stories for boys' magazines and melodramatic tales for the women's market. This was the pattern of her professional life until she retired from the stage and settled in Vancouver in 1909.

From her first public performance, the critics identified Johnson as "the voice of the Indian," a label on which she quickly capitalized. Yeigh began billing her as "the Mohawk Princess," and in November 1892 she donned the Indian dress that became a hallmark of her performances. Her costume consisted of a buckskin dress, fringed at the hem to reveal a lining of red wool and decorated at the neck with silver brooches, buckskin leggings and moccasins. Later she added a necklace of ermine tails. At her waist she carried a hunting knife and an authentic Huron scalp inherited from her great-grandfather. A red wool cloak hung from one shoulder. One sleeve was a long piece of fringed buckskin, attached at the shoulder and the wrist; the other was a drape of rabbit pelts. Johnson seems to have come up with this polyglot costume herself. She wore it during the half of her program devoted to Indian poems. For her non-Indian material, she wore a simple dinner gown.

In 1886, Johnson took the name Tekahionwake, which apparently meant Double Wampum. The naturalist, Ernest Thompson Seton, recalled that she complained to him once, "Oh, why have your people forced on me the name of Pauline Johnson? Was not my Indian name good enough?"[7] Actually, if anyone "forced" her name on her, it was Pauline's father, a chief at the Brantford reserve. He was a fervent admirer of Napoleon, and named his daughter after the French emperor's sister. (He nicknamed his eldest son "Boney" and his second son "Kleber" after one of Napoleon's generals.) Technically, the name Tekahionwake did not belong to Pauline. It was her great-grandfather's name; she adopted it as a gesture of identification with her Native background.

Johnson's White audiences loved these "authentic" Indian props. They thrilled at the war whoops, the dangling scalp, the name they could not pronounce, the poems of torture and war. She enjoyed immense popularity. Campers recited her poems by memory around their fires at night. "The Song My Paddle Sings" became an anthem for outdoors enthusiasts and a fixture in schoolbooks. It is possible that more Canadian children have memorized it than any other piece of verse. Her first biographer, Mrs. Garland Foster, claimed that a copy of her first book of poems was found in the packsack of a gold-seeker trekking into the Klondike over the Chilkoot Pass.[8]

The poet herself was ambivalent about her Indian "image." She recognized that her act depended on its exoticism. The public paid to see a Mohawk princess as much as a talented writer and recitalist. And she welcomed the opportunity to carry her message to a large audience. However, she did wonder from time to time if pandering to public taste was not stifling her growth as an artist. Writing to a friend, she confided that "the public will not listen to lyrics, will not appreciate real poetry, will in fact not have me as an entertainer if I give them nothing but rhythm, cadence, beauty, thought." Plaintively, she continued, "I could do so much better if they would only let me."[9]

Johnson could not abandon her Indian themes for fear of losing her audience. Nor did she want to. The purpose of her career, after all, was to proclaim the nobler aspects of Canada's Native people. "My aim, my joy, my pride is to sing the glories of my own people," she told Seton.[10] But in order to fulfill this purpose, Johnson had to make compromises with the expectations of her White public.

Johnson was a "White Man's Indian" in the sense that she had the polished manners of a well-bred, middle-class Victorian gentlewoman. "There are those who think they pay me a compliment—saying that I am just like a white woman," she once complained.[11] She had no desire to be considered anything but Native, but there is no question that Johnson was admired by so many Whites because she made it easy for them. Everyone she met remarked on her manners, her charm, her good looks. "She is tall and slender and dark, with grey eyes, beautifully clean cut features, black hair, a very sweet smile, and a clear, musical pleasant voice," Sara Jeannette Duncan informed her readers in the *Globe* in 1886. "I have always thought her beautiful and many agree with me. She has certainly that highest attribute of beauty, the rare, fine gift of expression. She is charmingly bright in conversation, and has a vivacity of tone and gesture that is almost French."[12]

Born to a Mohawk father and a white mother, Johnson grew up at their home, Chiefswood, a gracious colonial mansion set apart from the rest of the Six Nations Reserve on the Grand River at Brantford. Perched on a bluff overlooking the river, the house was surrounded with spacious, landscaped grounds. French windows opened onto the lawn where visitors played croquet. Each room had a fireplace, and there was a rosewood piano in the parlour. The family had three servants. Her father was the chief, but young Pauline had few friends from the reserve. She was encouraged to believe in the family's social superiority and because of her father's position she had many opportunities to mix with the White dignitaries who visited the reserve. Such an upbringing equipped Johnson with the refined sophistication that impressed so many of her White admirers and helped win acceptance for her Indian performances.

At the same time, Johnson was raised to be proud of her Native heritage. From her father she learned the great events of Mohawk history and heard the names of Brant and Pontiac and Tecumseh. From her grandfather, John Smoke Johnson, a veteran of the War of 1812 and a gifted orator, she learned the legends and stories of her people. It was his name she took as her own. No matter how far the music hall was from the longhouse, Johnson believed she was fulfilling an inheritance both racial and familial when she mounted the platform each night.

Critics and public alike admired in Johnson many traits which they believed to be distinctively Indian. Her stage presence and rhetorical skills were thought to derive from Native traditions of oratory. The image of Indian leaders giving eloquent speeches around the council fires was deeply ingrained in the White imagination. Likewise her simplicity was described as typically Indian, reflecting the innocence of a people uncorrupted by modern civilization. And the quiet dignity of her bearing betrayed the proud stoicism for which her race was famous.

To White critics, her poems and stories showed their Indian origins, not just in content but also in style. "Her singing sense she did not get from her white blood," remarked Mrs. Foster. "It is too evidently the product of the swinging paddle, the choral dance of the redman."[13] Most Whites thought that Indians were closer to nature than other people. Critics saw this reflected in the rhythms of Johnson's work, along with the intense passion which supposedly characterized all Indians, whether a passionate love of nature or a passionate sense of injustice. "Intense feeling distinguishes her Indian poems from all others," wrote Charles Mair; "they flow from her very veins, and are stamped with the seal of heredity.... Begot of her knowledge of the long-suffering of her race, of iniquities in the past and present, they poured red-hot from her inmost heart."[14]

What gave Johnson's work an added poignancy was the belief shared by most members of her audience that they were listening to the voice of a disappearing people. "The race that is gone speaks with touching pathos through Miss Johnson," was how the *Toronto Globe* put it.[15] In her stage performances, she personified the Vanishing Race and people strained to hear the final whispered message before it faded away completely.

Johnson, of course, was not the "voice" of the Indian. There were many Indians, and many voices. She herself knew that. "The term 'Indian,'" she once wrote, "signifies about as much as the term 'European' but I cannot recall ever having read a story where the heroine was described as 'a European.'"[16] Johnson, however, happened to possess the only voice that White society *could* hear. Other Native poets and orators did not speak English, did not aspire to a career on the concert stage. Natives were politically quiescent at the turn of the century. Pushed to the margins of public life, they could not get their concerns on the national agenda. Johnson, on the other hand, succeeded in capturing white attention, and while she had it, attempted to plead the cause of the native.

Johnson did not always sustain the angry sense of injustice present in some of her most popular poems. Occasionally she allowed herself to become as patronizing toward her own people as any White writer. In 1906 she paid a second visit to England, where the editor of the *London Daily Express* asked her to contribute some articles, one of which was called "A Pagan in St. Paul's." Recollecting a visit to St Paul's Cathedral, Johnson defends the dignity of Native religious practices and beliefs, but instead of doing so from the perspective of a sophisticated woman with some experience of the world, she adopts the persona of a naive "Redskin" who seems never to have ventured beyond the edges of the northern forest. "So this is the place where dwells the Great White Father, ruler of many lands, lodges, and tribes," her narrator marvels. "I, one of his loyal allies, have come to see his camp, known to the white man as London, his council which the whites call his Parliament, where his sachems and chiefs make the laws of his tribes, and to see his wigwam, known to the palefaces as Buckingham

Palace, but to the red man as the 'Teepee of the Great White Father.'"[17] Whatever the worth of her argument about Native religion, Johnson was clearly pandering to a stereotypical notion of the Indian as an artless, childlike innocent.

This need to satisfy the demands of a White audience stultified Pauline Johnson's development as a writer and limited her effectiveness as a spokesperson for Native people. Many of her stories appeared in *Mother's Magazine*, a popular women's magazine based in Illinois. "We want to picture only the best and highest," the editor told Johnson, "but we do want the good attractively presented." Johnson's stories conform to the melodramatic literary conventions of the period, but with a difference. Her brave heroines have to overcome not only social and sexual obstacles to win the man of their dreams, but racial obstacles as well. She often portrayed the traumatic effects of contact between Native and European in terms of a tragic love affair between a Native woman and a White man. One of her most famous stories was "A Red Girl's Reasoning," which she turned into a playlet for use in her performances. It is the tale of a marriage between a White man and a mixed-blood woman. The woman shocks polite society by divulging that her parents were wed according to Indian custom without the blessing of a priest. Their marriage is every bit as legitimate as any White marriage, she argues, but her friends are scandalized, her husband furious at her for being so candid. Her love for him dies and she leaves him. Realizing his hypocrisy, he tracks her down but she is adamant, and does not return to him. Pauline Johnson represented a shining example of Indian womanhood for her non-Native audiences, who saw in her the personification of Pocahontas, the Indian princess. According to legend, Pocahontas saved the life of Captain John Smith, a leader of the Virginia colony, when he was threatened by her people, the Powhatan. A paragon of virtue, Pocahontas later converted to Christianity. Her marriage to John Role, a White settler, helped to forge an alliance between the Powhatan and the colonists. The romantic story of Pocahontas inspired countless works of art, both low and high, idealizing the image of the Indian woman. She was painted often in European dress, much as Pauline Johnson appeared on stage wearing a formal gown; the Indian turned gentlewoman. The original Miss America, Pocahontas came to represent the beautiful, exotic, New World itself. Her story provided a model for the ideal merger of native and newcomer.[18]

Of course, not all the stereotypes of Indian women were this positive. Opposed to the princess there was the *squaw*, a derogatory epithet widely applied to Native women by non-Natives. In all ways the squaw was the opposite of the princess, an anti-Pocahontas. Where the princess was beautiful, the squaw was ugly, even deformed. Where the princess was virtuous, the squaw was debased, immoral, a sexual convenience. Where the princess was proud, the squaw lived a squalid life of servile toil, mistreated by her men. Non-Native writers described Indian women hanging around the margins of White settlement, drinking and prostituting themselves. This stereotype of the Indian woman as a low, sexual commodity—a "bit of brown" as the fur trade governor George Simpson put it— became increasingly common as Native people were pushed to the fringes of White settlement, neglected and powerless. Its tragic consequences were revealed in the case of Helen Betty Osborne, a young Native woman whose brutal murder by a gang of young Whites in The Pas, Manitoba, in 1971 was hushed up by the community for years.

In her own life, Pauline Johnson conformed to the princess stereotype. She gave great dignity to the Native characters in her poems and stories. They appear as honourable, proud people with strong family ties and long traditions. This was a rarity at the time. "Half of our authors who write up Indian stuff have never been on an Indian reserve," she complained in the *Toronto Sunday Globe*, "have never met a 'real live Redman,' have never ever read Parkman, Schoolcraft or Catlin; what wonder that their conception of a people they are ignorant of, save by hearsay, is dwarfed, erroneous and delusive."[19]

But Johnson herself only went so far. She presented the plight of the Red Man, but she demanded little from her White audience beyond sentimental regret, which was easy enough to give. The land may once have belonged to her people, but she was not asking for it back. Indeed, she was a fervent Canadian patriot who liked to mix her Indian material with odes to the National Policy, made-in-Canada manufacturing and the North West Mounted Police. "White race and Red are one if they are but Canadian Born" she wrote in *Canadian Born*, her second book of verse, published in 1902. These nationalist poems were among her most popular performance pieces. What could be more comforting for an Anglo-Saxon audience than to hear a Native woman singing the praises of Canada and the British-Canadian way of life?

Pauline Johnson wrote and performed at a time when the dominant image of the Indian in White culture was changing. No longer was the Indian the primitive savage. By 1900, most of Canada's Natives were pacified and living on reserves. The western frontier was closing. A wave of immigrant settlers was washing over the prairies, transforming grassland into farmland. Civilization had conquered the West and it was no longer necessary to mobilize public opinion against the frontier's original inhabitants. Having successfully subdued the Indians, Whites now could afford to get sentimental about them.

At the same time, many Canadians were beginning to have second thoughts about the industrial revolution which was transforming the country. Cities, they felt, were becoming polluted, crime-ridden and overcrowded. Jobs were becoming tedious and enslaving. There was a growing feeling that Indian character and culture had something positive to teach Euro-Canadians. Even as they reviled the Indian as brutal and ungovernable, many Whites had admired the nobility and independence reflected in the image of the "Redman." Indians were identified with the freedom, healthfulness and simplicity of the natural world. In the early decades of the twentieth century, Canadians who were unhappy with trends in their own society discovered in the Indian what they thought was an alternative lifestyle founded on an alternative set of values. Celebrity Indians like Pauline Johnson seemed to give voice to these alternatives and enjoyed enormous public appeal.

Notes

[1] This description is taken from Betty Keller's biography *Pauline: A Biography of Pauline Johnson* (Vancouver: Douglas and McIntyre, 1981), pp. 56-58, which is the source of most of the biographical material in this chapter.

[2] Toronto *Globe*, 18 Jan.1892.

[3] Ibid., 20 Feb.1892.

[4] Cited in Keller, p.71.

[5] Ibid., p.73

[6] Walter McRaye, *Town Hall Tonite* (Toronto: The Ryerson Press,1929), p.171.

[7] E.T. Seton, "Introduction" to Pauline Johnson, *The Shagganappi* (Toronto: Wm. Briggs, 1913), p.7.

[8] Mrs. W. Garland Foster, *The Mohawk Princess* (Vancouver: Lions' Gate Publishing Co., 1931), p.63.

[9] Cited in Keller, p.72.

[10] Seton, p.6.

[11] Ibid., p.5.

[12] Toronto *Globe*, 14 Oct.1886.

[13] Foster, p.96.

[14] Charles Mair, "Pauline Johnson: An Appreciation," *Canadian Magazine* (July 1913), p.282.

[15] *Globe*, 18 Jan. 1892.

[16] "The Indian Princess of Modern Fiction."

[17] Pauline Johnson, "A Pagan in St. Paul's Cathedral," *The Moccasin Maker* (Toronto: The Ryerson Press, 1913), p.13.

[18] Rayna Green, "The Pocahontas Perplex: the Image of Indian Women in American Culture," *The Massachusetts Review*, v.XVI, n.4 (Autumn 1975).

[19] "The Indian Princess of Modern Fiction."

Reprinted with permission from *The Imaginary Indian: The Image of the Indian in Canadian Culture*, Arsenal Pulp Press, 1992.

Bibliography

This list includes the Works Cited in the "Criticism" section, supplemented by works consulted by the editor and other useful sources on short stories and on individual authors.

Allen, Walter. *The Short Story in English*. Oxford: Clarendon Press, 1981.
Arnason, David, ed. *Nineteenth Century Canadian Stories*. Toronto: Macmillan, 1976.
Bader, A.L. "The Structure of the Modern Short Story." *Short Story Theories*. ed. Charles E. May. Athens: Ohio U P, 1976.
Ballstadt, Carl, ed. *The Search for English-Canadian Literature*. Toronto: U Toronto P, 1975.
—. "Susanna Moodie and the English Sketch." *Canadian Literature* 51 (1972): 32-38.
Barr, Robert. "How to Write A Short Story." *Bookman* (NY) 5 (March 1897): 42-46.
—. "Literature in Canada." In *Measure of the Rule*. Toronto: U Toronto P, 1973.
—. *Selected Stories of Robert Barr*. ed. Parr. Ottawa: U Ottawa P, 1977.
—. *The Triumphs of Eugène Valmont*. New York: D Appleton, 1906.
Beachcroft, Thomas O. *The English Short Story*. 2nd vol. London: Longmans, 1964.
Bennett, Donna, Russell Brown and Natalie Cooke. *An Anthology of Canadian Literature in English*. Toronto: Oxford, 1990.
Brooks, Cleanth and R.P. Warren, eds. Introduction. *Understanding Fiction*. 1943: New York: Appleton, 1959.
Brodie, Alan Douglas. "Canadian Short-Story Writers." *Canadian Magazine* 4 (Feb 1895): 834-44.
Canby, H.S. *The Short Story in English*. New York: Holt, 1909.
Davies, Barrie, ed. *At The Mermaid Inn: Wilfred Campbell, Archibald Lampman and Duncan Campbell Scott in The Globe, 1892-3*. Toronto: U Toronto P, 1979.
—. "Introduction." *At The Mermaid Inn: Wilfred Campbell, Archibald Lampman, Duncan Campbell Scott in "The Globe" 1892-3*. Toronto: U Toronto P, 1979.
Davey, Frank. *Reading Canadian Reading*. Winnipeg: Turnstone Press, 1988.
Daziron, Héliane. "The Preposterous Oxymoron: A Study of Alice Munro's 'The Dance of the Happy Shades'." *The Literary Half-Yearly* XXIV:2 (1983): 116-24.

Dean, Misao. *A Different Point of View: Sara Jeannette Duncan*. Montreal: McGill-Queen's UP, 1991.

———. "Political Science: Realism in Roberts' Animal Stories." *Studies in Canadian Literature* 21:1 (Summer 1996) 1-16.

Dougall, Lily. *A Dozen Ways of Love*. London: A.C. Black, 1897.

———. *Pro Christo et Ecclesia*. London: Macmillan, 1900.

Doyle, James. *The Fin-de-Siècle Spirit: Walter Blackburn Harte and the American Literary Milieu of the 1890s*. Toronto: ECW Press, 1995.

———. "Canadian Women Writers and the American Literary Milieu of the 1890s." *Re(Dis)covering Our Foremothers*. ed. McMullen. Ottawa: Ottawa U P, 1990. 30-36.

Dragland, Stan. *Floating Voice: Duncan Campbell Scott and the Literature of Treaty Nine*. Toronto: Anansi, 1994.

Dubrow, Heather. *Genre*. London: Methuen, 1982.

Duncan, Sara Jeannette. "American Influence on Canadian Thought." In *The Search for English-Canadian Literature*. ed. Carl Ballstadt. Toronto: U Toronto P, 1975.

———. *The Pool in the Desert*. New York: D. Appleton, 1903.

———. *Selected Journalism*. ed. Tausky. Ottawa: Tecumseh, 1978.

Duncan, Norman. *The Soul of the Street: Correlated Stories of the New York Syrian Quarter*. New York: McClure, Phillips, 1900.

Eagleton, Terry. *Literary Theory*. London: Basil Blackwell, 1983.

Eaton, Edith (Sui Sin Far). *Mrs. Spring Fragrance and Other Writings*. eds. Ling and White-Parks. Urbana: U Illinois P, 1995.

———. *Mrs. Spring Fragrance*. Chicago: McClurg, 1912.

Eichenbaum, Boris. *O. Henry and the Theory of the Short Story*. Trans. I.R. Titunik.1925: Ann Arbor: U of Michigan, 1968.

Faxon, F. W. "Ephemeral Bibelots." *Bulletin of Bibliography* 3 (1903-4).

Foster, Mrs. W. Garland. *The Mohawk Princess*. Vancouver: Lions' Gate Publishing Co., 1931.

Fowler, Alistair. *Kinds of Literature*. Cambridge: Harvard U P, 1982.

Francis, Daniel. *The Imaginary Indian*. Vancouver: Arsenal Pulp Press, 1992.

Garret, Robert Max. "Canadian Short Stories from Periodicals." *Canadian Bookman* 4 (Feb. 1922): 42-46.

Gerson, Carole. *A Purer Taste: the Writing and Reading of Fiction in English in Nineteenth- Century Canada*. Toronto: U Toronto P, 1989.

———. ed. *Vancouver Short Stories*. Vancouver: U British Columbia P 1985.

Gerson, Carole and Kathy Mezei. *The Prose of Life*. Toronto: ECW Press, 1981.

Godfrey, Dave. "A New Year's Morning on Bloor Street." *Dark Must Yield*. Erin, ON: Porcepic, 1978. 131-42.

Grady, Wayne. *Penguin Book of Canadian Short Stories*. Markham, Ont: Penguin, 1980.

Green, Rayna. "The Pocahontas Perplex: the Image of Indian Women in American Culture." *The Massachusetts Review*, v.XVI, n.4 (Autumn 1975).

Haliburton, Thomas Chandler. *A Historical and Statistical Account of Nova Scotia.* Halifax: J. Howe, 1829.

—. *The Clockmaker, Series One, Two and Three.* ed. Parker. Ottawa: Carleton UP, 1995.

—. *The Clockmaker.* Afterword by R.L. McDougall. Toronto: McClelland and Stewart, 1993.

Harrison, Susan Frances. *Crowded Out! and Other Sketches.* Ottawa: Evening Journal, 1886.

Harte, Walter Blackburn. *Meditations in Motley.* Boston: Arena, 1894.

Heble, Ajay, Donna Pennee and J.R. (Tim) Struthers. *New Contexts of Canadian Criticism.* Peterborough: Broadview, 1997.

Heyl, Laurence. "Little Magazines." *Princeton University Library Chronicle* 2 (1940): 21-26.

Hoar, Victor. *Morley Callaghan.* Toronto: Copp Clark, 1969.

Howells, William Dean. *A Hazard of New Fortunes.* 1890. Bloomington: Indiana U P, 1976.

Hutcheon, Linda. *As Canadian As Possible... Under the Circumstances.* Toronto: ECW Press, 1990.

Johnson, Pauline. *Legends of Vancouver.* Toronto: McClelland and Stewart, 1922.

—. *The Moccasin Maker.* Toronto: William Briggs, 1913.

—. "A Pagan in St. Paul's Cathedral." *The Moccasin Maker.* Toronto: The Ryerson Press, 1913.

Keller, Betty. *Pauline: A Biography of Pauline Johnson.* Vancouver: Douglas and McIntyre, 1981.

Klinck, Carl F., gen. ed. *Literary History of Canada: Canadian Literature in English.* Toronto: U of Toronto P, 1965. 2nd ed. 3 vols. Toronto: U of Toronto P, 1976.

Knister, Raymond, ed. *Canadian Short Stories.* Toronto: MacMillan, 1928.

Lampman, Archibald. "Mr. Thomson's *Old Man Savarin.*" *The Week* (9 Aug 1895): 880-81.

Lang, Marjory. "Separate Entrances: The First Generation of Canadian Women Journalists." *Re(Dis)covering Our Foremothers.* ed. McMullen. Ottawa: Ottawa U P, 1990. 77-90.

Laurence, Margaret. Introduction. *The Lamp at Noon and Other Stories.* By Sinclair Ross. Toronto: McClelland and Stewart, 1968.

Lawson, Alan. "Postcolonial Theory and the 'Settler' Subject." *ECW* 56 (Fall 1995): 20-36.

Leacock, Stephen. *Sunshine Sketches of a Little Town.* Toronto: Bell and Cockburn, 1912.

—. *Sunshine Sketches of a Little Town*. With an Afterword by Jack Hodgins. Toronto: McClelland and Stewart, 1989.

Leighton, Mary Elizabeth. "Performing Pauline Johnson: Representations of "the Indian Poetess" in the Periodical Press, 1892-95." *ECW* 65 (Fall 1998):141-164.

Leprohon, Rosanna. *Antoinette De Mirecourt*. ed. John Stockdale. Ottawa: Carleton U P, 1989.

London, Jack. *Martin Eden*. New York: Rinehart, 1908.

Lucas, Alec. *Great Canadian Short Stories*. New York: Dell, 1971.

McClung, Nellie L. *All We Like Sheep and other stories*. Toronto: T. Allen, 1926.

—. *In Times Like These*. 1916. intro. Veronica Strong-Boag. Toronto: U Toronto P., 1972.

—. *Sowing Seeds in Danny*. Toronto: William Briggs, 1908.

—. *Stories Subversive: Through the Field with the Gloves Off.* ed. Davis. Ottawa: U Ottawa P, 1996.

MacMechan, Archibald. *Head-Waters of Canadian Literature*. Toronto: McClelland, 1924.

McMullen, Lorraine, ed. *Re(Dis)covering Our Foremothers*. Ottawa: U Ottawa P, 1990.

McMullen, Lorraine and Sandra Campbell, eds. *Aspiring Women: Short Stories by Canadian Women 1880-1900*. Ottawa: U Ottawa P, 1993.

—. *New Women: Short Stories by Canadian Women 1900-1920*. Ottawa: U Ottawa P, 1993.

—. *Pioneering Women: Short Stories by Canadian Women, Beginnings to 1880*. Ottawa: U Ottawa P, 1993.

McPherson, Hugo. "Fiction: 1940-1960." *Literary History of Canada: Canadian Literature in English*. Gen. ed. Carl F. Klinck. Toronto: U of Toronto P, 1965. 694-722.

McRaye, Walter. *Town Hall Tonite*. Toronto: The Ryerson Press, 1929.

Mair, Charles. "Pauline Johnson: An Appreciation." *Canadian Magazine* (July 1913): 282.

Matthews, Brander. *The Philosophy of the Short-Story*. New York: Longmans, Green, 1901.

May, Charles E., ed. *The New Short Story Theories*. Athens: Ohio U P, 1994.

Meindl, Dieter. "Modernism and the English Canadian Short Story." *Rannam* 20 (1987):17-22.

Moodie, Susanna. *Life in the Clearings versus the Bush*. 1853: rpt. Toronto: McClelland and Stewart, 1989.

—. *Roughing It in the Bush*. 1852: rpt. Toronto: McClelland and Stewart, 1989.

—. *Voyages: Short Narratives of Susanna Moodie*. ed. Thurston. Ottawa: U Ottawa P, 1991.

Moravia, Alberto. "The Short Story and the Novel." *Short Story Theories.* ed. Charles May. Athens, Ohio: Ohio UP, 1976.

Mott, Frank Luther. *A History of American Magazines 1865-1885.* Cambridge, Mass.: Belknap, 1938.

—. *A History of American Magazines 1885-1905.* Cambridge, Mass.: Belknap, 1957.

Moyles, R.G., ed. *Improved by Cultivation: An Anthology of English-Canadian Prose to 1914.* Peterborough: Broadview Press, 1994.

New, W.H. "Back to the Future: The Short Story in Canada and the Writing of Literary History." *New Contexts of Canadian Criticism.* eds. Heble, Pennee and Struthers. Peterborough: Broadview, 1997.

—. *Dreams of Speech and Violence: The Art of the Short Story in Canada and New Zealand.* Toronto: U Toronto P, 1987.

— ed. *Canadian Short Fiction: from myth to modern.* Toronto: Prentice-Hall, 1986.

— ed. *Literary History of Canada: Canadian Literature in English.* Vol. 4. Toronto: U of Toronto P, 1990.

—. "Pronouns and Prepositions: Alice Munro's Stories." *Open Letter* 3rd ser. 5 (1976): 40-49.

Nichol, bp. *The True Eventual Story of Billy the Kid.* Toronto: Weed/Flower Press, 1970.

O'Higgins, Harvey. *Don-A-Dreams.* New York: Century, 1906.

Pache, Walter. " 'The Fiction Makes Us Real': Aspects of Postmodernism in Canada." *Gaining Ground.* ed. Robert Kroetsch and Reingard M. Nischik. Edmonton: NeWest Press, 1985.

Parker, George L. *The Beginnings of the Book Trade in Canada.* Toronto: U Toronto P, 1985.

Parker, Gilbert. *Pretty Pierre and his People.* Toronto: Copp Clark, 1897.

Pattee, F.L. *The Development of the American Short Story.* New York: Harper and Row, 1923.

Peterman, Michael. *This Great Epoch in Our Lives: Susanna Moodie's Roughing It in the Bush.* Toronto: ECW Press, 1996.

Pickthall, Marjorie. *Angel's Shoes.* London: Hodder and Stoughton, 1923.

Pierce, Lorne. *Marjorie Pickthall, a Book of Remembrance.* Toronto: Ryerson Press, 1925.

Polk, James. *Canadian Literature* 54 (1972): 102-04.

Pratt, Mary Louise. "The Short Story: The Long and the Short of It." *The New Short Story Theories.* ed. May. Athens: Ohio U P, 1994.

Reid, Ian. *The Short Story.* London: Methuen, 1977.

Roberts, Charles G.D. *Selected Poetry and Critical Prose* ed. Keith. Toronto: U Toronto P,1974.

—. *King of Beasts and Other Stories.* ed. Joseph Gold. Toronto: Ryerson Press, 1967.

—. *Kindred of the Wild.* Toronto: Copp Clark, 1902

—. "The Prisoners of the Pitcher-Plant." *The Haunters of the Silences: A Book of Animal Life*. Boston: L.C. Page, 1907. 84-91.

—. Vagrants of the Barren and other stories. ed. Ware. Ottawa: Tecumseh Press, 1992.

Sandwell, B.K. "The Short Story in Canada." Rev. of *Canadian Short Stories*, ed. Raymond Knister. *Saturday Night* 25 Aug. 1928: 7.

Saunders, M. Marshall. Saunders Papers. Address to Women Teachers' Association of Toronto, 26 Nov. Acadia University, Wolfville, Nova Scotia, 1921.

Scobie, Stephen. *Signature, Event, Cantext*. Edmonton: NeWest Press, 1989.

Scott, Duncan Campbell. *The Circle of Affection*. Toronto: McClelland and Stewart, 1947.

—. *In the Village of Viger*. Boston: Copeland and Day, 1896.

—. *In the Village of Viger and Other Stories*. Intro. Stan Dragland. Toronto: McClelland & Stewart, 1973.

—. *The Witching of Elspie: A Book of Stories*. New York: George H. Doran, 1923.

Seton, Ernest Thompson. *Wild Animals I have Known*. Toronto: 1898.

—. "Introduction" to *The Shagganappi* by Pauline Johnson. Toronto: Wm. Briggs, 1913.

Sime, Jessie Georgina. *Sister Woman*. London: Grant Richards, 1919.

Smith, A.J.M, ed. *The Colonial Century: English-Canadian Writing before Confederation*. 1973: rpt. with an introduction by George L. Parker, Ottawa: Tecumseh, 1986.

Stead, W.T. "The Novel of the Modern Woman." *Review of Reviews*, 18 (July 1894), 64-74.

Stedman, E. C., ed. *Victorian Anthology 1837-1895*. 1895. New York: Greenwood Press, 1969.

Stedman, Laura, and George M. Gould, eds. *Life and Letters of E. C. Stedman*. New York: Moffat, Yard, 1910.

Stringer, Arthur. *The Silver Poppy*. New York: D. Appleton, 1903.

Summers, Hollis, ed. *Discussions of the Short Story*. Boston: D.C. Heath, 1963.

Thomson, E.W. *Old Man Savarin: Tales of Canada and Canadians*. Toronto: William Briggs, 1895.

Todorov, Tzvetan. *The Fantastic*. Trans. Richard Howard. Cleveland: The Press of Case Western Reserve University, 1973.

—. "The Origin of Genres." Trans. Richard M. Berrong. *New Literary History* VIII:1 (1976): 159-70.

Traill, Catharine Parr. *Forest and Other Gleanings: The Fugitive Writings of Catharine Parr Trail*. Ottawa: U Ottawa P, 1995.

Van Kirk, Sylvia. *Many Tender Ties: Women in Fur-Trade Society in Western Canada, 1670-1870*. Winnipeg: Watson and Dwyer, 1980.

White-Parks, Annette. *Sui Sin Far/Edith Eaton: A Literary Biography*. Urbana: U Illinois P, 1995.

Williamson, Janice. "Framed by History: Marjorie Pickthall's devices and desire." *A Mazing Space*. ed. Neuman and Kamboureli. Edmonton: NeWest Press, 1986.

Woodcock, George. *The Century that Made Us: Canada 1814-1914*. Toronto: Oxford UP, 1989.